unforgivable

Mike Thomas was born in Wales in 1971. For more than two decades he served in the police, working in some of Cardiff's busiest neighbourhoods. He left the force in 2015 to write full-time.

Mike has previously had two novels published, was longlisted for the Wales Book of the Year and was on the list of Waterstones 'New Voices'. His second novel, *Ugly Bus*, is currently in development for a six-part series with the BBC.

He lives in the wilds of Portugal with his wife, children and a senile dog who enjoys eating furniture.

Also by Mike Thomas

Pocket Notebook
Ugly Bus

In the DC Will MacReady series

Ash and Bones

Mike
Thomas
unforgivable

ZAFFRE

First published in Great Britain in 2017 by
ZAFFRE PUBLISHING
80–81 Wimpole Street, London W1G 9RE
www.zaffrebooks.co.uk

A CIP catalogue record for this book is available from the British Library.

Paperback ISBN: 978–1–7857–6064–8
eBook ISBN: 978–1–7857–6065–5

1 3 5 7 9 10 8 6 4 2

Typesest by IDSUK (Data Connection) Ltd
Printed and bound by Clays Ltd, St Ives PLC

Zaffre Publishing is an imprint of Bonnier Zaffre,
a Bonnier Publishing company
www.bonnierzaffre.co.uk
www.bonnierpublishing.co.uk

For Toria, my Somebody

I should have gone to college
and gone into real estate
and got myself an aquarium.
That's what I should have done.

– Jeffrey Dahmer, presented during his trial,
Milwankee County Circuit Court,
January 30th to February 15th 1992

The hunter lifts his head to hear,
Now far and faint, now full and near . . .

– John Greenleaf Whittier
'Mogg Megone, Part II'

Wednesday

One

It was a beautiful day in a summer of beautiful days.

Late August, and everyone was accustomed to the temperature now: weeks of cloying heat making sweat-sheened brows and shirt-backs slick with perspiration the norm. Kaftans and loose-fitting dresses and sandals treading arid ground. Shorts and T-shirts and seared skin itching beneath knock-off football shirts, cheap sunglasses sitting above bright and genuine smiles. The world was a happier place. Upbeat. Lighter.

The sun does that to people, he thinks. For a little while, at least. Gives them just enough good times to bank the memories, ready to draw on during the harsh winter which lies ahead. Ready for the darkness.

He smells citrus and mint and smoked animal flesh as he slides from the beat-up car, reaches back in to grab his belongings from the dusty passenger seat. Breathes in the aroma as he shrugs on his rucksack, adjusts his baseball cap and shades, listens to the shouts from the vendors, to the various sound systems battling for attention: Berber flutes, the bouncing bass-twang of reggae, the percussive beats of drums iced with the *tsss* of finger cymbals, the music louder and more intoxicating as he wanders through the open entrance gates. Face downcast, he pushes through the sticky bodies of the crowd, through still air which seems to thicken and catch in his throat.

This market, this *souk*, is full. A noisy mess of colour and energy, of spices, preserved lemons and handbags, of shawls and carpets and a thousand pairs of shoes for sale. Clutches of people catching up and talking of family, of loved ones, of all the things which make life tick tock in that mundane yet wonderful way when you're a part of it. Tick tock. *Tick tock.* And the sun beats down and they swig at water bottles, sip at spiced tea and freshly squeezed orange juice, hands swinging plastic sacks filled with yams and figs, with third-hand clothing, with decade-old video games, with just-couldn't-resist bargains to be used once and instantly forgotten.

He finds the food stall immediately, drawn by the delicious smell drifting on smoke over the crowds: a makeshift grill beneath a sun-bleached canopy, trestle tables lined with earthenware dishes of tabbouleh, hummus, just-charred spiced sausages and myriad sweet pastries. Great shanks of meat hang from the creaking timbers, unbothered by the buzzing flies and casting long shadows onto the faces of the two Somali men – *brothers, they must be*, he thinks, eyeing them – who laugh and joke with glossy customers, with the mishmash of nationalities who have flocked here from surrounding towns and villages to cluck in their mother tongues over dried fruits and bowls of couscous.

Off to one side he waits a while. Just *is*, as unmoving as the air which warms his lungs. The people at the stall are so happy, emitting satisfied moans as they chew. The brothers moving this way and that, rolling wraps, slathering them with harissa, handing them over to grabbing hands. He finds one of his feet tapping to the music, glances around and sees garishly clad women dancing through streams of grinning people, an oily chancer hassling families for a paid photograph with the snake he has draped over one forearm.

Tap, tap. Tick tock. He begins to drift, such is the atmosphere. Momentarily forgets where he is. Starts to lose himself. A small part of him enjoying what is going on here. He looks down again, thinks of walking away. Leaving the market. Getting into the car and driving into the morning haze.

He is a moment from going home when he hears the unmistakeable sound of someone hawking mucus from the depths of their chest. Hears them spit the resultant phlegm, sees it land in the dirt just inches from his right foot. It sends a minute mushroom cloud of dust rippling outwards, one edge of it settling on the bulled toecap of his army surplus boot.

He glances up from under the brim of his 'ball cap. Notices the three figures. Three teenagers, all faded branded sports gear and leers. Staring at him. Motionless, like him.

He swallows. Moves through the crowd, moves away from them. No aggro here. Not today. He doesn't want it. Doesn't need it, not now of all times. And yet they follow him, move parallel with him, pushing through the throng, their belligerent faces bobbing over the heads of the people, seeking him out, their nasty, toothy grins visible over mops of hair and ponytails and braids and sunglasses. And he is trying to work out why, why him, why now, what do they want, what has he done to them, and then they are in front of him, one of them poking a finger into his chest, hard, and he remembers they don't need a why, and he needn't have done anything to them, and that is why he is here.

They circle him, step closer, uncomfortably close, invading his personal space, and one of them, a thickset teen with a shaven eyebrow, reaches out, grips his coat by the collar and yanks at him.

And this is a little inconvenient, but it was time to start anyway.

Deep breath. Deep, deep breath.

He pulls aside one flap of his jacket, shows them what hangs beneath.

Three pairs of eyes widen. The one with the eyebrow, his hand falls away. Lifts upwards, as if to ward him off. Head shaking. The three of them, backing away and into the scrum of oblivious market-goers. Their shouted warnings drowned by the music.

He smiles. Calmer than he thought he would be. Shrugs off his rucksack and places it on the ground. Reaches inside and pulls them out. One, two, three. Enough for now. Digs out his lighter, sparks it. Watches the dancing women, the happy families. Taps his foot and nods his head in time to the beat from a nearby sound system.

Lights one of the fuses and tosses the IED into the crowd.

Hoists his ruck to one shoulder, walks away, quickly, twenty feet or so, lights another fuse, tosses another IED, swivels on his heel, lights and lobs the third. Walks over to the stall with the Somali brothers, customers still gathered for the street food, joins the jam in front.

Waits, eyes unblinking behind his shades.

They're louder than he thought they would be, and he flinches a little as the bombs go off. The people in front of him at the stall, they hunch down, confused, the market suddenly quiet, just for a few seconds, and then the screams begin, and the wails can be heard over the music, and the people no longer wish to purchase food and scatter like rats, and the Somali brothers have stopped, mouths agape, looking past him, behind him at some unspeakable horror, one of them with a half-rolled flatbread hanging limply from frozen fingers.

Then they notice him. Standing there. Alone. A grin beneath his shades.

Head bobbing to the music. Foot still tapping away.

Tap, tap.

'Don't,' he warns, because he still has to finish this, but the brothers, they *know*, they're coming around the stall, advancing on him, grabbing hands raised and lips drawn back as they snarl and holler and he can't understand a word they're saying and he has no time for this so swipes back the flap of his jacket, raises the sawn-off he's tied to his shoulder and levels it at them. Neither man sees it. Two quick taps on the trigger and they both lurch backwards and out of sight. He notices blood in the tabbouleh, on top of the trestle table. Breaks open the shotgun, drops the spent cartridges into his jacket pocket. Reloads the barrels, racks them closed.

The building is at the back of the market, a thrown-together effort of breezeblock and chipboard and indifference. He heads for it, ignoring the screams and the rivulets of red, and when he reaches the door he kicks it open, quickly scans the interior: concrete floor, solitary desk and chair, titty calendars, television, all wrapped in the smell of chicken fat and cheap cigarettes.

A pair of wide, white eyes peeking over the rim of the desk.

He swings the shotgun around, aims at them.

The market owner. He bolts upright from behind the desk. One hand skywards in half-surrender, the other clamping a mobile phone to his ear. The dark skin of his face drenched with sweat, his underarms shadowy blooms of perspiration on the fabric of his lime polo shirt.

'Don't shoot,' the market owner pleads.

He drops the rucksack. Cocks his head. Listens. Can hear a voice on the other end of the line from where he stands: urgent, shrill.

Sir, where are you? We're tracing the call, but where are you?

'I won't,' he says, and sparks the lighter. Touches it to the fuse inside the rucksack. Tosses the whole thing to the desk and leaves.

He hears the door slam, the market owner yelling after him, quickens his pace, time against him. *Tick tock.* Breaks into a sprint, the rucksack going up in the office behind him, a colossal *whump* of an explosion, the earth quivering beneath his boots, almost throwing him forwards and off his feet, but he regains his balance and runs through the dead and the dying, looks around at what he has done as he goes, sees sprayed spices and torn baskets and punctured tinned goods, bodies and body parts, the music still playing, so incongruous, so surreal, and then he is out through the gates, running with the panicked crowd – mingling, disappearing – and he hears no sirens so yanks open the car door and dumps himself inside and starts the engine and drives away.

And it is such a beautiful day in Cardiff.

Two

All Inspector James Doolan could think was: *don't fuck this one up*.

Five years in, twenty-eight years old and a fast-tracker being groomed for better things – he'd already had the nod that he was looking at National Police Chiefs Council rank by the time he hit fifteen years in the job – he'd done all the courses, the classroom exercises covering hostage negotiation and crime scene containment, the practicals and hands-on riot training days where he'd suffered the sniggers and catcalls as the bottom-feeding PCs gleefully threw Molotovs and rubber bricks at his riot shield. He'd understood their enmity towards him: he was an accelerated promotion drone, the type hated by response cops and frontline departments who were at the coalface day in day out, who assumed he spent his hours hidden in an air-conditioned office formulating pie charts and massaging crime figures for the bean counters at HQ and the Home Office.

It made him want to be a better officer, to spend more time – any time that he could – on the street, to prove to any and all of them that he could cut it, that he wasn't just another clone, that they could rely on him. But his life, since joining, had been a whirlwind of examinations and self-reflective essays, of soft handshakes and knowing smiles from seniors with silver spaghetti on their epaulettes, of complete and utter immersion in every aspect of police policy and procedure, from filling out the most mundane of property labels to Multi-Agency Public Protection Arrangement strategy meetings about the latest shithouse rape merchant who'd decided to set up a squalid home in the division he now ran as its new bronze inspector.

Yet none of it had prepared him for this.

This was carnage.

Out of control.

They even had the army here, for Christ's sake.

The National Police Air Service chopper thundered overhead, whipping a rising funnel of dark smoke into a drab spiral which hung against the bright-blue summer sky. A fire still raged somewhere inside Bessemer Road Market and firefighters hovered outside the cordon tape, hoses poised and at the ready, unable to enter, frustration etched on their faces. Radios from ambulance crews, paramedics, fire and police officers crackled and bleeped, filling the air with metallic voices. TV crews jostled for space, interviewing members of the public who'd turned up to gawp or weep openly, questioning PCSOs who lined the police tape, even questioning each other when they ran out of people to collar, before turning to camera to opine and theorise for their ever-hungry twenty-four-hour-news junkies. So loud here, with everyone milling around helplessly, watching through the gaps in the metal perimeter fence as teams of firearms officers and army personnel worked the scene, moving quickly and quietly, Heckler & Koch submachine guns sweeping and clearing.

Over it all, audible and gut-scraping: the moans of the injured.

Still inside. Still untreated, twenty minutes after some lunatic had decided to attack the market. Nobody was allowed in, not until the Tac teams had declared the scene safe.

'Gold is still ten minutes away. She's asking for an update.'

Doolan looked at his companion: an unreconstructed dinosaur of a PC named Derek, who had been 'gifted' to him as his radio operator. Doolan knew it was because nobody else wanted to work with a slick career boy such as himself, and that management had nowhere else to place Derek, who was a lazy uniform-carrier from somewhere near Pontypridd who still described female officers as *split-arses* and *them lesbo types*.

Doolan shook his head. 'Tell her I'd prefer to have some CID suits here to take ownership of this thing.'

The PC arched an eyebrow, reached up to one of his radios. 'Really?'

'No, Derek,' Doolan sighed, more out of disappointment that Derek clearly felt somebody else would do a better job of running this incident. 'Tell her there is no update. Firearms are still clearing.'

'Bet you'd prefer to be in your cushy office, though,' Derek smiled. Added as an afterthought: 'Sir.'

Doolan turned to him. Thought about chewing him out. Decided against it. 'Just tell her.'

Derek shrugged, began to transmit. Hesitated. Placed a finger up to his earpiece, screwed up his face in concentration.

Doolan watched, eyes narrowed, as Derek's eyes did the opposite.

'What the fuck?' Derek blurted.

Doolan glanced upwards, saw the chopper suddenly peel away, nose down and heading west towards the coast at speed. Heard rapid footfalls and shouts and the roar of engines behind him, spun around to see paramedics sprinting back to their wagons, firefighters yanking open doors to their engines and clambering in, an ARV car printing tyre marks on tarmac as it powered out of the cordon. Mobile phones trilled and blasted ringtones, dozens of radios squawked in unison.

He looked back to Derek. 'What is it?'

'There's been another one.'

It didn't compute. Doolan shook his head, his stomach a knot. 'Another what?'

'The guy who did this . . .' Derek said robotically, finger still up to his ear. 'Same description . . . clothing . . . he just hit a mosque in Penarth. There are casualties . . .'

Doolan blanched. 'No. It can't be. He barely had time to get from here to there . . .'

Derek was glancing about. 'We don't need this now.'

'The city doesn't need this now,' Doolan replied. 'The Castle case. It's already enough. Too much.'

'Gold is diverting to Penarth,' Derek said, listening to a different radio.

'Good.' Doolan closed his eyes.

Wished, for the first time in his career, that he really was in a cushy office creating a pie chart.

Three

Bored.

Five of them sitting in the dock of Crown Court One. A row of apathy and barely concealed arrogance. Wrapped in oh-so-civilised black tie and white shirt combos which were only marginally less ill-fitting than the uniforms worn by the equally uninterested G4S prison officer civvies who bookended the accused.

DC Will MacReady saw their disgraceful sniggers and winks to their friends and *fam* in the public gallery. The sideways glances and wanker hand gestures and sullen stares at any police officer who happened to be in the courtroom. All of it in front of the deceased's parents, who had attended every day of every week since the trial began, shuffling in with backs bowed as if broken from the weight of it all, who had sat and listened, jaws tightening, as the prosecution barrister listed the injuries to their sixteen-year-old son, their kid who went out and never returned, their boy who suffered horrendous bruising and broken bones and multiple puncture wounds from a knife, one of which was delivered with such venom that it cleaved a rib clean in half before puncturing his heart.

Alexander Castle. Just sixteen, a high-achieving, sport-loving student, never in trouble in his life and on a night out with friends to celebrate finishing his GCSE exams. The antithesis of the teenagers fidgeting in the dock – all of them known to police for years, with myriad pre-convictions and much time spent *over the wall* in prison. Theft. Dwelling burglaries. Public order. Dealing. Dozens of street robberies where they pulled knives on anyone who dared resist.

It was wrong place, wrong time for Alex Castle. He'd been leaving a pub in Cardiff city centre, his unfinished pint glass left on the beer garden table and still warm from his grasp, when his friends had argued with a group of Asian males. A group of males who were part of a notorious Cardiff crime gang. A group of males who you did not want to cross.

It was all so predictable: his friends had run, and Castle – his naivety getting the better of him, his belief that as he had not been involved in the argument the gang would leave him alone – had walked away slowly, not looking back, not thinking to put distance between him and the five teens and twenty-somethings who were now following him along a row of parked vehicles.

Then they had set upon him.

Between two vans. Five of them, punching and kicking him until he went down. Stamping on his torso, his head, while he lay on the ground, then one of them – none of them had admitted wielding it – plunged the knife into Castle's prone body. Thirteen times, until his lungs were punctured and his hands were shredded with defensive wounds and the blade entered his ribcage and sheared through bone and tore through the pulmonary artery and then the five were gone into the night.

Castle had pulled himself upright, staggered across the road to his returning friends, walked in circles for a few moments, shaking his head, not quite believing what had just happened.

Said to one of his friends, 'I don't feel right . . .' and had given an incredulous laugh, his bloodied hands held out before him, the streetlights making his eyes glitter momentarily, a burst of adrenalin flashing in his pupils, and then they had dulled and he had sagged into their arms and was dead before he hit the ground.

The whole thing caught on the pub CCTV which faced out onto the main road. Only the attack itself was off-camera, hence the joint enterprise charges for the five, plus alternative murder and manslaughter charge sheets, and a court case which was now gripping the city and raising tensions as it dragged on.

The media were all over it, stirring the pot. A group of journos were clumped across the press bench, scribbling, typing onto tablets, live tweeting anything remotely interesting. Amongst them: Klaudia Solak, darling of BBC Wales. Occasional glances from her towards MacReady, who kept meeting her eyes, letting them linger before resuming glaring at the defendants.

The narrative: five Asian 'hoodlums' had knifed a 'fine young white boy' and everyone was going batshit. *Race murder. Hate crime.* Social media in meltdown. *Society broken beyond repair.* Far-right groups coming out in unwanted 'support' of the Castle family, rocking up each day outside Cardiff Crown in solidarity, then the left-wing Anti-Fascist opposition turning up en masse, the groups repeatedly bloodying each other as an increasingly thin line of police tried to separate them beneath a glorious summer sun.

MacReady had watched the pub CCTV recording on a loop for months, pausing and playing, forwarding and rewinding, hoping to catch something the others had missed, anything to push the investigation over the finish line, only stopping to answer the routine demands for teas and coffees and *don't forget the three bloody sugars, mun*, rattling around the office with mug-heavy tray in hand as Detective Inspector Fletcher and the Cardiff Bay CID team assembled their case.

He was sick of watching that tape. And after six weeks in a stifling Court One rammed with wigs and slick defence suits and air thick with dust motes, he was sick of watching the clowns performing in the dock. The investigating officers had given evidence, had stood in front of the jury and sworn on the good book and said what they had to say – which, in MacReady's case, had been very little, given that he'd bagged and tagged a few bits of evidence then sat in on two interviews – and were back to other crimes and outstanding actions and statements, arrests and file prep that probably should have been carried out two months ago.

Except him, of course. Still the new boy. No longer a trainee, but still a way to go as far as the higher-ups were concerned. And still being monitored. Nearly a year since 'it' had happened, yet nobody would ease up on him. Charlie Beck. MacReady could still picture it now: his detective sergeant slipping into unconsciousness in front of him on a cold concrete floor, dark red blooming beneath her hip and the thunderclap of a gunshot rattling around inside his skull . . .

And then the weeks and months of interviews and disciplinary notices and the lingering eyes on him whenever he entered a parade room or custody suite or CID office in another nick. And the DI, just last week, in the Crown's marbled lobby after MacReady had stepped down from the witness box and left the courtroom: *Get back in there, Will. Sit in till the end. See how things pan out. Bell me if anything goes south. And don't fuck anything up this time, right?*

This time.

From his right, a hissed whisper: 'Christ's sake, look at you.'

MacReady kept his eyes staring forwards, studying the royal coat of arms at the back of the court, ignoring the man sitting next to him: Detective Sergeant Paul Echols. Weapons-grade bellend and temporary – everyone hoped – replacement DS for Beck while she continued her recuperation. Echols had been seconded to the team in January when it became clear Beck was not rejoining them any time soon. Just to compound MacReady's misery, the DI had seen fit to make Echols sit in on the remainder of the trial as well. For no other reason, MacReady knew, than to keep Echols away from the rest of the team and to punish MacReady for saddling them with the prize prick by getting Beck shot and hospitalised.

'Face on you, man,' Echols whispered. Everyone was *man* to him, a drawled, intensely annoying Americanism and a peculiar affectation, given he hailed from an unpronounceable hamlet in deepest West Wales and the closest he had ever come to the US was watching crappy cop dramas on Netflix.

MacReady gave in, turned to the DS. Found his face about three inches away, saw the sunglasses propped on his carefully coiffed dark hair, could smell the coffee he'd sunk half an hour ago on his breath, stale and powerful. He recoiled and shushed Echols with a finger to his lips, a tip of the head to the judge who sat head on hand as he listened to one of the defence barristers waffle on about his client's concerns about disclosure.

Echols rolled his eyes. 'What?'

'I'm trying to listen,' MacReady muttered.

'You're putting the world to rights in your head, about this trial *and* your brother's. I can see it, and it's making you twitchy, and it's too early for me to deal with you being twitchy.'

MacReady shrugged. Said, not meaning it: 'Sorry 'bout that.'

'Don't be. You can't help it if wife-beating shithouses are par for the course in your family, right?'

'You're getting very personal here, Sarge,' MacReady said, but he hated to admit that Echols was pretty much on the money. Everybody on the force knew. MacReady pictured his brother, Stuart, the proverbial black sheep. An abiding problem, be it because of brawling while in drink, or begging MacReady to pay his rent, or assaulting his long-suffering girlfriend, Kirsty. Stuart was a man for whom *responsibility* meant ensuring he got enough beers in for his weekend, often spending what little cash Kirsty had saved for the children. His brother was here today, too. On trial, just down the corridor.

MacReady's thoughts quickly flashed to his father, the lifer. Everybody knew about him, too. It was hard to hide the fact your dad had murdered your mother and was currently serving a twenty-five-year sentence in prison.

'And you're getting right on my nerves,' Echols replied. 'So just fuck off and see him, yeah?'

'I don't want to see him. I'm quite happy here, thanks'

'And I don't want to see you. So . . . bu-bye, William.'

Echols had raised one hand, was bending his fingers up and down in an exaggerated fashion, waving MacReady off. Thin smile on his lips, his tanned face glossy with perspiration: a thirtysomething wide boy who was definitely warm as toast, and who, if he hadn't joined the job to chase criminals, would probably be the one being chased, running some Cardiff sink-hole estate as its low-level crime kingpin.

MacReady closed his eyes for a moment, pictured the usher holding Echols down while the courtroom – defendants, the bookish clerk to the court, even the judge in a flurry of wig hair – rose en masse and beat the DS to a pulp.

He savoured it for a few seconds. Opened his eyes. Glanced at Klaudia Solak.

Quietly left the court.

*

'How's it going?'

Indifferent nods and grunts of *alrigh'* from the trio of uniforms outside Courtroom Number Eight in the bowels of the building. Around them the court went about its business: people drifting in and out of anterooms, fire doors swishing open and closed, heels clacking on polished floor, a dozen conversations loaded with legal jargon and discussions about what to have for lunch.

MacReady recognised one of the response officers from a training day he'd attended a few months earlier at divisional headquarters, where the lucky few had sat through an interminable seminar on fingerprinting and bite-mark analysis on victims. No lunch to lighten the dour mood either, thanks to the austerity measures.

He felt their eyes on him; gossip and innuendo was the lifeblood of the service and MacReady's tale had been doing the rounds for a long time. Pretty much every officer in the city knew of him, or thought they knew him and what really happened to DS Charlie Beck in that basement garage last October. Thanks to the rumours and bullshit. And just to compound matters, here he was, drawn here because of somebody who managed to drag his family name through a river of mud whenever humanly possible, and annoying the officers who were hovering outside.

'Given evidence yet?' he asked them.

'Think we'd still be hanging around here if we had?' one of them replied, and followed it with an audible, irritated *tcch*.

'Y'know what it's like,' another offered. 'Airtight case, but the defence briefs'll try anything to get their scumbag client a not-guilty.' He looked away from MacReady. 'No offence, like.'

MacReady looked to the floor. Nodded. Mumbled a *'Scuse me* and pushed his way through the heavy double doors and into the court.

The room was brightly lit, modern. Cream carpets and polystyrene ceiling slotted with fluorescents, the benches and desks cheap, laminated. One of the newer courts, devoid of any of the atmosphere or sense of history you would find upstairs in what MacReady considered to be the proper Crown.

He stood at the back near the entrance door, watching the figure in the dock. Wiry and pale from weeks spent cooped up on remand, his eyes hooded and unreadable beneath the strip lights. MacReady knew he was staring right back, though. Staring right back and cursing him, just for the job he did, for being a copper, for being just like the men who had locked him up that night a few months ago, a rainy Tuesday when he'd been wetting the baby's head at the pub and downed those shots and necked those beers and rubbed that amphetamine on his swollen gums, before loping home to his girlfriend's house, where he woke everyone, woke the street, woke his girlfriend, who screamed and yelled, and he'd snapped – again – and grabbed her throat, and bang, there it was, before he knew what he was doing she was on the floor and out of it, nose crooked and pulsing blood, and he'd rubbed at his forehead, momentarily confused as to why it was throbbing until it dawned on him that he'd just smashed it into her face.

'You bastard,' MacReady said under his breath.

Stuart.

His brother.

On trial for assaulting Kirsty, his partner, in front of their children. After a night out celebrating the birth of his baby. *His* baby. Will's baby, now. A boy conceived last year as a business arrangement with MacReady's wife, Megan, so desperate was she for children, so money-hungry was his brother, and so incapable was MacReady of giving her what she so keenly wanted. Such was the mess it created – fracturing relationships, creating a chasm so wide between MacReady and his older sibling that they had not spoken for the better part of twelve months – that it didn't bear thinking about, even this far down the line. MacReady breathed deeply on the musty air and turned away. Noticed a ripple of energy in the public gallery as one or two journalists gathered their belongings, staring at phone screens with wide eyes.

MacReady saw Echols in the doorway, face set, mobile in his hand.

'We are leaving,' Echols said, voice quiet but tense. 'Right fucking now, man.'

Four

'My God, it's everywhere.'

MacReady held his mobile in one hand, used a thumb to scroll through the Google hits listed on the screen, used his other hand to grip the Jesus handle above the window as he rocked in the passenger seat; Echols was ninety-fiving it through the city centre, screaming with joy as if on a theme park ride, heading towards the Leckwith area, towards Bessemer Road. The market attack was all over the news websites, trending on social media, the numbing images already posted online by onlookers at the scene. Dribs and drabs coming in from the coastal town of Penarth too, from the Al Mahdi Mosque – same perpetrator, same MO.

Same butchery.

'Course it is.' Echols's voice was strained, one white-knuckled hand wrenching at the steering wheel of the unmarked CID car as he rounded a sweating cyclist. His other hand, repeatedly smacking the horn in lieu of blues and twos, a cadence of weak parps scarcely audible over the growling diesel engine and rat-a-tat radio transmissions – constant and increasingly shrill from officers at both scenes – thrumming from the in-car Airwave set. 'Look at who he's targeted. You can guess why, too. Some fruitcake getting so-called revenge for the Castle thing, I'll bet.

This'll go nationwide and right up the food chain.' A longer push on the horn as a car threatened to emerge from a road to their left. 'Come on, Will. Watch for traffic at the junctions.'

MacReady felt his phone vibrate, looked down to see the icon at the top left of the screen: a text message from Klaudia Solak:

> Getting all sorts from Bessemer. Stuck here re Castle.
> Updates?
> K xxx

He shook his head, was about to type a reply. Flinched as the phone was slapped from his hand. It rattled into the footwell, came to rest amongst the chocolate wrappers and tissues left by other users of the CID pool car and which nobody, ever, bothered to clean up.

'I ask you to do something, you do it, yeah?' Echols said, top lip curled as he leaned into MacReady. Echols's eyes never left the road, though. MacReady was thankful; the speedometer was nudging one hundred miles an hour. 'I want concentration, Will. Game faces on for this, not texting your wife about what you fancy for tea.'

MacReady pictured Solak, sitting in the courtroom. 'I wasn't texting my –'

'I don't care,' Echols said, spittle on his bottom lip, slowing the car to eighty as he weaved it through traffic towards a crossroads. '*Concentrate*. Make sure the side roads are clear. I kid you not when I say I'll sue you from the afterlife if you kill me in a POLACC.'

A POLACC. MacReady knew of several cops who had taken legal action against colleagues for causing *police accidents*, those collisions on duty involving police vehicles where the compensation for even the slightest of injuries was often considerable. He had no doubt Echols was a dab hand at playing the system. He bristled at the threat. Was yet more furious at the slap, the condescension. The fact that Echols was only on the team because of what had happened to Beck – his fault, he reminded himself again – gnawed at him afresh. An angry red coloured his neck, his cheeks, and he turned away, pretended to look out of the window, the mobile's screen glowing in the corner of his eye.

MacReady spent the next five minutes shouting *clear* at every junction and crossroads while Echols worked the car through mid-morning traffic, shoppers' confused faces turning to watch the parping, battered red Peugeot screech across sun-warmed streets. Echols slipped them south-west across the city, skirting the North Stand of the Principality Stadium, crossing the River Taff. A hard left through Clare Road's Edwardian terraced houses, snaking deep into the guts of the Grangetown neighbourhood. As they ran down the miles they could see it: a pall of thinning black smoke hanging over the warehouses and 4x4 showrooms of the industrial area at Leckwith, dulling the sunlight into a strange orange, the car interior deepening with shadows as if dusk had suddenly fallen.

'Man oh man oh man,' muttered Echols, eyes on the entrance to Bessemer Road as he killed the engine, tugged on the handbrake. 'On foot it is, then.'

So many emergency response vehicles. It was impossible to go any further. MacReady had never seen anything like it.

Strobes and fluorescent tabards into the distance, a morass of figures running this way and that, the street cordoned off at both ends. Police Community Support Officers lining the police tape, black-clad firearms officers strutting behind them with Heckler & Koch assault rifles cradled in their arms should anybody be foolish enough to ignore the PCSOs' warnings to stay back. The pavements lined with astonished market-goers and car sales staff, with office workers and overall-wrapped fork-lift truck drivers from the warehouses, a steadily increasing swell of members of the public – MOPs – watching silently with eyes wide, as if unable to comprehend what they were witnessing. Their demeanour spoke volumes: at any other incident – suicidal male threatening to jump from the top floor of a car park, a ruck outside a pub – there'd be some clown shouting the odds from the sidelines.

Now: nothing.

MacReady scooped his phone from the footwell, the text message forgotten. Followed Echols out of the car. Tasted smoke, the hot summer air thick with it, with flakes of ash spiralling from the heavens, making his eyelids flutter, his eyes water. Heard sobs and shouts. Saw paramedics huddled around a woman on the pavement, hands on her, wrapping her in gauze and bandages and applying pressure, pleading with her to stay calm, to sit still, the woman's face slack and blueish and open-mouthed, dreadlocked hair roped with blood, her left arm not there anymore, gone from the elbow with its tattered flaps of flesh and white nub of bone and she wasn't looking at it, was looking towards the market gates and shouting for her husband, her child, *where's mylittleboyohGodmyhusbandmylittleboyohGodohGod . . .*

MacReady thought of home.

This was hellish.

'C'mon, newbie.' Echols, looking over his shoulder at MacReady, the cockiness muted for once. 'You can wring your hands about it all later.'

The DS stomped away. MacReady watched him scuttle between army trucks and dog vans and ambulance first responder vehicles, all abandoned and empty, their occupants now part of the crowd working inside the cordon. A skinny special constable lifted police tape and Echols ducked into the insanity.

MacReady took a deep breath and trailed after him.

*

At the market gates was DC Warren Harrison.

Face dripping, jowls lined with soot, tie loosened and collar undone to show curled tufts of red-blond chest hair sitting above the balloon of his midriff. It was Wednesday, which meant white socks for the sandals he wore; the normally hyper-bright cotton of his ankle socks were now flecked a dull ash grey.

Harrison nodded a greeting. 'Right shit storm we got here, boys.'

'State of you,' Echols muttered, eyeing him.

'Been here a while,' Harrison replied pointedly. 'Give it ten in this heat and you'll have that shirt of yours off, mun.'

'Sergeant,' said Echols.

A shrug. Harrison: an old sweat who gave no fucks. 'Sarge.'

MacReady hung back a little. Let it play out between them again, a repeat of a repeat of their thrice-daily head-to-head which only served to prove – no matter how long Echols stayed in the department – they would never get along. It was tiresome, and counterproductive. Instead he tried to absorb what was going on around him, to find the slightest glimmer of order within a scene of total disorder: the idle of dozens of diesel engines, countless rubberised tactical boot soles slapping on tarmac, radios and shouts and the wax and wane of sirens. Two helicopters circling above the market, their news channel livery bright against a cone of smoke that now stretched across the southern half of the capital like a storm cloud.

Standing in a puddle of dirty water amongst thick coils of fire hose and empty medical bags was DI Danny Fletcher. Mac-Ready tuned out Harrison and Echols's pissing contest, let out a small sigh of relief that his detective inspector was already marshalling what needed to be marshalled.

He watched as the DI nodded down at a uniformed ranker MacReady recognised but whose name he could not recall. One of the new bronze inspectors for the city. Accelerated-promotion job, but one of the rare good guys on the scheme. The inspector talked and pointed and kept shaking his head, before using thumb and forefinger to repeatedly rub at his temples while Fletcher looked on. Just behind the DI stood the detective chief superintendent and detective chief inspector from Specialist Crime. Faces unreadable, yet pale and twitchy, the chief super mouthing something into a mobile phone, the DCI constantly brushing at the sleeves of her natty tailored suit jacket and looking skywards as if to curse the slivers of ash.

Fletcher nodded a final time at the bronze inspector and began walking towards MacReady and company.

'Guys,' MacReady muttered a warning.

Echols and Harrison stopped bickering as the DI planted his feet in front of them. An imposing figure, Danny Fletcher was rangy, but muscular with it, the coffee-coloured skin of his face pocked with acne scars. Hooded eyes moved this way and that, teeth chewing at the inside of his mouth. Grey satin shirt, charcoal trousers, a tie which complemented both. Sleeves rolled up, all business. A nod of his shaven head to each of them, a quick wipe at the sweat on his top lip.

'And?' Harrison asked him.

'OK, I've spoken to the on-duty bronze.'

'Dude looks like a lost lamb,' smirked Echols. 'Useless high-flyers.'

Fletcher arched an eyebrow at the DS. 'Doolan might be on the scheme but he's got nous. Credit where it's due and all that. And you might want to watch your tongue, Paul. Could prove awkward if the guy's ever shifted to CID and ends up as your DI.'

Echols rolled his eyes. 'As if. I'd put my ticket in before it ever happened.'

MacReady found himself wishing it would happen that very afternoon.

'So this is what we've got,' Fletcher said, ignoring his detective sergeant. 'Summer ethnic market here, a pretend souk, been going for over a decade, Cardiff's little week-long celebration of all things multicultural, blah blah, as we all know. Nine twenty, nine thirtyish this morning, guy walks into the market, faffs about for ten minutes like he's a punter.'

'Any description?' asked MacReady.

'Black clothing. Black shades. Black baseball cap.'

'So far, so clichéd,' said Harrison.

Fletcher waited a beat. Then: 'And white-skinned.'

'Told you,' said Echols, looking at MacReady.

Harrison shook his head. 'Cat. Pigeons.'

'Indeed. Hence the detective chief super looking a little bit nervous.' Fletcher tilted his head back to the pair of suits muttering questions at the bronze inspector. 'Anyway, Doolan's been busy, already got three significant witnesses,' he eyed Echols, as if daring him to say something, 'a group of wannabe gangsters from the Canton neighbourhood. All scrotes, all wearing shitty Sports Direct Lonsdale tracksuits they haven't washed for two years. He gets the feeling they were in here on the rob, but they appear to have picked on the wrong guy.'

'Our guy,' said MacReady.

Fletcher nodded. 'They fronted him up but he pulled what they say is a sawn-off shotgun from under his coat. So understandably they shit themselves and are on their toes, out of the market and next thing: boom, boom, boom.' He waved a hand in a wide arc at the market. 'This.'

'And the Penarth mosque?' MacReady asked.

'Pretty much samey same. Fifteen minutes after this, our man walks in, cool as you like, and then there's the explosions. I don't have a firm number on casualties there yet.'

Echols placed hands on hips and glanced around. 'He on foot? In a car? Might've left his ride here. Prints, DNA inside, yeah?'

'You serious?' Harrison's pudgy face wrinkled. 'He won't have left it behind, mun. He'd need the car to get to Penarth so quickly.' He scratched at his chest hairs. 'To do the mosque, you muppet.'

'You going to let him talk to me like this?' Echols asked Fletcher.

'Will you two fucking wind your necks in for five minutes?' Fletcher barked, looking from one to the other. 'There's no details of any particular vehicle. Plenty of them screamed out of here, but it's not unexpected though, don't you think? People were freaking. He could've spun into the distance in the Tardis and nobody would've noticed, given most of them were trying their best not to get blown up.'

Nobody spoke for a moment. MacReady could still hear the woman screaming for her family. He wished the ambulance would take her away so he didn't have to listen to it any more.

'We can go to the mosque now,' he said to Fletcher. 'Me and Warren, do whatever needs doing.'

'No chance,' said Fletcher.

'Cross-contamination,' Echols said, looking at MacReady as if he was intellectually challenged. 'You've been here, you can't go there. What's the matter with you?'

Fletcher placed a hand on MacReady's shoulder. 'Much as it pains me to admit it, Paul's right. One of the teams from Merthyr are taking ownership for now. Once it's been rendered safe and CSI have done their bit, we can make our way.'

MacReady nodded, refusing to look at Echols. 'That's a day or two.'

'At least. Meantime, we are here. The detective chief super has promised me more people. We have house to house and witnesses to round up. Plus making a list of every single car parked in this neighbourhood.'

'CCTV?' MacReady asked.

'Already tasked uniform. On their way to County Hall for the traffic camera recordings. We get to do all the businesses on this estate.'

Echols stopped glowering at Harrison for a second. 'And after that?'

Fletcher fiddled with the knot on his tie. A marked BMW was being ushered into the cordon by firearms officers and he watched with narrowed eyes as it drew to a stop. MacReady saw the passenger doors open and three males – sunglasses, neatly cropped hair, their plain-clothes getup a uniform in itself – emerge. After a few moments spent scanning the crowd one of them waved at Fletcher.

'That's the counter-terrorism spooks from WECTU and Special Branch,' Fletcher sighed, giving a limp wave in return. 'They're here to tell me what's after that. And what we've done wrong so far.'

MacReady turned to look at the officers from Special Branch and the Wales Extremism and Counter-Terrorism Unit. They were hands in pockets, chewing gum, staring at Bessemer Market: a medley of warehouses, storage units and outbuildings arranged around a central courtyard, where the ethnic market was being held. Encircled by perimeter fencing consisting of spiked, thin metal railings with a derelict security hut at the entrance gates. One way in, one way out. As a place to trap and maim a large number of people, it was almost perfect.

Through the gaps in the fence MacReady caught glimpses of Royal Logistics Corps engineers waddling in Explosive Ordnance Disposal suits, of pockets of firearms officers standing at the ready while the EOD-clad army specialists inched forward, of a pair of anxious paramedics tucked behind a redbrick wall. Beyond them, the remnants of a building burned despite the efforts of the fire service personnel blasting water through the fence from waste ground at the rear. In between, on the ground in what he could see of the courtyard, the signs of mass panic: spilled drink containers, half-eaten food, bags, coats, sunglasses and coins just dropped where people had stood.

A splash of bright red, spattered and drying on warm concrete.

MacReady looked to the left, at the low hut which had served as a security post. At the small roundabout behind it which fed traffic into the perimeter roads of the market. At the shapes beneath blankets: bodies, two of them as far as he could tell, a bare foot sticking out here, a clawed and bloodied hand there.

And then he heard it. Faint, barely audible beneath the din, but a sound he'd grown accustomed to hearing these last few months, that he'd become attuned to since his wife gave birth: a child crying.

'You away with the fairies again, William?'

Echols in his ear.

MacReady didn't even look at him. Cast his eyes over the nearby line of parked cars and mini-vans, the vehicles abandoned when their owners fled the market. 'Be quiet.'

'You talking to me like that, you –'

'Shut the fuck up, will you?' MacReady hissed. Placed a hand to hold an advancing Echols at bay. Crouched down, tuning out the racket of engines and sirens and a protesting detective sergeant.

'What is it, Will?' Fletcher, alongside him, bent at the waist.

'Wait one,' MacReady walked over to a people carrier, its white bodywork filmed with fine grey cinder. Paused with a hand on the bonnet, dust and ash beneath his fingertips. The crying. Louder now. 'Here,' he said, and dropped to his knees.

The boy was three years of age, perhaps a little older. Prone on the tarmac beneath the vehicle, kitted out in denim dungarees over a bright red t-shirt, head resting on arms and his face turned to MacReady. A fuzz of dark hair, fearful eyes leaking tears which cut through a face caked with black powder.

'Hey,' MacReady said. Gave a warm smile. 'You OK there? Playing hide-and-seek?'

'Daddy!' the boy cried.

'Jesus,' Fletcher said. He'd scooted down, was lying on the ground next to MacReady.

'We're going to take you to your daddy,' MacReady nodded. Extended a hand, slowly, not wanting to spook the kid. The boy's eyes shifted from MacReady to Fletcher and back. MacReady kept smiling. 'What's your name, little man?'

'I want daddy.'

'Come on,' MacReady urged. Hand almost within touching distance now. 'Come with us, I know just where your daddy is and he's waiting for you. I'll take you right to him, okay?'

The boy remained still. Silent now. Wide black eyes, blinking slowly, as if getting the measure of the two grown-ups gurning away at him. MacReady was about to give up and push himself upright when the little boy reached out with tiny fingers and gripped his outstretched hand.

'There you go,' MacReady said softly. 'Why don't you crawl out from under there and I'll take you to daddy, OK?'

The boy sniffed. Wiped at his nose with a forearm. Gave one last suspicious look at the adults lying in the dirt with him then wriggled forwards and out from under the people carrier.

'Wouldn't have heard that kid grizzling in a million years,' Harrison said.

Fletcher pushed himself to his feet, frowned at the grime streaking his shirtfront. He winked at MacReady. 'Well played.'

MacReady scooped the boy up into his arms; he was small enough to sit in the crook of one elbow, legs dangling and bumping against MacReady's midriff. 'Let's go find daddy, yeah?'

He ignored Echols's sarcastic handclaps as he headed towards the cordon. He'd not gone fifty feet when he heard her.

MylittleboyohmyGodit'smylittleboy . . .

Paramedics holding her in place, the woman with the missing arm tried to push herself upwards, to push the medical workers away, her remaining arm outwards, fingers pointing towards MacReady and the child he held against his chest.

'*Jordan!*' the woman screamed.

'Mummy!' the boy called, squirming, trying to break free.

MacReady walked over to the woman, trying not to look at her injury. At the needles and tourniquets and bandages enveloping a stump which didn't want to quit bleeding. He angled the boy, Jordan, away from it, hoping he wouldn't see. Lowered him to the pavement, let him free.

The boy ran to his mother. Her wounds forgotten as her son collapsed into her chest. That one good arm, wrapping him tight, fingers clamped around the nape of his neck.

'My baby,' she moaned. 'Oh, my little baby, my baby . . .'

MacReady didn't hang around. Nodded at the paramedics, walked away. Returned to his colleagues inside the cordon. Glanced around at the scene, trying to absorb it all. Sat down on his haunches, placing one hand to sodden, filthy concrete to steady himself; his guts aflame suddenly, as if he'd been punched there, the wind knocked out of him.

The woman was now screaming for her husband.

MacReady closed his eyes.

Pictured his family.

Five

Air con cool inside the nick, and welcome. Darkness had long since fallen yet the evening air remained warm and close to the point of being cloying, and it was a small joy just to escape it at last.

MacReady was worn out and filthy and reeked of smoke. He rode the lift to the third floor of Cardiff Bay, sharing the confined metal space with two response officers whose tired eyes never left their boots, whose hands were stuffed with reams of Manual of Guidance file prep forms and labelled exhibit bags. He recognised neither, which meant Job small talk was not forthcoming and he was glad because he couldn't face it.

The lift doors opened and MacReady stepped out.

A voice from behind him: 'You CID, bra?'

MacReady turned. The response officers hovered at the open lift door. One of them a late thirtysomething blond cop, watery blue eyes beneath thinning spiked hair, arms like he worked out a lot. In his hand and held out to MacReady was the paperwork he had spied on the way up.

He nodded at them.

The paperwork was thrust at him again. 'Drop these off for us then, yeah?'

MacReady let it hover in mid-air. He'd already learned from Harrison never to lay a finger on anything that you didn't want to become part of your workload. 'What is it?'

'Handover package,' the female uniform said. Thickset, face hard, eyes not even on MacReady as she spoke. One hand on the lift doors, her painted nails keeping them open for a quick escape. 'Wounding from this morning. It's already been passed from the early turn to the late shift to us, and I doubt anyone's even opened the case file. Our stripey says you lot need to take it on. Bronze is in agreement.'

'Are you serious?' MacReady gestured to a nearby window: through it the city skyline, pinpricks of white and red and yellow stretching across a blanket of black. In one corner there was a thick cluster of flashing blue lights where everyone and his dog was still working the market at Bessemer Road. 'There is no "you lot". Everyone's down there, or at the mosque, remember?'

The blond cop shoved the file into MacReady's hands; the female officer dumped the exhibit bags on top. It happened too fast for him. MacReady grimaced as they landed on his palms, wishing he'd pulled his hands away.

'Well, you're here, aren't you?' the blond cop smiled.

'I'm done for the day,' MacReady replied, hitching an elbow to stop a stray sheet of paper sliding from the pile.

The female officer gave a humourless chuckle. 'And we're just starting our night shift.'

'So give it to one of your team,' MacReady said, and raised the bundle of forms and bags towards them.

The response officers exchanged a quick glance. 'Team? Are *you* serious?' the blond cop asked. 'We're it. The two of us. For the next ten hours.'

The female stepped back into the lift, hand still on the door. 'And we already have three in the bin for processing. Plus seventeen calls outstanding, most of them since this morning, thanks to that.' She nodded at the window, removed her hand from the door.

'So if you want to take it up with our sergeant,' the blond cop said, joining his companion in the lift, 'feel free to point-to-point him on Airwave.'

'His collar number is nine-nine-nine-too-fucking-busy,' the female winked.

The lift doors slid closed.

MacReady waited for a moment, listening to the laughter emanating from the lift shaft. Looked down at the case file. Scanned the details quickly, flipping through a few of the pages. Noted the injured party was female, and thus far nameless. The IP's injuries: multiple puncture wounds, probably via a knife, the sort of attack which seemed ever more commonplace nowadays. Wondered if it was domestic abuse. The complete lack of any suspects or arrests meant plenty of ball-aching effort for whoever found the file in their in-tray.

He pushed through the doors to the suite of CID offices. Checked around: the suite deathly silent, nobody else in sight.

Smiled as he dropped the paperwork and exhibit bags on DS Echols's desk.

*

The CID's 'writing room' was a windowless box just off the main corridor; until the previous autumn it had been a store cupboard for a cantankerous cleaner's extensive selection of mops and soiled girlie mags, but the DI had seen to it that the moany old perv was booted elsewhere on the third floor in order to refit the place as an office. And, as was normal for the Old Bill, refit meant a new – and shockingly patchy – coat of paint, a scarred desk 'appropriated' from another floor, possibly while the user was out on their lunch break, and some cobbled-together IT equipment.

Charlie Beck seemed content enough in there, though. It was her designated space, created by Fletcher for her return to work on light duties, the DI having no intention of letting his star detective sergeant stray too far from the fold. He would not countenance a post-injury 'reintegration and familiarisation' stint in uniform for her, and MacReady understood why. People had a habit of never coming back from that quagmire of shitty shifts and uniformed social work, looking after large swathes of the public who were incapable of doing it themselves. The life got its claws into you, if you let it. Fletcher had argued vociferously with the divisional command team that Beck's recuperation would be speedier – and better for her, and the office as a whole – if she was part of the team, no matter how small or peripheral the position. He had tasked his favourite detective sergeant with the role of office manager – overseeing cases, managing workloads, giving myopic old-sweat DCs an objective view. Or, as Fletcher explained to MacReady during a pub visit, making sure none of the blokes on the team dropped a bollock.

It was also the room where MacReady had been served his disciplinary papers.

Late October the year before, paint pots and roller brushes leaning against half-completed walls, an unsmiling and mildly embarrassed detective sergeant from the force's Professional Standards Department explaining the reasons for the Regulation Nine notice. *The shooting . . . Independent Police Complaints Commission have asked us to do this . . .* Harrison, of all people, in there and acting as MacReady's 'police friend'. Everyone else too busy clearing their workloads after the Bob Garratt case.

'I'm really sorry about this,' the DS had shrugged at MacReady. 'It's just procedure so we can look into the circumstances of . . . you know.'

'Say fuck all, boy,' Harrison had advised bluntly.

MacReady stood in the doorway, doing the same now. Watching Beck for a moment. No light on, her face a glow of concentration at the computer screen as she mouse-clicked and tutted and shifted in her seat, pausing only to nibble at the skin around a thumb. Charlotte 'Charlie' Beck. Always on the move, even if she was sitting down. One booted heel tap-tap-tapping on the floor beneath her chair; MacReady noted it was her good leg doing it. Felt the guilt, acute as ever.

Your fault she's like this.

He glazed over, thinking back to last year, to Bob Garratt: a plain-clothes detective sergeant who'd been murdered on MacReady's first day in CID. Shot dead at point-blank range as he led his team on an early-morning raid. The shooting had shocked the city, but more was to come. Worse was to come.

And it had led MacReady and Beck to a filthy basement garage. To cold concrete and engine oil and the warmth of her blood on his fingers as he'd pushed against the bullet wound in her hip. And then the visits to hospital and Beck's home, her parents' pale, concerned faces slowly giving way to anger and recrimination, her girlfriend's quivering finger jabbing into MacReady's chest and asking questions to which he had no answer. After being served with papers: the taped interviews and statements and meetings with the force solicitor. Pointless emails and missed appointments by the useless Federation rep which made him wonder why he bothered paying his monthly subs. The point, that dark day in February this year, just six months into his detective training programme, where he considered putting his ticket in because it was abundantly clear the Job was going after him, no matter what good had come of the Garratt case, no matter how clean his disciplinary record, no matter how many people he was putting behind bars.

Then Fletcher had vouched for him. Pulled some strings, called in a few long-standing favours. Harrison, too, unbelievably. And then Beck herself. Letters and emails to whoever needed to receive them. Praise and absolution and the expression of a desire to move on and let MacReady continue to grow and learn with her guidance.

Months of it, seemingly endless, until one day Fletcher was at his side telling him he was off the hook.

A written warning. Management advice.

They'd celebrated over a cup of tea which they'd ordered MacReady to make by way of thanks. The advice had come from

Fletcher in his office later that day: *Don't be such a cock, next time, yeah? It's loads of hassle and I really hate all that paperwork.*

The gratitude he felt was only outweighed by the sense of relief, of a weight finally lifted; he'd gone home and slept for fourteen hours.

'You just going to stand there, numbnuts?'

MacReady blinked, Beck and the desk and the computer coming into focus. Found himself chewing at the inside of his cheek. Tasted something metallic in his mouth.

Beck was staring up at him, eyebrow arched.

'Sarge,' he said, and swallowed the blood. Exhaled, leaning against the doorframe, not sure if he could rely on his legs to hold out much longer.

'I could smell you from the corridor.' Beck swivelled to face him, gave a weary smile. 'A day of days, I gather.'

He wondered how much to say. What to tell her. If she'd heard enough already. The change in her since she'd been shot was barely noticeable, but it was there. Subtle things. The times she'd laugh a little too hard when the gallows humour about the latest sex assault or aggravated burglary incident started in the office. The slight hesitation when asked to view crime scene photos. MacReady sensed she was coping but her self-doubt, her mental brittleness, were proving annoying for her and were obvious to the hierarchy, which was why she was still on light duties. The perkiness, the jokes and name-calling were present and correct, and it was not quite a façade but there was certainly an undercurrent there. Something was off, and he worried for her.

It was the grand irony of police work: you spent so much time and effort not getting close to people – everybody moved on in the end – but one shared traumatic experience and an unspoken bond would develop, stronger sometimes than you had with your spouse or lover. Relationships and home lives often suffered as a result. MacReady could say things to his sergeant – who, in reality, he barely knew – that he wouldn't dream of discussing with his wife, Megan.

He offered a quick nod. 'Can't wait to get away but don't want to leave.'

'Then stay,' Beck urged.

'Believe me, I want to but Fletcher gave me the nod to go home. He's just this week signed me off as a fully fledged DC –'

'I heard, go you.'

'Thanks. *And* I'm still in best behaviour mode, so don't want to annoy him. Anyway I think he's got enough to deal with today, don't you?'

'He'd have enough just putting up with Echols,' she chuckled, then stopped when she saw MacReady's face. 'Not your fault, Will.'

He sighed. 'Nobody wants him here, least of all me.'

A wave of her hand. 'Well he is, so suck it up. How bad is it down there?'

The market. He pictured stiffening bodies beneath sheets. The bloodied stump of an arm. 'Horrific. I . . . I don't know . . .'

Beck waited, and when nothing more was forthcoming just reached across and gently squeezed at his forearm. She sucked air through teeth. 'Troubling times. We've got three confirmed deceased at Bessemer. And it's a right mess inside the mosque, apparently. I've been fielding calls from the team there. At least one bomb detonated but it was a smaller explosion, possibly partial, as if it didn't quite work properly. There's still a hell of a lot of damage, though.'

'Confined space,' MacReady said.

'Nice new red paint job on the walls.'

'I think I'm there tomorrow.'

'You lucky dabber. How did court go?'

MacReady rolled his eyes, but a small part of him was happy to talk about something other than Bessemer. 'Waffle and grand-standing from the briefs, as per. They –'

'Not Castle,' she cut across him. 'With your brother.'

He gestured at the empty chair next to hers; she nodded, and he slumped into it, glad to be off his feet. 'Wish he'd just duck his nut and plead. Torture for his ex and the kids, but Stuart doesn't really factor that into his limited thought processes. Other than that: waffle and grandstanding from the briefs.'

'The so-called justice *system*,' Beck smiled, and turned back to the computer screen; she winced, the tiniest of twinges, as she shifted in her seat.

'Hurrah,' he raised a weak fist into the air and shook it. 'So what you up to?'

'CCTV.' She nodded at the screen. 'Already got discs and hard drives coming out of my ears. Just started running through the Cardiff Bus recordings. They've got video and audio, so bonus. I'm supposed to start getting the ANPR camera data through at some point tonight.'

'You're staying?'

'From Fletch: long as it takes.'

'He's mad. You're mad.'

'Supplies.' She pointed to the floor; he saw a rucksack leaning against the side of the desk, zip partially open, packets of biscuits just about visible inside. 'Now off you go before you get too comfy, there's a good boy. You've a wife to get home to.'

He pushed himself up from the chair, glanced at the computer screen. Saw the paused CCTV image: the view from the front of a bus, just behind the driver and facing out through the large windscreen into the street. MacReady could see the industrial units, the car sales showrooms: Bessemer Road. Wondered if Fletcher or any of the rest of the higher-ups had even thought to consider what effect the contents might have on Beck.

'That I do,' he said, but wasn't sure what he had. He'd already called Megan, who seemed relieved to hear his voice; the market and mosque attacks were on every news channel. But the call had been awkward, and his blood had started boiling as it always did of late, and he'd ended it cutting his wife off mid-sentence.

'OK,' Beck muttered, almost to herself. She was lost to him again, face pressed up against the monitor, squinting and working the mouse.

He paused at the door. On the screen: the recording played, the sounds of passenger chatter and diesel engine as Bessemer Road rolled towards the bottom of the frame. The driver's left hand gripping the steering wheel. The gates of the market growing in size as the bus neared the entrance.

Then the loud bang. Two more in quick succession.

Beck flinched each time, her shoulders hunched.

MacReady stepped forwards and placed a hand on one of them.

'I'm sorry,' he said, and squeezed.

Beck didn't look at him, her eyes fixed on the video image she'd paused. Her hand came up and found MacReady's.

Stayed there.

Six

Gone eleven p.m. and he was met with the stillness of a sleeping house.

MacReady slipped in through the front door, timing it so there was no whoosh of traffic to follow him inside. Fingers tight around keys, mindful not to let them jangle. Eased off his shoes while standing on the mat, crept in socked silence along the wooden floor of the hallway, paused at the bottom of the stairs. Listened for a moment. Heard nothing but Megan's rhythmic breathing: the bedroom door would be open, just in case. Just so she could hear Finlay if he cried out or became unsettled.

In the kitchen he pulled the fridge's solitary lager from a shelf and popped the cap. Pulled hard on the bottle, sucking half of it down before wiping at his mouth with the back of an ash-smeared sleeve. For a moment it felt good, as if washing away the day, the alcohol hitting his empty stomach and giving an immediate buzz. Then he remembered the child at Bessemer Market, Jordan, hand jutting from beneath the people carrier, reaching for him. Needing him. MacReady looked at the ceiling. Thought about going upstairs, just to hold a tiny hand again. *He* needed it now, the closeness, the warmth and feel of another, like Beck had needed it not half an hour before.

The kitchen door opened. Megan, dark hair mussed, eyes scrunched to slits against the harsh spots dotting the ceiling.

'You're . . . here,' she said, voice a just-woken croak.

MacReady nodded. Noted she'd almost said 'home', and wasn't sure how he felt about her carefully worded greeting. Relief, probably. He held up the bottle. 'Just . . .'

He didn't finish but she nodded anyway, padded into the room, bare feet pale against quarry-tiled floor. Hesitated in front of him, as if gauging the mood. Trying to read him. Sighed, and folded herself into him, placed arms around his midriff, her head against his chest. MacReady tensed for a fraction of a second, an involuntary reaction, and not because of the filth caking him. Her hair smelled of fabric conditioner from her pillow, floral and exotic. He breathed it in. Forced himself to relax. Hoped she wouldn't hear the rapid thump of his heart.

'I know,' she said. Lifted her head to study him. Her mouth an inch away from his. Her face a blur. 'I'm so glad you're safe. I've been worried, Will. The stuff on TV, it looked so awful.'

MacReady felt her hot breaths on his lips. So close now, their mouths almost touching.

'I've never seen anything like it before. It made me want to be here.'

A nod from her. 'Do you want to talk?'

He twisted away, out of her arms, uncomfortable with the intimacy. Saw the flash of pain in her eyes as he did it, felt wretched for a second, but then Stuart was there, in his head, and what his wife had done with his brother resurfaced and the familiar resentment bubbled up and smothered any feelings of remorse. *Such a mess*. 'All I need to do is see Fin.'

'He's not long settled. It took me ages –'

'I'll be quick,' he snapped, instantly regretting it. He took another hit of the bottle, draining the thing. Placed the empty on the worktop and turned back to his wife. Softened his voice. 'And quiet. He'll never know I was in there.'

'No,' Megan said, eyes downcast, 'he probably won't.'

In the darkened bedroom he hovered over the cot, breathing quietly, his hair brushing against the garishly coloured caterpillars and bumble bees hanging from a mobile. Megan stood alongside him as he looked down on the small, unmoving form swaddled in a thin sheet.

Fin. Two-month-old Finlay William MacReady. A name he had always wanted for his own son. A son who he would love, would bring up properly, doing a better job – not hard, he admitted – than his own father had. A name Megan had pushed for anyway, in the delivery room as soon as Fin was in her arms and breathing his first. MacReady knew it was her way of trying to make amends. Of trying to make things better. He had fought her those first few weeks but acquiesced in the end, told her to go for it, just to stop her talking about it, just to leave him alone while he continued to try and make sense of Megan and Stuart's 'solution' to MacReady's infertility.

Fin was tucked in, flat on his back. Eyes squeezed tightly shut, one pudgy arm loose, a small popping noise coming from his nose. The hottest summer in decades and the kid had a cold.

MacReady reached in, let his fingers close around Fin's. Marvelled afresh at how tiny they were, how delicate. Wished that everything was normal, that he could just slip into bed alongside Megan and sleep properly for the first time in months, that he would wake to find Finlay sleeping between them and Bessemer was just a bad dream and his fucking brother had never been born.

'Stay, Will,' Megan whispered.

MacReady looked down at the baby. Around at the room which he'd paid to decorate. At his wife, her face a mask of shadows. He closed his eyes. The small boy beneath the car this morning. Reaching for him, calling for his father. MacReady wanted that. Needed that now, he knew. No matter the circumstances surrounding Finlay's arrival, as far as he was concerned he was the boy's father and would never let him go. But it was the grandest of ironies: for so long he had fought to be a good husband, had wanted to be a good father. Had stood by Megan during the pregnancy, at the birth. Had tried to be everything his own father was not. William MacReady Senior: alcoholic, domestic abuser, philanderer. Murderer. Unable to commit to any relationship, be it with his wife or sons or the string of lovers he trailed in his wake. And now here MacReady was, unable to commit to *his* wife because of his brother's intervention. Stuart, who seemed keen to replicate a father they both despised. A father whose actions still reverberated, twenty years later.

He'd fought so hard not to have a fucked-up family of his own, and yet here he was.

MacReady let go of Fin's hand. Opened his eyes.

He didn't know what to do any more so did what he thought was best.

'I can't,' he replied, and left the room.

*

Duncan Jones was drunk and sitting in his underpants.

'Oy, oy, Willy boy. Fancy a beer, amigo? Well warm still, innit?' Jones didn't wait for an answer. Turned back to the television, face slack and hands clawed around a PlayStation controller as he played the latest incarnation of FIFA.

MacReady surveyed the wreckage of the small lounge. Empty lager cans, half-finished bottle of budget supermarket whisky, plates and bowls and foil cartons with what looked like congealed takeaway Chinese food dangling from their sides, all of it on the cracked glass top of a coffee table. An ashtray loaded with fag butts rested on one edge; a fug of blueish smoke clung to the ceiling, as if one of the cigarettes had just been outed. Mingled with the delicate aroma was the faint whiff of body odour.

In the middle of it all, pale, sagging belly matching the tired cream faux-leather settee on which he sat, Jones cackled gleefully as he scored, then scratched at his groin. MacReady noticed the orange streaks on the plump man's skivvies, saw the remnants of a jumbo packet of cheese puffs on the floor.

'Not for me, thanks.'

'Good job really, *bach*,' Jones sniggered, and paused the football game. 'Ain't none left.' He patted about on the settee, found his crumpled pack of Marlboros. Slipped one into his mouth then, with a wink at MacReady, sparked it up and restarted the match he was already winning six-nil.

Jones clearly hadn't moved since MacReady had left for Crown that morning, other than to take a piss or, as he called it, *curl one out*. At twenty-nine he was just two years older than MacReady but already on the way to a second divorce, and his life revolved around shift work where he was a uniform – and not a good one – on the northern side of the city, or drinking and smoking himself into an emphysemic coma. The swagger was for effect, though: MacReady regularly heard Jones crying in his bedroom at night, evidently talking to an ex who had no intention of ever having him back.

He hovered behind the settee for a moment, hands on his car keys and wondering what on earth he had ever done to end up in this man's house, renting a box bedroom with a tiny window that afforded a view of a sprawling estate of identikit redbrick new builds and a McDonald's on Cardiff's eastern flank.

Desperation, he knew. There was nothing for him here, but at the moment it was marginally better than the place he used to call home. At the very least it gave him some breathing space, a place where the constant white noise in his ears would subside and where he could try to work out what to do next.

He tilted his head back and closed his eyes. Offered up a small prayer that this wasn't permanent. That this wasn't all that awaited him if he and Megan failed.

'Did you see it?' MacReady asked, looking down to the television.

Jones paused the game again, not altogether happy about having to do so. Shifted his sweaty bulk on the settee with a rubbery squelch, the ciggie hanging from one sticky lip and bouncing as he spoke. 'See wha'?'

MacReady raised his eyebrows. 'You serious? The market? The mosque?'

'Dunno. What about them?'

'We've had an attack, Dunc. Bombings. Some guy, he did the market at Bessemer Road, then drove across to Penarth and hit the Al Mahdi.'

Jones took a long pull on the cigarette, scrunched up his face, looked at the ceiling as if trying to remember if he'd heard anything. 'Nah,' he said eventually, and nodded at the wide screen as smoke drifted from the corners of his mouth. 'Been busy all day. Much aggro?'

MacReady exhaled. 'The entire world is at the scenes. You didn't get a recall to duty? Uniform knocking the door and telling you to come in?'

'How could I?' Jones frowned, as if MacReady was an idiot. 'I never answer the phone or the door on rest days. Fuck the job. And anyway,' he laughed, then let out a belch, 'I've been pissed since eleven this morning so I'm no good to anybody.'

MacReady left Jones to his FIFA tournament, dumped his car keys on the rickety bedside table in his room and lay on the bed fully clothed, studying the ceiling with its micro-cracked plasterwork. From the lounge came more cackles which disintegrated into deep gurgling coughs, accompanied by the roar of football crowds and commentary from the game. Jones might have been a useless plod but he could win Olympic gold at partying. MacReady knew the football-and-boozeathon could go on for hours yet.

He gave it ten minutes, the day spinning around him. The market, the bloodshed. Megan, Finlay. Echols and Stuart and waiting – waiting, again – at court for a result in the Castle case. MacReady checked the time on his phone. Hesitated, tapping

the top of the phone against his front teeth. After a few moments
he sighed and brought up his messages.

Sent: You still awake?
The reply was instant: Silly question.

'Fuck it,' he said, and reached for his car keys.

*

It meant nothing, and never did, and for that he was grateful. It
was a release, but MacReady had needed it. He rolled away from
her feeling lighter than he had done for days, draped his forearm
over his tired eyes and let it go. All of it, evaporating. Some solace
at last, away from the madness. No responsibilities, no small talk
or post-coitus cuddles required – she'd never asked for any of it
and he knew she was using him, much as he was using her.

Klaudia Solak had already turned her attention to her tablet,
tapping away at the screen, sitting up in the bed with back propped
against pillows, completely naked, a sheen of sweat on her breasts,
her top lip, the air con doing little to lower the sweltering temperature in the room. She couldn't be bothered to hide folds of skin or
ripples or even pretend to care whether he liked what he saw or
not. It made him like her more, and there was already plenty to like.

MacReady threw the thin duvet to one side, scooted off the bed.
Walked over to the window, looked out across the water, still unable
to believe the view from Solak's apartment. The waters of Cardiff
Bay and its marina, the pinprick lights of the English coastline in

the distance. He'd never bothered to check the cost of this place, but guessed they were probably changing hands for a cool half a million or more. For what was essentially a one-bedroom flat plus kitchenette – with an admittedly spectacular panoramic view of the sea.

He paused for a few minutes, tilted open the awning window, the weakest of breezes wafting into the room and across his skin. Sirens in the distance, faint yet constant, and he wondered how they were coping out there: the attacks meant staff would have been drafted in from all corners of the force, leaving the bare minimum to respond to calls from the public. He'd seen it before, albeit on a smaller scale, for high-profile sports matches, for ceremonial events and world leaders gathering for three-day jollies. Days off cancelled, people called in on overtime, shifts depleted right across every division just to cope. Just to give the impression there were lots of cops in one area. The reality was no uniforms to go anywhere else. Incidents racked and stacked, the Public Service Centre call handlers doing their best to deal with things on the phone, to fob people off, to use the old Bullshit Baffles Brains to convince the public they didn't really need the Old Bill to help settle their petty neighbour dispute.

While in uniform he'd always hated going into work for an early turn immediately after a major event or incident. You could guarantee the outstanding call list – some two or three days old – would be depressingly huge in number.

MacReady closed the window and climbed back onto the bed. Shifted onto an elbow and moved closer to Solak. Rested his head on her shoulder, eased a hand around her bare midriff; the simplicity of it felt wonderful. To have somebody to hold onto where he didn't have to explain or rationalise or try to work out if it was what she – what *he* – wanted. Solak was just like Harrison: she simply didn't give a shit.

On the iPad he could see images from Bessemer Road, see ten or more tabs Solak had opened lined across the top of the screen. A mixture of news reports about the attacks and articles covering the Alexander Castle trial.

'Still going,' he said.

She nodded. 'International now. And Facebook and Twitter have imploded.'

'I meant you,' he smiled.

'Got to keep up with the young guns,' she told him, squinting as she scrolled through a *Guardian* opinion piece that MacReady noticed was predictably anti-police. 'Everybody's a journalist nowadays.'

'It's just bloggers,' he yawned. 'There's a load of them out there.'

'You're wrong to dismiss them,' and there was a tone to her voice that caused him to look up at her. 'Print is dying. And anyone with a camera phone can record things as they happen. There's a new breed out there and they're after my job. Which is why I'm up at stupid o'clock cobbling together a piece for the website which'll generate some traffic.'

MacReady nuzzled into her arm. 'And there's me thinking it was because you enjoyed my company so much.'

'Yes, Will,' Solak snorted, without looking at him. 'My heart aches when you're not here with me. In fact, it aches when you *are* because you refuse to give me any info about your cases.'

He chuckled. It felt good. 'So what are this new breed saying?'

'Apart from you lot couldn't solve a kids' crossword puzzle?'

'Standard,' he shrugged.

'There's one in particular I follow.' Solak's finger swiped away the opinion piece, tapped on a different tab. A website appeared, filled with reams of text. The blogger's avatar was, unsurprisingly, a *V for Vendetta* Guy Fawkes mask; no name in the bio, either.

'Oh look, *Anonymous*.' He rolled his eyes.

MacReady skimmed through the piece on the screen. A wordy rant about the Castle trial, about race in the UK, and how the police have learned nothing since the Stephen Lawrence inquiry. Plenty of block capitals for emphasis.

'All seems a bit tin-foil hat,' he commented.

Solak pushed at him with her forearm. 'He's the best out there at the moment. You'd do well to read his work. Thorough, insightful. His pieces on the Alex Castle murder are pretty astounding. Most traditional media has been reporting what he blogs as fact. Much to the police's annoyance.'

MacReady studied the web pages she was now flicking through. 'Never read any of his stuff, if I'm being honest.'

Solak looked puzzled. 'That's odd.'

'Well, like I said, there's a load of them out there so –'

'No, I mean he's not blogged about today's attacks.'

'Might be waiting until he's got whatever info he needs, if he's that thorough.'

She shook her head. 'He's always got fresh content. *Always*. Something like today, it'd be straight up there. Some crazy idiot blowing up a mosque, and a market while an ethnic celebration was going on? With the Castle race murder trial as a backdrop? He'd be all over it. He'd just edit and correct as the day went on and more info became available.'

MacReady checked the time at the top of the iPad screen: gone one in the morning, and Fletcher had sent him home to sleep so he'd be in early to relieve night shift staff and pick up any ongoing actions or updates. He lolled sideways, onto his back. Rubbed at his face, tired now. 'I'm sure he'll pop up with the culprit's name tomorrow. And then we can all get some proper sleep.' He wriggled closer to Solak, yawned again.

She wagged a finger at him. 'Uh-uh. Don't get too comfortable, Detective Constable MacReady.'

He sat up, elbows on knees. Stared at her, incredulous. 'Serious? I've got to go? Now?'

'Them's the rules, my little sex toy. Time for you to make some room so I can make like a starfish.'

MacReady puffed air out between thinned lips. 'Well, this is just great.'

It was Solak's turn to yawn. 'Isn't it? You might want to shower before you go, though. You stink of horrible man juice and smoke.'

Seven

He sits amongst the detritus, the remnants of fast food and discarded bottles of alcohol and the thick stench of his own flesh, the television remote control resting on his naked white stomach, the matted hair around his filthy navel curling up along the handset, his eyes unblinking and on the images flickering across the television screen.

Smoke and misery and the pulse of blue lights. A breathless reporter, face smudged, his puny hands twisting at a microphone as he struggles to put into words what he has witnessed. What his eyes have seen that can never be unseen. His fey, bland voice battling to explain the unexplainable as inoffensively as possible. *Must not affront anyone. Must not fan the outrage. Be inclusive. Be diverse. Be bland with your tamed tongue.*

He laughs as he watches because it is written all over the man's twisted face: he wishes he was home with his loved ones. Wishes he was holding them tight. Wishes he could piss and moan and gnash his teeth live on the idiot box, railing against the horrors of this world, a world which he probably doesn't understand any more.

He's with the newsman on that count. The world is fucking insane. People are so inured, so numb, so disgracefully self-absorbed with their pouting selfies and endless cat pictures and stupid status updates, you have to do something spectacular to make them sit up and take notice.

And it is spectacular. He's been watching the fallout all day, clicking through the rolling twenty-four-hour news coverage, occasionally flicking back to the PlayStation to shoot up a few pedestrians or rip off a bank, turning back to the news again, revelling in a solid wall of unending chaos interrupted just the once when it all became too much for him and he had to masturbate into a half-empty beer bottle.

'That'll learn you,' he says to the television. 'That'll learn you, you fucks.'

The alcohol has finally hit him hard and he finds the words wrestling with his tongue, finds himself unable to stop the drool which leaks from his bottom lip onto his left nipple and he thinks about wiping it away, studies the spittle and his pinched pink areola for a minute or so while he decides if it's worth the effort, if he still has the energy after all that has taken place, and as the saliva soaks into his slippery skin he decides to leave it be. It is late, and he is exhausted now, the successes of the day finally catching up with him, the adrenalin finally – *finally*, more than fifteen hours later – spent, the TV screen suddenly shifting in his vision. He blinks the blurriness away, shakes his head a little. Glances around, at the mess he has created, the destruction he has wrought upon this room, a smaller version of the destruction meted out this morning.

'One more go,' he dribbles, and lifts up the remote control, carefully switches over to the game he's loaded, drops the remote back to his distended abdomen and reaches for the controller.

The shooter ready to go. His ammo maxed. The target building chock full of stuffed shirts and office drones and Powerfucking-Point pointlessness.

'Here we go, one more go . . .' he says and it won't be the same, could never be the same but should finish the day nicely, and he starts it up and is pushing through the company's glassed revolving door with semi-automatic cocked and raised but hears movement in the house, soft footsteps as if somebody is barefoot and padding around trying to be oh-so-quiet. *Not again.*

Then a voice from behind him.

'You still awake?'

Oh God oh God oh God please fuck off and die you miserable, boring cunt.

'Still going strong.' He follows it with a shrug, quick and resentful.

A pause. 'You need to get some sleep.'

He blinks slowly, the muscles in his face stiffening, his eyelids cast-iron shutters he is struggling to keep from slamming down. The booze streaking through him, pummelling him now. He feels a flash of anger, of *fury*, at being told what to do. Nobody can tell him what to do, not anymore. Not after the market and the mosque and all that he has planned.

All that he has planned.

It hits him: better to go quietly. Suck it up. Save it up. He could sit here and dial it up to eleven, give this fucker what for, but even in his paralytic state he knows it would be ruinous to do so. And he is so, so tired now. Dead on his feet. Was probably going to jack it in anyway.

So he stands, bare toes scrunching into crunchy snacks littering the floor, finger zapping the television off with the remote, one clammy hand yanking the PlayStation's plug out of its socket.

The other hand flies upwards, fingers pointing, until it reaches his forehead.

He salutes.

Laughs.

'Mission accomplished.'

Thursday

Eight

Banners and placards. Whistles and flags and loudhailers. Some loon dressed as a court jester, banging away on a humungous pair of bongos while he ignored the requests from *between-jobs* residents, hanging out of bedroom windows and clearly unimpressed with their unplanned early start to the morning, to shut the fuck up.

The chant: *If you're not part of the solution, you're part of the problem.*

Not as pithy as *All coppers are bastards* or even the time-honoured classic *Fuck the pigs*, but the Unite Against Fascism crowd seemed happy enough to recite it ad nauseam to the bongo beat, sun already warming their backs where it hovered over the James Street skyline behind them.

Five hours of broken sleep and MacReady was too tired to give a shit about what they shouted. Yet again it struck him as somewhat ironic that those bellowing and lobbing the odd piss-filled fizzy drink bottle or wooden stick at the police cordon were also being protected by the very officers they were abusing. A hundred yards away another sparse line of early-turn uniforms and drafted-in Public Order officers were just about keeping back a rabble of Britain First supporters and diehard English Defence Leaguers, whose failed placards and sandwich boards – *Respect Are Country; Muslins Out* – were being held by a clutch of shaved skulls in footy shirts who quite clearly wanted to bash a few Anti-Fash heads in. On the fringes, parked half on the pavement: an Armed Response vehicle, its occupants' gelled hair and shades in the windscreen. There'd be more across the city. Authorised Firearms Officers and Specialist Firearms Officers, in uniform and plain clothes, at major sites and shopping centres, at public transport hubs and the airport in the Vale of Glamorgan.

MacReady had always hated working demonstrations. Standing there for hours, deliberately blank while anyone and everyone called you from your hole to your pole. While ordinarily benign middle-aged middle-class types wished your family dead. Wished you cancer. Screamed into your face that you were racist, a murderer, that you'd helped cover up the murder of ninety-six football fans even though you hadn't been born when it happened and don't have anything to do with South Yorkshire Police. Their spittle landing in thick beads on your mouth, your cheeks. Ironic, again, that on most of the demos he'd worked he'd agreed with what they were protesting about. As a lowly plod you just had to stand there and take it, before going inside the nick to take it again from long-in-the-tooth colleagues and the senior ranks.

Sometimes he thought they should let the two sides get on with it. Just once. Let them pummel each other while the cops stood by and watched for a change. He was not the only one to think it, either. Bets were frequently made about who would win a rumble, with most cops leaning towards the 'pacifist hippies':

MacReady had seen they were more than capable of gouging an eye or biting off an earlobe if the urge took them.

'Top of the morning to you all,' he muttered and took the steps up to Cardiff Bay police station two at a time, dodging a thrown fruit juice carton as he went. MacReady recognised several faces in the crowd: a woman with ginger dreadlocks and several facial piercings, an earnest twentysomething man with thick-rimmed spectacles and the obligatory bright-red Che Guevara tee, the whey-faced overweight guy who – once again – was in a faded World of Warcraft sweatshirt and whose dark-ringed, unsettling eyes never left MacReady. All of them had been outside Crown for weeks, following the ongoing Castle trial, chanting about the rights of those in the dock. A new cause now, their shouts and demands geared towards justice – *when do we wannit? NOW!* – for the victims of yesterday's attacks.

MacReady buzzed, swiped and keyed in numbers, slowly working his way up and through the seemingly endless security checks and doors which always made him wonder how they would manage to evacuate sharpish if ever the building went up in flames.

The CID suite was empty, save for DC Warren Harrison sitting in the open-plan main office surrounded by swooping screensavers and piles of case files. It was a red socks day for Harrison today; they glowed beneath the straps of his sandals. He looked up at MacReady, grunted a greeting then returned to his bowl of Sugar Puffs, shovelling them into the gaping hole in his face as if he'd not eaten for three days. Tucked into his collar was a crumpled, sodden MG file form, a makeshift bib to prevent milk dripping on his tie.

'Am I early?' MacReady asked, draping his jacket on the back of his chair.

The spoon paused at Harrison's beefy lips. 'For what?'

'The briefing.'

'You having a laugh, mun?' Harrison shook his head. 'We started at eight.'

MacReady checked his phone: eight twenty. 'Ah.'

Harrison hooked a thumb at the window; MacReady could hear the noise from the street three floors below, bongo man clearly going for it. 'Even the crusties and skinheads were here before you. Pretty impressive given most of the unwashed fuckers are allergic to getting up before eleven. Anyway, everybody's up in Conference Room Two.'

'That the incident room?'

'For now it is, till they sort out all the equipment for the MIR.'

The Major Incident Room. Still being cobbled together. 'Shouldn't you be there?'

Harrison dropped the spoon into the bowl. Eyed MacReady. 'Yes. I bloody well should be. But I'm sitting here waiting for you, you clueless tosspot, because I knew you'd be late and need someone to tell you where it was all going on so you didn't get into any more bother with Fletcher.'

'Cheers, Wazza,' MacReady smiled. 'Owe you one.'

Harrison winked, finished the last of the cereal. Yanked off his file-form bib and crumpled it. 'Any bloody time. And you owe me one brew with three sugars.'

MacReady sighed. 'Of course.'

He glanced at his desk. With a sinking feeling noticed the case file he'd been handed by the two uniformed officers the night before. The case file he'd left on Detective Sergeant Echols's desk. The stabbing, with the Jane Doe injured party still in hospital. Beneath his chair sat the exhibit bags. On the file itself a Post-It note, Echols's scrawl across it: 'I will speak to you later.'

MacReady had no idea how Echols knew, but he knew. Which meant the file had been left untouched, other than for its short journey across the room to MacReady's desk as soon as Echols had walked in this morning. Which also meant the injured party and any other witnesses probably hadn't been visited by anyone from CID as yet. A trip to the University Hospital was on the cards. Meaning MacReady would be sidelined again, off doing things other than working the market and mosque attacks.

He swivelled his head to Harrison. 'You seen Echols yet?'

'Yep.'

'Is he a happy bunny?'

'Yep.'

'With me, I mean?'

'Oh,' yawned Harrison. 'Then no.'

MacReady puffed out his cheeks. 'Deep joy.'

*

MacReady feared for the Major Incident Room when it opened.

Cardiff Bay station's Conference Room Two was large enough to hold a fair few bodies under normal circumstances – its welcoming cream walls and plush carpets could comfortably host a jovial 'symposium' for a considerable number of senior officers, their hangers-on and a fine selection of crustless sarnies. After the attacks all pretensions of normality, something the upper echelons were usually adroit at maintaining no matter how pear-shaped things had gone, had evaporated.

MacReady had expected plenty of people for the first full briefing but this was ridiculous: they couldn't even get into the room. He stood back in the corridor as Harrison pushed at the door, grunting. Not noticing that it was thumping into the shoulder of a suit just on the other side.

The suit, an Asian male with a terrifically neat goatee and slicked-back hair, finally lost patience with an already out-of-breath Harrison clobbering him with a fire door and peeked through the gap.

'Do you mind?' he said, over the noise from within. MacReady was happy it was still conversations and war stories inside; it meant they hadn't started the briefing.

'Out the fucking way then, mate,' urged Harrison. A trickle of sweat down one temple. Sandalled foot tapping impatiently.

The suit arched an eyebrow that was as neat as his trendy beard. 'That's Detective Inspector Mate to you.'

Harrison tutted. 'Sorry. Out the fucking way then, sir.'

The DI held the door in place with his shoulder. Eyed Harrison through the thin sliver between door and frame. MacReady could see the weighing-up going on in the man's eyes: fat, arrogant Valley boy. Worth the hassle?

Evidently not. With a weary keep-your-powder-dry sigh the DI scooted sideways to create space for Harrison to open the door.

'Cheers, boss,' Harrison beamed. Ducked his head to Mac-Ready: 'Another reason to hate positive discrimination.'

'Jesus, Warren,' MacReady hissed.

It was sweltering inside the room, and awash with people MacReady didn't know. Crammed with the crisp white suits of the National Police Chief Council rankers, the natty two-pieces of detective superintendents, detective chief inspectors, and more DIs like the one at the door. A couple of armed forces guys. Plenty of *we-mean-business* aftershave and testosterone and caffeine in the air, offset just a fraction by a handful of female officers and upper-echelon civvies. The head of Corporate Communications, calmly making notes, and one of the top dogs from the Joint Scientific Investigation Unit, a supremely knowledgeable fiftysomething woman whose name MacReady couldn't recall but who had given a fantastic seminar which he had enjoyed sitting through a few months back.

MacReady thought he spied an assistant chief constable, but couldn't be certain as he'd never in his five years of service seen any of the force's leaders in the flesh. He recognised the police and crime commissioner from the television, had heard the horror stories. Ex-forces type, prone to shouting as if he was on the parade ground and needed to bust a few balls. The man had already dispensed with the services of a clutch of deputies and ensured a few superintendents had been sent on their merry way, tending their allotments and spending commuted pension pots after butting heads with him.

Clustered together in one corner near some windows were the trio of men who'd rocked up at the market the day before. Parachuted in from the Wales Extremism and Counter-Terrorism Unit. Not mingling types, clearly. There was a weird stillness about them as they surveyed the room, not talking to anyone, not talking to one another. MacReady was reminded of the identikit goons from the film *The Matrix*. The spooks were likely to grow in number too: Harrison had been grumbling about Counter-Terrorism security advisers and a couple of officers from the Met's SO15 who were already making their way west along the M4 from London to Cardiff.

Some of these people would leave after this morning, undoubtedly. Return to HQ once their deeds were done. Filter back to their respective divisions and stations and wait for the call to help out in any way that was necessary. Backfilling depleted shifts. Organising Public Order for the demos. Supplying bodies just to plug the gaps when the calls kept coming in and there was nobody to go because everyone was working the attacks. Still, MacReady knew that even if half of them disappeared they were going to have an interesting time fitting what remained, plus equipment, civilians and support, into a MIR that was smaller by half than the room they currently stood in.

'There they are,' Harrison said, and tugged at MacReady's sleeve.

He glanced in the direction he was being pulled as Harrison pushed through knots of detectives, saw Fletcher throwing them a hello across the sea of heads with a twitch of his eyebrows. MacReady grimaced when he saw Echols peer over the crowd, the detective sergeant's eyes narrowing at him.

'You made it,' said Fletcher when they reached them.

'Finally,' said Echols.

Beck stood alongside the DI. MacReady hadn't been able to see her amongst the scrum of officers. He smiled and she returned it.

'Sorry,' he said. 'Couldn't sleep properly after everything –'

'Least you got some,' Echols said pointedly.

Beck winced. Shook her head at MacReady. He looked from her to Fletcher to Echols. Washed-out skin, cracked red eyes.

'You haven't been home?'

'Slept on the floor in my office,' Fletcher nodded. 'Got about two hours.'

'In my chair in mine,' Beck shrugged. 'Same.'

'Grabbed a few hours on a hospital bench,' said Echols. He took a step towards MacReady, leaned into him. 'While I waited to speak to the stabbing victim whose case file you left on my desk.'

'It was nothing to do with m—'

'Night bronze came up to the office at two in the morning to see if anything had been done with it. He found me feet up and trying to kip, not ten minutes after I'd got back from the market. So I *had* to go to the hospital, didn't I? But before I left he told me his people had handed the file over to you, you assclown. So don't give me the clever-clever, right?'

'Paul,' Fletcher warned from behind Echols. A hand on the sergeant's upper arm.

MacReady recoiled a little, Echols too close for his liking. 'I'll deal with it, Sarge.'

Behind them, over by the window, there was movement, and a *shhhh* rippled through the crowd. The police and crime commissioner was climbing onto a chair, a piece of paper being folded and unfolded by pudgy fingers. The *Matrix* guys assembled alongside him.

Echols straightened, sucked in a chest full of air. Let it out slowly, staring out over MacReady's head as the PCC cleared his throat.

'Fucking right you will,' Echols muttered.

Nine

For all the man's media bluster about Cardiff's wonderful community spirit and the togetherness of the force he purported to control, the police and crime commissioner had seemed awfully keen not to be a part of either for any longer than was absolutely necessary. His speech had been as brief as it was hollow, a corporate jargon masterclass droned out before he dropped down from the chair to declare he had a 'Very Important Something' to be getting on with so couldn't stick around, sorry about that. No mention of the deceased. The wounded, their families. The emergency service personnel who'd worked twenty hours straight or more, who were still working, having not seen their own beds since yesterday. Several senior officers had clapped the PCC out of a side door before looking down at their hands as if mortified to find themselves doing it.

'Whatever it takes to rally the troops, I suppose,' Fletcher said.

The detective inspector crossed his legs at the knee, reclined his leather chair a little and turned to look out of his window, his face morose. MacReady watched him from the corner of the room, knew the DI didn't even believe it himself: they had decamped to his office after the briefing, after one ranker gave way to another, after an interminable line of headquarters types who hadn't worked a shift in decades and who appeared ill-equipped to deal with what had befallen the city. They'd offered nothing, and it had been in danger of descending into worthless farce until the fiftysomething civvy from the Joint Scientific Investigation Unit – Janice Goodwin, MacReady had remembered just as she introduced herself – had stepped up to embarrass them all further with a comprehensive list of forensic evidence they'd either gathered or were in the process of gathering.

'I dunno, boss,' Echols replied. 'Felt more like a "sort this out or I will sort you lot out" kind of pep talk from the PCC.'

'Man's got to get them votes,' Harrison said, picking at a dirty fingernail with his car keys. His thick tongue hung from the side his mouth as he concentrated, perched on the edge of a chair. 'Thought the chief would've shown her face for this, though.'

Echols slid into the chair next to him, making sure he didn't get too close. 'She's on her way back from some National Police Chiefs Council "Excellence in Policing" shindig up the north of Eng-er-land. Rushing, apparently.'

'And there's the COBRA committee this morning,' MacReady offered. 'Cabinet are convening about now.'

'Wow, another meeting,' Fletcher smiled.

'Tea and buns, the lot of them,' Harrison said. 'Tea and buns.'

'In fairness it's early doors,' Fletcher said, and scratched at his shaved head. 'And chaos across the board. Lots of people doing the headless chicken thing. Gold have only just opened up the command room in HQ. The Strategic Coordination Group haven't even got together yet. Half of the Cardiff Senior Management Team are still sunning themselves abroad or burning sausages outside a caravan down west Wales. To say we're on the back foot is an understatement.'

'Caught on the hop,' Harrison said, shoving his keys into a pocket.

Beck was leaning against the door, arms folded. 'So there was no warning?'

'Nope,' said Fletcher.

'No code word?' asked MacReady. 'Nothing at all?'

Fletcher continued to stare out at pale-blue sky. '*Nada*. The Public Service Centre has checked all calls into the three nines, the 101 system, even the force Twitter and Facebook accounts. There's absolutely nothing.'

Echols sat back, stretched his legs. 'Bar the usual fruitloops who are now overloading the system with calls that their sister-in-law's brother did it cos God's arse told him to.'

'There is that,' Fletcher said. 'They're drafting in staff on rest days, cancelling leave. Only so much you can do, though, after all the cuts.'

'We're going to run out of people,' Beck told him.

Fletcher gave a tired chuckle. 'We already have.' He swivelled around to his desk, scooted forwards so his stomach pushed against the edge. Sorted through the files piled there and opened one. 'OK. Four dead. Three at Bessemer, one at the mosque. It looks like the device at the Al Mahdi was a partial detonation, but still pretty powerful. Early word from Janice and her mob at CSI says our man was using crude homemade pipe bombs. Plus a shotty to take out a couple of stallholders. One or two wounded at the market are on the brink of shuffling off, and we have . . .'

he scanned the page with glassy eyes, '... thirty-six people injured, of varying severity. Everything from minor cuts and bruises where they fell over while running away to amputations and serious head trauma. All ages, male and female. The market owner is one of the Bessemer dead, a complete goner.'

'Surprised they could find anything of him,' Harrison said.

Fletcher ignored him. 'The imam from the mosque took the full force of the explosion and is probably on his way out.'

'We're lucky our attacker went in when he did at Penarth,' MacReady said.

Echols cocked his head. 'Lucky?'

'He's right,' Beck cut in, eyeing Echols who was clearly about to start. 'Morning prayers had long since finished. There was just a Classical Arabic class taking place. Five, ten people tops. Otherwise the mosque would have had more people inside it than Conference Room Two. Plus you've got the partial failure of the device. We'd be talking about even more casualties.'

'And we have a star witness,' Fletcher said, closing the file.

'One of those kids at the market?' asked Echols.

'At the mosque. I need him spoken to this morning. He saw the attacker, apparently. Description of white male, all dressed in black.'

'Snap,' said Harrison.

'Thing is,' Fletcher shook his head. 'Uniform took the witness's details but they let him wander off. And nobody has seen him since.'

'Fucking woodentops,' muttered Echols.

MacReady bit. Knew he shouldn't. 'You were one yourself once, Sarge.'

'Not as recently as you. And I don't let significant witnesses disappear into the bloody crowd. So wind your neck in, newbie.'

'Sorry to interrupt, but *anyone*?' Fletcher said, voice rising. The DI waited for a moment, looking from Echols to Harrison to MacReady.

'I'll go,' said Beck.

'No you won't, and you know it,' Fletcher replied. 'I'm sorry, Charlie. But I want you back on the CCTV and collating anything and everything that comes in. The detective chief super is already pushing for results, no matter how small. You're my oppo for the day.'

MacReady raised his hand. 'Happy to do it.'

'Good.' Fletcher slid the file across the desk towards him. He looked at Echols. 'It'll keep you two apart, which means I can enjoy my coffee in peace. Warren, seeing as you've failed to volunteer for anything for the six-hundred-and-twentieth time in a row, you can go with him.'

'I can't volunteer.' Harrison rose from the chair. 'I'm allergic.'

Fletcher shrugged. 'Well take a tablet for it because you're doing the talking and the writing. No fuck-ups.' He looked at MacReady. 'No offence, Will.'

MacReady glanced at a smirking Echols. Gathered up the file.

*

Harrison was still complaining fifteen minutes later.

'Taxpayers' money well spent.' He shook his head, pootling the CID car down the slip road after the Butetown tunnels, joining the stop-start mid-morning traffic clogging the link road. Window down, thick forearm lolling outside, air con full blast but doing nothing to dry his sweat-sodden shirtfront. 'I'm not being funny, like, but this Police Commissioner bollocks is, you know, bollocks.'

MacReady leaned the back of his head on the headrest, turned to watch the world drift by his window. The western fringes of Cardiff edged away to his left: the pontoons and moorings of the city's yacht club, the mazy green ribbons of marsh and miniature lakes of the wetlands reserve. Just beyond, the metallic white sail top glinting in the sunlight was the St David's Hotel and Spa, then the tubular blue warehouse of the Dr Who Experience, the shiny new BBC studios at Roath Lock. Nearly a year ago he'd been down there with Beck in the wind and drizzle while Specialist Search Team officers fished the putrid remains of a corpse from the Graving Docks. He shuddered. The smell had seemed to live in the fibres of his jacket for weeks afterwards until he had to dry clean the thing just to be able to wear it without gagging.

On MacReady's lap sat two files. Frustration, a flash of it, as he glanced at the one on top. The wounding. Jane Doe. Echols had carried on at him after the briefing, all the way down to Fletcher's office in the CID suite, nipping at his ear about cuffing stuff onto other people, *a piss-poor uniform trick*, and MacReady had said nothing because Echols was right.

He flipped open the handover file, took his first proper look at it. The first proper look anybody had taken, most probably.

Slimmer than slim for details: basic crime report, statements from the two response officers who attended after an anonymous three nines call to report somebody *not moving, think they've OD'd or somethin'*. The similarities to the Alexander Castle case were stark: the injured party was white, late teens to mid-twenties, numerous puncture wounds to upper torso, defensive wounds to her hands and forearms. Found unconscious in a lane not far from the southern concourse entrance of Cardiff Central railway station with its cashpoints and ticket machines. Jacket and jeans pockets turned out as if they'd been rifled. No identification at all. Echols had taken a spin to the University Hospital of Wales in the small hours to check on the IP's status, but found her sedated and out of it. He'd checked for any calls from concerned relatives that may have given the police a name and had cross-checked any new and outstanding Missing Persons reports. Got nothing. MacReady hadn't dared ask if his detective sergeant had bothered to arrange bagging and sealing of the injured party's clothes for forensic examination.

'Fiver says it's a robbery,' MacReady muttered. They were getting a lot of those lately. The latest iPhone or tablet were nice things to have, especially if you didn't have to pay for them. With a shake of his head he noted the location where the IP was found by uniform: a service lane between the railway station and the Brains Brewery complex. Another fifty metres northeast and it would be British Transport Police's area and therefore BTP's problem.

'You what?' Harrison asked.

'This.' He lifted the file. Pulled a face. 'My new case.'

'Nice for you,' Harrison said, drifting into the outside lane and causing a BMW to swerve to avoid him. Its driver cut past on the inside, sounded his horn and told Harrison what he thought of his abilities behind the wheel. 'You can bore me all about it after we've done the witnesses over here, like.'

Harrison nodded ahead. Across the bridge the town of Penarth lay on the headland, jutting out into the cold waters of the Bristol Channel. A quiet seaside enclave just west of the Welsh capital. Promenade, Victorian pier, the population affluent and a mixture of Cardiff commuters and the retired. Completely unused to most serious crime – cops stationed there joked how Penarth wannabe gangstas could just about manage drive-by name-calling – never mind a man walking into a place of worship and murdering people with what they now knew were homemade explosives.

MacReady closed the handover file for the stabbing, let it drop to the footwell. Opened what he had for the bomb attack at the Al Mahdi Mosque. A list of actions cascaded down from Specialist Crime, the incident and crime reports. DS Echols had checked Niche, the computerised record management system that held all the force's intelligence on suspects, addresses and vehicles, and printed out the one hit he'd found. Tucked at the rear were photocopies of the pocket notebook pages where a uniformed officer had made quick, jagged notes while speaking to their witness who had then decided to disappear.

'Nazir Uddin,' MacReady said, studying the paperwork.

Harrison accelerated as they passed the International Sports Village, headed towards the Cogan Spur roundabout. 'That our guy?'

'Only person who saw the attacker, by all accounts. Was on his way to the mosque, had turned the corner into Stanwell and saw the culprit walk inside. White male, slim, dressed in black with either a hood or baseball cap.'

'Sounds like our friend who hates coloured people.'

MacReady nodded. Ignored Harrison's outdated terminology; it was futile trying to change him. 'Says he heard a shout then explosions so he hid behind a parked car. Watched the guy come out again and run off into the trees along the side of the playing fields.'

'What about our witness?'

'He ran off too.'

'Chickenshit.'

'But he came back.'

'And then uniform let him bugger off again. Poor form, really. Almost as bad as leaving a handover file on your sergeant's desk.'

'Yeah, yeah,' MacReady sighed. 'It's been chaos, Warren. You heard the DI, there's only so many of us. Only so much we can do. Uniform will have been overwhelmed at scene.'

Harrison breathed deeply and spun the steering wheel; the CID car skirted the roundabout, heading left off the link road. 'So what's this Uddin guy's story?'

There was little more to the report than the one MacReady had for the railway station assault. Uddin's name was familiar, though. Vaguely. MacReady noted the man's address, couldn't recall ever attending there.

'I think I know him. Somehow.'

'Shit?'

'Nah,' MacReady replied. He closed the file. 'No pre-cons. Echols printed out what we've got. Uddin's a nominal on Niche but only as a witness for the Al Mahdi.'

'Squeaky clean?'

'Looks that way.'

Harrison thought for a moment. Then: 'That just means we've never caught him doing anything.'

MacReady rolled his eyes as Harrison took the turning for Penarth.

Ten

Stanwell Road cut through the heart of Penarth, from its pretty town centre of pubs and neat shops to the small housing estates in the 'burbs. A leafy route lined by a jumble of Edwardian and Victorian semis, grand cottages and palatial homes now changed into smart bedsits and flats. The much-coveted Stanwell School and its playing fields at the western end. A car journey from east to west would normally take a couple of minutes.

Not today, with emergency vehicles and sagging crime scene tape everywhere. The outer cordon cut the school playing fields and the road to the beaches at Lavernock in half, armed officers and a mixture of specials and PCSOs staffing the perimeter. The Al Mahdi Mosque sat in the centre of the inner cordon: an impressive modern redbrick topped with two colossal baubles of blue glass, its minaret – with a conical crown of matching glass – thrusting skywards. In its shadow was the town fire station, designated as the Forward Control Point. The station's forecourt held a clutch of fire trucks and council wagons, a forensic response vehicle and a shitty old Public Order van with its side door wedged open and a large tea urn dumped between the rear seats. MacReady was unsurprised to see a dozen or more people in fluorescent tabards gathered around the van holding polystyrene cups.

Harrison had wanted to swing by the Al Mahdi first. Mac-Ready told him there was nothing for them to do at the scene. That it would eat into their time. Harrison had argued that it wasn't the point.

'It'll get right on my tits, seeing what the bomber's done,' he said as they neared the outer cordon tape. 'Dinosaur like me needs a jolt to fire me up every now and again. It'll get me asking the right questions when we speak to Uddin.'

MacReady needed no jolt. No reminder of what he'd seen the day before. He ground his teeth and checked about as Harrison searched for a parking spot amongst the abandoned response cars and tech vehicles and CID motors. Lit candles and flowers everywhere, ribbons tied to trees and gateposts, this end of the street morphing into a makeshift memorial. Dozens of rubbernecking civvies and photographers took shots of anyone and everything. News crews and lone reporters lined up against railings which edged the western flank of the playing field, interviewing, talking to camera, grabbing passers-by and thrusting mics towards their mouths for their opinions, their horror. None of them paying any attention to Harrison's revving and wrestling with the steering wheel. Eventually he gave up with a mumbled *bugger it*, killed the engine with the car blocking somebody's driveway entrance.

'Look out,' Harrison said as they climbed out of the car. 'It's that fit news bird.'

'Hi, Will.'

Solak's voice. MacReady checked over one shoulder, saw her advancing towards them. Her cameraman – MacReady still hadn't asked Solak his name – waited in the shade of a sprawling oak with equipment at his feet, tipped his head back at MacReady in acknowledgement, regulation lit cigarette gripped between lips as he jetted smoke from nostrils.

'Hey, Klaudia.' MacReady briefly raised a hand, trying for casual, flashed his eyes wide before shifting them sideways in the direction of Harrison. Nobody on the team knew, thankfully. Matter of fact, *nobody* knew.

Least of all Megan.

No one would have guessed Solak was operating on three hours' sleep. Clear-eyed, hair swept into a loose ponytail, lips rouged to match the bright-red sleeveless dress she wore: she looked fabulous, and he thought of the night before, when she'd looked just as fabulous, and how put out he'd been when she sent him packing just as he was getting settled. How being used and abused – enjoyable while he was still in her bed – had left him feeling unexpectedly miserable as he'd left her apartment, the wretchedness compounded further when he'd arrived at Duncan Jones's house to find him borderline paralytic yet still bashing buttons on his games console controller.

'How . . . are you?' Solak asked.

'You know,' MacReady shrugged. He yawned for effect. 'Tired. Busy. Lots of driving about at all hours.'

'Poor thing.' She looked at the floor; MacReady caught the smirk as she did it. Head back up, eyes narrowed. She pointed at the Al Mahdi. 'So is it true the imam is dead?'

'Talk about straight down to business.'

'You know me. So is he? And it's the same guy at both attacks, yes? Some white supremacist targeting Cardiff's ethnic community? Revenge because of the Castle trial?'

She was exhausting. 'Where have you heard all this?'

'Sources, sources.'

'You mean online gossip.'

'Social media, detective. You should get on it.'

'Thought as much. Your secret blogger guy, I take it?'

'Still radio silence from him.' Solak took a step towards him, pushed her head towards his chest. Whispered: 'We can talk about it later, if you like.'

'Whoa, now,' Harrison called from behind MacReady. 'You got to go through our press office, see. No more questions, love.'

MacReady felt a hand on his elbow, Harrison guiding him away.

Ring me, he mouthed at Solak.

What for? she mouthed back. Winked.

They flashed badges and ducked the outer cordon tape. Walked the short distance to the mosque, Harrison pulling at the back of his shirt where his slick skin had sucked at the cotton for most of the journey. MacReady felt sun searing his neck, the day already hot, noon still an hour away.

Sobs and wails bounced along the house fronts, echoing towards them as they walked. The only noise in a normally bustling thoroughfare.

MacReady looked at Harrison. 'Families.'

'Get your sad face on then,' Harrison urged. 'Pretend your dog died.'

'I don't have a dog.'

'Then imagine it was Echols. That'd be really terrible, wouldn't it, eh?'

MacReady placed a hand over his mouth to hide the thin smile. It disappeared completely as they came up to the inner cordon.

'Look at this,' Harrison tutted, and shook his head.

Up close they could see the full scale of the damage: ornate narrow windows blown out by the blasts, fire-baked bricks and roof tiles, diamonds of glass embedded in window ledges, covering the front steps and pavement. Even outside, the blood spatters and thick red trails on handrails, across paving stones, into the street itself. MacReady pictured the injured dragging themselves out into the road.

'Guy just walked into the prayer room and set the bomb off,' he said quietly. 'They didn't know what hit them. Backs turned to the door, facing the imam.'

'Coward,' Harrison growled from beside him.

To one side, outside the cordon, the huddles of people. Families, relatives of the casualties. Embracing, shoulders shaking as they cried and wailed and looked to the heavens for answers that weren't forthcoming.

MacReady checked about, saw the security camera above the mosque's front doors. Another at the side, facing towards a small car park which contained a trio of battered wheelie bins. He wondered if Beck had the recordings yet. If she'd managed to dig something up for Specialist Crime. Other than a handful of street signs warning of speed cameras, there was nothing in terms of CCTV coverage. The mosque sat at a junction but was surrounded by residential houses and a lone pub-cum-hotel. No businesses, no council cameras the police could piggy-back for their own use. Plenty of uniform door-knocking would be going on to see if homeowners had installed their own kit, had perhaps caught something on tape or digital.

He breathed in the warm air, watched the crime scene investigators and techies shuffling in and out of the Al Mahdi entrance with plastic sacks and paper bags, with metal suitcases and recording equipment. Romper suits and booties and face masks beneath hoods, powder-blue matching the sky above them. The area around the mosque secured and sterile and speckled with yellow crime scene markers, full of damaged vehicles and shredded clothing and crusted bandages, frozen in time, at the exact moment Specialist Crime locked the place down.

'You want to kit up and go in?' MacReady asked. He turned to Harrison, found him with hands in pockets. Gloomy now, jaw working, making his jowls twitch. Watery eyes on the people who hugged and cried not ten feet away.

MacReady didn't know what to say, so waited.

After a while Harrison turned on his heel, car keys in hand.

'This witness,' he said over his shoulder. 'I'm ready to speak to him now.'

*

Penarth didn't do sink estates. The closest it ever had – the Billy Banks flats, a failed sixties development of communal dog-turd-encrusted grass patches and pebble-dash the colour of smog – had been demolished at the tail end of the noughties to make way for stratospherically expensive apartments and townhouses, replete with private security patrols and a propensity amongst the occupants to wear sailor hats and shorts, possibly because at least three of the buildings offered a glimpse of the Bristol Channel.

'Right at the bottom.' MacReady pointed towards the far end of the cul-de-sac. In the centre of the road two boys in replica football shirts kicked a ball back and forth, Liverpool versus Arsenal in the August sunlight, oblivious to the police car creeping down their street because of the terrible things that had occurred not three miles away. MacReady envied them their innocence. Everything so simple. Summer holidays seemingly endless, and joyously so. He remembered his own childhood: until he was six years old it had been Edinburgh, and the cramped conditions of a High Riggs flat, the drab car park beneath where he'd kicked a ball around just once with a father who'd preferred kicking out at anyone and everything else when the mood took him. And when in drink – which was most of the time – the mood took him a lot.

Nazir Uddin's address was an apartment on the ground floor of a three-storey, the building a whitewashed modernist cube peppered with tiny windows and a few balconies.

'Must be doing all right for himself, this guy,' Harrison said, eyes passing over the miniature footballers then along the street, the CID motor chugging in first gear. 'Well posh.'

MacReady had to agree: BMWs and Mercedes were the brands of choice, it appeared. A smattering of Audi SUVs dotted amongst them. All high-end and in various shades of black. Curtains and blinds were already twitching as their clapped-out Vauxhall coughed along. But something seemed a bit off: he checked the folder again, the photocopy of the officer's notebook.

'He's younger than me. Just nineteen. It's here, by the way.'

Harrison drew the car to a stop, checked the front of the apartment building, the hulking 4x4 on the hardstand. 'No way can he afford one of these places on his own. Unless he's one of them computer whizz-kid types, like. Maybe he invented something clever.'

'Maybe,' MacReady said.

'Maybe hacked government files and sold stuff to foreigners for loads of cash.'

MacReady hovered with one foot out of the open door. 'Or, you know, maybe he just lives with his parents?'

'Trust no one.' Harrison tapped the end of his nose with a finger, as if it would explain all, then got out of the car.

They knocked at Uddin's door, waited. Warrant cards in hands, ready for a flash. Smiling at silver-haired neighbours who – all of a sudden – appeared to realise they might have left their car unlocked, or simply had to take bins out, or fancied stretching their legs, so needed to stroll outside. Harrison, no patience as ever: he gave it thirty seconds then chopped at the woodwork with the side of his chunky hand. The door shook, the neighbours abandoned all pretence of chatting about pension plans and the weather and turned to look. The door jerked open a moment later.

'*What?*'

In the gap between door and frame: a muss of light-brown hair above a pinched, pasty face. Eyes puffy, squinting. No clothes on his top half, from what MacReady could see. Skin dense with freckles, a couple of tats on his shoulder and bicep. The man had quite clearly been asleep. Probably in bed. Was a tad miffed about being woken, to say the least.

'Nazir?' Harrison asked.

Again: 'What?'

'Mr Uddin?' MacReady held up his warrant card. Already a sinking feeling in his guts.

'Jesus.' Eyes flicking to MacReady's ID. 'Are you Job?'

MacReady lowered his card. Was thrown. 'Um ... I'm DC MacReady, this is –'

'And I'm a firearms tac advisor, and I've been working Bessemer Market since yesterday morning, and I got to bed,' a quick check of the watch on his wrist, *'two and a half hours ago.'*

Harrison sniffed. 'Ah. Sorry, man.'

'Looks like we were given a duff address by a witness,' MacReady told him.

The man looked from MacReady to Harrison. 'You check the voters' register before coming out here? Niche to check who's at this address? Any of that really important special magic CID stuff you lot do?'

'Um ...' MacReady said again. He had the Niche printout Echols had done: it said Uddin lived here.

'CID.' The tac advisor shook his head. 'Brains Department. Fucking useless morons, the lot of you.'

He slammed the door. MacReady heard the stomp of feet inside, fading as the man retreated into the apartment. Turned to see the neighbours look away.

'Well, this is excellent,' he said to Harrison. 'Shall we knock a few doors? See if anyone knows our star witness?'

Harrison thrust hands into pockets, exhaled. His interest had evaporated. 'Nah. Uddin's thrown us a boner. If that's even his name. And he's not from these parts, I'll bet on it.'

MacReady knew the response teams were under the cosh, had very few numbers, were being run ragged by bosses who cared only for figures and stats and made-up crime clear-ups for a shitty government who seemed desperate to ruin the service so they could flog it off to their private-sector chums. But for the first time he found himself cursing them for not detaining Nazir Uddin – or whatever his name was – and checking his details before letting him walk. It was basic, student-officer-level stuff. And they hadn't done it.

He pulled a business card from his wallet, slipped it through the tac advisor's letter box. Wasn't expecting a call from him any time soon. Then MacReady's mobile buzzed; he fished it out of his trouser pocket, checked the screen: Beck calling.

'Hey, numbnuts. Hospital just called the Public Service Centre. Your Jane Doe's mum and dad showed up earlier this morning.'

'So we have a name,' MacReady replied.

Beck *mmm-hmm*ed down the line. 'Heidi Paxton. Twenty-two years of age, lives with her folks in the Whitchurch area.'

'Never heard of her.'

'Neither have any of our systems. Blanks everywhere. You ready?'

MacReady tucked the phone under his chin, pulled out his notebook and pen. Scribbled down Paxton's details, the names and mobile numbers of her parents as Beck reeled them off in his ear. 'Cheers for this,' he said once she'd finished.

'She's still in a bad way, by the way. The family are staying put with her for now, so I've been told. I'll call again if I dig anything else up.' The line cleared.

MacReady slipped the phone and notebook away, watched the footballing kids: still hoofing the ball back and forth. 'My Jane Doe is no longer a Jane Doe.'

'So?'

'So what now?'

Harrison thought about it for a moment or two. 'Mid-morning snack?'

*

Traffic and roadworks plus a fifteen-minute stop at Tesco Extra in the claustrophobic sprawl of chain stores and roundabouts at Culverhouse Cross just so Harrison could pick up his 'snack' – jumbo sausage roll, crisps and two cans of Coke Zero, because *I likes to do my healthy bit* – meant it was gone midday by the time they pulled up outside the University Hospital of Wales.

MacReady had tried calling Heidi Paxton's parents using the numbers Beck gave him, but both went to voicemail; understandable if they were deep within the maze that was the

UHW, where mobile signals were a luxury. He'd followed up by phoning the DI, giving him the updates about Nazir Uddin's address and Paxton. Fletcher had ranted and raved for a full two minutes – MacReady had counted the seconds, watching as Penarth receded into the late-morning haze – about people fucking the police about, pausing only to slurp noisily at his mug of tea. Eventually he'd ordered them to the University Hospital to join the rest of the teams of officers talking to anyone from the market and mosque who *could* talk – and before they tried speaking to Heidi Paxton or her family.

'Priorities, Will,' he'd sighed, appearing to have finally calmed down, before shouting at somebody in the office then killing the call.

As ever the UHW entrance was a gridlock of ambulances, parked taxis at the ranks and cars dropping off visiting relatives of the bomb victims, the main doors flanked by clouded clumps of smokers and a lone, empty wheelchair. Harrison bullied a taxi driver out of a space, dumped the Vauxhall in it. Thrust his warrant card out of the window and warned the driver he'd have his car towed if he moaned any further.

'Official police business,' he barked. 'For the bombings, fucko.'

MacReady slipped down in the passenger seat and looked the other way.

Lack of sleep had finally caught up with him, and he needed the energy; in the concourse he grudgingly fed four pound coins into a vending machine for a pack of cheese and onion sandwiches. There was no change forthcoming, and as they made their way into the bowels of the hospital, biting at the flaccid bread as he walked, case files tucked under one arm, MacReady regretted not joining Harrison inside the supermarket.

They paused at the lifts, waiting for one of the sets of doors to open. MacReady dumped the half-eaten sandwiches in a bin, shifted the files to his hands.

'Need to see my wounding IP while we're here.' He was surprised at the lack of enthusiasm in his own voice. It was a nasty attack, a Section 20 or Section 18 assault, or *wounding* as they all referred to it, yet he couldn't help but wish he hadn't been riding the lift the previous night with the two uniforms looking to cuff a job onto CID. Onto him. He was on borrowed time as far as Bessemer and the Al Mahdi were concerned, he knew it. Unless he could put the stabbing to bed quickly.

Harrison kept jabbing the call button. 'Yours or ours first, then?'

MacReady looked down at the files. 'Ours. Fletcher says keep with the bombings.'

'No probs, butty. We'll go see your injured party after lunch.'

The lift door opened. 'We . . . we've just eaten, Warren.'

Harrison's expression was one of mild horror. 'Yeah, right.'

With a Major Incident declared, casualties had been conveyed to all corners of south Wales. Both the market and mosque had seen people with grazes, bruising and shock shipped to Llandough Hospital just outside Penarth. More to the Minor Injuries Unit in Barry, up the sticks to Merthyr's Prince Charles, east to the Royal Gwent in Newport. Two or three victims with severe burns ended up down west, at the Tempest High Dependency Unit in Swansea's Morriston Hospital.

The rest were here, at the University Hospital. Filling up the Intensive Treatment Unit. The emergency surgery and trauma wards. Some still in trolley bays in A&E, which had been closed to all other patients, such was the overwhelming number of injured.

'I've told the rest of your people: just don't go upsetting them.' The diminutive charge nurse pinched at the bridge of her nose; she looked exhausted, glasses shelved atop her curly fringe, her pixie-like frame sunk behind the nurses' station at the entrance to Ward A2. She was swamped with clipboards, paperwork, folders and files. People buzzed left and right along the corridor, the phone trilled constantly and she ignored it.

MacReady nodded. Heard soft moans from somewhere, could smell detergent in the air. 'We'll go gentle.'

'To be honest most of the poor sods won't even know you're there.' She gave a tired smile. 'But I appreciate it, thanks.'

Harrison checked with the two detectives from Specialist Crime who were interviewing IPs in the anterooms off the main corridor. They hadn't reached the ward yet.

'I'll take left, you go right,' Harrison said as they entered A2 proper. MacReady noted that of the eight beds on Harrison's chosen side, six of the occupants were out of it. Hooked up to drips and monitors and equipment he couldn't begin to understand. No talking to be done there.

'No problem,' he said. At least it gave Harrison the chance to stuff his face in the block's ground floor restaurant after he finished speaking to the casualties.

The male in the nearest bed was all mottled black skin and bandages, poorly looking and deep in thought. Wiry frame, mid- to late thirties with legs splayed beneath a thin sheet, turned slightly to one side to stare out of the third-floor windows at a cloudless sky. His back was to MacReady. He could see a scatter of sticking plasters and raw scabs sprinkled across it, fanned out over his shoulder blades up to his neck. Glass cuts, perhaps. Shrapnel injuries. Too small and numerous to be wrapped in dressings.

'Having a good look, bra?' The accent, broad Cardiff.

MacReady blinked. 'Sorry. Didn't mean to sneak up on you.'

The man shifted so he could see MacReady. Gestured at his bandaged abdomen and chest. 'Bit twitchy about surprises at the minute, know what I mean?'

'Bessemer? Or the mosque?'

The man swallowed. 'The market, mate. Happy days, eh?'

MacReady gave the thinnest of smiles as the man chuckled humourlessly. He pointed to the chair next to the bed. 'Mind if I . . . ?'

The man regarded him for a second. Nodded. 'You Old Bill, yeah?'

'Is it that obvious?' MacReady dropped into the chair, placed the folders on the floor at his feet. Pulled out his notebook, pen.

'Can always tell. It's the way you scuffers are, you know? All stiff and tense like you've all got sticks wedged up your arses. Even when you try to look relaxed it's like you're stressed about looking relaxed.'

Known to police, MacReady thought. He could always tell, too. Judging by his matter-of-fact manner, the man was more than used to dealing with plod. Comfortable, even. Long-in-the-tooth cops and veteran villains were always the same: easy in each other's company, in the way they spoke, as if there was a mutual grudging respect for surviving the game for so long. He shifted his eyes to the bed board, noted the man's name: Peter Corlett. Had never heard of him, quickly scribbled it down to check on the system later.

'Bay CID. We're just asking a few questions. If you're up to it, that is.'

Corlett's feet moved beneath the sheet. 'Don't normally talk to your lot, know what I mean? Been on too many demos, been slapped about too many times for telling it like it is. Getting locked up for carrying a bit of personal, what a load of bollocks. But yesterday, some of your guys just came running in and pulled me out, while it was still on fire and everyone was screaming and pissing blood. For that . . . you know. For that, we can talk.'

'If it means anything . . . if it helps, I'm just the same as you. I can't make sense of what happened.'

'How could you make sense of it, mate?' Corlett asked. 'How could anybody?'

'Did you see anything? See the man who did this?'

'Look, all I know is one minute I'm enjoying the tunes and dancing about with my boy on my shoulders, next thing I'm on the floor with glass and metal bits in my guts. Rest is a blur of people telling me to calm down and sticking needles in me veins, and then I woke up in this place.'

Corlett talking about his child made MacReady think of Finlay. He hadn't seen him, spent time with him properly, for weeks. The situation wasn't likely to improve in the near future, either. Not now. 'Lot of people not as lucky as you.'

Corlett chuckled, and for a second MacReady didn't understand what was so funny, then realised there was nothing funny because the man's eyes were brimming with tears.

'Yeah, lucky as fuck,' Corlett said. Irritation and sadness in his voice now. Face creasing, one hand up to his eyes to wipe at them. 'I'm so lucky one of the bombs went off right next to my missus, who's now sucking on a tube in intensive care and might not make it. If it wasn't for her getting her fucking arm blown off it would have taken out me and our kid instead.'

The woman outside the market. Her left arm, shredded to the elbow.

Screaming for her husband, her child.

'Your boy . . .'

Jordan.

'With his grandma,' Corlett said. 'Not a scratch. Can you believe that? Bombs going off all over the place and all he gets is a banged-up elbow where I dropped him. Still beating myself up about it. Boy's my world.'

'I'm glad,' MacReady smiled. Felt a sudden longing for Fin. Just to hold him for a few minutes. Just to feel him in his arms. 'I'm so glad he's safe.'

Corlett fixed MacReady with a stare. 'What I said earlier . . . that I don't normally talk to your lot. Well, the paramedics told me one of you found my son. Took him to my wife. Found him and took him to her before she, y'know, before she . . .'

The man visibly crumbled, legs drawing up beneath the bedsheet. MacReady looked away. Saw Harrison leaning against a wall as he spoke to his only conscious witness, smiling and nodding and generally having a bit of what he would probably call *banter*.

He slipped his notebook into his trouser pocket. There was nothing for him to learn here. Nothing Corlett could tell them. All MacReady was doing was precisely what the charge nurse had asked them not to: upsetting people. It was too soon. Too soon, but the Senior Investigating Officer and the rest of the hierarchy wouldn't care about that. Politicians would already be demanding results, putting on the pressure. The media would grow more critical, more intrusive as the hours slipped by.

'I'm sorry,' MacReady said, looking up again. He reached out, hand hovering at the foot of the bed, just inches from Corlett. Not sure if he should touch him. Not sure what good it would do. Not sure what the reaction would be. Wondered if it was more for him than the casualty he was talking to.

MacReady let his hand drop anyway, gently resting it on the man's forearm. Held it there. And there was no reaction, no movement or snatching away of his arm. For a minute they were motionless, MacReady staring at the floor, Corlett's wet eyes back on the pastel blue rectangles of Ward A2's windows.

'Are you . . . done?'

Harrison, at his shoulder. The tone dubious, and not a little amused.

A sigh from MacReady. Didn't turn around. 'Not yet. I take it you are.'

'All finished.' A clap of hands. 'You need me to speak to some of this lot now?'

'No, I'll meet you in the restaurant.'

He waited for a reply, an insistent offer of help to question the other patients in this half of the ward, perhaps an update on anything he had managed to glean from his one fully alert casualty, but nothing was forthcoming. A second later MacReady heard the faint yet unmistakeable squeak of Harrison's sandals as they faded down the corridor. He was gone for his food without as much as a *see you later*.

MacReady eased his hand off Corlett's forearm. Slipped a business card out of his pocket, placed it on the bedside.

'Please ring me if you think of anything,' he said to Corlett. 'Anything at all. Even if you think it's not important, it might be really helpful to us.'

When Corlett didn't reply MacReady picked up the case files from the floor. Looked across to the next bed: another male. Asian guy, early twenties, hair matted and sweaty. Lying flat on his back, eyes open and unblinking, staring at ceiling tiles. Hooked up to IV lines and monitors, sheet up to the middle of his chest, arms tucked into his ribs. Arms that were too short, somehow, and wrapped with gauze and bandage at the wrists.

It took MacReady a moment to realise both hands were missing.

'Christ,' he whispered.

'From the mosque, I think,' Corlett said to him. 'Woke up this morning and he'd appeared next door.'

MacReady nodded at Corlett, turned back to the Asian male. Stepped across. 'Hi. I'm really sorry to bother you . . .'

Nothing. Eyes fixed on something above him. Mouth a thin slash across the bottom half of his face. Whereas Corlett was a jumble of emotions and struggling to maintain a façade – practice for when his boy visited, perhaps – this one exuded something altogether more pure. Rage, it seemed. MacReady could sense the raw anger coming off the man in waves.

He checked the bed board: no name.

Tried again. Introduced himself. Asked: 'Is it OK to talk?'

Corlett: 'Good luck getting anything out of him. He's been awake all morning and I haven't heard a peep. He won't even answer the nurses or doctors.'

MacReady wedged the folders under one arm again, tucked his hands behind his back. Out of view. 'I don't want to bother you but –'

The male lifted his head, dropped it back to the pillow. Lifted it, dropped it. Kept doing it, banging the back of his skull into the fabric. Faster, harder, hard enough to make a hollow thud each time, hard enough to make the bed shake, a strange keening sound coming out of his mouth, the cords on his neck thick and prominent and his eyes wide and on the ceiling, the whites huge and bulbous.

'Whoa, whoa,' MacReady said, and backed away. 'It's fine. It's OK.'

He glanced around, at a goggle-eyed Corlett, at patients who'd woken in the other beds. All of them, staring at the male, at MacReady who was just about to call for staff when two nurses ran into the ward.

And the male stopped. The noise died in his throat. The nurses hadn't touched him yet he became still. Those golfball eyes burning into thirty-year-old ceiling tiles once more.

Corlett rolled onto his side, facing away from his neighbour. 'I'd be a bit pissed off if I was him. Least I can still grab my beer and smokes when I get out of here.'

A nurse turned to MacReady. 'You'd best be gone,' she urged.

He took a breath. Nodded once. The other victims would have to wait. For him to return, or for another interviewing team from Specialist Crime. 'Of course.'

As he reached the ward doors Corlett raised a hand.

'Hey, hang on.'

MacReady stopped, face downcast. Braced himself for it. He could feel Corlett eyeing him. 'Yeah?'

'Just . . . if you find out who that copper was who found my boy . . . just tell him thanks, man. Thanks from me, yeah?'

MacReady didn't turn around.

'I will.'

*

Heidi Paxton was the next floor up, in the Adult Critical Care Unit.

MacReady took the lift again, looking forward to getting out of here: he'd already had enough of this hospital, of this day. As he left Ward A2 he'd collared the beleaguered charge nurse – frostier than she had been due to the episode with the Asian male – and asked what she had on the man, which was little more than nothing. Came in with one hand missing, another mangled so badly it had to be amputated, and nothing in the way of ID. Was found in the mosque's prayer room amongst the rest of the victims, clothes shredded and skin perforated from the blasts. Understandably, he'd been less than chatty since he woke from the operation to find his piano-playing days were over.

She'd glanced up with a fixed smile. 'We're still trying to locate next of kin. But then there are half a dozen more just like him.' And she'd gone back to ignoring the telephone's incessant ringing while she typed at a computer.

Things were becoming frustrating, enough for MacReady to leave a mildly irritating Harrison filling his guts in the restaurant while he went it alone and got what he could from the stabbing victim. He rested against the lift wall, the metal cool against his skin, his clammy hand gripping the case files. Penarth and Nazir Uddin had been a waste of time and effort, unless you considered pissing off a firearms tac adviser a result. Harrison's reluctance to knock on a few doors was also niggling at him; he decided to return that afternoon and do it himself. A few more hours would give the firearms officer the chance for sleep and he might be a little more amenable later in the day.

MacReady opened the stabbing case file. Shook his head once again at the paucity of information. Resolved to get this sorted one way or another as soon as possible – if he got some headway on it today it would free him up to work the attacks.

A ping, the doors opened. MacReady closed the file, shifting sideways and up against the wall, making room. A male, silver-haired, pale-faced yet sweating, guiding a woman in a wheelchair into the lift. The couple didn't notice him. MacReady gave them a quick once-over: the woman blonde, her slim frame bound in a tight, bright-pink cardigan, her deep-seated sobs muffled, face pressed into the stomach of her male companion who flickered his anguished eyes to MacReady then away. Mac-Ready quickly looked at the floor, stepped out of the lift and into the ward. So much misery and sorrow in this place now. He felt a pang of regret, of a need to be with someone. Pictured Megan and Finlay. As tense and uncomfortable as it would be between them, he'd happily spend the rest of the day at home.

Even sitting in Duncan Jones's hovel with a lukewarm beer in his hand would be an improvement on this.

At the nurses' station he cleared his throat, introduced himself. A male nurse this time. Just as harassed. Another phone ringing and ringing.

'I'm here about the female who was brought in yesterday. Multiple stab wounds, found at Cardiff Central railway station?' MacReady checked his notebook. 'Heidi Paxton.'

The nurse pulled a face.

Bad news.

MacReady groaned. Glanced over his shoulder at the lifts. Realised. 'Her parents?'

A slow nod from the nurse. 'As you can imagine, they needed some air . . .'

Eleven

MacReady gave up waiting and took the stairs.

Took each flight at speed, almost tumbling as he went, thinking about the Alex Castle trial. Thinking about Heidi Paxton. Thinking: *here we go again.*

A murder now. And he knew without doubt: this one would wallow in the background of the public's consciousness, an afterthought almost, the media's attention completely focused on the bombings. Heidi Paxton's death a page four article at best, a footnote, something which MacReady was going to have to push to get out there. Push to find witnesses, never mind who killed the girl. It was the way it worked, he understood, that on any other day, at any other time the senseless death of a young woman would make headlines.

But this wasn't any other time. This was the worst possible time for Paxton, and for her parents. And for the police.

For me, trying to catch whoever did this, MacReady thought.

Paxton's parents had already left the lift by the time he hit the ground-floor lobby; its doors were sliding shut, probably to return it to the Critical Care Unit, where he'd pressed the call button not three minutes earlier. At the far end of the main corridor: a flash of silver hair, the pink cardigan, at the top of the ramp which dropped down to the concourse and shops. MacReady walked quickly, scooting in and out of the flow of visitors and medical personnel. Lost sight of the pink amongst the crowd when he reached the concourse. Scanned the shops, the packed seats outside them. Saw nothing. Hazarded a guess.

He was right. The woman in the cardigan and her husband were outside in the smokers' area, cigarettes already lit, cheeks drawn as they sucked hard and inhaled deeply. Getting that air they needed, the world continuing to turn as theirs fractured, the sun still shining as their lives dimmed. Both had that haunted look, that thousand-yard stare MacReady had seen so many times working uniform: when attending the hated 'death message' calls, while dealing with fatal RTCs, when sat filling in forms in an overwarm house where the *he-always-seemed-so-happy* father had decided to rig a pipe between the running car exhaust and driver's window in the garage, or hanged himself from a wardrobe pole.

Relatives who'd just seen their loved one slip away all wore the same glassy-eyed, unbelieving expression initially, seeing nothing, their minds shocked into numbness. You could never tell if they were going to collapse with laughter or just collapse. A few years back, while a student officer, he'd had to tell a young wife her husband and infant son had been mown down and killed by a Cardiff bus while out buying her Christmas presents; she'd taken one look at MacReady as he'd removed his helmet and offered his condolences and burst into hysterical laughter, eyes wild and fingernails clawing at her cheeks.

'Mr and Mrs Paxton,' MacReady said, and they started, the woman dropping her cigarette. It bounced on the toe of her shoe; her withered legs didn't move as tiny red sparks danced around them, around the wheelchair's footrest. 'I'm so sorry for your loss.'

The Paxtons stared at him. MacReady bent over a little to catch his breath, felt the bloom of sweat on his forehead, his top lip. Realised he looked like a maniac, dug out his warrant card and showed it to them. He extended his other hand to shake. Neither took it.

'So you're the police,' the husband said, studying MacReady's warrant card. The words clipped, refined. His tone almost accusatory. He was motionless, hands at his sides, fag burning away between curled fingers, smoke creeping up along his hip, the midriff of his powder-blue shirt.

The Paxtons were middle-class late-fortysomethings – the husband average everything: height, weight, looks, a slight gut on him as if he enjoyed a beer or three; the wife clearly wheelchair-bound yet otherwise unremarkable bar a thick, ragged line of scar tissue that ran from the cleft of her chin to the crease at the left side of her mouth.

MacReady introduced himself. 'I'm the officer dealing with Heidi's case.'

'*Dealing?*' Mrs Paxton asked. Again, that tone. She pulled another cigarette from a pack of Silk Cut, lit it and inhaled. Exhaled as she spoke: 'That would imply one of your lot is actually looking after my daughter's case. Managing it. On top of it.'

'Where have you *been*, for God's sake?' the husband asked. He rubbed a hand through strands of neatly coiffed hair, pushing his fringe to one side. 'We've had to do everything. *Everything.* Nobody knew where my daughter was and –'

The woman reached up, hand on her husband's chest, shushing him. 'We've been ringing and ringing everywhere since last night. Friends, family. All the hospitals, then all the police stations. Call after call after call for hours and hours. Not one of you could help. We had to find Heidi ourselves, my poor girl . . .'

The last few words bled into one another, and MacReady saw it happen as if in slow motion: the woman's face and neck seemed to sink into themselves, lips drawing down at the corners of her mouth as she wailed at the sky.

'I'm so sorry.' MacReady checked around, conscious that they had an audience of smokers, paramedic crews and taxi drivers, one of whom – thanks to Harrison – would take great delight in seeing Heidi Paxton's parents rip into a copper. 'It means nothing to you, I know, but after yesterday . . .'

'I don't *care*,' the woman cried. Loud now. Loud enough for heads to really turn. For a security guard to poke his head out of the entrance to see what was going on before clearly deciding it was too griefy and slinking back into the hospital. 'I want my little girl back, I want her back now please. Now. *Pleaseplease-pleasepleaseplease* . . .'

She was lost, and MacReady silently cursed himself for dragging his feet. This was no unimportant incident. Even taking the market and mosque attacks into account, the delays were inexcusable, and now they had missed that twenty-four-hour golden period. He saw himself dumping the file on Echols's desk and laughing at his detective sergeant. Imagined a pissed-off Echols doing the bare minimum at this very hospital in the small hours of this morning, before slapping an angry note onto the file and tossing it onto MacReady's desk.

'I'm going to find who did this,' he said quietly.

'You'd damn well better.' The husband puffed smoke from his mouth, threw the half-finished cigarette to the floor. Leaned down and embraced his wife. 'Christ, I don't even smoke . . .'

*

He'd got little more from Heidi Paxton's parents.

Not at that moment. They were gone, vanished into a nightmare he hoped he'd never have to contend with: losing your child. They were very different scenarios but he knew he couldn't afford to lose Finlay from his life. Not now. He already considered the boy his own. But it was a very real prospect. He didn't want to admit it, but he could feel himself drifting away from Megan, yet Megan and Finlay were a package deal.

MacReady had stopped questioning the Paxtons after a couple of minutes, told them he'd ring one of their mobiles to schedule a time to call at their home, placed a business card into the husband's cold palm. Offered his condolences once again, watched them disappear into the hospital concourse. He'd dug out his phone, called the DI to give him the 'good news', got no reply. Called the Ops Room and asked to speak to the civvy working on the incident console dealing with the stabbing. Updated them with Paxton's full details, that she was now deceased, that the parents were aware and had been spoken to. That arrangements had been made to statement them later today or tomorrow, and the scene of the attack needed to be re-searched and photographed, sealed if necessary. That he needed a family liaison officer to contact them to arrange a home visit to check on their welfare, and a hospital liaison officer to make his way to the Critical Care Unit to do the honours with the coroner's paperwork while the parents were still at scene – without the coroner file there could be no post-mortem.

After that there was nothing to do other than collect Harrison and listen to him grumble about being overfull all the way back to Cardiff Bay police station.

The CID suite was deserted again, and Beck's hidey-hole office looked distinctly abandoned, which meant only one thing: the Major Incident Room was up and running and she'd been shifted upstairs.

'It's like a chief constable's retirement party in here,' Harrison said, before walking straight back out of the door.

MacReady hovered at his desk for a moment, looking at the property bags from the Paxton stabbing. *The Paxton murder*, he corrected himself. He thought about opening them, checking the contents. They'd been dabbed and photographed, listed and labelled by uniform. Were just waiting, now. Waiting to be paraded in court as exhibits, if it got that far. Waiting to be handed back to Heidi Paxton's grieving parents, probably in a year's time, to resurrect the horror of it all just as some of it was beginning to fade.

Waiting for MacReady. Because there was nobody else now.

He looked around the room, out of the window at the city skyline, at the scuds of clouds pocking the blue. Dumped the case files he'd been carrying around all morning on his desk and followed Harrison out of the suite.

Where the CID offices were empty and silent, the Major Incident Room felt like most of the city's police and civilian staff had decided to flock there en masse: MacReady stood at the threshold with both door and mouth open, gaping at the sheer number of people milling about or seated at workstations. Landlines and mobiles rang, keyboards rattled, faces studied computer screens and televisions, wading through reams of incident reports and actions and data on HOLMES2 – the Home Office Large Major Enquiry System. Overalled techies knelt in front of desks, frantically cabling IT equipment together even as it was being worked on by detectives. At the furthest end of the room a coterie of top brass hovered in front of whiteboards, studying the scrawls of marker pen, the lists of places and times and names – so many of them – of casualties from both sites.

In amongst the madness he spied the team – Fletcher, Echols and Harrison – deep in conversation, deep into mugs of tea. Beck, standing just off from the other three, hands on hips, watching one of the three large television flat screens bolted to the walls; news reports rolled across two of them, a map of the city glowed from the third. Her eyes drifted across to MacReady and he motioned for her to come over.

'So you've moved out of your Hobbit hole,' he remarked as she neared.

'Not enough room. I now have a team. Three nerds fresh from HQ to help me search CCTV for our man in black.'

'They spoil you,' he smiled.

'Well you're not here for me to boss around so they gave me some other sad sacks. Any joy with Paxton and her family?'

'You mean Warren hasn't told you?'

Beck shook her head. 'He just came in, made tea, moaned there were no biscuits.'

MacReady rubbed at tired eyes. 'Code blue this morning.'

'Poor girl.' Beck winced. Tipped her head into the MIR. 'That'll cheer everybody up. Fletch is already talking about taking early retirement.'

'It's the last thing we need right about now, I agree.'

'Crime goes on and all that,' Beck shrugged. 'You going to be okay with it? Because you *are* it for the moment, Will. They've opened up Gold Command at HQ for the bombings and there's even talk of some of us being shunted up there for the duration.'

MacReady shuddered. Headquarters in Bridgend was the last place he'd enjoy working out of. Errands for the strategists and careerists, mostly involving nipping across the road to Tesco to pick up sandwiches for their lunch. He needed to keep his head down as much as possible until the powers that be had chosen who was being transferred.

'You're on top of the CCTV, Sarge, Cardiff Central Railway – do we have coverage of the location Paxton was found?'

She shook her head. 'Uniform already tried. The service lane is a small blind spot. About seventy, eighty metres off the car park. There are a couple of cameras under the canopy for the southern entrance of the station to cover the concourse doors, and we have a camera further south, on Penarth Road. But they were all facing the wrong way. Everything was switched to look west yesterday morning.'

'Towards Bessemer Market.'

'Your girl picked the wrong time to get robbed.'

MacReady grunted a sigh, looked beyond her, into the MIR. Caught Fletcher glancing across, the DI's eyes narrowing as MacReady raised a hand in acknowledgement. 'British Transport Police? Any cameras the Train Ticket Police know of?'

'I called. Nope. And the Automobile Association building has a couple but they only cover their entrances. Same with Cardiff and Vale College. Even rang the gatehouse at Brains Brewery for you. They have recording gear at their front gates but they face down at the road to monitor traffic in and out. Nobody has anything on the location. It's an old access lane from the seventies, and nobody really uses it.'

MacReady's shoulders slumped. No CCTV at the scene. CCTV cameras right across the area to be checked, to see if Paxton could be spotted. To see if her attacker or attackers were also caught on camera. No resources whatsoever to plough into it. Just him, sitting around watching video recordings yet again, getting nowhere fast. And he'd promised the parents miracles. 'Thanks anyway. Appreciate it.'

Beck studied him for a second. 'You seem down.'

He threw a look into the Major Incident Room. 'Just wish I was in there. You know?'

'You're not *banned*, you idiot,' she grinned. 'Just busy. Like we all –'

'Wait, the cashpoints – they have cameras, right?'

'Most, but not all.' She cocked her head. 'Why do I sense a *please, Sarge* inbound?'

'Would you be able to do the honours? Check with the banks to see if they have cameras fitted to the cash machines?'

'Will, I am beyond busy –'

'And the ticket machines, too? Get one of your new nerds to check with Network Rail, see if they have mini CCTV? Please?'

'You're reaching here,' she warned him. 'I've been through the new entrance myself. The ticket machines and cashpoints face out into the car park. In completely the wrong direction.'

'It's worth a shot. And I'll do the rest of the camera stuff myself, check if I can find Paxton wandering about. Most of the recordings have been collated by now anyway, right?'

Beck held his gaze for a moment. Then: 'You get the names of the banks on the cashpoints, I'll make the inquiries with them.'

'I love you, Sarge,' MacReady smiled.

'I hate you, Will,' Beck replied. 'And it's going on page seventeen of my To Do list, not right at the top, OK? Because clutching at straws doesn't even cover it.'

Fletcher appeared behind her. 'You harassing my secretary, William?'

Beck turned, mock disgusted. Punched the DI on the shoulder. 'Dickhead.'

'Harsh,' Fletcher rubbed at his upper arm. 'But true.' He looked at MacReady. 'How is your robbery doing?'

MacReady shifted his eyes to Beck. Back to Fletcher. 'I tried ringing from the hospital.'

Fletcher spun at the waist, arced his hand at the MRI. 'Been a bit tied up –'

'It's not good news.'

'I only want good news. Bad news is banned as of –'

'She died this morning.'

'Oh.' The DI visibly sagged. Exhaled a long, weary breath. 'Well, that's just terrific, isn't it? Completely wonderful.'

*

The Crown Court liaison officer was your typical old sweat: nothing needed to be hurried, and any sense of urgency had been beaten out of him years ago – probably when the CPS decided to No Further Action yet another airtight case he'd spent four months working on, or a newly promoted looked-like-a-teenager inspector rocked up at the climax of a particularly brutal pub brawl to tell him off for not wearing his tie – when he'd realised the job was a load of fucking nonsense. MacReady had ground his teeth while waiting for the CCLO to dig out the details, then ended the call without thanking him. Not that the man would have cared.

In short: in light of the attacks, and given the increased security risk in the capital, the Alexander Castle trial was being shifted elsewhere. All trials were being shifted elsewhere, in fact. That meant his brother, too. MacReady had called just to find out how Stuart's assault case was going, but the old sweat had yawned and huffed and puffed and told him *R v Stuart MacReady* – along with every other trial in Crown – had been adjourned as of right now. New locations were to be Newport or Swansea, or even over the border in Bristol until Cardiff came to its senses and – the liaison officer had said, with no trace of irony – *you lot pull your finger out and lock up this bomber, like.*

You lot. As if the old fart wasn't one of them.

MacReady was beginning to hate the description.

He tilted his chair back, placed the heel of one shoe on his desk and tented fingers beneath his chin. Closed his eyes for a moment and listened to the noise, to the chants and shouts from outside, still going strong, although the bongo man appeared to have had enough sun and called it a day. For that he was eternally thankful.

Beneath his desk the brown-paper evidence bags containing Heidi Paxton's property rested to one side. MacReady opened his eyes and stared at them for a full minute, wondering if CSI would turn anything up from the prints. From DNA or fibres. He leaned sideways, opened a drawer, rooted around, pushing file forms and boxes of paperclips and various items of crap he'd accumulated over the last year to one side until he found the battered cardboard box. Took a pair of latex gloves, stretched them over his clammy hands. Dropped his foot to the floor and sat forward, picking up the first bag, a large sack which was as light as it was bulky. Checked the exhibit label.

The contents: blouson jacket. The next paper sack: T-shirt. Then one containing jeans, more with underwear, socks, and a small rucksack. All bloodstained. Paxton's clothing, taken off her at A&E by uniform, ready for forensics. He picked up the last bag. Heavier this time. The feel of hard edges through the thick paper lining.

The exhibit label had the same handwriting, compact and clear. Listed were the rest of Heidi Paxton's belongings.

£7.62 in cash. Smartphone.

MacReady sat back into the chair with the evidence bag on his lap.

Recalled what Beck had said.

Your girl picked the wrong time to get robbed.

Wondered what sort of street robbers leave behind somebody's smartphone.

Twelve

Unamused faces at the rear of Cardiff Central railway station.

People were turning up to catch trains only to find the southern concourse and its surroundings sealed with crime scene tape. The day a new one, yesterday's horrors already fading for most. Life moved on and the mundanities needed attending to. There were places to go. Things to do. What happened was terrible, but it had happened and that was that.

A lone British Transport Police uniform acted as the lightning rod for commuters' ire as they realised a terribly draining 500-metre walk around to the north entrance was on the cards if they wanted to get where they were going. BTP had armed officers on the platforms to deliver the old *public reassurance*, and had provided more bodies to assist on the cordon, presumably out of relief that Heidi Paxton had been gracious enough to get stabbed just off their patch, and therefore they didn't have to deal with her murder. The extra boots on the ground hadn't even made it to the railway station, though – the rankers in the Major Incident Room had seen fit to whisk them across to Bessemer Market first thing to help with knocking doors, arguing that they were better put to use as part of the regional Mutual Aid mobilisation which was now in effect.

Inside the sterile area two paper-suited technicians huddled over a clipboard, their faces burnished circles of concentration beneath elasticated hoods; the Paxton scene had been wide open to the public – and probably contaminated beyond all forensic opportunity – for well over twenty-four hours, but MacReady knew it had to be done all the same. Specialist Crime hadn't felt likewise, clearly reluctant to release the CSIs from the mosque until Fletcher had intervened and pressed their case for tech assistance with Paxton's murder inquiry. A grateful Mac-Ready had just spoken with the CSIs for ten minutes, stressing the importance of finding something, *anything*, Heidi Paxton's inconsolable parents – and what he'd promised them – foremost in his mind as he'd talked.

It was almost inconceivable, but Central was the busiest railway station in the city – in Wales – and other than the anonymous three nines reporting Paxton collapsed, not one telephone call had been received about the attack. An attack which took place during morning rush hour, when hundreds of people would have walked past her. When any one of those hundreds could have seen – could have *been* – the attacker.

MacReady gave a consoling nod to the BTP plod, climbed into the CID car and lowered the driver's window. From above, wafting over the new embankment wall and down to the car park, the sounds of a hectic station doing what it was supposed to do: the overlap of jostling tannoy announcements, the deep reverberation of freight wagons, of passenger carriages, of a seemingly endless procession of train services heading to all corners. Beneath it a low whine: another civvy – all pinstripes and rouged whisky

drinker's skin with a Very Important Thing in London to get to –
was pissing and moaning to the Transport plod about the infini-
tesimal inconvenience to his afternoon travel plans. MacReady
was tempted to get back out and tell him just why the back doors
of the station were closed. Wondered if the entitled fucker would
even care. He thought about Heidi Paxton lying in the mouth of
the service lane, bleeding out, the commuters' heads down and in
Facebook Land, too busy to notice. Thinking she was homeless, or
hassling for small change and not worthy of any attention.

Such was the way of things nowadays.

MacReady clocked the trio of cash machines outside the
new south-side building: two Barclays, one Royal Bank of Scot-
land. Two squat silver automated ticket machines alongside the
ATMs. Sent a quick text to Charlie Beck to let her know. Rang
the Ops Room, asked the supervisor there to check the 999 call
record for the incident: male or female voice on the recording,
the telephone number, service provider, any cell site. Anything
they could think of, anything he could pick up and work with
when he got back to the nick.

He headed out of the car park and across Callaghan Square,
his Airwave handheld bleeping with incessant transmissions
from the passenger seat as he drove south towards the bay via
the long sweep of Lloyd George Avenue, trying to clear his head
of Heidi Paxton for a while. Trying to focus on the bombings.
Even if Harrison didn't, he wanted to speak to the tac adviser
again. Just this one thing to get out of the way. Even if it was
the last work he did on the market and mosque attacks before –
voluntarily, or under orders – shifting his full concentration

onto the Paxton murder. It was just after three: there'd been no call from the angry firearms officer but plenty of time for the guy to have grabbed some sleep.

To his right the sunken maisonettes of Hodges Square flashed past. MacReady thought about the DS Bob Garratt shooting last year, and all it had led to.

He sent another text to Beck as he was driving, adding his thanks for her help.

*

No street footballers this time.

The sky above Penarth a thick quilt of ribboned cloud, dulling the sun to a pale orange, shifting everything to shadow. It had moved in from the sea as MacReady drove across the bridge from Cardiff Bay, an off-white fringe fogging the horizon. The late afternoon now hazy and close. MacReady wondered if rain would come with it. A storm to clear the air. To clear things a little. Found himself, as he knocked doors in the affluent cul-de-sac with its Beemers and Benzes and ridiculous SUV street tanks, willing the rain to fall, if only to beat away the punishing heat for a few hours.

Not one of the residents who answered his knock knew of Nazir Uddin. The shake of heads, the suck of air through teeth about the bombings, *a terrible business, is that why you're here? My goodness, someone from here is involved?*, MacReady politely refusing to answer, thanking them for their help, telling them not to worry after seeing it in their eyes.

It had become achingly clear within a few townhouses that Uddin had never lived here. Every occupant of this rarefied reserve was a retired sixty- or seventysomething – and white. Uddin would have been remembered. After half a dozen addresses MacReady was just killing time, time none of them really had, just to make sure the tac advisor was awake and fully *compos mentis* when he spoke to him.

The 4x4 was still on the hardstand. The man hadn't returned to work yet.

MacReady walked across. Rapped lightly at the door, not wanting to set him off again. When it opened a crack he was met with a sandwich. Then above it, mouth working, the firearms officer's bone-tired face.

'Sorry for earlier,' MacReady offered, warrant card raised.

'Ah.' A wave of the sandwich. 'Never been a good sleeper off a night turn. 'Scuse the munch. Grabbing something before . . .' A tilt of the head in the general direction of Cardiff. 'Y'know.'

MacReady knew. 'No rest for the wicked.'

An exchange of nods and the door drew open.

The tac advisor was Ken Cullen, a mid-thirties, ten-years-in PC, hailing from the north of England and normally based at HQ as a firearms trainer but drafted in as soon as Bessemer went up. Ex-forces, MacReady guessed: the man was squat, muscular, all neat and squared away in his joggers and tee. Speech measured, no-nonsense. A stillness about him as he sat in the middle of the sofa, hands clasped and elbows on knees, sandwich finished – quietly and efficiently – before they'd reached the lounge. His eyes were the only thing that moved, shifting from

MacReady to the case files he had on his lap and back again. Cullen had showered not long before MacReady arrived; a fine mist hung at the top of a nearby doorway and the place smelled of citrus.

'I'd offer coffee,' Cullen said, a huge yawn stretching his face. 'Or tea. But I don't have any in. Glass of water?'

MacReady shook his head. Glanced around from the armchair he'd dropped into. Cullen's apartment was well ordered and compact, much like the man himself. No personal touches or family photos. No books, DVDs, ornaments or knick-knacks. Just the basics: wide screen, coffee table, the chairs they sat on, a thick brown carpet which sucked up the weak light allowed into the room by a tiny window. It had the feel of a space rarely occupied for long periods of time. MacReady could understand that. Lot of cops' places barely felt like homes, more hotel suites for transient and often sleeping men and women. The lack of tea and coffee was not surprising; MacReady knew if he checked the man's fridge he'd probably find empty shelves, bar some token bruised fruit and a jar of something that should have been binned months ago.

Cullen's voice, still depths of Sheffield: 'So you're working it?'

MacReady turned to look at him. 'The market?'

A gesture at the files, a nod from Cullen.

'At the moment.' MacReady didn't feel the need to add *probably for the next hour, at the most.*

'Fucking crazies about,' Cullen muttered. He was still looking at MacReady but had gone elsewhere. Glazed over. Was looking inwards, as if remembering something.

'You heard any chitchat about who we're looking for?'

Cullen's eyebrows leaped upwards. 'You're asking me?'

'I'm kind of on the periphery,' MacReady offered, cursing himself, the uniforms who dumped him with Paxton's handover package. 'You know how it works. New boy and all that.'

'Lone wolf, what I heard on the grapevine,' Cullen shrugged. 'HQ talking about the far right, them nationalist types who don't like the blacks and Asians and stuff. Who's the Swedish guy who took out the government buildings then shot them kids on the island?'

'Anders Breivik,' MacReady nodded. Thought it best not to correct Cullen about Breivik's nationality.

'That'll be the one. Some mad fucker like him. Or that David Copeland who did the gay bombings in Soho back in the day. Whispers are they're putting surveillance onto a load of targets, doing the follows and phone taps. Old Welsh Defence League fruitbats, anyone who's ever popped up on Special Branch's radar for racist threats on Twitter and all that nonsense. All rest days and leave cancelled for the foreseeable. But then you probably know all this.'

'I don't know any of it,' MacReady sighed.

The faintest of smiles played with one corner of Cullen's mouth. 'Bet you make a great brew though, right?'

A laugh from MacReady. Cullen had him sussed. 'Exceptional tea skills.'

'Good lad.' Cullen leaned back a little. Shook his head. 'Right mad fucker we're talking about, though. Market, boom, boom, boom. Straight across to that mosque, quick as you like, then the same again. Fast, effective, no messing.'

'You sound like you . . . admire him, or something.'

Cullen tilted his head to one side, studied MacReady for a moment. His voice, harder still: 'Not admire. Not in the slightest. But you've got to respect the guy's tactics, his planning. The market owner might be the only witness who saw his face . . . and he's gone, mate. As well as all the market CCTV recordings. Gone, in teeny tiny bits. All that evidence. Then while we're stepping over body parts inside Bessemer he's hitting them people down in Penarth. Unbelievably quick, he was, getting over there. Like I said, got to respect the guy for his balls.'

The market owner. MacReady didn't even know the victim's name. Just what he'd managed to pick up from within the MIR: that the man had been on the three nines when he was hit, leaving a dead line whistling in the earpiece of the Ops Room civvy who'd taken his terrified call. No names mentioned or shouted. No recording of the attacker's voice before the call cleared. And any security recording equipment had been spread over a forty-feet radius and in minute pieces by the blast, much the same as the market owner.

'Lot of damage,' MacReady said. 'For a bunch of homemade bombs.'

A snort from Cullen. 'Know a lot about them, do we? Expert on the old Improvised Explosive Devices?'

'I just mean –'

'You seen the damage just one of those things can do? Just a mix of crap from your house, nail varnish remover and a few other bits and bobs, they could take half this street down. Ever seen the videos on the web? Googled "Mother of Satan"?'

'No, I haven't –'

'Then with all due respect you know fuck all, mate. And I went in there. Chummy lobbed three of them, at least. Carnage doesn't even begin to cover it . . .' Cullen tailed off. Eyes looking inwards again. Mumbled: 'Not seen anything like it since Afghan when we were clearing routes for Op Barma. Missed a few every now and again, buried under tyres or roadside clay. Messy doesn't even cover it when they go off under your legs . . .'

MacReady had guessed right about Cullen's military background. He shifted in his seat, interested now. 'But the building at the rear of the market? It went up, completely gone. It's not as if the attacker had a suitcase full of explosive.'

Cullen nodded. Knew where MacReady was heading. 'Propane canisters in the office, by all accounts, feeding a couple of portable heaters the owner used during the winter months. Only added to the power of the blast. And it was pretty powerful already.'

MacReady felt his phone vibrate in his pocket. Ignored it.

'So you find your man?' Cullen asked. 'Uddin, was it?'

MacReady rubbed a thumb over the outline of his phone, impressed Cullen remembered the name given the circumstances of the previous visit. 'Nope. That's what I'm here for, actually. He witnessed our guy hit the mosque in Penarth. Apparently.'

'Apparently?'

'Response officers collared him, took bare minimum details, let him walk. Nobody's seen him since.'

'Top police work,' Cullen sniffed. 'And you're at my place because?'

MacReady jerked a thumb around the lounge. 'Uddin – if that's his real name – told uniform this was his address.'

'Well, it's not.'

'We checked Niche,' MacReady said quickly, thinking of Cullen's outburst this morning. 'Uddin's shown as living here.'

Cullen stood, an abrupt movement, as if standing to attention. He looked down on MacReady. 'Well, he's not. And I haven't a clue who he is. And I'm due back in for an evening turn, so . . .' A glance towards the front door.

MacReady pushed himself up to his feet, sensing he'd already been dismissed. A dead end here, with an ex-forces wallah who wanted him gone sharpish and didn't seem to be the type to suffer any messing around. He didn't understand why Uddin had given the address, though.

'One thing,' he paused at the lounge door. 'Do you own this apartment?'

Cullen laughed, a strange, strangled choke as if he'd begun snoring then thought better of it. 'I get a lot of overtime in my role, but not enough to buy one of these places.'

'Renting?'

'Indeed.'

MacReady squinted about. 'You got details of the owner?'

'Nope,' Cullen replied. 'But I've got the rental company I go through.'

In three steps Cullen was at a small table behind the sofa, rifling through its lone drawer. It took him a couple of seconds to find what he was looking for. Handed it to MacReady.

The piece of paper had a fancy letterhead: Asma Residential. Offices just across the road in Penarth town centre. Couple of landline numbers, an email address.

MacReady stared at the company name. The professional layout – not to mention the office location – reeked of high-end properties. He wondered how on earth Nazir Uddin, a nineteen-year-old, was linked to Cullen's very expensive apartment. Just what he'd been doing, giving it as his home address to uniform. How he knew the exact contact details . . .

And then it clicked.

'May I?' he asked Cullen, who gave an uninterested shrug.

MacReady pulled out his mobile, saw he had a text message, got on with dialling the first number for the rental company. A female voice answered after three rings. Well spoken, bordering on plummy.

'Can I speak with Mister Uddin, please?' MacReady asked.

'Who's calling?'

'It's Mister Cullen.'

MacReady glanced at a frowning Cullen. Frowned himself as he was placed on hold, a short burst of horrible nineties boy-band gloop in his ear. Then:

'Mister Cullen? This is Aadhil Uddin.'

MacReady allowed a small smile. 'Not Nazir Uddin?'

'Not . . .' The man's voice faltered. 'You are looking for my son?'

'Is Nazir your son?'

'Yes, I . . . Who is this, please?'

MacReady killed the call. Exhaled. Checked the clock on his phone: twenty past four. It gave him plenty of time to make the short drive across the town and speak to Nazir Uddin's father before they shut up shop for the day. He jotted down the company's address and contact details in his notebook, handed the letter back to Cullen. 'I'm done here, thanks.'

At the front door MacReady turned around to offer his hand to Cullen. 'Appreciate your help, Ken. If you do think of anything, or need a favour sometime, just drop me a line.'

The tac adviser shook it: firm, sharp pumps of MacReady's hand as he cocked an eyebrow at him. 'Did some boning up on you, after you gave me your name this morning. Thought it rang a bell. You the shooting guy, right? Got your oppo shot during that thing in the limo rental place last year?'

MacReady closed his eyes. Sighed. 'That'll be me.'

That bizarre laugh from Cullen again. He let go of MacReady's hand.

'CID. The fuckin' Brains Department.'

MacReady opened his eyes. Cullen had quietly closed the front door and was gone.

*

The text was from Fletcher, the DI asking where he was and what he was getting up to. No swearing or block capitals with this one, so MacReady knew it was safe to ring him.

'Still out and about?'

Fletcher's grunted words in his ear as MacReady eased the car out of the cul-de-sac, swung the steering wheel and headed for the main drag of Windsor Road, where Asma Residential was located.

'Just firming up on a few things.'

Fletcher waited a beat. 'What have I told you about telling porkies? That sounded really rubbish, Will. "Firming up"? You know I hate that Sweeney bollocks.'

MacReady winced. 'Look, I'm in Penarth.'

'Penarth? You've already done Penarth today. I've got tasks for the place tomorrow. Warren and DS Echols are speaking to the occupant of the address Nazir Uddin gave to uniform. Wazza mentioned a tac adviser.'

'Yeah, we spoke to him briefly this morning.'

'Okay. Leave the rest of it with us, Will.'

'It's just around the corner, boss, I can –'

'Update the Incident Room with anything you've got. Log it all on HOLMES2 when you get back to the nick. That's it.'

'You sure?'

'That's it. For now, at least. You're pretty much all I have at the moment, Will. OK?'

MacReady didn't understand. Rolled his eyes. 'I understand.'

'Just get onto this stabbing. Your full attention. Specialist Crime have designated me as Senior Investigating Officer on the system, so you're my eyes and ears at the moment. You on your way to the Paxtons? Charlie said you've made arrangements to speak to them about their daughter.'

MacReady moved the phone away from his ear. Used his thumb to press at his left temple. 'I'm on my way there now.'

'Good. Then we're done.'

The DI ended the call. MacReady reached the junction for Windsor Road. A right turn took him back towards Cogan, to the interchange and the bridge over to Cardiff where the Paxtons waited for him. A left turn took him onto Windsor Road, where Aadhil Uddin was still at work and might know the whereabouts of his son.

MacReady drummed fingers on the steering wheel. Looked up and out of the windscreen, at sky which had darkened, closing in.

Turned left.

*

Eye-watering.

MacReady stood in front of Asma Residential, shirt sucking at his skin, the heat of the day thickening around him. Storm clouds now but still no rain. He shook his head at the apartments and houses displayed for sale and rent in the bay window. Made a mental note never to bother coming here if looking for a place to live. Three hundred and fifty thousand for a one-bed overlooking the marina. A grand a month for an unfurnished rental *with view of the pier!* just off the seafront. A flat in the same block as Klaudia Solak's, on sale for a cool half a million. Not London prices, but then not a lot could match that madness. There was nothing here he could ever afford, all the same, even if the miserable government reversed all the cuts to his pay and conditions. Ken Cullen must have been pulling in some serious overtime – or fiddling a second job on the side – to manage the apartment he was renting.

MacReady had a quick read-through of Nazir Uddin's details. Tucked the file under his arm and pushed through the front door, a bell tinkling quietly above him as it opened. The interior was small but chic, with an air of relaxed efficiency. Wood floor, polished oak desks with nothing but MacBooks and a couple of smiling suits, a male and a female. Two doors at the rear, both ajar, a glimpse of a kitchenette through one, *Manager* on a sign on the other. Around the sales duo rows of tall carousel display racks, rammed with pictures and specs of yet more unaffordables. Water machine. Magazine rack: *Ideal Home*, *What Mortgage*, couple of trade mags. Coldplay twanging blandly from speakers in the ceiling.

'Mister Uddin around?' MacReady asked, looking from one smiler to the other.

'Did I hear my name?'

Aadhil Uddin was just as smiley as he emerged from the manager's office. A small, well-fed man, pot-bellied and sporting a spectacularly dense moustache. Decked out in black, tasselled patent loafers, tight slacks and a shirt with bizarre diamante swirls on the shoulders. He proffered a hand: his wrist chinked with silver bracelets, a thick watch.

Out came MacReady's warrant card and the smile faltered.

'Follow me,' Uddin urged, all teeth and sudden fluster.

His office was a box, no bigger than Beck's back at Cardiff Bay. Desk, three chairs, a filing cabinet. Photographs of properties affixed to a cork board. A solitary photo of a laughing woman on the desk: Uddin's wife, MacReady assumed, eyeing the plump fiftysomething in the frame. MacReady waited for him to close the door, breathed in the woody aftershave Uddin had clearly applied upon hearing his name.

MacReady took a seat next to the door, paperwork file balanced on knees.

Uddin remained standing. Looked anxious. 'We're just about to call it a day.'

'This won't take long.'

'Pointless staying open, really. Things are a little slow at the moment. People are nervous after yesterday. Not many about. I think you're only the third person through the door today, and it's not even for . . .' He gestured at the property photographs.

'Understandable. And kind of why I'm here.'

'The bombings?'

'I'm on the team working them, yes.' MacReady just came out with it. 'Do you know where Nazir is, Mister Uddin?'

Uddin blinked. 'My son?'

'He was at the Al Mahdi Mosque. Or at least somebody was there who gave Nazir's name, date of birth and the address of one of your rental properties to uniformed officers at the scene.'

'What rental?'

MacReady gave him Cullen's apartment address. 'The occupant has never heard of your son.'

'What . . . Wait, was it you that rang a short time ago?'

MacReady flashed an apologetic smile. 'I wanted to be sure you were who I thought you were.'

Uddin slipped into his chair. Raked stubby fingers through hair as glossy as the loafers on his feet. His skin suddenly washed out. 'Please don't tell me my son is involved in any of this.'

'If he is, it's as a witness. At least that's what we're going with. It's just that he – if it was him – vanished as soon as he'd spoken to police. And now we don't know where he is. Which, as you can understand, is making us a little concerned as to why.'

Uddin lowered his head towards the polished desk top. Let it hang there for a moment. MacReady could see his breath misting the varnish. He spoke without looking up at MacReady: 'Do you have a description? Of the boy who spoke to the police officers?'

MacReady opened the file. Scanned the printouts, the Niche entry for Nazir. There wasn't much of it. 'Male, nineteen years, slim build, Arabic appearance, it says here. Hair shaved sides and back, long on top. Left ear pierced, left eyebrow has two shaved lines.'

Uddin hoisted his head upwards. 'That sounds like my son.'

'Sounds like?'

'It might be, it might not. It's complicated.'

MacReady closed the file. 'Try me.'

'I can't be sure because I haven't seen him. Not for a while, at least. Some months. Maybe May was the last time? But his ear, it had the diamond earring in it. And his eyebrow, that stupid thing, he was always doing it.'

'Do you have a photograph of Nazir we could use?'

Uddin leaned back in the chair, created some room so his hand could slip into a trouser pocket. Pulled out a wallet. After a second of digging inside it he pulled out a small photo. Handed it to MacReady. 'I'd like it back. It's the only time I get to see him nowadays.'

MacReady took a quick look at Nazir Uddin. Ear piercing, shaved eyebrow present and correct. Didn't recognise him, slipped the photograph into the file. Asked: 'Why don't you see him?'

Uddin looked aggravated. 'Look, my son is going through a difficult patch. Not that he wants for anything, but he's . . . lost his way. He was always a good boy but lately it hasn't been easy. Certainly not for my family.' His eyes shifted to the photo frame to his right, settled on the woman's picture for a few seconds. He gestured at it with a hand, bracelets clinking. 'My wife, Asma. I named this place after her. Everything was going so well for so long. But now . . . she is worried sick.'

'Nazir's a teenager,' MacReady offered. 'He'll work his way through it.' Stuart flashed into his thoughts. His brother had lost his way and then some. Was yet to work his way through anything other than women who he knocked up or about, despite nudging thirty years of age.

'We are a very close-knit community here, officer. We behave. We do things right. But Nazir's antics have been noticed. By family, friends. By the elders at the mosque. He has drifted away from us all, both in body and mind. The mosque, sometimes he goes, mostly he doesn't. It was the same at home for a while. Sometimes he stayed away for weeks. Then he finally stopped coming home at all.'

MacReady hooked a leg over one knee. 'You think drugs?'

'Not drugs.' An emphatic response. Uddin looked mortified by the suggestion. 'Nazir never drank or smoked. Certainly never touched any of that other rubbish.'

'Then I don't understand.'

He sat forwards, held MacReady's gaze. 'I think it's safe to say my son is the naive sort, Officer MacReady. Easily led. And not a little bit of a fantasist. So if I tell you I have heard he has been spending some time with, shall we say, undesirable elements in *your* community, I am sure you will understand.'

MacReady gave a slow nod. *A fantasist.* Something nagging at him about Nazir Uddin again, something so familiar about the name, but it wouldn't click into place. 'Of course.'

'Nazir is my son, and I love him, but he is a strange one. He pretends to be brave but he's a coward. Wastes all day on his computer, typing drivel, playing stupid video games and pretending to be a soldier, a superstar football player. A *wizard*. And he likes to create stories. Just last year he was bragging to people in the mosque about how he went abroad, how he trained in the mountains, and now he is back he is waiting for the order to strike –'

'I take it you've informed the authorities about this?'

'I haven't because I don't need to.'

MacReady thought he might scream. 'Your son's a returning jihadist and –'

A laugh from Uddin. 'I don't need to because it's a nonsense. Like everything with Nazir. My son wasn't training with guns and bombs in the desert. He was in London with his uncle, help-ing to renovate one of our properties there. I rang my brother every day. Nazir was working very hard. He especially enjoyed painting ceilings.'

'You seem quite relaxed about this,' MacReady said. A dull throb behind his right eye now. Headache on the way.

Uddin shrugged, threw hands out wide. 'It hurts me to say this but I have made peace with the fact that my son is an idiot. We all have. We are resigned to it now. But I would still like him home with us.'

'Would you like to report him missing?'

Uddin ignored the question. Looked to the door next to Mac-Ready. 'If it is fine with you, I am closing for the day.'

MacReady stood, tucking the folder under his arm. He wanted out of here. 'We need details of friends, family. Anyone he might be staying with. Telephone numbers, email addresses, the lot. My colleagues will be here to speak to you further. Tomorrow. Early.'

'Not you?'

'Not me,' MacReady muttered, thinking of Heidi Paxton. 'Not me at all.'

Thirteen

The Paxtons' house looked like any other in the Whitchurch area: neat, detached, gated. Surrounded by stone walls and lush greenery, a colossal oak throwing a canopy over the entire façade. The lawn, pared and shaped, fringed with beds of colour. The driveway paved and clean and home to a nearly new Volvo hatchback. A nice house in the nice middle-class neighbourhood residents called 'The Village', and far from the council estates of Ely and Adamsdown and Llanrumney. A place where violence rarely found you.

Heidi Paxton had gone elsewhere to find it. And inside the house would be different from all the others now. Would never be the same again.

The rain had finally fallen, heavy and thick, as MacReady battled back into Cardiff through rush-hour traffic. He was glad, and had left the driver's window open for several minutes, fat drops cooling his forearm as he crossed the bridge, riding beneath thunder all the way, thinking about the Paxton case and what the fuck he was going to say to her parents. When he called to let them know he was en route, Simone Paxton, Heidi's mother, had answered; she didn't respond to anything he said, and it had a taken a moment for MacReady to realise she'd been crying quietly on the other end of the line the whole time.

The rain had stopped now, as abruptly as it had started, and MacReady stood at the gate with Paxton's case file gripped in one hand, eyeing the solitary bunch of flowers leaning against one wall. The card, soggy from the downpour, tucked in cellophane speckled with water: *Rest in Peace Beautiful Friend xxx*. He waited, just for a moment, enjoying the noticeable drop in temperature, the lack of stickiness for the first time in weeks, the sudden freshness of the air he breathed. Dropped his head back, stared upwards: the clouds above him already ebbing, shifting to show pockets of blue evening sky.

He didn't notice until the approaching figure was a few feet from him and unlatching the gate. Silver-white hair, same loose-fitting shirt. It was Heidi's father.

'Thanks for coming,' Mark Paxton said, voice low, unemotional, and ushered MacReady in. The man looked drained, aged after just a handful of numbed hours spent trying to make sense of the senseless. He didn't linger for a reply, just turned and walked with a stoop back to the front door of the house. The gate stayed open; MacReady was about to ask him if he wanted it left that way but instead he shut it, following the man up the driveway.

The inside of the house was warm and musty, almost overwhelmingly so. Its windows sealed, curtains drawn against the outside world. Time stopped in here, a place of silence and sorrow and elongated shadows. The lounge dimly lit, a single floor lamp throwing out a miserly glow in one corner. Simone Paxton sat on one end of an oversized sofa which ran the length of the longest wall, pink cardigan absent. Fag-stuffed ashtray and mobile phone on the arm of the furniture, empty wheel-chair next to her and within reach; she didn't glance up when MacReady entered, her face partially hidden by long blonde hair which had become matted. Her fingers squeezed a balled tissue that she dabbed against glassy, downcast eyes.

'I do apologise about the mess,' she said. 'People have been traipsing through here all afternoon.'

The room was immaculate. Clean, comfortable, borderline cavernous, bookcases crammed with tomes, a grand fireplace which MacReady was glad remained unlit. He turned to Mark Paxton, who placed a hand on his wife's shoulder.

'We've had a lot of visitors,' Mark Paxton said. There was something not quite there about the man, as if he'd slipped his moorings. 'Family members, Heidi's friends. Everyone calling. Word seems to get around much faster nowadays.'

'Nothing from you people though,' Simone Paxton said point-edly, eyes still avoiding MacReady. 'No calls or updates or even a visit from one of your family officers, or whatever they're called.'

'Family liaison officers,' MacReady said. Cursed inwardly. This was the first he'd learned of the FLOs not showing. 'I'm so sorry, they've been requested but we're really stretched after yesterday. I'll make some calls before I leave –'

'We're managing,' Simone said. 'We don't need our hands held. And I don't care one iota how stretched you lot are, to be perfectly frank.'

At this she looked up at him. Gave a fuck-you smile. Mac-Ready took it, knew he had to. Knew the police deserved her venom.

He turned to Mark Paxton. 'All I can tell you is we're doing everything we can with what we have. I've just spoken to the Senior Investigating Officer, a detective inspector, and he'll be attending here as soon as he's free from the bombings. For now, though, if it's OK with you both,' he glanced at Simone Paxton, 'I want to run through a few things. And I'd just like to ask you some very basic questions. It would really help us a lot.'

Heidi's father lifted his head in the direction of an armchair opposite the sofa. MacReady nodded a silent thanks and squatted onto the seat. Hovered on the edge of the cushion, not allowing himself to get comfortable. Folder in his hands, moist fingertips leaving prints on the brown cardboard.

'I want a press conference,' MacReady began. 'Are you up to doing it?'

Mark Paxton shrugged; he was drifting, MacReady could see it. His wife had her anger to sustain her for now, but Heidi's father was unravelling in front of him.

'If you think it will make a difference,' Mark Paxton offered. Another hopeless shrug. He took a seat on the arm of the sofa, knitted his fingers atop his thighs. Simone Paxton's ashtray almost toppled over; she moved it, and her mobile, to the floor by her feet, sighing at her husband.

'I want Heidi out there,' MacReady went on. 'Tomorrow morning if possible. First thing. It's the ideal time to do it: Cardiff is already swarming with media. Local, national. Even some international. I'm going to grab as many of them as I can and sit you down in front of them. As wide as we can go.'

A low snort from Heidi's mother. 'Nobody will care. Not now. Not with people being blown to bits by a lunatic. My daughter will be a footnote in the newspapers, at best.'

'I'm telling you I won't let that happen.'

'You won't have a choice,' she replied.

'But will you do the press conference anyway?' MacReady asked. Kept his eyes on hers. Pleading. Willing her to agree.

After a few seconds: 'Yes.'

'Mister Paxton?'

Mark Paxton blinked. 'Yes?'

'Will you do the press conference for me? Tomorrow morning?'

'Oh,' he puffed out cheeks. 'If you say so, yes. Would you like a cup of tea, by the way?'

MacReady studied the poor man for a moment. Checked across to Simone Paxton. She'd resumed staring at thick cream carpet.

'I . . . sure, as long as it's not too much trouble.'

He didn't have long before Mark Paxton crumbled, and this would be over. He watched as the father wandered off into the bowels of the house, heard the faint chink of teacups. Sat silently for a minute, counting the seconds in his head, listening to a kettle bubbling. Then he leaned forwards, pulling out a pen and opening the case folder.

'I really need your help here, Mrs Paxton,' he said, keeping his voice low. Shifting his eyes to the lounge door, to the hallway which led to the rear of the house where Heidi's father clinked and stirred and ran taps. 'I've dealt with so many of these,' a lie, 'and I can see your husband is not coping with it very well at all.'

Her head snapped around to him. 'And you think I bloody am?'

'That's not what I'm saying.' Hands up, palms outwards, soothing her. 'At all, I promise. It's just I can see you're more capable of answering questions at the moment. You're angry, and that's good. Angry with me, with the police. So stay angry, please. Hate me if you want. It'll keep you focused, meaning I can get a lot of helpful stuff from you. I need it. Anything and everything you can think of about Heidi. I need it right now.'

Simone Paxton kept her eyes on him, lips pinched as she stared, the tendons at the sides of her mouth rippling beneath pale skin. Wanting to snap at him. Wanting to rake his face with her fingernails because there was nobody else to do it to. He could see it in her eyes, that almost uncontrollable urge. Then she turned her head away from him.

Said, 'Ask me whatever you want.'

MacReady clicked his pen.

Heidi Paxton had no reason to be attacked and killed. She had no enemies, wasn't being bullied, was liked by everyone who met her, and the few friends she had were loyal and extremely close to her. No boyfriends, in the romantic sense. Spent most of her time in 'The Village', occasionally venturing into the city centre for nights out. Nobody had been hanging around or stalking her, calling at the house or making calls. No online issues either, and Paxton was – as with most people her age, MacReady excluded – busy on social media, with Twitter and Facebook profiles. No debts or any money problems. Left school with a brace of A-levels but declined an opportunity to go to university. Enjoyed a drink, but was outspokenly anti-drugs after losing a school friend to a heroin overdose a few years earlier. According to her mother – and father, when he had a lucid moment – Heidi was just a normal young woman. Bright. Happy. Focused. Working online from her bedroom via some sort of content website, doing data entry for a pittance while trying to decide what she really wanted to do with her life.

'We've been supporting her for a little while, I suppose,' Heidi's father said. 'We don't regret it at all. We have the money.'

'Cardiff Central railway station,' MacReady said. Sipped at sweet tea, fought the urge to shiver. Mark Paxton had loaded it with sugar without asking if MacReady had wanted any. 'Did she normally travel to or from there? Or visit the area?'

'Not as far as I'm aware,' Simone Paxton replied. 'If she was going shopping or out for the evening in the city centre she'd catch the train from here to Queen Street Station. But she could have gone a little further. Changed trains at Central. I don't know. We didn't keep tabs on her day and night. She's twenty-two.'

'Perhaps for work or friends at the college?'

It was Heidi's mother's turn to shrug. 'Perhaps. I don't recall her having any friends or acquaintances who went to the college, though. What is south of the city centre anyway? Butetown? Riverside?' She shuddered; MacReady said nothing. 'And if she wanted to visit the Bay she'd have changed trains at Queen Street.'

MacReady checked his notes: enough to be getting on with. Speaking to friends and other family members. Interrogating her phone for calls and contacts and pings as she moved across the city on her final morning. Following up on the content website she worked for, her Facebook and Twitter followers and posts. Checking more CCTV, the railway stations, shopping centres, her bank account and any credit cards . . . and it was just him.

'What about a brother or sister?' he asked. 'Any siblings I can speak to?'

Silence. The Paxtons motionless. A sudden tension between them. MacReady cocked his head, looking from one to the other. After a few long, quiet seconds Heidi's mother glanced up at her husband. He continued staring ahead, at curtains blocking out sunlight in the window.

'None,' she said eventually. She blinked, several rapid flutters of her eyelashes. Fresh tears forming there. 'She . . . she had a younger brother but he was killed in a car accident when he was fifteen.'

MacReady shut his eyes, just for a moment. Just to let it sink in. Both Paxton children, gone. It was unimaginable, the depth of tragedy visited upon this family.

He opened his eyes, breathed deeply. Thought of Finlay. Once again thought how despite all that had gone on with Megan and Stuart, he'd not know how to cope if something like this happened to Fin. He looked at the Paxtons with fresh eyes: how they kept going was beyond miraculous.

He shook his head. 'I'm truly sorry for –'

'I was driving the car when he died,' Simone Paxton said. Squinted at the wheelchair, down to her emaciated legs. Up to her husband. A fingertip to the ugly scar, tracing it from mouth to chin. 'I got the better end of the bargain, I think.'

MacReady swallowed. Searched for words, something to say. Could find nothing. Wished he was anywhere but here. Wished the FLOs would turn up *right now* so there was somebody else to soak up this unending heartbreak. To share the load a little.

'This is why we pay her a monthly allowance,' Mark Paxton explained, still not realising he was referring to his daughter in the present tense. 'She does everything for her mother. Acts as sort of a live-in carer. We don't begrudge paying her a penny, as she's so helpful. The online work . . . well, we just let her get on with that. It keeps her occupied, and gives her something to focus on other than us.'

'Did she work from her room all day?'

Nods from Heidi's parents.

A click of MacReady's pen. The overwhelming urge to move, to get out of this lounge. To break away from this misery. 'Can we take a look at Heidi's bedroom?'

Mark Paxton swallowed. 'I'd rather not.'

'That's fine, we can do it another –'

'I mean you go ahead. Just don't ask me to come with you, please. I can't.'

MacReady chewed at his bottom lip as he watched it happen: Heidi's father finally crumpled. Placed hands up to his face and wept, shoulders shaking, sobbing uncontrollably on the arm of the sofa.

Simone Paxton embraced him, her hands slipping around his waist. It reminded MacReady of a few hours earlier in the hospital lift, but this time it was Heidi's father that needed comforting. Simone pulled him down and close, whispered something into his ear, the palm of her hand resting against the side of his face for a moment. He nuzzled against it, apologising. Telling her he was sorry for not being there to save their daughter, their son. That he was a failure as a father. Simone Paxton quietened him, ran fingers through his hair. Gestured for MacReady to take the stairs to Heidi's bedroom.

It was gut-wrenching to witness and MacReady was happy to turn away.

Heidi's room was a capacious loft conversion replete with en suite, huge bed, walk-in wardrobe and panoramic dormer window looking out at Whitchurch village and the greenery of the Common. It was clear Heidi had been left to do with it as she pleased: on top of the simple décor – white walls, wood beams and tasteful furnishings – over the years it had been personalised to the nth degree. Photographs, cork boards with myriad pins and notes and reminders. Dozens of posters showing rock groups and DJs, Pokémon characters, *Game of Thrones*, the walls just about visible in places. Clothes and trainers and makeup everywhere, littering the bed, a beanbag, the floor with its selection of garishly coloured rugs and throws. Television at the foot of the bed, cables and wires and connectors hooking it up to a home cinema rig, complete with surround sound. Beneath the window: a desk with a shabby laptop, its lid peppered with stickers and symbols. Notes everywhere, handwritten, typed. Screwed-up balls of paper. Live gig ticket stubs, flyers for a new nightclub due to open in the city centre promising yet more BOGOF drinks deals and 6 a.m. finishes for uniform to contend with.

It was the typical bedroom of someone in their late teens or early twenties. Messy, busy. All of it paused. Still. Waiting in stasis for an occupant who would never return. There were bedrooms like this across the city now, after the market and mosque. Lives just stopped. More cops standing in lounges and dining rooms and kitchens, awkwardly offering condolences to horrified relatives. Things just lying where their owner had last used or touched them. And MacReady took care not to touch anything. Wanted this bedroom left as it was, for CSI to do their magic, for techies to check her computer equipment. For him to return here, which he'd need to do, over and again, as things developed, as the case opened up or closed down on him.

And most of all for Heidi Paxton's parents.

Then it hit him: he didn't even know what she looked like. Her physical description. It hadn't even registered. And it was indicative of the police's – of *his* – lack of investment in the case. He pictured the parents, two floors below him, grief-stricken at the loss of their child. Another child. Their only living child. He felt disgust at the way things had played out here. Disgusted with himself.

He checked the photographs dotted around the walls, a multi-photo frame by the side of the bed. A happy, contented young woman featured in all of them; he could see her mother in Heidi. A handful with her parents. One astride a white horse. Shots taken at the beach, at parties, in pubs, where she draped arms around friends. Her hair blonde but streaked with green, small nose piercing, trendy specs over bright-blue eyes. Intelligence in them, her eyebrow arched in most of the images, as if she was laughing knowingly at something or someone.

MacReady had touched nothing but needed this. He selected a photo from a clutch near the laptop. Picked it up. Stared at it for a few seconds, one finger brushing at the glass.

'Hello, Heidi,' he said quietly.

Slipped the photograph into the case file.

Glanced around the bedroom again.

What on earth happened to you?

*

While the city edged towards sleep the police station bustled.

It was gone ten p.m. when MacReady arrived back at Cardiff Bay, its offices and corridors and public rooms alive with activity, with clumps of rankers, clusters of detectives from all corners of the force, a token drunk sleeping on a foyer bench and dribbling onto the carpet, uniform unwilling to lock him up because that would mean paperwork and court appearances and provide the guy with meals and a cell bed for the night, which was just what he wanted.

MacReady had spent the evening statementing Simone Paxton, the pair of them ensconced in the kitchen on either side of a table in the breakfast nook, both trying to ignore Heidi's father as he'd shuffled and snuffled from one room to another, lost in his thoughts, making tea for nobody. MacReady trying to take no notice of the rumble in his guts where he'd skipped food once again. It had taken close to three hours just to get the bare minimum from the mother – a taste of Heidi Paxton's ante-cedents, history, some names of her main friends who might be worth speaking to, then the rundown of her final night and the morning she left to go into the city. MacReady had cajoled and prodded as gently as he could, making sure he had some lines of inquiry at least, until Simone was spent and he'd stopped writ-ing on the MG11 statement form mid-sentence. They'd resume when she was up to it, he'd promised her, mindful that she needed some rest if there was to be a hastily assembled press conference tomorrow. Before he left he'd dialled the Major Inci-dent Room and demanded a family liaison officer be diverted to attend for the night. An exhausted-looking plain-clothes FLO who MacReady didn't recognise had rocked up fifteen minutes later while he was sat in the car going through the Paxton file. They'd exchanged curt nods, a pair of busy Busies, and Mac-Ready had driven away.

Alone in the CID suite yet again. A solitary fluorescent buzzing overhead. Blinds still open at every window, the greys and blacks of the cityscape studded with amber streetlights. MacReady plonked himself into the chair at his desk, dropped Paxton's file into a drawer, noted a thickening pile of paperwork in his tray. Saw several new emails when he fired up the workstation. Clear plastic sleeves containing DVDs, envelopes with antiquated VHS tapes inside, the recordings he'd requested from the council's highways department, from stores and businesses and shopping centres, in an effort to try and trace Heidi Paxton's movements across the city, all neatly piled on one corner of the desk. He ignored it all, rubbed at weary eyes with the heels of his palms.

After visiting the Paxtons he ached to hold Finlay.

MacReady yawned and began typing: an email pinged to Special Branch and WECTU about Nazir Uddin. He had no clue if Aadhil Uddin was being straight about his son spending time decorating a property in London. MacReady wanted to leave nothing to chance if the kid really had gone abroad. As an afterthought he copied in Fletcher, Beck and Harrison, pressed send. Swapped out to Niche and updated it with his inquiries regarding Paxton. Logged into the HOLMES2 system for the bombings and added everything he had on Nazir Uddin, his father, and the father's business premises. Topped it off with a précis of his conversation with Aadhil Uddin. Enough for Harrison and Echols to work with in the morning. To work the father further. Put the arm on him if need be. MacReady reclined the chair, laced fingers behind his head. Stared at Nazir Uddin's name.

And not a little bit of a fantasist . . .

The father's description. But MacReady knew of Nazir Uddin and, for the life of him, could not remember why.

He let the room hum around him for a few minutes, enjoying the air con, eyes on the name on the computer screen. A sigh when nothing came to him. Instead he powered everything down, grabbed his slimmer-than-slim case file for the bombings, eased himself out of the chair.

The Major Incident Room was the antithesis of the CID office: MacReady had to press through more starched white shirts and clip-on ties gathered in one place than he'd ever seen in all his service just to get to the centre of the room. The air reeked of coffee and burned toast and takeaway food. Amongst the mass of bodies and desks and IT equipment he found Fletcher and Echols hunched over a table, scrutinising a map of the streets around Bessemer Market. Alongside the map, reams of incident printouts, the sheets of paper well thumbed and curling, Fletcher muttering and pointing from incidents to map and back again.

'The wanderer returns,' the DI said, glancing up. A pallor to Fletcher's face, his olive skin drained, tight across his cheekbones. Tie off and shirtsleeves rolled up on the same shirt he'd worn since yesterday. Fletcher hadn't been home yet, MacReady knew.

Echols's chest heaved just a little, a small groan slipping from between his lips as he looked MacReady up and down. 'You all over that murder of yours? Been holding hands with Mummy and Daddy while they grizzle?'

'All over it,' MacReady replied. Added as a silent afterthought: *Fuck you, Paul.* 'And I've done all I can with your witness Nazir Uddin.'

Fletcher tilted his head, one eye half-closed, as if in pain. 'What d'you mean, you've done all you can?'

Echols chuckled, shaking his head. 'Here we go.'

'Look, I was there,' MacReady offered. Threw in a little white lie. 'I had to drive past Uddin's father's business to get back to Cardiff. Seemed mad not to so I just called in for a few minutes.'

'We have tasks to go to Penarth tomorrow,' Echols said, straightening. His brow had furrowed, face darkening. 'Speak to the occupant of that address. The firearms goon. Find out what the score is, man. Now you're duplicating work. Confusing everyone.'

'I'm not confused. At all.'

Echols bristled. 'Cheeky little twat.' It was loud enough for people's heads to turn.

Fletcher stepped between them. 'I asked you . . . *told* you to drop everything and concentrate on the Paxton girl.' He leaned back to the table, fists resting on the map's surface. Dropped his head and looked away from MacReady.

MacReady opened his file. Quickly scanned through his notes. 'Occupant of the address Nazir Uddin gave to uniform at the mosque bombing scene is Ken Cullen. Firearms tac adviser based at HQ. Doesn't know Uddin, but rents the apartment from a company in Penarth called Asma Residential. I went there. Asma Residential is run by Nazir Uddin's father, Aadhil Uddin. He owns the property Cullen rents, which is probably why Nazir gave it as an address when uniform questioned him. He panicked, I think. Anyway, the father provided a full description of Nazir, some background information, but doesn't know where his boy is at present. He's going off the rails a little, by all accounts.'

'We could have done all this –' started Echols.

'Well it's done, and on the system,' said MacReady. He reached into the file. 'And here's a photo of Nazir for circulation so we can pick him up and find out what he's playing at. The father wants it back once we're finished with it.'

Fletcher heaved his tall frame upwards, took the photograph MacReady was holding. Studied it. Shifted his red-rimmed eyes to MacReady. 'Right. Now please tell me . . .'

MacReady flashed a half-smile. 'Then I went to the Paxtons. They're devastated, obviously, but I spoke to the parents at length, searched the deceased's bedroom, copped an eleven-pager from the mother, which we'll finish when she's ready. Made sure an FLO was at scene overnight prior to me leaving. And they've agreed to a presser tomorrow. First thing in the morning, hopefully. All of this is also on the system for you to look at if and when you have a few minutes out of this madness.'

MacReady inhaled, needing it. Looked from Fletcher to Echols.

After a moment: 'OK,' Fletcher nodded. Threw MacReady a look that said *Good. But don't push your luck.*

'Anybody told you you're a cocky bellend?' Echols grunted.

MacReady sniffed. 'Is the sarge about?' Emphasis on *the* as he looked at Echols.

'In her swanky new office,' Fletcher replied, and turned back to the map. 'Right next to the toilets. Call it a day once you've spoken to her, Will. And in early tomorrow if you've got a press conference to sort.'

MacReady eased sideways through the crowd of civvies. Fingers tapped busily at keyboards, phones rang, someone shouted about a coffee run, hands going up behind monitors, seeking that extra jag of caffeine needed to push them on into the small hours, the room a swirl of different conversations and calls for resource deployment, for updates about actions delegated to officers, for Armed Response vehicles to carry out hi-vis patrols as a deterrent. He noted the hastily thrown-together casualty whiteboards had been replaced with a couple of large office display panels – one marked Bessemer, the other Al Mahdi. Their blue fabric held neat rows of pinned photographs: the dead and injured from both sites.

MacReady hovered in front of them for a moment. Looked at the names and faces of the deceased, the injured. The smiles, the laughter, the bright eyes. Like Heidi Paxton. Gone now, just like her. Dead at the mosque: *Aaliyah Ghaffari, 19 years. Shaykh Hafiz Yusuf, 68 years.* So the imam had succumbed to his wounds. He scanned the wounded, almost a dozen of them. Male, female, young and old. Saw a familiar face, remembered it from the hospital ward. The male, hands missing, who'd become so upset when MacReady tried to speak to him. Still no name for him yet though.

On the second board, Bessemer Market: *Daacad Farah, 28 years. Daahir Farah, 26 years.* The brothers taken out with the shotgun. *Dennis Afolabi, 47 years.* The market owner, obliterated in the explosion.

And at the bottom: *Shakima Corlett, 26 years.*

The wife of the man MacReady had spoken to at the UHW. Jordan's mother. She'd died at the hospital.

MacReady closed his eyes and thought about Megan, how he'd feel if he lost her for ever, even after all that had gone on. Pictured Finlay again. Nose popping as he breathed, struggling with his first cold, chubby arm hanging loose from the sheet which enveloped the rest of his body. Remembered the woman at Bessemer, her arm ragged and ruined, pleading for the return of her husband, her son. The bodies at the market entrance.

'Christ,' MacReady whispered.

Beck's temporary new office was bigger, but just as hot and cramped as her broom cupboard in the CID suite due to the extra staff and equipment brought in to pore over hour upon hour of CCTV. He glanced around a room which resembled an explosion in a home entertainment store. Racks of DVD players, flat-panel televisions of various sizes, tapes and speakers and wires and remote controls everywhere, Beck's so-called nerds in the midst of it all, a troika of beards and achingly hip spectacles inches away from computer screens that played security footage collected from across Cardiff.

Beck stepped over to him, knew what MacReady was thinking as soon as she saw the look on his face. 'Wait until tomorrow. Got two more joining the crew, which means there'll barely be room to breathe in here.' She leaned in, conspiratorial. 'I bet they're both bloody hipsters, too.'

MacReady looked from Beck to the beards. 'D'you really need all these people? All this . . . stuff?'

She placed hands on hips, hitched an eyebrow. 'Will, we've had over two hundred DVDs, Blu-rays, VHS tapes and digital recordings on memory stick arrive since this morning. To add to the seventy-plus we got yesterday. To say I'm not looking forward to tomorrow's internal mail is an understatement.'

He gave a shake of the head. 'Crazy. So no joy with our man in black yet, I take it?'

'Still working through Bessemer. Council is a *nada*, Cardiff Bus cameras likewise, other than what you saw where one of their single-deckers caught the sound of the explosions. None of the nearby businesses have cameras that face directly onto the market entrance or car-parking area so we're a bit stuck in relation to any vehicle. Assuming he was in a vehicle, given that he got to Penarth so quickly. We're working outwards now. Fletcher and Echols are cross-referencing incidents created on the Captor computer system with a map of the city, seeing if they can pinpoint any locations where a vehicle is seen driving erratically and if there's CCTV that covers the area.'

'I'm sure something will come up,' he smiled. Beyond tired now.

Beck gave a small laugh. The beards turned to look at Mac-Ready.

'Something I said?'

'Why d'you think there's so many people out there?' she asked. 'Developments, developments.' A wink, and she ushered him further into the room. MacReady was already regretting dropping by, the heat was almost unbearable, and there was not really anywhere for him to go in there. Instead he shuffled forwards a couple of feet and parked his backside on the corner of the nearest desk.

Beck fiddled with a DVD player remote; the television next to her showed a HD recording, the scenes skipping backwards at speed. She stopped it with jab of her thumb on the play button.

'Nothing for Bessemer yet, but here's the Al Mahdi.'

MacReady remembered the security cameras. Two of them on the mosque walls, one facing front and out onto Penarth's Stanwell Road, the other into the small parking area at the rear. The television was showing a silent recording of the mosque's front entrance from the morning of the attack.

He leaned forwards, squinted as it played.

Nothing for a few moments, the time showing 9.47 a.m., Stanwell Road in Penarth normal as usual, a handful of moving vehicles passing across the frame, the tree-lined roadside chock-full with parked cars, sunlight falling through leaves and branches to dapple tarmac. No foot traffic. No people at all. The seconds ticking on the screen, nudging towards 9.48 a.m.

And there he was.

Enter stage left: a black-clad figure. Jacket, combat trousers, baseball cap, shades. Gloved hands gripping a rucksack. Head down, stride purposeful. Heading towards the front doors of the Al Mahdi.

Tick tock. 9.49 a.m. on screen.

Then the image fuzzed, rolled, the camera clearly shaking violently. Sparks and dust and what seemed to be glittering diamonds – shattered glass – spraying out onto the pavement, across the bonnets of the cars. Smoke billowing upwards, fogging the screen, whiting it out.

Beck paused the recording. 'That's pretty much it. Smoke and dust in the air for a good while, obscuring everything. I can play it on for five minutes or so, if you're desperate to see people with their legs missing dragging themselves out of the mosque.'

MacReady exhaled. Shook his head. 'What a shitty world we're living in.'

'We have stills going out to all the news agencies tonight. Pictures of chummy as he goes in. Blown up – if you'll excuse the phrase – as best we can while keeping the picture resolution.'

MacReady thought for a few seconds. The release of the stills was great, and would be major news overnight and certainly for the morning. But it could mute any public interest in the press conference for Heidi Paxton. Might swamp it until it was completely forgotten. He checked some of the TV screens around the room: 'What about the other mosque camera?'

'The parking area?' Beck replied. 'Same kind of stuff when the explosions go off. There's dust everywhere for two or three minutes. Can't see a thing. Plenty of time for our guy to disappear into the surrounding area.'

MacReady shifted around, continued studying the televisions and monitors, most of which displayed paused video recordings. 'What about neighbouring premises?'

'Done them all,' one of the civvies piped up. 'No sign of your man approaching the place or after he runs away. Just empty streets and rows of parked vehicles.'

'We're working on the assumption that he was CCTV-smart, knew the locations of cameras in the area,' Beck offered. 'And that he still had his car. So until we know what car we're looking for . . .'

The civvy nodded. 'Needle in a haystack made of needles.'

MacReady ignored him. 'I don't care about our guy. I'm thinking about another guy. You say you've viewed every other recording in the area?'

'Pretty much,' Beck nodded. 'We focused on the mosque location first, just because it's more . . . sensitive, as far the bosses are concerned. Community relations and all that.'

'Did you see anybody hiding behind one of those parked vehicles?'

Beck screwed up her face. 'Hiding?'

MacReady nodded. 'Asian or Arab male. Late teens or early twenties. Hiding behind a parked car near the mosque.'

'Not at all,' said Beck. She turned to the civvies; three heads shook in unison. 'We've watched them on loop for most of the day. There's nobody hiding behind any car on any of them. Anywhere near the mosque.'

MacReady pushed himself up from the desk. The room hotter still.

Beck studied him, one finger twirling a hank of hair. 'What are you thinking, Will?'

He craned his neck, looking for Fletcher in the scrummage of the MIR.

And not a little bit of a fantasist . . .

'I'm thinking why our supposed star witness told uniform he saw the attacker go into the mosque,' he gestured at the paused television screen, 'when he wasn't even at the scene when it happened.'

*

An amber-tinged paleness to the bedroom, window blinds yellowed rectangles from street lights, the thin cotton sheet clinging to his thighs and tangled at his feet. Finlay next to him, a warm, unmoving bundle now, fed and rocked around the room until his cries subsided and sleep retook him.

On the other side of Finlay: Megan. Breaths light and long, her right hand twitching occasionally on the pillow where it had come to rest near her face.

MacReady had driven here, not knowing what to expect, not really knowing what he was doing but unable to stop himself seeing Fin. Had lifted the boy out of his cot just to feel him, just to hold him.

Just to hold on.

And Finlay had woken and cried and MacReady had shuffled guiltily as Megan burst into the room, sleep still on her and in her, her worried expression slowly morphing into one of shock at seeing her husband holding her baby, then confusion, then hope.

MacReady watched them both now. Watched for a long while. One came with the other, that package deal. His thoughts drifted to the Corlett family. The little boy under the car, Jordan, and his father, Peter in Ward A2. *Boy's my world*, he'd said, and MacReady had seen it in the man's eyes, that conviction, the certainty that Corlett would do anything to be with and protect his son. Corlett's wife, Shakima, her body ruined at the market and now lying in the University Hospital mortuary. Their lives ripped apart through no doing of their own. All MacReady had ever wanted was a family like that, the chance to do things right when all he'd known of fatherhood as he grew up was somebody doing it so, so wrong. And just when he thought he had it, it was snatched away from him by his brother and his wife. He had been humiliated in the process. And he wasn't sure he could ever forgive Megan. If he could get over it, accept it. He was trying his best, but he didn't know if it was going to be enough. If he had the strength to live with what had gone before.

He traced a finger along Finlay's arm. Thought of Klaudia Solak. Of work. Of using Solak for the Paxton press conference.

Of using her while she used him.

MacReady rolled onto his back.

Stared into the gloom.

Friday

Fourteen

Lukewarm water in the shower, full blast, drenching him. Cooling him. The previous evening's rainfall a blip, it seemed. A fleeting period of lower temperature before normal, blistering service resumed. MacReady leaned into the tepid spray, palms against cold tiles. Nails digging into grout. Eyes shut, thinking about this morning.

They'd woken early, a wriggling Finlay rousing them just after six a.m., the room already stifling. Megan had offered to squirrel Fin away so MacReady could grab another hour but he'd thanked her for the offer and climbed out of bed. Sleep wouldn't come to him again. Too much to do. Not least spend a little time with Finlay before disappearing into work. He'd yanked up a window blind, instantly felt warmth on his naked torso. Nothing but powder-blue sky above a horizon tinged with reds and purples, a burning half-sun creeping over distant hills that flanked the east of the capital. A beautiful day, again. Then he'd ambled downstairs in just his underwear, a small part of him glad to be home, if only for a short while. Just being normal, doing normal, mundane things. Stuffing Marmite on toast into his mouth. Gulping at sweet tea. On a brightly coloured mat he'd played with Fin, pulling faces and squeaking various soft toys. Making him laugh. Trying to forget about Stuart and Megan, how they'd conspired to bring the boy into this world. From the lounge doorway Megan had watched, wringing her hands, her mouth formed into a nervous smile. He'd known she was there, had avoided looking directly at her. It would have led to discussing their current situation, when all he wanted was to enjoy a few simple moments with Finlay.

MacReady stepped out of the cubicle, skin speckled with water and face doughy, the shower doing nothing to wake him properly. Heard his mobile ringing in the pocket of his trousers, bunched on the floor near the door. He dug out the phone, Fletcher's number on the screen.

'Hang fire with the presser,' the DI said. No *Good morning* for MacReady. Fletcher all business, already. 'I've been across to the Paxtons, introduced myself as the Senior Investigating Officer. Wanted to get in there early to see them with the FLO in tow. They'll do it, but not until this afternoon. Need a bit more time to gather themselves, maybe catch up on some sleep. The old man especially, he's still in bits.'

MacReady nodded, feeling not a little odd talking to his detective inspector with everything hanging out in the wind. He pulled a towel from the rail next to the sink, slipped it around his waist. 'It's for the best,' he said, sitting on the toilet seat. 'The mosque photo is all over the news. Heidi's parents don't stand a chance this morning.'

'True, dat,' Fletcher yawned in his ear. 'More space for them this afters.'

'You been home yet, boss?'

'Course I fucking haven't. And who are you, my mother? Anyway, good work with them yesterday, Will. The father is a zombie, but Simone Paxton – I get the feeling she was pretty impressed with you, all things considered.'

'She was still pretty frosty when I left but she'll come around. I was just about to head across to speak to them, actually.'

'Stay put. There's nothing for you to do. The day family liaison officer is already on duty at the house and I've arranged for CSI to make their way. So take a load off this morning. Have some lunch and get back in here for two-ish.'

'A late turn? I've got loads I can be doing this morn–'

'Came from the detective chief superintendent in Specialist Crime. He's been butting heads with the division's higher-ups about money, because they're already pissing and moaning about their budget, would you believe. All these bodies are really expensive, apparently, and they don't want to incur any more overtime costs. So you're two till midnight. The press conference is scheduled for four, which gives you plenty of time to prep the Paxtons then do whatever you need to do afterwards.'

MacReady gave a quiet sigh. 'Are Harrison and Echols . . . ?'

'On their way to Penarth to speak to Uddin's father? Yes. Which means I only have to get rid of motormouth Charlie Beck for the day and I can have some peace and quiet for a change.'

MacReady laughed, but Fletcher had gone.

In the lounge Finlay gurgled and drooled in a bouncer chair as Megan handed MacReady another mug of tea. He told her about his shift change, sipped at the drink.

'Go back to bed, then. You look exhausted.'

MacReady chuckled at Fin. 'Wouldn't want to miss this.' He looked at her. 'And I'm not the only one who's exhausted.'

Megan shrugged, a *Comes with the territory*.

'You go back to bed,' MacReady told her. 'I'll take him out.'

'Take him out?'

'Yeah. Give you a break. Just for a few hours.'

'A few hours?'

He arched an eyebrow. 'This repetition game isn't much fun, y'know.'

Megan clutched her hands together. 'I'm not sure.'

'What, that I can't be trusted to look after him?'

'It's not that,' Megan offered, hands twisting at her navel.

MacReady felt a pinch of anger. Placed the mug on a table. 'Then what?'

'I mean you've never . . . This is all so sudden, you coming here and spending the night with us and I don't know what to make of it all–'

'I just want to take our son out for a while,' he snapped.

The words hung between them for a moment.

Our son.

MacReady turned away. Looked at Finlay, eyeing them from his bouncer. 'Your son. Our son. Whatever. I'm just trying to do what feels right here. OK?'

Megan studied him for a good while, the pair of them standing in silence, the only noise the faint creak of the baby's chair. Then she stepped forwards and hugged MacReady. Pulled him close. Held him tight.

Into the crook of his neck, said: 'OK.'

MacReady stood with arms dangling at his sides, watching Finlay.

*

Inside the St David's Centre it was gloriously cool, the sweat under MacReady's arms, on his back quickly drying as he took in the procession of passers-by from his seat outside the Mexican restaurant. Shoppers, diners, people just drifting through and happy to be out of the scorching lunchtime heat, an endless parade of shorts and tees, of halter tops and summer dresses and sunglasses perched on heads. The second floor of the Eastside café quarter awash with punters, with yet more of them filing in and up on the sky bridges and escalators. It felt good to see the centre so full. To see the market and mosque attacks had failed to scare people away.

While Megan had gathered bags and nappies and bottles for Finlay, MacReady had made a few phone calls during the morning, keen to push on with inquiries for the Paxton case despite being out of the office. Firstly to the inspector in the Financial Investigation Unit at HQ, for an order enabling him to look at any bank accounts Heidi Paxton might have held. Then to Beck, to see if any of Great Western Railway's ticket machines or the banks with ATMs at the rear of Cardiff Central station had come up with images – there was nothing yet. Then to the old sweat Crown Court liaison officer to be told the Alex Castle trial was yet to resume, that it was likewise with all other trials, including Stuart's.

Then as he'd pulled away from the house, a quick call to arrange lunch.

'He's completely out of it, bless him.'

MacReady glanced down at Finlay in his buggy. Definitely out of it, at last. He'd cried continuously since leaving home: in the car all the way into the city centre, as he was wheeled along Queen Street's pedestrianised shopping avenue, past Cardiff Castle and then the entire length of The Hayes before finally succumbing to overtiredness as they'd entered St David's. By that point MacReady was more than a little frazzled, silently blaming the kid for waking so bloody early and wondering why he'd offered to take him off Megan's hands.

It had been an interesting hour, to say the least.

He looked up at Klaudia Solak. 'So what are we eating?'

She studied the menu while MacReady studied her. Felt the last of the tension seep out of him as he regarded her: legs crossed at the ankles and leaning back in her chair, raven hair loose around the nape of her neck, relaxed and tanned and unbothered by pretty much anything. Her eyes narrowed a little, working their way down the list of Tex-Mex concoctions.

'A mojito sounds good,' Solak said finally. Winked at him. 'For the heat, of course.'

'Of course,' MacReady smiled. 'Unfortunately I have work at two. Murder victim's parents plus press conference plus booze? That doesn't equal good.'

She chuckled. 'Well, I'm already in work, and I *am* having a cocktail for lunch. And what is it with you new breed of CID officers? If you stabbed one of the old lot they'd bleed lager. It's a poor show, Willy.'

MacReady sighed and picked up his menu. Burritos. Burgers. Chargrilled wings. He doubted Solak would want anything. She seemed to survive on coffee and adrenalin. 'You sure you can help me out with this?'

'If in doubt, hit the nachos.'

'Very funny. I mean the Paxtons. With everything else that's going on we're going to be drowned out and then ignored unless someone runs with it. Come on, Klaudia. I need you pushing it hard.'

She signalled to one of the waiting staff. 'What about the bombings? Is there anything you can give me that's not already out there?'

'This is a young woman we're talking about. I'm struggling as it is, so don't use her as a bargaining chip, not now. Just tell me you'll –'

'Mojito,' Solak smiled at the young man who appeared at their table. 'Double the rum and flavour it with mango purée. And he'll have . . .' She pointed at MacReady.

He ordered a water. Thought quickly, his stomach griping, breakfast a distant memory after Finlay's early start. 'And nachos to share.'

'Hope you're hungry,' Solak remarked as the waiter slipped away.

MacReady ignored the comment. 'Just tell me you'll pick this Paxton thing up. Keep it out there as best as you can. You should see the parents, Klaudia. What they're going through.'

'No different to lots of other parents and family members at the moment.'

He shook his head. Glanced around at people eating at tables, at the stream of foot traffic through the titanic mall. Down to Finlay, one hand twitching as he slept. 'They've got nothing now. Nothing. You'll see them this afternoon. They're just . . . hollowed out.'

They were quiet for a few minutes, Solak nodding a thanks when her drink appeared on the table. She lifted it to her lips, eyed MacReady as she sipped. 'What are we talking about here? What's the angle, the hook? Because it's going to need one to stand out. People die all the time. The rest of the world will tweet about it once, sulk it got no retweets or the hashtag didn't get any traction, then move on. It's the way things work.'

'How about a family tragedy?'

She shrugged. 'They all experience tragedy. With the market alone we've got enough tragic family stories to tide us over for several weeks. And that's before I even think about the Penarth attack, or the racial aspect of the bombings.'

MacReady pushed at his forehead, frustrated now. 'It's the second child they've lost. Heidi's brother was killed in a car accident a few years back.'

'OK. A little more interesting.' She leaned forwards. 'I sense there's extra?'

MacReady exhaled deeply. He hadn't wanted to elaborate further, or mention Simone Paxton at all. 'The mother was driving the car at the time. The crash put her in a wheelchair for life. And she blames herself for her son's death.'

Solak took another sip. 'And there's your angle.'

'So you'll look after them for me? Keep Heidi out there until I find who did it?'

A pause. Then she nodded. 'You owe me, MacReady.'

'I finish at midnight,' he grinned. 'I can call over later. Help out with that debt.'

Solak gave an exaggerated yawn into the palm of her hand. 'I feel an early night coming on.'

'I won't stay long. It'll be very fast.'

'No change there, then.'

That throaty chuckle of hers. It made MacReady laugh aloud. She was so deliberately annoying, so confrontational, so wilfully stubborn, yet he loved being with her. He couldn't recall the last time he'd felt so relaxed. For a second or two he found it hard to look away from Solak, and – not for the first time – she caught him staring. Held his eyes. The chuckle dying, a warm smile replacing it as she blinked and swallowed then finally glanced away. As if, just for a fleeting moment, she'd allowed a glimpse of how she really felt about him and had been surprised by it herself. It was an odd feeling: exhilarating and special, yet it filled MacReady with guilt. Again he checked down at Fin. Closed his eyes and thought about Megan. His wife. At home, worrying about Finlay on his first trip out with MacReady when she should be catching up on some much-needed sleep.

His thoughts turned to his brother. Stuart, who had ruined everything.

The mess they were all in.

MacReady heard it before seeing it: a rattle of metal, loud enough to register over the hubbub of diners, of muzak, of sing-song announcements over the shopping centre PR. He frowned at Solak, turning to look around. Worked out where the sound was coming from, climbed out of his seat and walked the few feet over to the railing. Found Solak by his side. Checked back at Finlay. Checked down to the ground floor.

Below them the security grille for the Eastside entrance was lowering, a steady clank and chime as metal fed through runners towards the floor. MacReady watched as the grille locked into place, sealing the glass doors. A handful of shoppers stopped in front of it, confused, and shrugged at each other before laughing and walking off to find another way out.

'That seem odd to you?' he asked Solak.

She pulled a face. 'You really need to relax more.'

'It could be something.'

'And it's probably a faulty security fence thingy.'

He forced a smile. 'That the technical term?'

'It is now, yes.'

They returned to their seats, MacReady's pulse a little faster now. He dug out his mobile before he sat. Mulled over dialling the three nines just in case, or maybe getting hold of someone in the Major Incident Room, finding out if they'd had any reports of suspicious activity in the city centre.

A dull *whump* from somewhere inside the bowels of the building shook him from his thoughts. Shook the cutlery on the table. Just the tiniest tinkle of steel. Enough to make MacReady sit upright.

'Someone's set fire to your nachos,' Solak muttered, and downed the rest of the mojito, ice crunching in her mouth.

MacReady checked around. Nothing untoward. Food and drink being delivered, being eaten. Music playing. A hundred conversations, myriad coloured T-shirts and lobster-red flashes of skin passing by. No tannoy announcements or alarms.

'This isn't right,' he said quietly, and wheeled the buggy closer to him.

Placed a hand on Finlay's chest, feeling it rise and fall.

Fifteen

So heavy, all this clothing. This rucksack. So hot.

Under cloudless sky he strides towards the entrance, across sculpted lawn and immaculate block pathways, the open space peppered with bag-laden shoppers, with Pret-stuffing businessmen, with giggling teens who sit beneath trees and sup on lattes, on iced drinks, smartphones never more than a few inches from their faces. People forget so quickly. Yesterday, the day after Bessemer, the Al Mahdi, they were fearful. Of enclosed areas, of large gatherings. He saw it on their faces: in railway stations, on buses, in the city centre's pubs and bars and clubs. A tension there. Anxiety fizzing beneath the surface. Casting sideways glances. Watchful. Nervous. Trying not to appear so.

Now not one of them looks at him. Widens their eyes as they take in his appearance. Reels backward in terror as they push themselves away from him. Even after the news reports this morning, the photograph that is everywhere. There is nothing. Not a flicker of recognition, of anything remotely close to vigilance. Just ignorance and apathy and self-absorption, shocking in their measure, and deserving of punishment.

The skin between his shoulder blades prickles, a square of cold sweat. Head low, tucked into the raised collar. Baseball cap too tight on his head, pinching at hair and scalp. Sunglasses heavy across the bridge of his nose. Hands wrinkled and sopping inside leather gloves that he has jammed into the pockets of his jacket. The hiss of white noise in his ears, growing louder with every step.

This heat. Unbearable. He pauses after pushing through the glass doors, as the temperature-controlled air envelops him. Cools him a little. He savours it, checking about as he stands in his outfit. The jacket one he used to wear when tasked with stopping anyone seeking to do the very thing he was about to. When protecting the public. Serving them. The jacket is the only thing that might identify him. It's a minor oversight, he realises now. Just like the market, the mosque, there have been no warnings, no coded telephone calls. He has nothing else on him. No wallet. No phone. No ID of any kind, other than what they might take from his fingertips, from his mouth for DNA, if they captured him. If they took him alive.

If.

Again, not a single head turns towards him as he stands, motionless bar the rise and fall of his chest, at the entrance to the shopping centre's café quarter. Restaurants, eateries. Two entire floors of chain brands selling their overpriced, reheated wares to consumer zombies with their bags crammed full of expensive tat. Mouths chew at egg noodles, pasta, overpriced *funky chips* and pulse-ridden Super fucking Foods. The sight of it almost makes him do it right here, right now. He closes his eyes behind the sunglasses. Breathes deeply, listens to the white noise, the thump of his heart just-about-audible beneath.

Removes the security card. Congratulates himself again on his foresight. How he removed it long before they removed him. Swipe at the pad, the *Staff Only* door giving a slight tremor as its locks disable. A quick shift of the rucksack, higher onto his back, and he pushes through.

He's in.

Inside it is breezeblock and concrete, piping and ventilation ducts. The real world behind the consumerism curtain. Health and Safety signs and strip lights, the warren of dim corridors leading him through the guts of the building to the shopping centre's security control room.

He hesitates outside the door. Listens. Hears the faint bleep of a radio. So many hours spent inside this room. Long nights and impossibly early mornings. Days flicking between CCTV cameras, between PR staff channels, between the pages of magazines he'd help himself to on the rare occasions he wandered out to the stores in the Grand Arcade. So many hours waiting for his thirty-minute break, so he could take the escalator to the first floor and sit at a table inside the restaurant. Sit and wait for the small moment that made working here worthwhile.

And then it had all gone horribly wrong.

He'd not meant to do it. Had misread the signs. Had apologised and bowed and scraped and disgusted himself at the depths he was willing to sink to just to save his shitty job. And it had all been for nought.

And now here he is.

Another swipe of the card, the faintest of clicks as the door unlocks. He leans down on the handle, opens the door and steps inside. A quick, soundless movement, so practised is he at it.

It's just one of them sitting there. Seat reclined, hands cradling the silver bristle of his head, all comfortable as his jowly mouth works a wad of gum. He recognises him but can't recall a name: an old fart, ex-RAF or army or whateverwhocares. Another one who couldn't hack not being able to tell people what to do once he'd retired. Another weakling who pined for a uniform, any uniform. Yet another chubby bore who'd drone into the small hours repeating war stories that made his teeth grind.

The man doesn't hear the door open. Doesn't even see him out of the corner of his eye, such is his lack of awareness. Instead he is yawning and switching across CCTV cameras covering the Hayes Arcade. Following a blonde as she weaves through shoppers, past display windows, talking into a phone. Shorts, tight vest top, sandals. An acre of late-teen flesh, little left to the imagination. The man is laughing quietly to himself, muttering and casually punching in camera numbers to pursue his quarry: *You fuckin' beauty, look at you, you fucking –*

'Hey,' he says.

The old fart starts, eyes widening in alarm. Drops his chair down, boots clomping on carpet. 'What the f—'

He swings the rucksack down from his shoulder, lowers it to the floor. Smiles. Sees the shocked expression, the horror at being caught following the blonde morph into a look of relief.

'Shit, mun, I thought I was in trouble there,' the old fart chuckles. He leans over, elbows on knees. Exhales, his rubbery lips vibrate a little. He glances up, still chuckling, but then the frown starts to form and his eyebrows knot and he cocks his head to one side as he finally remembers. 'Hang on, I thought you were –'

'Always wanted to do this,' he tells the guy and punches him in the face. Hard. So hard he hears bone crunching, the guy's nose caving in, splintering beneath gloved knuckles.

Comical, almost, how the old fart squeals and falls backwards, taking the chair with him. He lands on his back, soles of his boots pointing heavenwards, heels knocked together, one castor wheel swivelling. The small room smelling of piss where the unconscious man's bladder just went on him, blood and tissue flecking the wall.

The noise in his ears, louder now. That hiss, blocking out everything. He checks the control console, the familiar layout of switches and dials and finds what he is looking for.

Presses the buttons.

Watches via the entrance cameras as security grilles start to lower themselves over the glass doors. As a few heads turn, people looking at each other, confused, then back to the wall of thick stainless steel squares rolling towards the floor.

No Exit.

He pulls one of the IEDs out of the ruck. Checks the door: nobody. Not yet. Too busy selling or buying or stacking shelves with shit people didn't want or need and would never use. Too busy to notice they were now trapped inside.

In the corridor he slings the rucksack onto one shoulder and lights the IED. Rolls it into the room. Stares for a few seconds, the fuse sparking, alive, mesmerising. For a moment he just waits there. Hovering. Everything in his life now shrinking in on itself, simmered down to this.

When the fuse is nearing its last he slams the door shut and scampers away.

The explosion occurs just as he ventures back out into the main thoroughfare. At first it is as if nothing has happened. Busy here now, the lunchtime rush, people still shovelling food, the entrances locked down by security grilles and either going unnoticed or causing no concern whatsoever. When the low thump is heard – loud enough to make a few people cower in their seats, he notes with a smile – he takes the escalator to the first floor. To the marbled walkways and pavilions packed full of places to lunch. Packed full of people.

To the restaurant he has come here for.

Spices and herbs on the air already, even before he reaches the second level. He sniffs at it, breathes in the aroma of onion and garlic and rich sauces, the masala and cumin and turmeric. Strangely, even amidst all this, he is suddenly hungry. Wonders, just for a second, if he has time to sit at his usual table and ask the waitress for a few nibbles. Engage her in small talk, just like he used to do . . .

The thought catches him out. Makes him bend over at the waist, nauseous, at the top of the escalator. Makes him wonder if he really wants to do this. He sucks in air, waits for the light-headedness to pass. Stands upright, pushes the sunglasses back onto his nose. Swallows hard. Paces towards the restaurant, towards its wide entrance, towards the tables of customers and smiling waiting staff, their skin dark above bright white shirts and red bow ties.

Deep breaths. Deep breaths. You can do this. You have to do this.

The red neon of the restaurant sign: *Kurry Korner.*

An abominable name for an abominable place.

He stares at it. Time ticking. Breathes in, great lungfuls, then turns away. Presses his gloved hand against his lips, bites at the leather. Turns back to the restaurant. To the staff.

Thinks, teeth clenched: *You fuckers. You deserve this. All of you.*

Slips the rucksack from his shoulder and reaches into it.

Sees something reflected in the window. The briefest of flashes.

A shape, advancing toward him.

Then the air is knocked from his lungs and the world tilts sideways and before his vision turns to black he hears screams, sees diners rise from their chairs, eyes wide.

And the rucksack.

The rucksack, skittering away from his grasping fingers.

Sixteen

Blues and twos and crime scene tape carving The Hayes into cordons, a fleet of vans and response cars and Joint Firearms Unit 4x4s lining the pedestrianised area with its now-empty shops and bars and restaurants. Crowds of onlookers, ten to twelve deep, held back by lines of uniforms as they gawped at and filmed the façade of St David's.

A Royal Logistics Corps wagon partially blocked their view; behind the white Leyland DAF truck, three army Ammunition Techs kitted up while two more rigged a bomb disposal robot, ready to enter the centre to carry out Render Safe procedures on the rucksack, on any other devices they might find. Black-clad armed cops wielded G36ers and ballistic shields, providing cover, scouring neighbouring buildings, rooftops, Special Forces advisers mingling with them, gesturing as they gave orders. A steady stream of sweating civilians being shepherded out of the shopping centre doors by pairs of firearms officers, their faces contorted in terror.

'Exciting, innit?'

MacReady, down on his haunches, leaning against a low bollard in the shadow of the giant arrow-and-hoop Alliance sculpture. Exhausted now, that post-adrenalin plunge. He didn't look up at the voice, could see the sandals, the bright-blue socks, the oddly hairless and waxy Valley boy's shins. Harrison, standing in front of him, decked out in three-quarter-length shorts because *fuck you, it's hot and I'll wear what I want, mun.*

'Not really, no,' he said. Pain in his shoulder, his collarbone. Inside the shopping centre MacReady had hit the guy at full pelt, hit him with all the strength he could muster. Knocked him out cold before he could reach into the rucksack. All the while thinking how the man in black could just be an ordinary punter. How it could be a huge mistake. How he was going to explain being at lunch with Klaudia Solak.

What he was going to say to Megan.

She was here already. Standing at the back doors of a Police Support Unit van on the fringes of the outer cordon, buggy at her heel, a squawking Finlay held close, her arms wrapped tightly around him. A reproachful look in her eyes as she rocked her baby and nodded at whatever Echols was saying to her. They'd called her straight away, just to reassure her, to let her know MacReady was okay. That Finlay was fine. She'd driven into the city centre despite being asked not to.

She'd seen the reports on television.

Solak had filmed the entire thing. As soon as she'd killed the three nines call to report the attacker, she'd switched to the camera on her phone and hit record, even wheeling Finlay closer to the action so she could get a better shot.

MacReady, sprinting through crowds of shoppers, barging people out of the way. Hitting a male decked out in black duds, shoulder first, taking him at the side of his face, a sickening thump audible on camera. The man in black dropping to the floor, legs gone, out cold. A rucksack spinning away across polished marble floor, restaurant patrons scattering. Security guards and shop staff joining in, one of the restaurant waiters – as ever, unsure who was who and what was what – punching MacReady in the back of the head, MacReady yelling *Police, I'm the fucking police*, a heaving tangle of arms and legs, a soundtrack of shouts and screams and the currently famous off-duty detective constable turning the air blue.

It had gone viral. Been picked up and played on loop by all the news channels.

Solak was still reporting live: over by the Central Library building, lanky cameraman filming her, microphone in hand, head shaking and mouth working as she breathlessly relayed what had happened, what was going on during the lockdown and evac of the centre and its surrounding buildings.

MacReady shook his head. So much for getting Heidi Paxton into the spotlight.

He checked Megan and Finlay again. Stayed put, not going over to them. Too many news crews on the scene. Too many cameras to pick up their faces as they talked. As she yelled at him for abandoning Fin while he played hero.

'You OK, Will?'

He looked up, squinting into sunlight. The DI stood with hands on hips, Fletcher's face in shadow, unreadable.

MacReady pressed the back of his head, his scalp tender where he'd taken that hefty clout from the Kurry Korner waiter. After learning the full facts, the man had been so embarrassed by what he'd done that he wouldn't stop apologising. After ten minutes of it MacReady had to tell the guy to bugger off.

'Suppose I'd better get writing a statement,' he offered. Dropped his hand from his head. Noticed the tremble in his fingers.

'Will it explain why you were having lunch with that news bird?' Harrison asked. All innocent, one sandal casually sweeping at the ground.

Fletcher squatted next to him. A smile at the edge of his mouth but concern in his eyes. He stared hard at MacReady. 'There is that.'

'It's because he's a bloody idiot.'

Beck, from above. MacReady looked up, bracing himself. Harrison had filled him in moments before Beck screeched up in a CID car: after the 999 calls and Solak's shaky-cam footage she'd demanded to be let out of the office. Fletcher – all of them – had seen her expression. Had been too scared to say no.

'Look, Sarge –'

Beck made as if to grab him by the collar of his shirt, Fletcher and Harrison placed hands on her, held her back. She straightened. Raised a hand. *Leave me alone.* She closed her eyes and turned away from them.

'You're full of surprises today, Will,' Fletcher remarked. He looked around The Hayes, at the crowds, at the prisoner transport van with its open doors; in the cage at the rear paramedics were treating the bomber for what one had described, making no effort to hide her delighted grin, as a *nasty face wound.* 'You catch our guy, which believe me we are all eternally grateful for. But then you go spoil it by lunching with a total gobshite journo who now has you all over the news.'

'And you're a daddy,' said Harrison. 'That one's a humdinger.'

'I thought my life was complicated.' Fletcher swivelled his head back to MacReady. 'Is there anything else you might like to tell me?'

'That I need a holiday?'

'You got plenty of sun here, kiddo,' Fletcher gestured to the sky. 'So did our guy say anything before you sparked him out?'

A shake of the head from MacReady. 'Didn't really give him much of a chance.'

He ran through it again as he stared at the ground. The man in black realising – far too late – that MacReady was upon him. The shoulder into his face, a dull smack, the man's head whipping sideways, sunglasses flying, baseball cap shifting slightly, his eyes rolling upwards. The nonsense that came after it: members of the public, security, a lone undercover firearms officer who rocked up far, far too late, all of them getting involved.

In the minutes that followed, after shouting at Klaudia to leave with Finlay immediately, at security and staff to start clearing the building, before uniform and firearms and lots of other people with weapons finally showed up, MacReady had sat with legs splayed and back against a pillar, drawing ragged breaths as he'd taken a look at the unconscious bomber.

Male, white. Late twenties to early thirties at most. Head shaved beneath his cap. A light stubble around his jawline. Wearing a jacket that matched those on the security guards who'd waded in. MacReady didn't recognise the man, had never seen him before, but the guards had.

'You must be joking,' one of them had almost laughed. 'Tim?'

MacReady had been incredulous. 'You know this fucker?'

'Oh my God, yeah. Total bellend on a power trip. He was sacked a while back.'

Timothy Coe.

Their bomber.

Cuffed and stuffed in the back of the van. MacReady glanced over at the authorised firearms officers flanking the open doors, assault rifles slung over forearms.

'I want in on the bombing case,' he said to Fletcher. 'Give Paxton to someone else.'

The DI pushed himself upright. Scanned around, hands back on hips. A deep breath, then: 'Much as I'm grateful for what you've done today, you've got no chance.'

'I really want to be a part of it, boss.'

'You forgetting about your grieving parents, Will?'

MacReady lowered his head. The press conference. The Paxtons. They'd be at the station already, waiting for him. For a pack of journalists who had no intention of leaving The Hayes until all this was over.

'Later, then? Hand the murder over to another officer once I'm done with Heidi's mother and father?'

Fletcher sighed and began to walk away. Stopped and turned to MacReady. 'All you need to think about is what you're going to wear in front of the cameras.'

MacReady looked down at his clothes. Shirt, trousers. Clean, presentable, despite the impromptu lunchtime scrummage. 'Was going to chuck a tie on and be done with it.'

'Jesus,' said Harrison. 'Why d'you think we've not come that close to you, or given you a pat on the back for catching our fella, or allowed Charlie to strangle you for sleeping with her friend?'

'I'm not sleeping with her.'

Harrison snorted. 'Aye aye, course you ain't.'

MacReady exhaled; it was pointless bickering with Harrison. He thought for a second about why nobody had come near him. *Forensics*. Locard's Principle. Covering all the bases: they wanted his clothes. They'd want the clothes off the backs of everyone who came in contact with the bomber during the struggle.

'I've got nothing to change into,' he told Fletcher.

'Can your wife do the honours and nip home for . . . ?'

MacReady looked from Fletcher to Megan and back to the DI. Arched an eyebrow.

'Ah yes,' Fletcher smiled. 'Abandoning your kid to go rassle with a bad guy.'

'Paper suit it is, then,' Harrison smirked. 'Should look good on the telly.'

Beck leaned down to him, her anger palpable. 'Serves you bloody right.'

*

In the end MacReady called Duncan Jones, waking him from sleeping off a night turn. As ever, his housemate was completely unaware of what had taken place in the city, and had been more concerned about not getting his nine hours in the festering pit he called a bed. After griping for a few minutes Jones had reluctantly made the trip to Cardiff Bay police station with a plastic carrier bag containing a selection of MacReady's clothes.

'You coming home tonight, or what?' Jones asked as he handed over the Asda bag, as if they were some sort of couple.

MacReady stood before him in a paper suit and beyond-cheap flip flops normally handed to prisoners who'd been relieved of everything they wore; he exhaled heavily when he caught the amused faces on the MOPs and waiting briefs peppering chairs in the foyer.

Home. Hearing Jones use the word to describe the drab house MacReady was dossing in made him doubly miserable. He checked the bag's contents – fresh shirt and trousers, both well crumpled now, a pair of mismatched socks – before thanking Jones with a weary smile, thoughts drifting to Megan. She'd bawled him out over the phone and was now refusing to answer his texts or emails. Not that he could blame her for doing it. Putting Finlay in such a situation was ridiculous to the point of neglect, yet when it happened he'd not really had the luxury of time to think things through. There was the bigger picture, but he could understand why she couldn't see it.

And Megan was yet to learn about his little rendezvous with Klaudia Solak. If she did, his temporary arrangement with old Dunc would quickly become permanent.

'Probably not, no,' he replied.

'Tshh,' Jones huffed, heading for the door. 'Got the beers in for you specially, too.'

A trio of rankers – one of them the divisional commander himself, a chief superintendent more memorable for his championing of LGBT issues than anything remotely police-orientated – collared MacReady for five minutes just after he left the foyer, shaking his hand and thanking him for what he'd done while eyeing his paper custody suit with suspicion. He returned their smiles, silently willed them to go away. He was drowning in work now, and their appreciation of his efforts meant nothing.

It was nudging three o'clock by the time he changed, slipping out of the paper all-in-one at his desk in the CID suite. The Paxtons were in the building, being looked after by their family liaison officer and prepped by a press officer from HQ's Communications Team, but MacReady couldn't head down to meet them yet – he fired up the computer, began typing his arrest statement, fingers rattling keys as he flew through what had happened in St David's, wanting it on Niche as soon as, so the investigating officers – Fletcher, Echols, whoever from Specialist Crime – would have something to work with when they interviewed Timothy Coe.

MacReady's hand hovered above the keyboard when he came to explain why he was there, knowing that down the line his lunch meeting with Solak would come up. Maybe even in court. During a trial which would be covered by national and international news crews.

It was going to be excruciating.

Then there was what he did to Coe. Taking him out without so much as a how-do-you-do. Despite the circumstances – he'd already been told IEDs had been found in the rucksack – MacReady knew he'd be served with papers. Coe would make the complaint, the Regulation Nine disciplinary notice would come down the pipe, swiftly followed by the predictable *Guardian* articles about police brutality while the *Mail* would wait and see which way the wind blew amongst the public and politicians before deciding on hatchet job or God-bless-our-boys-in-blue piece.

MacReady finished the statement twenty minutes later. It was rough and ready, but enough. He uploaded it to the system, pushed himself away from the desk and bent forward, hands dangling between his thighs.

Both hands, shaking now.

*

Danny Fletcher asked: 'Are we ready?'

'We're ready.'

Simone Paxton, face set, eyes fixed on the double doors. She'd given MacReady a weak smile as she said it, but it did nothing to calm his nerves. He'd spent the last half hour with the Paxtons in a small office off the main corridor, an FLO in support, the DI – jazzed on caffeine and the arrest of Coe – taking time out from the Major Incident Room to sit in as MacReady explained the process, explained what to expect during the press conference, when in reality he wasn't expecting much of anything at all. The incident was still ongoing at St David's shopping centre and he assumed the majority of journos would still be at The Hayes for coverage.

MacReady looked from Simone to Mark Paxton, the paleness of their faces aggravated by the corridor's fluorescents. Ducked his head, a quick nod of support, of encouragement. Silently hoped they wouldn't be disappointed. With the media turnout. With how it went.

With him.

'We're all set,' said the press officer, a tall, attenuated streak of a man, all crisp suit, bequiffed fringe and louder-than-loud tie to match the gaudily coloured frames of his spectacles. He was like a jolly kids' TV presenter, a twitchy clown gurning as he prepped for the cameras.

Fletcher goggled at the man for a second. 'Let's go.' A glance at MacReady, eyes narrowing. *You OK?* it said.

MacReady gave him the thumbs-up.

Heidi's father took hold of the wheelchair handles but Simone shook her head.

'No,' she said softly. Dropped her hands to the rear wheels and gripped them. 'Thank you, but I can do this. I don't want their pity. I want them to see we're strong.'

Mark Paxton hesitated for a second before leaning down to kiss his wife. When he straightened MacReady saw the raw grief in his eyes. The man was still falling apart.

They pushed through the double doors and into the room.

It lit up. Rapid staccato bursts, bright and eye-watering. Mac-Ready placed a hand up to his forehead, shielding his eyes from the glare of the arc lights and photographers' flash guns.

The conference room was full of media.

He was staggered.

In the midst of the crowd of journalists he saw Klaudia Solak. Up on her feet, watching MacReady as he walked the short distance to the table and chairs set up for the briefing. She tilted her head, waved a hand around her, at the rows of her colleagues, as if to say *Will this do*?

After what she'd done at St David's it mattered that she'd come good.

And then it went bad.

Even before they could introduce themselves, the questions. Flying at them, reporters yelling over one another, raising hands.

Not one aimed at the Paxtons.

All at MacReady: *how did it feel to arrest the bomber? Why was there no extra security? Were you worried about your own safety? Are you concerned people will think you went overboard when you attacked him?*

They knew it was him from the shopping centre. MacReady reeled. Turned to the Paxtons. Saw astonishment there. Heidi's father blinking rapidly, not understanding. Simone shaking her head, eyes glassy, all too aware that the journalists had turned up, but not for them. Not for their daughter.

Solak, flapping a hand: 'DC MacReady ... DC MacReady, what can you tell us about Heidi Paxton? I believe there –'

She was drowned out. MacReady sat watching her mouth move but could hear nothing she said. Saw her face crack with frustration. Silently thanked her for what she'd done. For what she was trying to do.

The press officer raised his hands, trying to mollify them. 'Guys, please. Can we *please* ... ? Guys?' The last word a shout lost in a sea of shouts. When they ignored him he slumped back in his chair, breathed a theatrical sigh.

MacReady felt it then. A tremble in his thighs. The muscles contracting, a series of spasms that caused him to squeeze at them with slick fingertips. He pulled at his collar, at the sudden tightness of his tie. Felt the flutter of his heartbeat against the damp cotton of his shirt. Felt the nausea.

Pictured Coe. The man in black. Running at him. Hitting him. The rucksack, full of explosives.

The noise in the room dulled, voices slowing, flowing into one drone, a recording played at the wrong speed. The flashes, now behind MacReady's eyes. He gripped the edge of the table, managed to push himself out of his seat.

'Will?' Fletcher's voice, low and drawn out, his detective inspector's face a shifting collage of black and white pinpricks.

'You'll have to excuse . . .' MacReady managed, unsteady legs carrying him through the double doors and into the corridor.

Fletcher's hand on MacReady's shoulder. 'You should go home.'

He was crouched, one hand placed to the floor to steady himself. His vision slowly returning to normal, the flashes ebbing. He could smell himself, the tang of fresh perspiration. Feel it, across his brow, trickling down his spine, under his armpits. 'I'm not going anywhere.'

'Will, you're sweatier than I get after rolling around with my better half,' Fletcher said. 'You're in shock. I've seen this before. What you've done today, at St David's –'

MacReady forced himself upright. Palm of one hand against the cool wall. Just in case. Repeated, 'I'm not going anywhere.'

Fletcher studied him for a good while. 'I should be ordering you to clock off.'

'There's too much to do and not enough of us to do it. Sending me home doesn't help anybody. You know that.'

A sigh from the DI. His gaze falling to the floor as he stood, thinking. Then he nodded. 'Take ten minutes. Go get a drink, some tea, plenty of sugar. We'll resume this,' he gestured at the double doors, 'when you're good to go.'

'I'm not going back in. This is for Heidi. If I'm sitting there not one of them will ask about her. It'll be all about me. About Coe. And I don't want to put her parents through that.'

Fletcher stared into MacReady's eyes. Inhaled, a long, deep breath. 'OK. Sit tight. Get yourself together. I'll head back in and do the honours.'

MacReady felt relief wash through him. His legs, no longer shaking. 'Thanks.'

'Any time, hero,' Fletcher slapped him on the top of his arm. Walked towards the double doors. Over his shoulder: 'Just don't go fucking dying on me out here, though. I'm too busy for more paperwork.'

Seventeen

They rode in convoy.

Sirens wailing, squelching. Blues strobing across roofs, head-lights flashing. Cutting through late-evening traffic, running reds at junctions, forcing cars and buses and motorcycles to pull in, to mount pavements. People stopped, gawped, heads turning as they screamed past, a cacophonous line of 4x4s and marked wagons heading out of the city, spearing through the rush-hour vehicular clog that was Western Avenue.

Revs redlining on the CID car, its careworn diesel engine struggling to keep up. MacReady, foot to the floor, tailing the rearmost firearms truck. His window down, the day sweltering still.

'How long?'

Beck's hand white-knuckled the Jesus handle as MacReady cut the steering wheel left to round a startled cyclist; the car's rear tyres shrieked, losing traction for a second. He righted the motor, threw her a quick glance. It was the first time she'd spoken since they'd left Cardiff Bay.

'Few months,' MacReady replied. This was like confessing to his wife. Possibly worse. 'Maybe a bit longer.'

She sniffed. Said nothing, staring out of the passenger win-dow, the mammoth tube and glass monstrosity of Tesco Extra slipping by, its sprawling car park full as always. MacReady gunned the Peugeot, taking the bridge over the River Taff at sixty. The traffic ahead snarled, waiting for lights to switch to green outside the Metropolitan University.

'I should have told you,' he said.

Beck snapped her head around to glare at him. '*She* should have told me. She's my friend, Will. We've been friends since school. And she knows damn well – you both know – that you two getting it on is going to cause no end of problems.'

He'd never seen her so angry. Not even after he got her shot. 'It doesn't have to be a problem, though.'

'But it *is* a problem. You know it is, because you've both kept it quiet. Both of you should have said something at least, if only so that I could cover your arses when word got out. Because word always gets out.'

The firearms trucks slowed, MacReady did likewise. Snaked through the crossroads, past static commuters frowning at them through windscreens, Beck's head left and right, checking for oncoming civvy vehicles, for any driver – radio volume to the max and singing as they crawled home from the office – who might have missed the sirens.

'I hope to God you haven't been blabbing about work,' she said. The convoy picked up speed again, haring west, taking the outside lane. 'Fletcher will gut you alive.'

'What do you take me for?' he asked, genuinely offended.

'Like I said earlier. A fucking idiot. And I'm acutely aware of how Klaudia operates, too.'

'Well, I haven't, all right? She asks, I say nothing. She pretends to sulk, I ignore it. It's not that kind of . . . relationship, anyway. If you can call it that. Not much talking goes on.'

Beck shook her head, muttering to herself. 'Wait. What about your wife?'

He twisted his hands on the steering wheel. 'I know.'

'Jesus.' Beck shook her head. 'You have a *kid*, Will. One you didn't seem to think was important enough to tell us about. Your team. *Me*. After all we've been through. That's before we even start to think about your poor wife.'

'It's a bit complicated –'

'Oh, don't give me that crap. You disgust me. I wish I'd left you back at the nick.' She folded her arms. Turned back to her window. 'It's not as if you're even safe to drive at the moment.'

The press conference. Losing it in front of the journalists. In front of the Paxtons. Fletcher handled it like a pro while MacReady had paced the corridor, sipping water from a plastic cup. When it was done – Heidi Paxton the only topic on the table, much to the hacks' irritation – he'd shuffled, embarrassed, as Simone Paxton had thanked him for what he was doing. For what he was trying to do. Then she'd pulled him down to her, placed her arms around him. Hugged him. And MacReady had closed his eyes and sworn to himself that he wasn't going to rest until he found the person who murdered Heidi. He'd gone straight to the CID suite, sat at his desk while others remained empty, had gone through Niche, through any and all of the actions that he had, found nothing to move forwards with: nothing from the banks, from CSI about Heidi's bedroom, her smartphone, everyone busy, the entire force stretched to breaking point. When Klaudia sent a text he'd replied, thanking her for what she'd done while bollocking her about filming everything, and it had descended into an argument, so he'd turned his phone off and shoved it in his pocket. When Fletcher dropped by the suite and asked him to chaperone Beck while she attended the Section 18 search of Timothy Coe's flat as exhibits officer – she was out of the box now, and refusing to go back in, but couldn't drive because of her gammy leg and the DI had nobody else to do it – MacReady had snatched the car keys from the DI's hand before he'd finished telling him not to get involved and *stay in the bloody car while they do the Eighteen.*

MacReady turned right, following the convoy onto Waungron Road, the wailers echoing back at him as they passed under a railway bridge.

He took a deep breath. 'As I was going to say, it's a bit complicated at home.'

'I'm not interested anymore, Will. Really I'm not.'

MacReady told Beck everything anyway. About Megan, Stuart. About Finlay. About him living with Drunken Duncan at the moment. How Megan had allowed him out with Fin for the morning, only for MacReady to go launching himself at the armed lunatic who'd been blowing up Cardiff and Penarth, literally leaving Klaudia Solak holding the baby.

He shrugged when he finished. A huge weight lifted. Glanced at Beck.

She was staring at him, mouth slightly agape.

MacReady swallowed when she reached across and squeezed at his hand.

*

Fairwater.

Leafy, busy, a sprawling suburb of homes and schools and parkland just before western Cardiff petered out into a tapestry of forestry and farmers' fields. The south-eastern side neat semis and apartments and the blemish of the police station, a mixed orange-brick and prefab square lump that resembled a hideous layer cake, and which MacReady assumed had cut the value of the surrounding properties by at least half when it was built. The north-western side boxy terraced efforts packed into maze-like streets, old council houses and squat cubes of compact flats that resembled Soviet Bloc accommodation.

Timothy Coe's Last Known Address was among the flats.

It was all they had. His LKA obtained from the records – if a solitary sheet with limited information could be called *records* – at the security firm Coe had been working for before they sacked him. Echols was still liaising with the firm, finding out the reasons for Coe's dismissal, but at present Beck's file from Specialist Crime was as slim as the one MacReady had carried around while looking for Nazir Uddin.

Coe had given them nothing as he was booked in at the custody suite. Remained silent, staring straight ahead. Refused to answer questions. On the mapping system, the electoral list, on Niche and PNC: no trace. No photos, no listing as a nominal for any crimes, or even as a witness or complainant. Completely absent from any of their records, including Special Branch and the Welsh Extremism and Counter-Terrorism Unit. From any of the UK security services' systems, including MI5. Wasn't on a watch list, wasn't pegged by the Met's National Domestic Extremism and Disorder Intelligence Unit. Had never even been on their radar.

In other words Coe was, like the 7/7 London bombers, a cleanskin.

Nobody knew anything about him.

Beck had been firing off emails to so-called partner agencies – the DVLA for a driving licence search or link to a vehicle, the Department of Work and Pensions for any kind of benefits or allowances; anything to expand on what little they had – when MacReady came knocking to chauffeur her across the city.

'Warren said he was just smiling,' MacReady said, glancing out of the car window at the housing estate spread out in front of them. They followed the Armed Response and other vehicles into the street, a hilly strip of tarmac dotted with tiny one- and two-beds, a community centre at its block end boasting an expansive car park and perimeter walls coloured with graffiti tags and murals. 'Calmer than calm, as if he was enjoying a little daydream or something.'

'That's what they're always like,' Beck said. 'In my experience, anyway. Especially for the serious crimes. Soon as they're locked up and you get them in the cells, they either fall asleep or sit there smiling. As if they've finally accepted it. Like they've made peace with being caught.'

He nodded. 'Having to constantly look over your shoulder for the law gets tiring in the end. But even Wazza said it was odd. Unnerving was the word he used. And when a cynical old bugger like Warren Harrison admits to being unnerved, my alarm starts to sound.'

The convoy drew to a sudden halt in the car park. MacReady jammed his foot on the brake, heard gravel kick up at the underside of the car. 'This it?'

'Staging area. Kit up here, out of sight. Go in fast. We have no idea if this is Coe's address, but if it is we're taking no chances.'

'What's the intel?'

'That's the problem. There is none. No contact number to put a call in. We don't know what we're walking into, who's in there, or what gifts he might have left unwanted visitors.'

MacReady hoped she was careful. 'Want me to come with?'

Beck was half out the passenger door. In front, specialist firearms officers and Public Order trained uniforms were decamping from vehicles. Army bomb techs were unloading their robot friend, Trumpton were slipping on chemical and biological hazard gear in case Coe had decided to leave a dirty bomb surprise rigged up. Counter-Terrorism advisers and specialist-search-trained PolSA teams huddled together, heads down, listening as one of the spooks talked, everyone pulling on gloves and gathering evidence sacks. A small army of dark suits and black tactical gear, just for Coe. When all they could scrape together for Heidi Paxton was a wet-behind-the-ears DC and a pair of family liaison officers working double shifts to cover.

Around the corral of emergency services vehicles faces appeared at windows, figures on doorsteps, a couple of grey-faced old fellows sucking on roll-ups as they watched, squinting beneath blue smoke. A lone tracksuit, hood up and loping by in the evening sunlight, loudly hawking a mouthful of phlegm at the pavement, his predictable and pathetic little *fuck you* to the Five-O.

Beck narrowed her eyes at MacReady. 'Don't even think about leaving this car.'

'Another pair of hands won't hurt –'

'Stay put. Fletcher told me to keep you out of this. And I don't need your protection, thanks all the same.'

'So what am I supposed to do? Act as parking attendant?'

'Someone needs to keep an eye on the vans.' She pretended to think. 'Or, I don't know, you could swap dirty texts with your new girlfriend or something?'

He winced as Beck slammed the door on him, marched over to the firearms inspector, disguising the pain she felt in her hip, MacReady knew. No room for signs of weakness on a job like this. At any time in this job, in fact. He watched her for a moment, chatting away, clearly relieved to be out of the bubble of the police station. She was no CCTV analyst, not a nine-to-fiver, and being cooped up in an office was slowly draining the life out of her.

MacReady switched his PR to the dedicated firearms channel, leaned back in the seat and listened, arm hanging out of the window. Heard the measured tones of the Ops Room radio operator, linking up with the officers he was now staring at. Talk of PCSOs and Specials currently setting up roadblocks in and out of the estate. Firming up on identified points of entry, the layout of the flat. Requests to cut electricity, to check with the council if they had located a keyholder. All of it buzzing away, battling against the in-car Airwave set which continued to blurt out Grade 1 emergency calls across the city. MacReady sighed when nobody responded after repeated requests to response officers for attendance – there simply wasn't anyone to go.

Fuck this government and its cuts.

Loaded with Hecklers and ballistic shields, the black-clad specialist firearms officers moved off, towards the main drag and its clutch of low-rise flats. A line of them, crouched, running. Beck, the WECTU officers, the water fairies of the fire service, and the army 'bot following behind. MacReady shifted upright, feeling a flutter in his gut.

Then a voice on the firearms channel: 'Radio silence, please.'

One of the wrinkled smokers called across to MacReady.

'All 'appening here, boy.'

MacReady nodded a patient smile and turned away. Pictured Beck, fingers twitching, watching the heavily armed officers surround the target building. The transmissions, fuzzing from the firearms channel: 'Team Two on Black, no movement . . . No movement at front . . . Bronze, we are approaching the communal door. . .'

He couldn't stand it. Climbed out of the CID motor, Airwave set in hand, Fletcher's warning to *stay in the bloody car* still with him as he paced on the tarmac, cutting a line between two firearms wagons, out of sight of the old fellows puffing on their rollies.

'Team One to Bronze, communal door has been opened by a neighbour, we are evacuating the neighbouring flats. Still no movement in the target premises.'

'He don't stand still, does he?'

One of the smokers. MacReady glanced about for something to do. Anything to get away from the car park. To get closer to Coe's block of flats.

He spotted a walled waste bin area, tucked behind the block. Obviously shared – the handful of refuse bins had various flat numbers painted on their green flanks. And there were no fire-arms officers nearby. Nothing for MacReady to meddle with. He paced over, opened a sagging wooden gate – its lock long gone – and stepped inside. Began lifting lids, poking at plastic sacks with the tips of his fingers, not sure what he was looking for, if anything. The PolSA people would be in here imminently, pulling out everything, cutting open these bags, rifling through the lot.

MacReady heard the old guys, their broad Cardiff accents:

'He's going for the bins now, mun –'

'I knows, you think he's hungry?'

The cackle of their laughter, one of them breaking into a hacking cough.

'What are you doing, Will?' he asked himself.

From his PR, the voice an octave higher: 'Team One to Bronze, premises breached, entry gained. Conducting search.'

They were in.

MacReady hovered, surrounded by the detritus of other people's lives spilling out and under his feet. He listened, PR hissing white noise, giving the occasional bleep. Several minutes passed, the smokers quiet now, the only sounds the faint swish of traffic from the A4232 dual carriageway, the occasional squeal of laughter from children in The Dell at Fairwater Park.

Then Beck's voice: 'Premises clear.'

MacReady gave a sigh of relief. Pushed open the gate, stepped out into the car park. The old smokers, gone. A pair of firearms officers, head to toe in black and Kevlar and weaponry, ambling back to the line of police vehicles. Someone else to play security guard. To watch for locals – gathering quickly, like they always did – trying to key the bodywork of a van or put a windscreen through. Someone other than him.

'Fuck this,' he muttered. Strode over to the CID car, opened the boot. Reached into a holdall, pulled out latex gloves, booties, a paper hairnet. Flashed a smile as he passed the sweat-sheened firearms plods on his way to the front of Coe's block of flats.

The communal door, lined with *Heddlu Police* tape. An authorised firearms officer rocked up outside, H&K hooked over his shoulder. Couple of suits MacReady didn't recognise on the far pavement, talking with a handful of people whose eyes flicked at the building, their expressions anxious. Coe's neighbours, no doubt. Wouldn't be long before the media joined the party. He flashed his warrant card at the firearms wallah, slipped the hairnet on. Pulled the booties over his filth-encrusted shoes, stretched latex over fingers and thumbs.

Ducked under the police tape.

The place was the antithesis of the apartments MacReady had visited in Penarth. Pebble-dashed, the awful façade broken up by cheap aluminium windows of mismatched sizes, its entrance porch a bizarre pointed hood of faux wood tiles and rusted metal struts. The communal hall and stairs a gloomy column of cracked linoleum steps and battered handrails, a faint odour in the stale and unmoving air that reminded MacReady of chip fat and the unclean restaurant kitchens he'd visited so many times for burglary and damage calls while in uniform. His footsteps echoed upwards, everything amplified, bouncing off the rubber floor and scuffed cream walls. Voices from above, from Coe's flat on the first floor. Beck's amongst them, asking for more photographs, for video, to record what they had found.

MacReady took the stairs three at a time, ignoring the techies who returned the favour as they went the other way, bags and files in gloved hands. Pulled out his mobile as he went, fired up the camera. He wanted to record this. Wanted to get a feel for the place, wanted something he could replay whenever he needed to.

Timothy Coe's entire flat was no bigger than Heidi Paxton's bedroom. Small lounge with kitchenette, one bedroom, minuscule bathroom with no bath but a shower cubicle – a carnival of soap scum and calcium streaks on glass – squeezed into the corner. Busy, CSI and suits and firearms in every room. Front door a ruin from the enforcer ram. Crime-scene kits on the floor next to a pathetic-looking sofa, its cushions deflated and miserable. MacReady couldn't help but think of Duncan Jones and the house he was currently sharing with the man.

'I guessed fifteen minutes, so you've done pretty well.'

Beck, in the doorway to the bedroom. Shaking her head, but MacReady could see the smile beneath her face mask.

'Held out as long as I could, Sarge,' he shrugged. 'You're not a CCTV analyst, and I'm no parking attendant. Just don't tell Fletcher.'

She gave him a latexed thumbs-up. A wink.

MacReady kept the recording going. Panned around. Coe's bedroom was obviously the nerve centre. A single bed – no more than an adult cot – to one side, a small rectangular window on the other. Wood panelling covering the walls, the ceiling, dark and knotted, muting what limited light managed to bleed in from the outside world. Between bed and window sat a large table and rickety chair. Coe's workstation. On its surface, notes and wires and a solitary piece of metal pipe, about two inches in diameter. A faint smear of white crystalline powder, no more than a few milligrams. Tools and schematics and a printout of the St David's Centre floorplan. A half-and-half cork and whiteboard nailed to the wooden wall pinned with scraps of paper, filled with whorls of marker pen, with exclamation marks, with the rantings of a man who clearly held a few grudges. Coe had the same kind of posters and flyers for local events but otherwise the contrast was huge: where Paxton's room was bright and positive, everything here seemed raw with anger.

'The mother lode,' said MacReady, and turned the camera off. He nodded at the tiny amount of powder. 'That drugs?'

A shake of Beck's head. 'Army guy says it's TATP.'

MacReady scrunched up his face. 'And that is . . . ?'

'Acetone peroxide. Homemade explosive, apparently.'

MacReady took a step backwards. 'Ooo-kay . . .'

'The amount you're looking at would barely light a ciga-rette. And there's no more in the flat, so it looks like Coe used pretty much all of it for the pipe bombs he was carrying. Keep your grubby little latex fingers away from it, though. I want it photographed *in situ*. And it's supposed to be really unstable and can go *poof* at any time. Wouldn't want to singe your lovely fringe.'

'That's . . . interesting.' MacReady swallowed. Pictured him hitting Coe at speed. The rucksack – full of pipe bombs packed with this stuff – sliding away.

Beck eyed him. 'Yes, you're a very lucky boy. Anyway, we've found a mobile phone, too,' she tilted her head back towards the lounge, 'plus some boys' toys. Gaming junk, PlayStation, what have you. His laptop is the main thing. There has to be some stuff on there. With the rest of this on the table it should be more than enough to tie him to everything.'

'What's that?' MacReady asked, pointing at a piece of A4 already secured in a clear evidence bag.

'Suicide note. Farewell note. Whatever. Basically Coe saying a very brief goodbye to a world he hated and that he thinks hated him.'

MacReady looked around the room. Out of the window. 'What about the car he used? Any keys found in here?'

'Not yet. Firearms are going to sweep the side streets, see if any sus-looking motors are parked nearby. We'll see if we can get a match on any of the ones seen leaving the market scene. That's all I can do until the DVLA come back with anything.'

'That's if he registered the car properly.'

Beck nudged him with her elbow. 'Let's keep the good vibe going here, OK? We got our man. Or more specifically, you got our man. He's in the bin, Fletcher and the HQ bods are putting the arm on him. There were no nasty surprises waiting here for us. So we won, it's over. Yay for us, right?'

MacReady studied the table. The St David's floorplan. The warren of corridors behind the stores. The security room, where Coe murdered his old colleague, an ex-forces guy named Foster, before dropping the centre shutters and blowing the recording equipment to pieces. All so meticulously planned, he could see now. Points of entry and egress. The locations of security foot patrols at specific times. CCTV coverage. Even the amount of first-aid-trained staff on duty at any given time of day.

None of it removed. Coe had just left it for anyone to find. No booby traps, no IEDs primed to go off if and when the police put his door in.

MacReady cocked his head as he studied the scribbles and scraps.

'What I can't work out is why there is just the one attack plan.'

Beck turned to look at him. 'Meaning?'

'There's nothing here for Bessemer, or the Al Mahdi. Not that I can see, anyway.'

'Maybe he cleaned them up before moving on to this one?'

'But why?'

Beck threw an arm around. 'It's not exactly a penthouse here, Will. There's barely room to stretch out on the sofa.'

'I mean, why bother?' MacReady pointed at the suicide note. 'He expected to be taken out, either by his own bombs or by the police. Why would he give a shit and clean up? You'd think there'd be at least something from the other attacks. It doesn't make sense.'

Beck was silent for a moment. MacReady likewise.

He dug out his phone and dialled.

'It's me,' he said into the mobile. 'Just a quick one: Coe. He talking yet?'

'*Nada*,' Fletcher's voice in his ear. 'Same old same old. I'm in the custody suite now, waiting for his brief to turn up so we can chuck an interview into him.'

'Is he still all calm and happy and weird?'

'Sure is. I've just been watching him on the cell CCTV. He's sitting on the bench and smirking. Almost like he's laughing at something.'

'Maybe it's at us,' MacReady said quietly.

He clamped the phone to his ear. Looked from Coe's table to Beck.

Back to the table.

Eighteen

He sits, smiling to himself. A calmness about him. At last.

Developments today meant things had to be brought forwards. The timeline, altered. The strategy, modified. Never satisfactory, having to juggle or rush, but the planning had always been meticulous, had allowed plenty of wriggle room. There had been some unease, certainly during the early hours of this afternoon, but those moments of anxiety were already fading from memory. No more worrying. No pervasive fear of getting caught. No more constantly glancing over your shoulder in the street, or at your front door, waiting for it to explode in on itself with the force of their boots and metal tools, with their rasping screams designed to make you cower . . .

His work here is almost done. Things are drawing to a close. And this is different.

When they expect one thing, give them another.

The sun is falling, slowly, finally, casting the buildings in an auburn hue, angling towards the rooftops of the shabby flats and innumerable takeaways in the city's student quarter. He studies the alleyway with its overstuffed bins and spiny jags of graffiti, its rear gardens wild with foliage and university debris left behind by the last load of marauding undergraduates. A lonely place, a neglected and forgotten strip of cracked concrete between two side roads where nobody bothers to tread.

Where starting this is perfect.

It rests there on the ground next to a council wheelie bin. Such a small thing. Waiting for him. The relief he feels at getting it here safely – getting *himself* here safely with it, such is its volatility – is almost overwhelming. He closes his eyes for a moment, swears he can feel its latent energy from a hundred metres away, a rhythmic throb that jangles his guts, his thighs, behind his eyes. Slumps lower in the driver's seat, iPad in hand, the app he needs already opened and ready.

He is parked up in Cathays, just outside the city centre, away from the prying eyes of the powers that be, their cameras yet to invade much of this neighbourhood. He has studied the coverage, knows the blind spots. Is in one of them. Made his way here through more of them. Slipped the car into a parking space amongst a line of other nondescript vehicles, just another guy going about his business in an area swamped – already so many of them cluttering the streets, arriving early for the new academic year – with teens and twentysomethings who wouldn't notice somebody like him anyway, such is their narcissism, these students who know everything about nothing, who presume the world wishes to know what they are thinking, what they are wearing, what they are eating and who they are fucking.

The iPad screen: a view of gravel, weeds, the alleyway from an extremely low angle, the base of the nearest bin almost visible. The clock shows 19:42. He grips the tablet's bevelled edges, fingertips sweaty on its aluminium body. Sucks in a long breath, the car interior warm despite the air con. Prickles of perspiration on his forehead, his temples. A heady mixture of fear and excitement that he finds adrenalising, that he wishes he could bottle.

It's time.

He swipes the icon at the top and the image on the screen judders, shifts. Pulls away from the dirt and dust of the ground, lifting upwards for a bird's-eye view, the alleyway appearing in all its miserable glory.

He thumbs the right side of the screen, the faint picture of a joystick, and the view shifts as the drone yaws in that direction, the on-board camera turning to face the city centre. A tilt of the tablet, forwards, and the drone rises higher still and for a moment it is breathtaking: the Civic Centre with its Portland stone City Hall and National Museum, the shopping malls and parks and castle grounds beyond, red spatters of setting sun on the wavelets of the River Taff. Cardiff in true HD brilliance from the air, a sight he has never seen before and which makes him a little sad about what he is about to do.

He guides the drone south, gliding over railway tracks, the Welsh Government buildings, the lawns and monuments of Alexandra Gardens, then into the heart of the city centre. Hovers for ten seconds above the New Theatre in Park Place. Busy down there, as always. Heavy with clueless coppers, with taxis, with foot traffic drifting away from the pedestrianised shopping streets, with bar-hoppers and foodies.

With smiling faces, sitting in wicker chairs outside the cocktail lounge, outside the burger bar opposite. Drinks on tables, plates of food balanced on laps, *al fresco* in the dying embers of the evening, waiting for the evening performance in the theatre.

He stares at them via the camera.

Zooms in, lip curling.

These fucks with their middle-class bollocks, with their air kisses and box seats for a pair of scenery-chewing luvvies, with their predilection for Prosecco and martinis, with *pre-show nibbles* and ludicrous selfies.

The latter alone is enough to make him go postal.

He tilts the iPad, backwards this time and the drone drops slowly, heading for street level. He moves the joystick, the screen showing the theatre's façade, the entrance doors of Jongleurs comedy club, then into the bottom end of Park Place.

Into the outdoor dining areas.

It's funny, for a little while. People see the drone, point at it and giggle. One of them, a brash, drunken sort, his face chargrilled from sun, a smear of mayonnaise on his lips, he even reaches up, tries to grab it. A table of diners break into song, thinking it is for one of their party, and he can see what they are mouthing: *Happy birthday to you, happy birthday to you* ... Clueless, the lot of them. Arrogantly assuming it will never happen. Not here, not now.

Not to them.

And they laugh and a mile away he laughs because he can't believe he managed to get this far without killing himself and angles the iPad forwards and the drone shoots skywards, just for thirty feet or so, but it will do, the height is enough, just the smallest of knocks will do it, just the tiniest of impacts will set it off, and he stops laughing, pushes himself hard into the car seat, beyond excited now, and tips the tablet backwards again.

Watches the screen blur as the drone plummets towards the ground.

Mother of Satan.

Hears it.

Feels the car, the ground beneath him shake, even where he is sitting.

Nineteen

Two dead. More than forty injured.

The casualties, the victims, there were so many the ambulance service ran out of wagons to send. Taxis, civvy cars, police vehicles, even a single-decker bus: anybody with a working set of wheels had been collared to rush people to accident and emergency. The University Hospital's A&E department full now, and closed to any other members of the public in the region. The shouts had gone out on all channels ten minutes earlier: every officer retained on duty. Nobody to go home. All rest days cancelled for the foreseeable. All annual leave, likewise. They were drafting in further Mutual Aid from other forces. More soldiers and support, making their way from Hereford, from Tidworth. All roads in and out of the capital were in the process of being closed by roadblocks, a so-called ring of steel being put in place.

Horror beneath the brilliant purples and blues of dusk: upturned seats, knocked-over tables. Crockery and drinking glasses, smashed and scattered, hamburger buns and condiment bottles among the shards. Shattered windows the length of the street and beyond. Ground peppered with rubble, a ceiling of dust clinging to the air at roof height. On the front of the Thistle Hotel an alarm sounded, an unending electronic howl. Beneath the bleeping, the sound of somebody – a man – crying uncontrollably.

The pavement, charred and cracked where the explosion took place. The adjacent walls and few remaining windows smeared and splattered with blood, the waning light turning the reds a deep brown.

MacReady had heard the first calls while he'd waited for Beck outside Coe's flat. The Public Service Centre swamped with niners, with members of the public reporting the explosion. Not enough call handlers to cope with the demand. The 999 system almost breaking down.

They'd driven back into the city centre faster than they'd travelled west to Fairwater.

He tried to take it all in, feeling a numbness in his chest. Just inside the cordon at the junction of Park Place and Queen Street, crime-scene tape dancing in the light breeze and knocking against his lower back. His mobile in his pocket, buzzing, buzzing. Megan, or Klaudia, or both. More people flooding the mobile networks with calls, texts, emails, searching for loved ones, panicking, wanting to know. Wouldn't be long before it all crashed due to overload, and the buzzing would stop, and he would be grateful.

Beside MacReady, Beck, Fletcher and Harrison. DS Echols, his cockiness noticeably absent, was pacing in a circle, raking fingers through hair and gabbling on his phone while he updated the Major Incident Room with what they knew.

'Think the chief constable might have to cancel tomorrow morning's *we caught the bomber* press conference,' Harrison said.

Fletcher didn't look at him. 'Shut up, Warren. Just shut the fuck up for once. All right?'

'Coe is in custody,' said MacReady. 'We have our man.'

'We have *a* man,' replied Beck. 'You said it yourself at Coe's place not an hour ago. Why just the one set of plans for St David's?'

'Well, now we know,' said Fletcher.

MacReady glanced at the alarm, wished it would stop its bleating. He couldn't think straight. Needed to make sense of this. What they were dealing with.

Harrison sniffed, fidgeted with his belt as he pulled up his three-quarter-length trousers. 'Word from the first on scene is that witnesses were banging on about something dropping from the sky. One of them quadcopter jobbies.'

'A drone,' clarified Beck.

'Which would need someone to pilot it,' said MacReady.

Fletcher let out a long, miserable sigh. 'Can't remember the custody sergeant giving Coe the chance to play with one in his cell.'

Beck was shaking her head. Laughing, no humour in it. 'We were all amazed at how quickly he got from the market to the mosque in Penarth. This explains it.'

MacReady felt winded. He bent over a little, holding onto the skin above his hips.

'It wasn't the same man.'

*

The station was like the city in microcosm: in full lockdown mode. Officers on fire doors, in stairwells. Deployed in lifts, patrolling the perimeter on James Street and Dumballs Road. No protestors outside. The pavements deserted, bar the lines of vehicles parked on kerbs. Armed Response trucks, army wagons, media vans.

People were scared to leave their homes now.

It was nearly eleven p.m. when she arrived. Ushered inside by full-kit firearms officers guarding the entrance. A small, slender woman in her early twenties, timidly looking about with huge, dark eyes, peering from under the curve of her fringe. Head lowered slightly as she walked in through Cardiff Bay's front doors, still wearing her work outfit: black trousers and shirt, bright orange waist pinny replete with pockets and pens and fingertip smudges.

'Thank you so much for coming in.'

MacReady really was grateful, was on his feet and walking over to her with hand extended. Faria Begum. Server at the Kurry Korner restaurant in St David's. Nothing but a sliver of nerves topped with a pained smile as she slipped her tiny fingers into MacReady's hand and let him shake away. She'd been spoken to at the shopping centre, albeit very briefly, by one of the other CID teams after Coe's arrest. What she'd alluded to, the handwritten notes the officers made, had been raised by the Action Allocator in the MIR and the request for a full statement had come soon afterwards. Timothy Coe's custody clock was already ticking and they needed anything they could to throw into him in interview, so – in Fletcher's words – *it's all hands to the fucking pump, bro*. The DI had stressed this was to be MacReady's last task before returning his full attention to the Paxton murder. After the scene at Park Place, after the revelation that there was someone else running around out there blowing people up, MacReady was itching to do something. Was happy to work on into the night. Would sleep – like most of his colleagues had already been doing – on an office floor if need be.

The downside: Beck wasn't available. The ever-growing collection of items from Coe's flat – all of which needed bagging, tagging and affixing with property labels – as well as liaising with whatever CSI they could find that wasn't examining the scenes at Park Place and St David's and supervising her team of CCTV people was keeping her fully occupied, meaning that MacReady was lumbered with Detective Sergeant Paul Echols as his interview partner.

'Well, hello,' Echols smiled, leaning down to Begum and offering his own hand.

MacReady noticed the woman hesitate, then shake Echols's paw anyway. He grimaced when his DS winked at her. Even now, after all that had happened, Echols couldn't rein it in.

They ushered Begum into the police station proper, out of the public foyer and into a small office. It was old-school time – every computer terminal was in use and offices were full of other witnesses, with detectives surviving on caffeine and vending-machine chocolate – so MacReady had reams of MG11 and MG11a statement forms, plus a few pens. His wrist ached at just the thought of what he was going to have to write.

'You mentioned to our colleagues that you knew Timothy Coe?'

Echols, straight in there. Nothing to engage with Begum, or establish a rapport, or anything close to following the investigative interviewing framework. No offer of something to drink. No checking if she was ready, or comfortable, or that she was aware she could leave at any time and she was just a witness. A significant witness, at that.

'I . . . Not really,' Begum replied. Hand raised to the side of her face, where she began twisting a coil of hair between fingers. Her eyes downcast, looking at her lap.

'So you didn't know him? Or you did know him?' Echols asked. His tone, forceful already. Begum blinked a few times, turning her head away from him.

MacReady threw Echols a look. Ignored the narrowed eyes, the arrogant scowl he got in return. 'Do you need a glass of water, Faria?' he asked.

Begum shook her head. Glanced at MacReady then away. 'Not for the moment, thank you. It's really late and I'd like to get this done quickly if that's OK. After everything that's gone on today I . . . I just want to be at home.'

Her voice, a near whisper. MacReady had to strain to hear the woman. 'It's understandable. There's been a lot of scary stuff happening out there.'

'But you've got him now, yes?' Begum asked. She stared at MacReady this time, her eyes near-pleading for an answer in the affirmative. 'I saw you, you arrested him, yes? It was you, wasn't it? You grabbed him –'

'Grabbed is one way of putting it,' said Echols.

MacReady ignored it. 'Yes, we've got him.'

'And you're going to keep him locked away?'

'We're going to try our best to, yes.'

'But . . . what about the explosion this evening? I don't understand . . .'

'We're not sure but we think it was a timed bomb, set by Coe a couple of days ago.'

Echols, eyebrows hitched skywards for a second. Muttered: 'Interesting.'

Begum exhaled audibly. 'So this is over.'

It wasn't a question, more Begum confirming it to herself. Convincing herself. MacReady and Echols exchanged glances. As he nodded at Begum, MacReady willed his detective sergeant to keep quiet about the drone, about the second bomber. Not only would it make Begum clam up, and possibly leave the station, it would mean word would get out before any official press conference or decision on a media strategy could be arranged to explain – and contain – new developments.

A beaming smile on Echols's face, forced and entirely unconvincing. 'You've got to give us everything you have on this Coe joker, all right?'

It was clear – and understandable – that Begum had taken an instant dislike to Echols. She was refusing to meet his eyes. Obviously not wanting to talk to him.

'So what can you tell us, Faria?' MacReady asked, keeping it gentle. He could feel Echols tense next to him, upset about MacReady trying to take the lead. Unable to see the bigger picture, yet again. MacReady wished the DS would just piss off back to the MIR. 'Anything can help. You have nothing to worry about now, but we need to get as much information as we can so it keeps Coe in a cell for a very long time.'

Begum's bony shoulders rose and fell. Her fingers, still entwined in that length of jet-black hair. Her voice, so quiet: 'You know how it's only when you get to know somebody, even just a little, you realise how you're never going to have anything in common?'

MacReady felt Echols's eyes on him. Heard: 'You're not wrong.'

He gave a thin smile. Cast a sideways glance at the man next to him. 'Oh, definitely.'

A quick shrug from Begum. 'Well, that was what it was like with Timmy. With Coe.'

'Timmy?' Echols asked. 'So you were friends.'

'We were and then we weren't. When I spent more time with him it was obvious we were different kinds of people.'

She was being gracious, MacReady suspected. It was endearing, but not helpful.

'Can you elaborate a little more, Faria? For example, how did you first meet?' MacReady pretty much knew the circumstances, but wanted her to talk, to relax into some kind of rhythm, so he could draw as much out of her as possible.

'He was a security officer at the shopping centre. He'd already been working there a while before I started at the restaurant. I'd been made redundant and needed the work, the money, so applied to be a waitress, a server, whatever it's called, at most of the places in St David's. Most restaurants and cafés in the city centre, to be honest. I'd just about given up when I got the Kurry Korner job . . . that was about six months ago.'

'And Coe?' asked Echols. 'Where does he come into this?'

Begum didn't look at him. 'Timmy . . . Coe, he used to come and sit in the restaurant every now and then. At first, anyway. He had a favourite table which was in my section. After a while he was there every time he had a meal break. Always at table forty-nine. Always something from the starter menu and a Coke or Sprite. Just enough to keep him there for half an hour or so. I kind of guessed he didn't have much money to spend, like me.'

'So you got talking,' MacReady said, scribbling notes, bullet points, for later. For when the real writing began.

She sighed. 'Yes, we did. He seemed nice enough. It was the usual small talk at first, always polite, asking me how my day had been, stuff about the weather . . . You know, boring, typical chatting. It just kind of grew from there, a bit of flirting, until we knew each other's names, backgrounds, could have a laugh and joke together. He used to tell me about his army days, all the things he'd got up to. He always cheered me up . . .'

Echols stood, paced over to and leaned against a wall. 'He told you he'd been in the army?'

'Served in Iraq and Afghanistan, so he said.'

'News to us. And I would imagine to his ex-employers at the security company. Was he ever rude, or threatening?'

'Never,' said Begum, staring at Echols for the first time. 'He was a gentleman. At least until, you know, it happened . . .'

Begum's face fell. Her cheeks, reddening.

MacReady dropped his pen to the desk, leaned down a little so he was closer, so he could see her as he talked. 'We've been given a rough idea of what he did by the security company, but . . . could you elaborate, Faria? If it's not too distressing?'

She was finding this incredibly difficult, MacReady knew. Could already sense what was coming, too. He'd done enough of these types of interviews.

'He got really aggressive towards the end,' a note of sadness in her voice. 'I didn't want to have anything more to do with him, but he wouldn't accept it. He kept coming to the table in his break, trying to talk, but I didn't want to. And then the final time he began pleading, really begging and crying . . . then getting angry and shouting about me, about the world being against him and he didn't have anyone, that kind of thing. Then before I knew what was going on he was touching my hand, then my legs, then he was pretty much groping me in front of the other customers. It was obvious he wasn't going to stop and it got so bad some of the other staff ran over to help out. The guys there were great. *Are* great. Timmy was going . . . well, mental, so in the end they told him he was banned. When he still refused to go back to work they threw him out, literally threw him onto the concourse outside the restaurant, but he still wouldn't walk away. He was standing there, making all sorts of threats about what he was going to do.'

'Threats?' MacReady asked.

'It was nonsense, really. He kept going on about how he's an underdog that nobody listens to. How people like him were rising up, that the world was going to listen to them instead of shouting them down and making fun. He was ranting about those riots that happened in London a few years back and how it was just the start. It was ridiculous, really. You know all this Brexit business, and that Trump guy in America? How his supporters were saying they had finally spoken and the world was going to listen? It was all a bit like that. So anyway, of all things, the centre security had to come and rescue us from one of their own guys.'

'And that's why he lost his job,' said Echols.

'Why wasn't this reported to the police?' asked MacReady.

'I still . . .' she began. 'I knew the shopping centre, the security company, they'd get rid of him. That he was going to lose his job. I thought that was enough punishment for him, and didn't want to waste the police's time.'

'You should have come to us, Faria,' MacReady said.

Begum nodded. 'He'd been so nice up until then.'

'They usually are.'

'And I was scared,' she blurted out. 'By that point I found him quite frightening. I wasn't sure what he would do, or what he was capable of. If he'd come back again the next day and attack me. I mean, look at what he *has* done now. So I didn't take it further. I hoped he'd realise what I'd done for him by letting it go, but all it did was make me nervous from the moment I woke up to the time I went to bed. Always looking over my shoulder for him. Even now, even though you people have him.'

MacReady made a few more notes, biting down the urge to scream. He understood her logic, but if Begum had called them they might have been able to stop Coe. Might have learned of his plans. Might have found something that led them to Coe's accomplice who had just destroyed half of Park

Place. MacReady turned back to her. 'OK. Rewind a little. Tell us about the time you spent together outside work. What the build-up was to him playing up in the restaurant.'

'We went out two or three times. Well when I say out, I mean we only went out for one date to a cinema in town . . .'

In town. The Cardiffian's way of describing the city centre. Coe had chosen to spend his very first evening with Begum – after chasing her for weeks, if not months – sitting in a darkened auditorium and not speaking to her.

'Anything good?' Echols asked. Bored now, MacReady knew. He wasn't even trying to hide the yawns.

'A superhero film. One of those remakes of a remake of a remake. So unoriginal I can't even remember the title. *Spiderman* something?'

MacReady waved it away. 'What about the other times?'

Begum gave a dejected chuckle. 'We went to his flat in Fairwater. This tiny place, just a man cave. Nothing but a television and computer stuff, really. No pictures of family or friends. Nothing. You should see it.'

I already have, thought MacReady. Pictured Coe's flat. Thought of Ken Cullen, the tac advisor in Penarth, and his apartment: just as spartan. Closed his eyes for a second and thought of his own miserable pit in Duncan Jones's house. Not much difference between any of them, he realised with despair.

Echols gripped the back of a chair. 'What did you get up to in the flat?'

'We didn't *get up to* anything,' she shot back. 'Both times he ordered takeaway – a curry to share, of all things – then he would turn on his PlayStation and show me how to play football games, or how to kill soldiers and blow up buildings. Like he thought it would impress me.'

'Did you play the games with him?' MacReady asked. Was reminded of Duncan yet again. And of Nazir Uddin's father, describing how his son *wastes all day on his computer, typing drivel, playing stupid video games and pretending to be a soldier, a superstar football player . . .*

'At first. For an hour, the first time I went to the flat. Just to, I don't know, show willing, I suppose. It got very boring very quickly, to be honest. I like Facebook and have some games on my phone, but those things aren't for me. Then he just . . . got on with it. Was kind of happy for me to be there, but was just as happy playing his game as long as I stayed and watched. Do you know what I mean? It was pretty weird.'

'What did you talk about when he was doing this?'

'That's the thing,' Begum frowned. 'He didn't talk. At least not to me. He'd have a headset on, one with earphones and a microphone. He'd be shouting and laughing and saying *yes, sir* and *will comply* and all these other things. Talking online as he played.'

'Do you know the name of the person he was talking to?'

Begum shook her head. 'No. And it was more than one person. I could tell. I'm no gamer but their IDs were flashing up on screen and it was obvious there were quite a few of them.'

Echols straightened. 'So what you're saying is that basically Coe is a sad geek who has no friends.'

Begum looked at MacReady, turned her head to stare at Echols. 'I'm saying he has plenty of friends, actually. If that's what you want to call them. If I had to describe them I'd say they were more of a team.'

MacReady stopped writing.

Narrowed his eyes at Begum.

Felt the slightest shiver in his guts.

*

'So he's a Walt,' Echols said.

'A what?' MacReady asked.

'A bullshitter,' offered Fletcher.

MacReady was none the wiser. He checked around the CID suite, at the DI who had decided that the Major Incident Room was too cramped with sweat-soaked bodies to think straight so had sought solace in his own office for an hour, leaving Beck and Harrison up with Specialist Crime to sort through the mountain of crap they'd removed from Coe's flat. According to MacReady's antiquated computer terminal it was a few minutes to two in the morning; he'd finished handwriting Begum's statement just twenty minutes earlier and still had to transfer it – every word to be retyped – to the system before he clocked off. Tiredness had wormed its way into the marrow of his bones, and he ached for his bed.

Any bed, with anyone. Even Duncan.

'It's a forces phrase,' Echols added. 'At least it used to be, but it's in wider use now. Means a Walter Mitty type, someone who lies and embellishes stuff, like their service in the army. Where they fought, medals they got. Or how good they are as a detective.'

MacReady rolled his eyes at the barb.

'We get a couple every now and again,' said Fletcher. He was feet up, visibly relieved to be back at his own workplace with its well-worn grooves and comforting stains. 'Civvy weirdo dresses up as a traffic cop, tapes homemade flashing lights and woo-woos to the top of their Vauxhall Astra. They love pulling people over and telling them off for speeding.'

MacReady shook his head. 'Why on earth would anyone ever want to pretend to be a traffic black rat?'

'Why would anyone want to be a real one?' laughed Echols.

Echols was still chuckling to himself while MacReady sent text messages to Megan and Klaudia. Let them know he was safe, that he was still working. Didn't mention that it was no longer on the Park Place bomb, a fact he was thoroughly miserable about, even if it meant not having to spend a single second more assisting Echols. The DS had thanked Begum for her time then left MacReady to get on with statementing her, and even though his wrist now ached he'd been happy to be left alone. He'd been grateful for what she'd given, and had arranged for an Armed Response vehicle to drop her home safely.

He'd found the DI ensconced behind his desk when he returned to the office, and Fletcher had pretty much thanked MacReady for his input then banished him to his desk to work on Heidi Paxton's murder. Added, as an afterthought, to check on anything else that may have filtered in – the stabbings, robberies and sexual offences – from a similarly overstretched uniform in the last few hours.

'You can't do anything with any of it,' the DI had muttered. 'But make sure you cover our arses as best you can.'

Echols was now busy on the phone, the DI likewise with his thoughts and gazing out of the window at the darkened bay, at the necklace of harbour lights strung above the surface of the water. Beneath the desk, at MacReady's feet, sat Paxton's belongings in an array of evidence bags. He still hadn't shifted them to the property store. Was reluctant to do so. They were a reminder that he had a dead young woman on his hands and parents he'd made a promise to. He looked more closely, saw the new scrawl on the one of the evidence labels: someone had worked the bag it was attached to, had timed and dated it earlier this evening, while they were at Coe's flat.

Heidi Paxton's smartphone was inside the evidence bag. CSI and the Hi-Tech Crime Unit had done the business.

MacReady powered up his computer to check emails. Ignored the reams of reminders and warnings that his CS incapacitant spray needed replacing, that his e-Learning training password had expired and he couldn't do any more online courses, that an assistant chief constable he'd never met was being promoted to deputy chief, meaning he was even less likely to encounter the woman at any time during his service.

He eventually found the email from a techie, who, if he'd been in the room at that time, MacReady would have kissed.

The civvy had cracked Paxton's mobile, had the PIN code for MacReady to input whenever he needed. Had even charged the thing ready for use. MacReady fired an email back, profusely thanking the Hi-Tech Crime guy and promising a beer or five if they ever crossed paths.

He pulled latex gloves from his drawer, opened the evidence bag, reminded himself to annotate what he'd done and when on the label. Fished out Paxton's phone: a relatively new model Samsung. Checked the PIN on the email.

1805.

He stared at the computer screen, phone in hand. The PIN immediately rang a bell. He sat back, tapped at the phone's screen to enter it as he tried to recall why it chimed with him.

As the Samsung fired up, MacReady remembered. Brought up Niche, the Paxton file. The as yet unfinished statement from Simone Paxton. Scrolled through the pages, nodding, knowing he was right, that he had to be.

And there it was: 18 May. *1805*. The date Heidi Paxton's brother, Jonathan, was killed in the car crash. Heidi had used it to remember, he was sure. To think of her brother every time she tapped in the PIN. But why? Just to commemorate him? For some other reason? The only person who knew was the phone's owner, and she wasn't with them any more.

Straight away, buzzes and bleeps. The phone catching up, flashing notifications, the missed calls, texts and emails. A WhatsApp message. Dozens of Facebook Messenger alerts and Twitter direct messages. All of it coming through, a deluge of it now the phone was properly live again. MacReady knew there would be calls from friends, family. Anybody whose lives Heidi Paxton had touched in some way. He placed the Samsung on his desk, let it play out. After five straight minutes it stopped vibrating.

'Thank Christ for that!' Fletcher called, eyes closed and chair reclined.

MacReady spent the next half hour scrolling through everything, mindful that he still had Faria Begum's statement to add to the system for Specialist Crime. But Paxton's phone was rammed with info – despite what her parents had told Mac-Ready, and her apparent lack of interaction with the real world while tucked away in her bedroom each day. Heidi had been a very busy young woman.

Her contacts list alone was over 300 strong. He skimmed them. Her mother, father, doctor's surgery, a takeaway. *Harvey, AJ, SazzaG, Vicky,* it went on and on, putting his own circle of friends and acquaintances to shame. Her most recent calls had been to her parents, to a couple of restaurants, to a taxi company. Several to *SouljahBoy* in the days leading up to her death.

A boyfriend? One her parents didn't know about?

MacReady scanned the incoming calls list. *SouljahBoy* again. Numerous calls this time. Long ones – fifteen, twenty, thirty minutes. All the night before she died. More the morning of the attack, when Heidi would have been travelling into the city centre.

SouljahBoy.

MacReady sat forwards, felt the shiver of adrenalin in his chest. Finger hovering over the contact. He looked over at Echols, at Fletcher. Neither paying him any attention, as usual. Fletcher on the cusp of dozing off in his chair.

He dialled. Placed the phone to his ear.

When it rang his mouth went dry. Was he about to speak to the last person to see Heidi Paxton alive?

''Ello?'

The voice in his ear. Deep, not a boy's, despite the contact name.

'Who's this?' MacReady asked. Thought: *just blag it.* Hoped he sounded calm.

A pause on the line. 'Who's this?'

'Who's this, please?' MacReady tried again.

'You tell me first,' was the reply.

MacReady screwed up his face. He'd heard this voice before. Recently, too. Tried to summon a face to go with the words – the pitch and tone of them, so annoyingly familiar – that played over and over in his head. Could feel his heart hammering against the cotton of his crumpled shirt.

'This is DC Will MacReady of Cardiff Bay CID,' he barked, 'and I would like to know who I am speaking to, please.'

A few seconds of silence.

'Fuck me, mun.'

MacReady's mouth fell open. 'Wazza?'

'Yeah, it's me, you muppet,' said Harrison. 'I'm upstairs, talking to you on Timothy Coe's phone. How the hell did you get this number?'

Saturday

Twenty

Four hours was nowhere near enough, but it was all MacReady got.

An airy whine woke him in his reclined chair, legs splayed beneath the desk and a rivulet of drool on his chin. The cleaner pushed her vacuum around him, not even looking in his direction, she'd seen enough sleeping coppers in her time. He lifted his head and glanced around. Echols absent, thankfully, while Fletcher was already up and pacing the carpet in his office, nodding and *uh-huh*ing into his mobile, cup of coffee in his other hand.

It hit him again. Heidi Paxton and Timothy Coe knew each other.

MacReady sat upright, adjusted his chair. Gave a sheepish smile to the cleaner, wiping at the drying spittle with a sleeve. It had taken him – taken all of them – a good hour after that phone call to discuss what it meant. Where Paxton fitted into this chaos. Harrison and Beck had come down to the CID suite, away from the madness of the MIR, so they could talk it through. Just between them – the team, no spooks or Specialist Crime for now – so they could come up with some reason for MacReady's murder victim to be linked with Coe and his as-yet-unknown accomplice.

In the end, they had nothing. Short of ringing every contact in Heidi Paxton's list, or waking her poor parents and pummelling them with questions at three in the morning, the new information had to be added to Niche and HOLMES2, then passed up to Counter-Terrorism and the rankers in the Major Incident Room so they could make the decision what to do with it.

Then they'd crashed and burned, Fletcher in his office, Echols beneath his desk, MacReady – just about managing a wave as Beck and Harrison disappeared upstairs – in his chair, which he reclined just half a second before finally succumbing to exhaustion.

A paper plate with two piece of soggy toast appeared on the desk in front of him.

'Breakfast,' said Fletcher from behind him.

MacReady eyed the plate, craned his neck to look at the DI. 'Thank you.'

Fletcher placed a hand on MacReady's shoulder. Left it there for a few seconds then walked away. MacReady watched him go, watched him slump into his chair and stare out of the window, at another bright-blue sky.

He sent a text to Megan, checking she was OK, that everything was good with Finlay. No calls, not at the moment. Just a message to let her know he was still sucking air. She replied immediately, obviously up with Fin already, her day long started.

We are fine. Please stay safe. X

Short, to the point, but a reply nonetheless. MacReady yawned and stretched. Folded a limp piece of toast in half and bit into it. Brought up the internet on his computer, scrolled through the news reports of the Park Place bombing. The horrific photographs. The shaky videos – all shattered glass and the smoke and screams of the immediate aftermath – posted to YouTube. The requests for info, for witnesses, for blood donations to help the injured – not just from last night, but those still being treated from Bessemer Market and the Al Mahdi Mosque. Amongst it all was Klaudia Solak, on Twitter and banging out tweets from the scene outside the New Theatre.

MacReady sent her a text:

> Don't you ever sleep?

Another quick reply:

> Only when you call around, lover. Anything for me?

Always digging. He smiled and shook his head. Turned off his phone.

There was nothing for MacReady to do. Certainly not with the bombings, and now Heidi Paxton had been kicked up to Specialist Crime – with Fletcher of the opinion they might very well fold it into their inquiry – even that had been taken out of his hands for a while. Thinking about Paxton, he finished the piece of toast, brought up his work emails.

Someone at HQ was in the office early, thankfully. There was one from the Financial Investigation Unit. The FIU had sent a full rundown on Heidi's bank account.

MacReady skimmed through the text of the email, opened the attachment. Chewed more toast as he read. Stopped chewing, the bread mushed against the inside of his cheek, as he took in the figures. Recalled what her mother and father had said.

How she worked online from her bedroom, doing data entry for a pittance.

We're supporting her for a little while . . .

MacReady swallowed the toast, turned on his mobile. Found the number for Simone Paxton. It was nudging eight a.m.; he hoped she'd be up.

She sounded tired when she answered. MacReady had been updated by the FLO that she wasn't sleeping, that any sleep she did get was frequently interrupted by Mark Paxton sobbing them both awake or, as he continued to fall apart, knocking over furniture while he drunkenly roamed the downstairs of the house, shouting for his daughter. He felt guilty for ringing, for interrupting her if she'd been grabbing some rest, but it needed to be done.

'The bombs, it's terrible,' Simone Paxton said down the line. 'I can't believe what I've been watching. Those poor people, so many of them. What on earth is the world coming to, Will?'

'We're doing everything we can to stop it,' he said. Changed tack quickly. 'And I'm still working flat out for Heidi, which is kind of why I'm ringing. Do you mind if I ask a few more questions?'

'Of course.'

'Heidi's job – we touched on it, but not in any detail yet. Do you have any idea how much she was earning doing this online work?'

A pause. Then: 'Very little, really. They pay in dollars, and she was getting a few hundred each month, if you added up all the contracts she had with various people and businesses. Some of them were for as little as three dollars an hour.'

Three dollars an hour. MacReady looked at his computer screen again.

'Your husband mentioned that you helped out. Did you give her cash, or transfer money into her bank account?'

'Both. Mostly bank transfers, though. We'd usually put a large sum in her account at the beginning of each month, but Mark would always be dipping into his wallet for ten or twenty pounds if she asked for it. Train fares, things for her computer or phone, stuff like that.'

'Did she have any savings?'

'None. I mean, she had about six hundred at one point last year but spent it on a new laptop and phone. We argued about it, the waste of money, when she already had both. Since then it's just been the money we gave her and her earnings from this website.'

'Do you mind me asking how much would be transferred at the start of the month?'

Simone Paxton *umm*ed down the line. 'Maybe two hundred? I'd have to ask Mark, but it would certainly be around that amount. We helped, but still wanted her to try and stand on her own two feet.'

MacReady shook his head. 'So never more than, say, two or three hundred pounds?'

'Three hundred. Maximum. Definitely.'

'Look, I have to go, Simone. Thanks for this.'

MIKE THOMAS | 250

'I . . . Is there a problem?'

'Not at all,' he lied. 'I'll call you later. Once I've worked through a few things.'

MacReady ended the call. Tapped at the computer keyboard, scrolling through the pages of data from the FIU.

'Boss, you want to come take a look at this?' he called to Fletcher.

The DI was back on the phone; he muttered a thanks and goodbye, walked across to MacReady's desk and perched his backside on the corner of it. 'This going to tip me over the edge?'

MacReady shook his head. 'You've read the stuff I've gathered on Heidi Paxton, right? Her job and finances?'

Fletcher nodded. 'Lovely girl, works from home, doesn't earn much but her parents sort her out for dosh. That about cover it?'

'Pretty much.'

'I sense a *however* coming my way.'

'I've just spoken to her mother. They sort her for dosh, but to the tune of a couple of hundred quid each month. Three hundred, tops.'

'Not much, when you think of it.'

'No,' said MacReady. His finger, pointing at the monitor. 'And she had no savings at all, according to Simone Paxton. Which doesn't explain this.'

Fletcher squinted, leaned in a little. Eyes skittering about as he studied what was shown on MacReady's screen.

'The fuck?'

MacReady sighed. 'I've done a quick skim through. Gone through statements for the last year for her Barclays account.

When she died she had more than thirty thousand pounds in there. All accrued in the last ten months, via hefty lump sum payments every few weeks.'

'Someone was paying her.'

'And it wasn't the Bank of Mum and Dad.'

'Who, then?'

MacReady looked up at the DI. 'And for what?'

Fletcher breathed in through his nose, a deep chest full of air. Regarded MacReady with worn-out eyes, the normally olive skin around them bloated and pale. 'Were there any withdrawals on the day she was murdered?'

'None.'

'Any time since?'

'Nope. The account has been dormant since she was found with the injuries. No payments in, no withdrawals. No activity whatsoever.'

Fletcher absorbed the news. 'So it wasn't a robbery. She wasn't done for her money.'

'It could be that someone is planning to take the money out, but they're biding their time.'

'Not wanting to draw attention to themselves until all this dies down, maybe.'

'Maybe. But I'm going to ask the bank to put a marker on the account for us. If there's any activity they'll let us know immediately.'

'Sounds like a plan. But first, perhaps you should make sure all this is put to Coe when you go into interview.'

MacReady flinched. 'I'm interviewing? I'm just a DC –'

'Not interviewing per se. I've just got off the phone to the detective chief super. They've formally arrested Coe on suspicion of murdering Heidi Paxton so they can question him about it. Put some more pressure on him, see where it goes. The DCS has seen your update about the girl, and the WECTU officers have studied it as best they can, but both are of the mind that it might be better if you sit in on the next one.'

'I can brief them,' MacReady offered.

Fletcher wrinkled his nose, waved the suggestion away. 'You've been working it since the start and we really do not have time to be doing bloody briefings or bringing people up to speed for the next three hours. Custody clock and all that. And there might be something you pick up on, or something the Specialist Crime guys miss, that you can advise upon during the session. Even ask some straightforward questions. You know Paxton better than any of us, after all.'

The huge amount of money in her bank account? MacReady didn't know her at all, it seemed. Neither, clearly, did her parents. He said nothing, nodded.

'This chunk of change she has squirrelled away lends even more weight to you going in there,' Fletcher said. Jabbed a thumb at MacReady. 'But just to assist, maybe chuck a few questions into him and nothing more, OK? No pushing buttons or getting your arse in your hand when Coe goes *No comment* for the tenth time, right?'

'Scout's honour.'

'Were you even in the Scouts?'

'Never,' MacReady smiled.

Fletcher rolled his eyes and walked back to his office.

*

MacReady made for the lifts, everything he had on Paxton – her mother's still-unfinished statement, the bank details, the list of calls made to and received from Timothy Coe's mobile, and pretty much nothing else – in a folder tucked under his arm. A call on his phone just as he was just about to press the button for the custody suite level. It was Beck.

'Where are you off to?' she asked.

MacReady's finger hovered over the -1 button on the lift wall. 'Cells.'

'They finally locking you up for cheating on your wife with my friend?'

'Hardy-har. I'm sitting in on an interview with Coe.'

A brief pause. 'You might want to drop by here first, then.'

The tone of her voice made him shift his finger to the button for the next floor up, where Beck's team of CCTV researchers were based next to the MIR. 'Something interesting?'

'Very. So get a move on, tea boy.'

Including Beck, there were now six people crammed into the room designated for CCTV research and investigation. MacReady felt the warmth – screens and whirring boxes and overheating skin in the boxy room – from the doorway and was reluctant to enter until Beck demanded that he join her at a desk.

'Came through fifteen minutes ago,' she said, tipping her head at the computer terminal. 'Pull up a chair.'

MacReady sat next to her, his detective sergeant scooting across a little – he noticed the look of discomfort on her face as she moved – to give him room. Around them the beards were heads down, surrounded by half-drunk mugs of tea, soft drink cans and chocolate bar wrappers, scrutinising television flat screens and computer monitors, shifting recordings back and forth, back and forth. Painstaking work, studying frame after frame, making notes as they went, searching for anything they could find amongst the thousands of hours of CCTV they had collected or received over the last three days.

Beck used a mouse to move a slider at the bottom of her screen. 'Know what an IP cam is?'

'Nope,' MacReady replied. On the screen, what appeared to be people zipping in and out of the picture, staring at the camera itself, Beck working the slider, the images moving at high speed, too fast for MacReady to see anything other than blurred faces and flashes of colour from clothing.

'Internet protocol camera,' she told him. 'Digital video, but sent via the internet or a computer network to a server for viewing or storage.'

'A netcam, then.'

'Yep. And this is from one of the cashpoints outside Cardiff Central railway station.'

'So it came through?' MacReady asked, inching closer to the screen.

'Took them a while to dig it out and email the relevant clip to us. It's really high quality, too. I just need to find the right spot . . . Here we go, watch.'

She let the recording play at normal speed. MacReady rested his elbows on knees, chin cupped in his hands as he took it in: the car park at the rear of the railway station, a brilliant clear sky above it, the grey stone and tinted glass monolith of the British Gas building at Callaghan Square in the distance. All in remarkably sharp detail, as were the people walking up to the cashpoint. The camera picked up everything. A small queue for cash, the bizarre facial expressions of commuters waiting in line, people rifling through wallets and handbags and pockets for their bank cards, a couple arguing in the middle distance while struggling to remove luggage from a beat-up hatchback. In the top left corner of the screen the time showed 9:34 a.m.

'This is crystal clear,' said MacReady. 'But not much help if we don't catch sight of Heidi Paxton, if I'm being honest.'

Beck said nothing, held a finger up to her mouth. *Quiet*.

He arched an eyebrow and turned back to the video. More punters, walking up to the cashpoint, inserting cards, fiddling with buttons and squinting at a screen MacReady and Beck couldn't see. Pulling out cash, shoving it in pockets, folding it into purses. The queue, seemingly endless.

Then Beck pressed a button on the keyboard; the recording slowed considerably, shifting forwards a half-frame at a time.

'There you go,' she said.

MacReady looked at the man withdrawing money. Male, white, grizzled hair. In his fifties and apparently fond of working out: his forearms were corded and lean, his shoulders rounded humps of well-defined muscle.

'A silver fox,' MacReady said.

'If you say so.' Beck waited, head cocked, staring at MacReady.

He shifted his eyes back to the screen. Studied the male again. Saw nothing other than a very fit middle-aged guy standing in front of a cash machine.

As the recording crept forwards: a figure appearing on the right-hand side of the image. Behind the silver fox's left shoulder. Just a sliver of a face at first, then a hand. An arm, the right side of a male's chest, his torso wrapped in black. His legs, obscured by the good-looking fiftysomething's muscular frame.

Then the full face came into shot and MacReady's mouth flopped open.

It was Timothy Coe.

'My God,' he whispered. Turned to Beck. 'He was there when Heidi was murdered.'

'That he was,' Beck smiled.

'Pause it. Freeze it, whatever you do with this thing. I need a still or screen print or something. For Specialist Crime. The interview. This could change everything.'

Beck was nodding, pointing at the time: 9.36 a.m. 'Well it certainly means Coe didn't do Bessemer Market. He couldn't be in two places at once.'

'But this doesn't make sense.' Beside him the recording chugged onwards, frame by painfully slow frame. 'We're working on the assumption that Coe did Bessemer, and his accomplice did the Al Mahdi Mosque. There simply wasn't enough time for him to get across the city to Penarth. But if Coe didn't hit the market, who did? The same person who just used a drone to take out half of Park Place?'

'Look, Fletcher is aware of this, and I've passed it onto the MIR for you. Other than that, I really don't know any more.' A weary shrug from Beck, her hand on the keyboard ready to stop the recording. Already looking about, yet more work to be getting on with, despite feeling beat.

MacReady glanced at the recording. Froze in his seat.

'Wait,' he said. Grabbed Beck's hand before she could shut the video down.

She turned to him, saw his wide-eyed expression. Shifted her eyes to the computer screen. 'What is it?'

MacReady watched a second figure move into frame from the right. A short time after Timothy Coe. Male. Late teens. Dark skin, with an earring in his left ear. Eyes wild, mouth split into a manic laugh.

With two lines shaved into his left eyebrow.

MacReady closed his eyes. Heard the voice.

I think it's safe to say my son is . . . easily led. I have heard he has been spending some time with, shall we say, undesirable elements in your *community . . .*

MacReady opened his eyes.

Stared at Nazir Uddin.

Twenty-one

A sterile custody suite for Coe.

Every other prisoner bailed, or turfed out as No Further Action, or shunted to cell complexes and bridewells in Merthyr, in Bridgend, to anywhere else in the force area that could house them. All the people answering bail that MacReady had seen in the foyer last night, gone, along with their slippery defence solicitors. Every single one of the station's sixty *hotel rooms* empty, save for the very first in the wing nearest the booking-in desk – the cell rigged with state-of-the-art gubbins to monitor their special guest.

Heroin dealers with a penchant for firearms. Multiple rapists. A prison visit to question a dead-eyed lifer – in for murdering his girlfriend and with nothing to lose – who'd shivved a chaplain across the bridge of his nose, the razor-blade-and-toothbrush combo effortlessly removing both of the man's nostrils. MacReady had interviewed all of them and more over the last year on CID, and not once had he felt as uneasy as he did now. Waiting off the main custody area in a kitchenette with a detective inspector from Specialist Crime and an officer from Counter-Terrorism. One of the interview teams grilling Timothy Coe.

Coe was still silent. Refusing to answer anything put to him. Accepting only glasses of water since arriving in custody.

Nothing to eat. The only words coming out of his mouth saved for the ears of his solicitor when they conferred in a private room before and after interviews.

Time was getting on. The initial forty-eight hours fast bleeding away, then it was the rigmarole of applying to magistrates, to judges, for extensions to the time they could keep him in the bin. And there was the very real possibility that the Metropolitan Police would shift everything to London under the terror umbrella, something the hierarchy were keen to avoid by putting this to bed soonest. HQ had already made it known they wanted this resolved here, in force, to reassure the local public and media, to demonstrate that the region's police could do the job just as well as Met terrorism specialists, even for something like this.

MacReady had just finished passing on everything he now had about Heidi Paxton, her links to Coe, her swollen bank account, the litany of phone calls. The images – printed out by Beck, and still fixed in MacReady's mind – of Nazir Uddin walking just behind Coe, across the car park at the rear of Cardiff Central railway station, from the direction of the service lane where Paxton was found a short time later. Laughing together, just minutes before the bombing in Bessemer Market. Twenty minutes before the attack on the Al Mahdi Mosque.

Uddin was involved. Wasn't at the mosque when it was attacked – Beck's CCTV recordings bore that out – but was at scene immediately after the bombing. Must have made his way there in order to speak to uniform, to give them his details and describe what he saw. But why? And what was he doing with Timothy Coe, their supposedly racist would-be bomber? Mac-Ready hoped Coe would cave. Would give them something to explain why Nazir Uddin had decided to go to Penarth. Where Uddin was hiding now.

And the name still nagged at MacReady. Something about it, so familiar.

'Anything else?' asked the detective inspector, a portly man named Evans, all glistening skin and permanently troubled expression, his manner brusque and accent more Valleys than Warren Harrison's.

MacReady closed his folder and shook his head. In a chair next to them the suit from the Welsh Extremism and Counter-Terrorism Unit stroked a pen across the pages of a notebook, not looking up. He'd not spoken a word yet, not even to introduce himself, just radiated woody aftershave tinged with base notes of self-importance.

'Watch and listen at first,' the DI said to MacReady. 'Anything jumps out at you, slip me a note. If you think I'm missing anything, give me a nudge. Otherwise sit tight until I'm done, then you get to have a go about your dead girl.'

'Got it.'

'I mean it,' Evans warned. 'I don't do impulsive. And I know who you are, and what you did last year.'

MacReady was about to protest but the detective inspector turned and left the room. The WECTU officer clicked off his pen, got out of the chair and slipped after him.

MacReady waited a beat, quietly seething at the insinuation he couldn't be trusted, that the incident with Charlie Beck still reverberated, then followed them out of the kitchenette.

*

Timothy Coe was a nobody.

MacReady hadn't had the opportunity to take a good look at him until now. Yesterday, at St David's, it had been all twisted, twitching limbs and the slack-jawed, eyes-half-closed expression that came with unconsciousness. Since then MacReady had been otherwise engaged, and Coe had been hidden from view: in ambulances, in a police van, in his cell, where he'd sat and rocked and mocked them silently.

MacReady's nerves dissipated as soon as he walked into the interview room and saw Coe sitting in a plastic chair.

The man was no monster. More a disappointment.

Washed-out skin stretched over a scrawny frame, wrapped in a cheap beige sweatshirt and jeans; clothes brought from his flat to replace the paper suit he'd worn for most of yesterday after Coe's brief had complained about her client being cold. A face so bland as to be immediately forgettable: light-brown hair in a home haircut style, light-brown eyes, a shadow of light-brown stubble hooking under his jawline. Nothing distinctive about him at all, bar the nasty injury on his cheekbone, courtesy of MacReady. Coe was the guy the world took no notice of.

Until now.

Coe glanced up as MacReady and his colleagues entered the interview room. That smile Beck had mentioned, curling the man's lips slightly at the corners. Serene, but his eyes were red-rimmed and wouldn't settle on anyone, anything, as if he was jacked on amphet. His legal team, already assembled at great public expense, flanking him. His solicitor, her assistant, a tall, cardigan-wearing woman – even in this heat – from Social Services, looking apologetic and a little lost, as if she'd found herself on the wrong side of the table and didn't quite know what to do about it.

Detective Inspector Evans and the WECTU suit sat opposite Coe and company. MacReady closed the door and pulled a chair over to it, sitting away from his colleagues. Waited, pretending to read through the notes in his folder as they made small talk with Coe's legal team. Pretended some more as Evans fired everything up and started proceedings: the recorder, the opening spiel, the caution, asking the people present in the room to introduce themselves – MacReady learned the Counter-Terrorism spook was a detective constable called Chris Williams.

Coe stared at him when MacReady stated his name for the recording. The man's eyes, thinning into slits for a few seconds, then shifting elsewhere when MacReady refused to look away.

And then they were off. Evans, using open questions. Who, what, where, why, when. His voice clipped but calm. MacReady listened, was quickly up to speed with where the interviewing teams were with their prisoner – in previous sessions they'd tried to cover his flat, his background, his work experience as a security guard at St David's shopping centre – which, as was more or less immediately apparent as Evans put question after question to Timothy Coe, was pretty much nowhere.

The homemade devices. His religious and political leanings. Friends, relatives. Places he frequented, things he did in his spare time. The reason for his attempted attack on the restaurant. On and on, Coe remaining silent throughout. That smile, already annoying.

After half an hour Evans leaned back in his chair, ran a thick hand over the plump curve of his stomach. Threw a sideways glance at MacReady. Turned back to Coe.

'How do you know Heidi Paxton?'

The smile never faltered but MacReady saw it instantly: the briefest of twitches in Coe's right eye.

Fucker, he thought.

There was no reply from Coe.

Evans caught it too. Shifted forwards, staring at the prisoner. Williams, the WECTU officer, sensed something and looked up from his scribbles, interest piqued at last.

'Why were you at the rear of Cardiff Central railway station three days ago,' Evans asked, 'just after nine thirty in the morning?'

Nothing. MacReady ground his teeth. He'd expected a bit more piss and vinegar from the detective inspector, but he was going easy. Being respectful, even. Obviously saved the attitude for junior officers with whom he could play tough guy. And this was MacReady's territory, it had been agreed before they came in.

Coe continued to smile away.

Williams finally spoke. MacReady almost flinched.

'How do you know Nazir Uddin, Timothy?' The WECTU man's voice businesslike to the point of being monotone. 'We know you've been running together. We're interrogating your computer equipment and will find whatever you have been doing with him.'

Stick with Heidi, MacReady silently urged. *You saw the reaction. Lean on him.*

Coe's chest pushed in and out, his mouth clamped into that smirk, his eyes drifting around the ceiling as Evans pointed at him.

'Was it Uddin who piloted the drone, Tim?' Evans asked.

Tim. Like they were best buds. MacReady gave a small shake of his head.

'Do you know where Nazir Uddin is now?' Williams cut in. 'His family is worried, Tim. We're worried. He needs to come in, so he's safe.'

Evans puffed air through rubbery lips. 'We have both you and Nazir Uddin in central Cardiff when Heidi Paxton was attacked. We're in the process of comparing forensic evidence gathered from you with the Paxton scene. Is it going to match, Tim?'

MacReady fidgeted in his seat; this was painful. The DI was weak and the Counter-Terrorism officer was jumping about too much with his questions, not pushing Coe at all on any single point. Not focusing on one strand at a time. He opened his folder, wrote in the corner of a blank sheet. Ripped the corner off and handed it to the DI.

Evans took it, saw the large pound sign. MacReady wanted him to stick with Heidi Paxton, put the arm on Coe about her bank account, about the hefty sum of money and where it came from. Maybe even get a word in edgeways himself.

'Thank you, DC MacReady.'

MacReady felt someone looking him. Checked up to find Timothy Coe regarding him again at the mention of his name, those shifty eyes suddenly still. The smile, present but dimmed.

A flash of something across Coe's face – anger, perhaps.

MacReady returned the stare. Saw it happen: the smile finally slip at the moment of recognition.

Coe knew who he was. That MacReady was the copper who'd taken him out.

He was rattled. And now was the perfect time to capitalise on it.

'Why were you ringing Heidi?' MacReady asked. *Fuck the note.*

Evans threw him a withering look, the torn piece of paper disappearing as his hand formed into a fist.

Coe was motionless. Breathing softly, bugging eyeballs on MacReady.

'And why was she ringing you?' he continued. 'There are numerous calls on her phone from you. The night before she died. The morning she was murdered. And she called you, too. Many times. How did you know her?'

Nothing but the heavy breaths of Evans next to him. Williams was arms folded and looking at the floor.

'Were you giving her money? Paying her for something? Was she working for you, or somebody you know? Because there's a hell of a lot of cash sitting in her bank account right now, and nobody can explain why it's there.'

The smile, returning again. MacReady wanted to launch himself across the table and pummel Coe until he begged him to stop.

'I interviewed an old friend of yours,' MacReady gave a broad smile in return. 'It was quite illuminating. How you behaved in front of her. What she thought about you. And the lies you told her. Your army days, Mister Coe? The ones you made up to impress a woman? Isn't that right, SouljahBoy?'

Coe's eye twitched again. Beneath it the smile, pasted on his mouth.

'Is that why you killed Heidi Paxton? Because you were dumped by a woman who finally found out what a fraud you are, what a faker –'

'*Officer*,' the solicitor cautioned. A slow shake of her head.

MacReady ignored her. 'She knew what a complete loser you are, right? You couldn't even pull a waitress in a stupid curry restaurant . . .'

A sharp intake of breath beside him, Evans's face colouring slightly. The WECTU suit, sighing audibly. Coe's solicitor still shaking her head, but more vigorously now.

'. . . so decided to take it out on a defenceless young woman who'd spent the last few years looking after her mother and –'

'People react to fear, not love.'

It was Coe.

The room seemed suddenly airless. Still. The only movement the Social Services woman's wide eyes, panning left and right, the rest of her scared to shift even a millimetre.

MacReady watched as Coe tilted his head. Spread his arms outwards.

The smile broader than ever.

Coe's solicitor broke the spell. 'I'm, er . . . I think this might be a good time to take a comfort break.' She looked at her client, at his spread-eagled arms and beatific smile. Back to MacReady. 'Can we terminate the interview? Please?'

*

'So talk me through it,' Fletcher said, as he closed the main CID suite door.

Locked it.

Fletcher, Beck, Harrison and Echols. They'd come down from the MIR after lunch, had been waiting for MacReady to return to the offices after the interview, for an update on Timothy Coe, for news of some kind of breakthrough. He'd walked in to find Fletcher on the phone again, rubbing at his temples and eyeing MacReady with displeasure – Evans or Williams, obviously on the other end of the line.

'It went quite well,' MacReady offered. Checked around. Harrison stuffing his face with a prawn sandwich, Beck pretending to be busy, Echols staring at MacReady, face set with hostility.

'Right,' Fletcher said, drawing the word out. He sighed, dropped himself into a chair next to MacReady's desk. '*Quite well* as in, you're never interviewing Coe again? That sort of *quite well*?'

MacReady exhaled. 'Least I managed to get him to say something.'

'There is that.'

'You should have seen them,' MacReady shrugged. 'That DI, Evans, he was weak as piss. And the spook, I don't even know what game he was playing. The pair of them, shifting from one topic to the next, no build-up or effort to put the arm on Coe. All nicey-nice, to a guy who was prepped to blow up the city's biggest shopping centre. There was no pressure on him at all. Nothing. At least until I had a crack at him.'

'This is the part', Fletcher leaned forwards, looked into Mac-Ready's eyes, 'where, if anyone asks, I got all discipline-happy and told you off for your behaviour in the interview room, right?'

MacReady narrowed his eyes, studying Fletcher's. 'Um . . . right.'

'And for riling my colleague Detective Inspector Lloyd Evans, who has just been bending my ear on the blower, which meant I had to talk to the prick –'

'Prize prick,' Harrison muttered, one cheek stuffed like a hamster's.

'Prize prick, thank you, DC Harrison,' Fletcher nodded, 'for ten minutes, which is ten minutes of my life I will never, ever get back.'

Beck glanced over. 'He's right about Evans being weak as piss, too. If that helps.'

'There,' said Fletcher, and pushed himself out of the chair. 'You've been told.'

MacReady shook his head, confused. 'Is . . . is that it?'

'My fuckin' thoughts exactly, man,' Echols called across the room. 'Is that the way we do things round here?'

Fletcher placed a hand to his chin, held it there while he pretended to think.

'Yes. Now, while the gang's all here, why don't you three,' he pointed from MacReady to Harrison to Echols, 'get your tiny little minds together on Nazir Uddin. You've all spoken to his old man, you've been poking around. Tell me something, please. I have to be upstairs sharpish to update the SIO with anything we have.'

Echols and Harrison swapped glances.

'Well, he's full of shit,' Echols offered, reclining in his chair and swinging a shoe up to the desk. 'Everyone we've spoken to says that he can lie for Britain. Is always making stuff up.'

Harrison slipped out his notebook, thumbed through its pages. 'The father told us pretty much what he told Willy-boy. Added that they fell out late last year because Nazir thought his old man was being too strict and over-protective. There was tension between them about the business, too. Apparently Nazir wanted to play a bigger role in the property empire but Daddy wasn't having any of it. Thinks his kid is useless, basically. The dad still doesn't want to report him missing, either. And we've checked with the family members in London and Nazir was definitely with them.'

'Not jihadist training in Syria, then?' asked Beck, head peeping over her computer.

'Nope. Plenty of coving and hanging doors, though.'

'We've liaised with Special Branch, and they have no record of him at all,' said Echols. 'Clean as a whistle.'

Another cleanskin, thought MacReady.

'No flights, either,' said Harrison, flicking over a page in his notebook. 'We did the last two years, he didn't leave the country once.'

Fletcher sighed. Turned to MacReady. 'Did Coe say *anything* in the interview about why he had Nazir Uddin with him the other day?'

'Nothing. Just that one line, *people react to fear*, or whatever it was. Nothing else.'

'I've spoken to most of the people who attend the mosque,' said Echols, 'and Warren did the kid's friends and acquaintances. The overwhelming response was that Nazir is a huge fantasist. In his own little world, either sat drooling in front of a laptop or blagging his way through real life. Hates us too, by all accounts. Really anti-police, and has openly told people he'd do anything to make our job harder than it already is.'

'Probably applied to join the Job and failed to get in,' offered Beck.

'Yup,' nodded Harrison.

'Jesus,' Fletcher muttered. Looked around the room. 'Fine. I'll précis it for the chief super but make sure you upload what you have to the system too. It'll give them something to work through while I'm otherwise engaged.'

'You on a jolly?' asked Beck.

Fletcher shook his head. 'I wish. The Alex Castle trial has been shifted to Newport Crown. It restarts Tuesday morning, after the Bank Holiday. I've got meetings with the CPS about it. As if we haven't got enough to be –'

'Wait,' blurted MacReady. He sat upright, gripped the arms of his chair. 'The Castle trial. That's how I know him.'

Confusion on Fletcher's face. 'You know Alex Castle? What?'

'Nazir Uddin,' MacReady said. He swung around, rattled at the keyboard with fingers which shook slightly. 'The name, it's been nagging at me since day one. I knew I'd come across him before. I can't believe I didn't remember sooner.'

Fletcher walked over, stood behind MacReady. 'Uddin was involved? I've never heard of him before, and I'd know the name if he was part of the case.'

'Look,' MacReady said, pointing at the screen. 'This is Uddin's Niche record. Pretty slim on info. He was only created on the system a couple of days ago, by the uniforms who spoke to him after the Al Mahdi went up, so not surprisingly they didn't have much to go with. I'm kicking myself here, because I didn't really take much notice of it. But we were treating him as a star witness, right?'

'He wasn't a scrote as far as I was concerned,' Fletcher said. 'So my radar was off. But go on, you've got my attention.'

'And we've been using this Niche record, since the mosque.'

Fletcher, face in hands, talking through fingers. 'Please don't tell me –'

MacReady clicked out of Uddin's record, back to the search results. Clicked again, wincing inwardly. 'I should have double-checked, because this one,' he pointed at the screen again, to another hit on Uddin's name, 'is a duplicate nominal entry, created a couple of years back.'

An audible groan from Fletcher. 'Nazir Uddin.'

'Same guy, but this time he gave a different DOB and address. His *correct* date of birth and the address at the family home, where he was obviously living before he fell out with them and did his disappearing act. It's all old stuff,' MacReady said, moving his mouse and clicking each incident. 'He has three Occurrences, where he's a reporting person in one and a complainant in two others. All three were closed as No Further Action by the response officers who dealt with them. When he was a reporting person for damage to a local park playground, the uniforms who went there were pelted with stones. And when he was a complainant where he told response he'd been racially abused, both times it turned out to be a load of nonsense. Attention-seeking, wasting police time, whatever you think he was up to, each Occurrence was closed as No Further Action because he was deemed an unreliable witness.'

'Bloody hell,' Harrison was at Fletcher's side, peering at the monitor.

MacReady shifted and clicked the mouse. 'Then last year he was a supposed witness at the start of the Alex Castle case. Rang Ops Room to say he'd been at the pub when it all went off, then saw the rumble outside. Said it was a gang of white lads that did Castle. Skinheads, racists, shouting about getting their country back. This is why his name rang a faint bell with me. I heard the name once, when the incident was in its early days.'

Fletcher was chewing at his bottom lip. 'How didn't we know about this?'

MacReady turned to look at Echols. Let his gaze stay on the detective sergeant for a few seconds, then turned back to the computer screen. 'Inquiries were made which proved Uddin was nowhere near the pub when the gang attacked Castle. He was written off by uniform, warned about providing false information. And we didn't look at him any further because the CID officer who was tasked to follow it up agreed with response that Uddin was full of shit. Except for a brief mention in the intelligence text pages he wasn't officially linked to the Castle investigation on the Niche system, so – bar that one CID officer – we never dealt with him.'

Fletcher squinted as he took in the details on screen. The collar number of the CID officer who spoke to Uddin. The skin on the DI's neck, his face, reddening as he turned to look at Echols.

'My bad,' Echols held his hands up, dropped his foot off the desk. Gave an uncomfortable cough, as if to clear something wedged in his throat.

'Didn't it fucking ring a bell with you, Paul?' Fletcher asked, incredulous. 'Not at any time when you were out and about speaking to Uddin's friends, his family? That the name was fucking familiar? That it was you who spoke to him and wrote him off? That you printed out the wrong bloody Niche record and we've been wasting our time with it ever since?'

Beck's head sunk below her computer screen. Harrison stuffed hands in pockets, whistled as he turned to look out of the window.

'No offence, boss,' Echols swallowed. 'But these names, they're all so similar, right? I mean, it only dawned on me this last minute while Will was talking – good work there, buddy, by the way – that I'd had dealings with him last year. It was only a five-minute chat –'

'My office,' Fletcher said.

Echols looked crestfallen. Sniffed, eyes to the floor, unable to look up. 'Really?'

'Really,' Fletcher replied. 'Because that's the way we do things round here.'

The DI's door slammed shut, the blinds came down. Both failed to drown out Fletcher as he bellowed. MacReady hitched his eyebrows at Beck, who mouthed a *good*. Harrison took the seat Fletcher had just vacated.

After several minutes Fletcher's door opened. A shell-shocked Echols stepped out, unlocked the main suite door and walked off down the corridor.

'He's making a brew to make up for being a twat,' Fletcher flashed a grin. 'So what are we talking about? Uddin is using deliberate misdirection?'

MacReady's fingers hovered over the keyboard at his detective inspector's comment.

'Sarge,' he said to Beck. 'You got the mosque recording to hand?'

'The bomber?'

MacReady nodded, climbed out of his chair and walked over to Beck's desk. Harrison, breathing heavily behind as he followed him across the room. Fletcher dumped himself into a spare seat next to Beck as she clicked through her video files.

'This is the front camera,' she said.

There he was. Their black-clad figure, striding towards the main doors of the Al Mahdi Mosque. Average height, slim-to-average build. Hat, jacket, shades, his gloved hands clutching the top of a rucksack.

'Pause it,' MacReady said.

Beck clicked her mouse button; the video halted. 'And?'

'Uddin was definitely there a short while after the attack, yes?'

Harrison nodded. 'I showed the photograph to the pair of uniforms who spoke to Uddin. They said it was definitely him who was there, and who gave them the only description of the bomber that we have.'

'Yeah, *white male, slim, dressed in black . . .*' MacReady moved in closer to the screen. 'Can you go forwards frame by frame? Slow as possible?'

Beck clicked on a drop-down menu, made the adjustments. 'Tell me when.'

After a couple of seconds MacReady said, 'Stop. Right there.' His face, almost pressed against the monitor.

'See something?' Fletcher asked. There was undisguised tiredness in his voice now. He'd had enough, the days of adrenalin and snatched sleep finally taking hold of him.

'Do you have the images we sent out to the media?' MacReady asked Beck. 'The ones we enlarged?'

More clicking and dragging from Beck. An image of the mosque bomber flashed up, filling the screen. The picture good quality, despite its size.

Harrison gave a bored sigh. 'You going to faff about or just tell us what's up? Are you thinking this is the guy who did Park Place, too?'

Fletcher pushed the heels of his palms into his eyes. Rubbed for a few seconds. Looked around, stretching his face, he looked utterly exhausted. 'Yeah, come on, Will. Because I'm due to brief the Specialist Crime detective chief super in about ten minutes, and there'll be questions a go-go about what we're doing to stop this turd doing it again.'

MacReady pictured Park Place, the epicentre of the blast, the surrounding buildings and businesses. 'I think we're mistaken about the reason.'

'The reason?' Fletcher asked.

'For the attacks. All of us, the police, the media, the government – we've been working on the assumption that this is a race thing. That it's been sparked by the Castle case, and our nutter –'

'Nutters,' Harrison offered.

'And our nutters,' MacReady continued, 'are targeting BME people in retaliation. The ethnic market, the mosque. The Indian restaurant in St David's Centre. We just assumed they were revenge attacks by a lone wolf. But Park Place . . .'

Fletcher twirled a finger. *Hurry up.* 'Your point?'

MacReady turned to look at him. 'Well, if it's racially motivated, if it's a deranged white guy out to murder people of colour because of the Alex Castle murder, why blow up a fake American burger chain and an overpriced cocktail lounge owned by Cardiff's biggest tax-fiddling businessman – who happens to be white?'

Fletcher stood quietly for a second. Absorbing what MacReady had just said. Then: 'I need more than this to take it upstairs.'

'Well, I think Uddin lied to us again.' MacReady extended a finger to the computer screen, traced it along the arm of the mosque bomber, to the hand that held the rucksack full of homemade pipe bombs. Where, when the attacker had swung the rucksack backwards, a tiny gap had appeared between the bomber's sleeve and glove. 'Why, I don't know. What he was there for, I don't know. Why we didn't double-check all this, instead of running with the assumption it was a race war starting, again, I don't know. But what I do know is Uddin told us a white male blew up the Al Mahdi . . .'

Fletcher leaned in close. Stared at the gap MacReady was pointing at.

'And that looks like dark skin.'

Twenty-two

While Harrison and a chastened Echols headed across Cardiff Bay for Penarth and Nazir Uddin's family, MacReady took the city's back roads towards Whitchurch.

Towards Heidi Paxton's parents.

The long route. Country lanes and fields of crisp, sun-dried grass. Pockets of houses, the River Taff to his right, the M4 visible to the north, the first green slopes and old slag heaps of the Valleys beyond. He needed time to think. How much to tell the Paxtons? What to ask without giving away the fact that their daughter – their quiet, loving daughter – was somehow connected to the attacks which had caused panic across the Welsh capital and beyond? Any last shred of energy they had, any vestige of courage to see this through, would evaporate if they learned that Heidi had been involved.

And MacReady was beginning to think it might be out of his hands anyway.

He skirted Cardiff's western flank, windows down, a breeze cooling his forearms as he cut across the river and joined the A470 to head south. Letting the CID car drift along, letting his mind do likewise. The first time in days, it seemed, that he'd had space to let his thoughts wander.

Timothy Coe knew Nazir Uddin. Heidi Paxton and Coe also knew each other – their mobile phones bore that out. But what had their relationship been? And the money in Heidi's bank account – where had it come from, and why?

Then there was Nazir Uddin. Police-hater. Perpetual bull-shitter. When they finally found him, at the least he would be arrested for attempting to pervert the course of justice. The mosque attacker definitely wasn't white. Specialist Crime author-ised image enhancement on the hurry-up, but with time against them Beck had emailed the Technical Support Unit at HQ, told them to drop everything else while they worked on the mosque CCTV still using specialist software. All the changes made to the original – the sharpening of edges and mapping of colours, the noise reduction and decreasing motion blur – could be written up in a statement by the techie as and when. The senior inves-tigating officer just wanted the image done, and fast. Twenty minutes after she'd emailed the original, the enhanced version dropped into Beck's inbox for them all to see.

Uddin's lies had made them blind to what was in front of them; they'd ignored it, had gone with the narrative of a lone-wolf white male, a far-right, ethnic-minority-hating nationalist. Their very own Anders Behring Breivik.

In fact, it was a black or Asian male.

That solitary, minuscule patch of dark skin between the sleeve and glove.

MacReady came off the Coryton interchange and accelerated into Whitchurch village. Had it been Nazir Uddin all along? Did he, somehow, get from Cardiff to Penarth quickly enough to attack the Al Mahdi? And was it Uddin who was responsible for the drone attack in Park Place yesterday evening?

It had to be. *Had* to be.

Coe and Uddin, working together. But to what end? And if it wasn't racially motivated, why? There had been no code words, no Virginia Tech-style manifesto sent to news outlets, no motives or claims of responsibility from either man. And where the fuck was Uddin now?

So many questions. Too many. MacReady wanted to be shaking Aadhil Uddin until he coughed to his son's whereabouts. Not Harrison doing it, not that useless Echols. He wanted to be in Penarth himself, right now, putting the arm on the whole family until Nazir was located.

Fletcher had sensed MacReady's mood, told him to go and see Heidi's parents.

'They trust you,' the DI had said as the room cleared following the viewing of Tech Support's enhanced photograph. 'There's a connection there. Tell the parents personally that their daughter is now part of this larger investigation and we have someone in the pokey for it. We're going to be stripping out her bedroom, so tread carefully when you advise them, all right, Will? Lay the groundwork for us to come in but don't go spooking the poor bastards. The old man, for one, I don't think he can take much more before he just curls into a ball in the corner of his bathroom.'

Tread carefully. MacReady pulled up to the kerb. *Yeah, right. And how am I supposed to do that? Heidi's parents aren't stupid.*

Blinds and curtains drawn, still. The Paxtons' house with its eyes closed against the outside world. Mark Paxton at the door MacReady had just knocked on, a ghost of the man he'd met at the University Hospital just two days ago, as he shuffled backwards, opening the door wide. MacReady nodded a thanks and stepped into the hallway, breathing on sour air.

Simone Paxton pulled him down, pulled him close, as he entered the lounge.

'It's good to see you, Will,' she said quietly into his ear, arms folded around his shoulders. Palms of her hands pressing against the middle of his back; he could feel the desperation there, as if she didn't want to let go. He wondered when Mark Paxton had last hugged his wife.

MacReady held onto her for a good ten seconds, eyeing the family liaison officer who watched them from the kitchen doorway. Mug in hand, sorrowful expression on his face. MacReady hitched his eyebrows, gave a weak smile.

'I have some news,' he said, and eased from her embrace. His throat suddenly dry. He swallowed, checked from Simone to Mark Paxton. The father, eyes on something only he could see, not even looking at his wife, at MacReady. Simone Paxton staring up at MacReady, hands wringing atop her useless legs, already a glimmer of something there – hope, perhaps. Or worry that she was daring to let herself hope.

'Please let it be good,' Simone Paxton said, her voice unsteady.

'It's good,' MacReady replied. A smile for her benefit. His words, chosen very carefully. 'We have a male in custody in connection with Heidi's murder.'

Simone Paxton tilted her head back, drew air in through an open mouth. Closed her eyes. 'Oh, thank God.'

It was as if someone had flicked a switch. Mark Paxton was at MacReady's side in an instant, holding onto his forearm, fingers tight. Eyes, bright and lucid and glittering angrily, locked onto MacReady's. 'Who is it? Do we know him?'

'No, you don't know –'

'Is it somebody from here? One of her friends?'

His fingers were clamped against MacReady's skin. Painfully so.

'Mark,' MacReady soothed. 'You don't know him. I don't know him. He came to my attention . . . to our attention yesterday, and this morning he was arrested on suspicion of murdering Heidi. That's all I can tell you.'

'Because that's all you're allowed to bloody say, yes?'

'Because that's all I know at the moment,' MacReady lied.

Mark Paxton's hand fell away as he stalked off and dropped into an armchair. Began sobbing. MacReady looked at his forearm, red welts there. Looked to Simone Paxton, saw the tilt of her head, her bottom lip trembling as she regarded her broken husband. Heard footsteps, the family liaison officer walking back into the room to squat down and place an arm around Mark Paxton's shoulders.

'We need to take a look at Heidi's bedroom again,' MacReady said. Trying to talk as softly as possible. 'When I checked it the other day it was because I was treating her case as a robbery that had gone wrong. But due to new information that's come to light we need to search the room with a fresh set of eyes.'

'You said *we*,' Simone Paxton said. 'Who's *we*?'

'Are you happy for Heidi's bedroom to be searched, Simone?'

'I . . . Of course, if it helps, anything to help. But who's *we*, Will?'

MacReady swallowed again. Keyed the transmit button on his Airwave handset.

Said, 'You can come in now.'

The unmistakeable sound of diesel engines, the sharp *scree* of brakes from the street, audible even through windows, through thick curtains. Then the clatter of the front door against hallway wall. The thump of boots on tiles, the drumming of rubberised soles, the swish of paper booties, loud and jarring in this place of drawn-out silences and shadows.

Simone Paxton's glassy eyes drifted past MacReady, to the lounge door.

Widened. Shifted back to MacReady.

'You said you have someone in custody in connection with Heidi's murder,' she said. 'You said he came to your attention yesterday . . .'

'To our attention, yes.'

'To *your* attention, you said. And yesterday was when you tackled that man in the shopping centre. In St David's.'

'Simone –'

'Don't lie to me, Will,' Simone Paxton cried. 'Not now. Not *ever*. You're the only thing we have to hold onto at the moment. What was my daughter involved with? Tell us. Tell us, *please*.'

MacReady stood motionless. Felt eyes burn into him: the Paxtons', the family liaison officer's.

'We'll just crack straight on then, yeah?'

The man at the lounge door was tall, buzz-cut blond, flabby. A once-muscular frame gone south, bulging in all the wrong places beneath his black PolSA uniform overalls. Two pips on each shoulder.

'Yes please, sir,' MacReady replied. 'The bedroom is right at the top of the house.'

The inspector considered the scene in the lounge for a few seconds. Sniffed. Started saying something then thought better of it. Began to turn away.

'Please,' MacReady said, and the Territorial Support Group inspector paused. 'Please be as careful as you can. With her things. We're trying to keep it low-key here.'

The inspector glanced over his shoulder. Nodded towards the front of the house.

'Good luck with that,' he said, and made for the stairs.

MacReady stepped over to the window. Pulled back the curtains, just a little.

Saw Klaudia Solak on the pavement outside, thumb working the screen of her mobile.

Felt his phone buzz in his pocket.

MacReady eased the phone out, looked at Solak's text message.

Are you in Whitchurch? We've just followed your mini-army from Cardiff Bay . . .

He turned to Heidi Paxton's mother and said, 'Simone, I'm truly sorry.'

*

It was the moment the Paxtons finally realised their daughter was never coming back.

Her room was completely cleared out, anything and every-thing Heidi Paxton had ever touched, brushed against, laid eyes on. MacReady had watched, standing in their lounge as search officers trampled up and down stairs and out into the street, carrying the television, the bed and its bedding, a gaming rig. Everything from the rugs and throws to a used sponge that had been in her en suite, bagged and tagged and taken away. CSI technicians moving in immediately afterwards, humping sacks and equipment and cameras to the dead woman's room.

It was like defilement. The removal of the last remaining parts of her personality.

And the Paxtons had been inconsolable.

They'd understood, though. MacReady had explained why they were stripping Heidi's bedroom back to its walls. Had sat down next to them, held Simone Paxton's hands, talked quietly for an hour about forensic opportunities, about having to break things down to build them back up again as part of the case. So he could find out who killed their daughter. All the while avoid-ing how she might be linked to the bombings in some way. He'd wanted to spare them that pain.

It had been exhausting to do it, and they'd thanked him as he left, but as he'd pulled the front door of their house closed and stepped into the sunlight he'd caught the sobs and imagined them clinging to each other on the sofa as they wept.

*

MacReady stood at the window in the half-light, naked body slick with sweat, the sun setting on another shitty day. Behind him Klaudia Solak lay prone on her bed, arm draped over a pillow, foot dangling off the edge of the mattress. Watching him intently, one eye obscured by a whorl of dark hair. Scrunched beneath her shiny skin a thin cotton sheet, tangled and warm from their lovemaking.

'They would've found out sooner or later,' she said, and rolled onto her back. MacReady could just about make out her reflection in the glass; it was faint, ghostlike. Her soft curves shimmered in the weakening sunlight, and his breath caught in his throat.

She was beautiful. Despite what she'd done at St David's, he knew she was good for him. And after the misery of the Paxtons she'd been the person he'd sought out upon finishing work.

Not Duncan Jones, asking him to put some beers in the fridge so he could spend the night drowning his sorrows. Not Megan, begging her to let him spend some time with Finlay.

It had been Solak.

'I'd have preferred later.'

'Sometimes it's best to just get it out in the open,' she offered.

'Like we are now?' he asked, not turning around to look at her. 'With Charlie? With my job?'

He heard springs shift in the bed, knew she was moving around again. 'Perhaps.'

MacReady nodded without turning to look at her. Placed a hand up to the glass, tilted the window open further. The sea breeze, cool on his face, his chest. The water between Cardiff and Penarth reflecting the sun onto him, a glorious mélange of oranges and reds and yellows.

'It's all so . . .' he said, but couldn't finish. Closed his eyes.

He didn't hear her until she was behind him. Felt her slipping her arms around his midriff, pulling herself to him. Her head, nestling between his shoulder blades. No jokes or teasing or sarcasm. Just her warm breaths on his skin, her face pressed tight, arms squeezed tighter.

'I'm getting a little concerned about you, Will,' she said quietly.

'Me too,' he said, and chuckled.

'It'll come good,' Solak offered, holding him close. 'Eventually. It always does.'

MacReady shook his head. He thought about Timothy Coe, still refusing to speak. About the Paxtons. About his marriage.

'I'm not so sure that it will.'

Solak took hold of MacReady's upper arms, turned him around to face her. 'I can help you, you know.'

'I thought the agreement was not to talk shop,' he replied. 'That these are just our, what did you call them, *shared therapy sessions*?'

'We can put Coe everywhere for you,' Solak said, squeezing his arm. 'Just give me something I can use, something different, and I can make sure he's never out of the public's consciousness, not until someone comes forward with more information. Like today. What's the connection with the house in Whitchurch? Nobody would talk to us.'

MacReady tried to wriggle from her grasp. Felt a surge of anger at Solak, still looking for an angle, an in. Something she could use, for their investigation, for him, but mostly for herself now the world's media had descended and she'd morphed into the little fish in a big pond. 'This is why we have an agreement.'

'You know yourself it'll die away in a few days. Zero coverage. The public will move on now you have your man. The pressure is officially off. Your own chief constable said it at his press conference this morning – you need all the help you can get. I can be that help. I won't let Coe fade away.'

He thought about the presser the chief had given: a brief statement, taking no questions. Deliberate vagueness. Describing Coe as the man they were looking for. That he was being *extremely* helpful to police.

And no mention of a second bomber.

'Klaudia, you don't understand –'

She let go of him. 'You don't seem to understand, Will. I'd be doing this for you. I hate seeing you like this and I think I –'

'Coe is not the only bomber.' MacReady winced as it came out. Placed thumb and forefinger up to his closed eyes and pushed at the lids.

Silence for a few seconds. Then: 'Are you fucking *joking*?'

MacReady looked down at her. 'This stays between us. Promise me. *Please.*'

Solak took a step back from him. Regarded him with utter astonishment. 'So the chief con lied?'

'Not lied, as such,' MacReady shrugged. It felt odd that they were naked now. The mood had changed, and he cast his eyes around, looking for his clothes. 'It's a hedging of bets, a gamble. The chief constable and his team, they came up with it after speaking to the SIO, with the head of Communications. They're convinced they can break Coe, get him to tell us who the other bomber is, where he is.' He didn't mention Nazir Uddin's name to Solak. After the revelations about MacReady and Solak's relationship following the foiled St David's attack, any leaks and Fletcher would be looking straight at him. 'If he doesn't give it up by Sunday night, maybe Monday morning at the latest, they're going to go public. Give out whatever we've got while people are off work for the Bank Holiday. Larger audience. They felt it was the best strategy.'

'Some strategy,' Solak replied. Her voice had risen slightly, incredulous. She was pacing back and forth in front of him, her nakedness completely forgotten. 'What if your prisoner doesn't talk at all? If there's another attack, what then? You lot are going to look pretty bloody stupid. Not to mention incompetent.'

'They don't want to spook the public further, and are hoping something – Coe, forensics, I don't know – will lead us to the other bomber before he hits us again. I'm not totally in the loop so I don't know what they're cooking up or what they've got up their sleeves. But, believe me, the pressure is most definitely not off.'

'Christ,' muttered Solak. Her head, shaking from side to side. 'I dread to think of the legal ramifications if there's another bomb and more people are killed.'

MacReady walked over to the bed, lowered himself down to it and covered himself with the twisted sheet. 'Why do you think the chief was so ambiguous?' he asked, eyes left and right, following Solak as she paced in front of the window. 'But it's a risk, I agree. I sat in on the interview with Coe this morning. Anything we throw at him, he's refusing to reply. I just hope the hierarchy know what they're doing.'

'The public need to know, Will. They should be in the loop. Even though they think you have "your man" in custody, there are still a lot of really frightened people in this city right now.'

MacReady thought about Coe, about what he'd said. The only thing he'd said during hours of interviews. The arrogance of the man, sitting with arms spread. Grinning.

'*People react to fear, not love*,' MacReady sighed. He was tired now. Glanced about, searching for his shoes, his trousers. Became aware that Solak had stopped pacing.

He turned to look at her. Found her staring at him, head cocked. Eyes narrowed.

'What did you just say?'

Her expression, he couldn't work it out. Shock, maybe? 'I, er, it was something Coe said. The only thing he said, actually. I was pressing him about something and he just came out with it.'

'People react to fear, not love. Yes?'

MacReady nodded. 'Have I said anything wrong, Klaudia?'

Solak wasn't listening. Was striding across the bedroom, eyes flitting right then left, searching for something. She stopped next to a small armchair, bent down, came up with her iPad. Marched over to the bed, to a confused MacReady. Sat next to him, the mattress bouncing a little.

'Look at this,' she urged. Swiping and typing. On the screen: a website, amateurish but jammed with text. Coverage of the Alex Castle trial. Posts on the police's handling of the case. References – all in angry block capitals – to Stephen Lawrence, to Mark Duggan, to *rising up and fighting the power*. His thoughts flickered to Faria Begum, what she'd said about Coe, ranting and raving outside the restaurant about *how people like him were rising up, that the world was going to listen to them . . .*

MacReady skimmed the sidebars, saw lots of political topics, social justice campaigns, anti-government rants. 'I remember. This is that blogger whose work you're so enamoured with.'

'And look at this,' she tapped her finger on a link on the sidebar.

Up flashed one of the blogger's articles.

The title: *People React to Fear, Not Love.*

'My God,' said MacReady. He leaned in, read through the piece. It was well written, articulate, but the content troubling. 'It's like a manifesto for the bombings.'

'Yup,' nodded Solak, looking from MacReady to the screen. ' "When mankind can't find truth, untruth is converted to truth via violence." Which is nice, isn't it? Anyway there's lots of stuff about taking power back from the elites, the establishment. By any means necessary. The struggle, and all that. I remember reading it a few months back and laughing about it. Doesn't seem so funny now.'

MacReady looked at the date it was posted. Eight months ago. 'What are the most recent entries from this guy?' he asked.

Solak continued flicking through the website. 'I told you. He was adding fresh content a couple of times a day, but there's been nothing since the night before the first bomb –'

'Fuck,' MacReady said. Felt his skin prickle. Felt his guts lurch. 'Will?'

Solak, studying him now. iPad forgotten.

MacReady groaned a *Nononononooo*. Squeezed his eyes shut, balled his hands into fists, lowered his forehead onto the knuckles. Pictured Timothy Coe and Nazir Uddin. Pictured a bedroom – spacious, private – where the occupant spent significant amounts of time alone on a laptop, earning a pittance. Thought of a bank account, containing a major amount of money that couldn't be explained. Of grieving parents who had no clue what their daughter was up to in her room.

Of the blogger's website, which hadn't been updated since the day of the first bombings.

Since Heidi Paxton was murdered.

MacReady turned to Solak. 'You're sure it's a guy writing that thing?'

She shrugged. 'I always assumed so. Why?'

MacReady checked around. At the detritus – clothing, paperwork, bunches of keys, abandoned as they had rolled around the room. Remembered Solak's question:

What's the connection with the house in Whitchurch?

'I really need to find my phone,' he told her.

*

'I'll make some more coffee.'

Gone one in the morning in the CID suite. MacReady gave Beck a thumbs-up, not taking his eyes from the laptop screen in front of him.

Heidi Paxton's laptop. Recovered from her bedroom. Removed from its evidence bag after authorisation from the senior investigating officer. Cracked by the HQ technician who now sat beside MacReady.

Its contents enough to confirm that Heidi was Klaudia Solak's favourite blogger. All the articles, the comment pieces, the thoughts and observations from the blog were there, in Word documents, on the dead woman's computer.

'Two sugars for me,' the techie said. MacReady glanced at him: early thirties, good-looking if you ignored the blond power-ballad hair, and clearly keen on Beck. The man's brows dovetailed, eyes following Beck's backside as she traipsed over to the tea makings.

'You've got no chance,' MacReady muttered out of the side of his mouth.

'Married?'

MacReady couldn't be bothered explaining. 'Something like that.'

He'd called it in from Solak's apartment, the DI telling him to come back into work so they could run everything by the detective chief superintendent. By the time he'd returned

to Cardiff Bay the Major Incident Room was full of specialist crime officers and most of the station's senior command
team, a motley bunch of pips and spaghetti-shouldered clones
plus hangers-on, most of whom hadn't stayed up this late for
a decade or more. It had taken MacReady five minutes to give
details of what he'd discovered, before the SIO clapped his
hands together.

'You work it,' he'd said, pointing at MacReady. Checked his
watch. 'It's just after eleven. I'll authorise overtime for you plus
one –'

'Sergeant Beck,' MacReady had said, then pointed at Paxton's
laptop, at her PlayStation and its controllers. 'And I'll need tech
support, sir. In case those are protected or encrypted.'

'Plus a civvy for the laptop and game console, then,' the detective chief super replied. Jabbed a finger at the people gathered
in front of him. 'The rest of you – home. We start again in the
morning with whatever DC MacReady can dig up for us to use
when we next interview Coe. Zero-seven-hundred hours start,
ladies and gents.'

And the Major Incident Room had cleared, Harrison grumbling about not getting any of the overtime, Fletcher visibly
relieved to be going home and getting some sleep in his own
bed for the first time in days; he had a trip east to Newport for
his urgent weekend CPS strategy meeting at nine a.m., ready for
the Castle trial restart. When the last person was out of the door,
MacReady and Beck made straight for the CID suite.

'Better biscuits there,' she'd smiled.

Now, MacReady shifted his attention back to the laptop. Wondered what he was going to say to Heidi's parents. If there was any way he could avoid telling them that their outwardly timid and loving daughter had been a full-blown internet warrior, a borderline anarchist with an online life and alternative personality they simply would not have recognised.

Would, in fact, be horrified about.

He'd been working the laptop for two hours straight. And it was all there: Paxton's rants, her musings and diary entries, the scraps and thoughts and inner workings of a mind that seemed completely at odds with the picture of the young woman Simone and Mark Paxton had painted. MacReady was getting ever further down the rabbit hole; one article would lead to another internet link, to a particular date on her calendar, then onwards, deeper, until the opinion pieces and snippets of paragraphs and draft Facebook posts morphed into caps-lock rages that screamed off the screen.

They were yet to fire up Paxton's PlayStation. It was already too much, even for two of them. A team working around the clock would take four or five days to wade through a quarter of what MacReady had managed to dig up on the laptop alone, to work out the reasons for the attacks. Why Coe and Uddin had chosen their targets and why.

And they didn't have four or five days. Nazir Uddin was still out there.

Beck, at his side. 'I think it's safe to say she seems . . . a little odd.'

'Thanks, Charlie,' said the techie, taking the mug she offered. Smiling up at her.

'This stuff is just . . .' MacReady took the mug from Beck's hand, shook his head. 'I can't even describe it. It's like it's not her.'

'You never knew Heidi, Will. You can't possibly know what she was really like.'

The techie chuckled. 'Nobody knows what people are really like, though, do they?'

They ignored him, so he sipped at his coffee.

Beck took a seat, rolled closer to MacReady. 'So tell me, how did you find out about Paxton being the blogger again?'

MacReady pictured Klaudia Solak. Naked. 'Just . . . digging about.'

'That digging again,' Beck replied coolly.

'Look at this, though,' MacReady said. He aimed his pen at the screen. 'She's set the system to delete her search history, cookies, everything she comes into contact with online, every two hours. And she's systematically cleared her emails. Nothing in the inbox, drafts, bin, nothing. All of them deleted. No contacts. A total wipe. She's tech-savvy all right, and has been very clever. Means we don't have email or IP addresses. But she's clearly talking to or about people,' he clicked a different tab, brought up her Google calendar, 'right across here, where she's added text entries.'

Beck squinted as she read one of the notes. '"2pm, Greyf, NCP, SouljahBoy." There's Coe, again.'

'And that'll be the NCP car park on Greyfriars Road. She was meeting Coe there.'

'Possibly to collect the money?'

MacReady shrugged. '"NUman, 7pm, The Village." There's lots of mentions of this NUman person.'

'And The Village is Whitchurch. She's been meeting him or her there.'

'"NUman",' MacReady took a slug of coffee; it was scalding, but he held it in his mouth, ignored the pain, his eyes on the name. 'Why the capital letters?'

Beck nudged MacReady with her elbow. 'Nazir Uddin. It's *got* to be.'

'Nice. So she was meeting our wanted man regularly.'

'Yeah. Until two months ago.'

A handful of clicks on the mouse, MacReady cross-referencing dates on the calendar with documents in Google Drive, on Word. Checking through reams of text, skimming titles and opening paragraphs. His heart thumping.

Then: 'There.'

He sank into his seat, giving a small shake of the head.

Beck read the words on the screen. The rambling, stream-of-consciousness text Heidi Paxton had tapped out on her keyboard the same day she dumped Nazir Uddin.

'My God, she was seeing him,' Beck said.

'And she ended the relationship,' MacReady nodded. 'And now she's dead, and her ex is probably the one who did it.'

'For breaking up with him?'

'You're asking that as if you don't know these things happen, Sarge.'

'There must be more to it than that.'

'D'you want me to take a look at her console?' the techie asked. A beaming smile at Beck again. 'Might take me a little while to get it running properly, open up her account on the system.'

Beck nodded. 'That'd be great, thanks.'

'Not a problem. Not a problem at all. I can cross-reference those usernames you've got there, too. *SouljahBoy* or whatever.'

'They're usernames?' MacReady asked.

The techie shrugged, one hand sweeping at his ridiculous golden mop as he glanced at Beck to see if she was looking his way. 'Looks like them to me. I may be wrong, but I can run through her friends list on the PlayStation Network, just to check.'

MacReady had no clue what the man was talking about. Nodded anyway, assuming he was just showing off to Beck. 'Thanks.'

The techie wandered off towards the desk with the Play-Station, whistling as he went.

'Here.' Beck took the mouse from MacReady, scrolled up and down the calendar, the weeks and months shifting in his vision. Names, times, meeting places. Dozens of nicknames. When she stopped scrolling the calendar showed September of last year. 'There's a huge amount going on here. Right up until about ten months ago. And then it just . . .'

'Drops off a cliff,' MacReady nodded. Studied Paxton's sched-ule. Busy. Beyond busy. Reminders, notifications, notes to finish articles, meet so-and-so, post blog entries. All of it dying away in the September.

'Weird,' Beck said. 'It's like she was a huge part of it up to a certain point. And then there's nothing. Like she was cut adrift or something.'

'What's weirder is that just as all the entries stop is when the money began appearing in her account. From the September. All those big amounts, where someone was paying her.'

MacReady swigged coffee, mulling over what they'd found. Felt overwhelmed by it all, felt the fatigue in his muscles, in his mind. Worried that the tiredness would make him – make them all – miss something.

'Want to come see?' the techie called across the room.

'Already?' MacReady asked.

'Magic fingers,' he replied, waggling them for effect and staring at Beck. MacReady wondered if he should put the man out of his misery.

MacReady joined the man in front of a small television, the PlayStation set up next to it whirring away, the techie's equipment – a morass of wires and black boxes – jumbled at the rear of the machine. MacReady saw the familiar icons spread across the screen; he'd seen them enough times while Duncan Jones faffed with his own console at home.

'I've had a quick look around the cross-media bar,' the techie said, using a controller to whizz it back and forth, 'and there's very little on it. No photos or music, nothing on the Spotify app or any playlists. And there's no video uploads. She has some game data on the system – *Call of Duty*, *Grand Theft Auto*, *Minecraft*, that sort of crap – but her browser is the same as on the laptop: wiped. No search history, no predictive text entries from previous searches. It's real clean, to be honest, almost like it's just come out of the box.'

'Please tell me there's a *but*,' MacReady sighed.

'Well, her PlayStation Network account throws up a few nuggets. I've got her online ID here,' he shifted his thumb on the controller.

MacReady saw it on Paxton's account details: *SHYG1rl*.

'I'm starting to think she was taking the piss,' he said.

The techie shifted his eyebrows upwards. 'Lot of it about. But anyway, those names you've got on the laptop? They're on here too. A few messages from them in her message box, but it's the same kind of stuff that she's got on her Google calendar.'

'Which doesn't really help us at all, other than provide yet more confirmation that she knew Timothy Coe and Nazir Uddin.' MacReady rolled his eyes and began to walk back to Beck. 'Thanks for your help, though.'

'And there's these two.'

MacReady paused. Turned to see the techie pointing at the screen. 'What two?'

The techie urged him to take a look. MacReady placed his hands on the edge of the desk. Leaned in close to the television.

RakKap and *RookSTAR*.

'She has no friend requests,' said the techie, 'no list of players met during online games, no interaction with anybody on the network – other than these four. It's like a little closed group or something.'

Four names. *SouljahBoy. NUman. RakKap. RookSTAR*. A private club, of which *SHYG1rl* had been a member. Until she was murdered.

'There're more of them than we thought,' MacReady whispered to himself.

'Will,' Beck called. Urgency in her voice.

At the desk he saw she'd shifted the calendar to the current month of August.

'Look at this,' she said.

MacReady saw the entries on the laptop's screen. 'Christ.'

Bess/AlMahdi. St. D's. N.Th8re.

'She's got the bombing locations listed,' Beck said. 'Bessemer Market. The Al Mahdi. St David's. And the New Theatre.'

He scanned down, blinking rapidly.

Saw *Venus*. Listed for Sunday 30 August.

For today.

Sunday

Twenty-three

Darkness. Eyes closed.

He listens to the whine, the feed of traction cables, the electric motor going about its business and then above it the unzipping of kitbags, the clickety-click of metal on metal, of things ratcheting and locking and then a loud ping and his stomach knots and he can't tell if it's because the elevator has just stopped or the enormity of what he is about to do has finally hit him.

He knows what is coming.

Eyes open.

Body armour over suit jackets, assault rifles locked and loaded: his four companions stand at the elevator doors, the circular green light above them showing '2', their faces set, waiting, a curious mix of determination and serenity, as if this is an inevitability, that it simply must be done, that this is all they exist for. One of them barks at him but he ignores it, checks his weapon, thinks about reloading, remembers the magazine is full.

Then the doors open.

And they are out.

No fuss. No yelling or running; he can't, even though he wants to, even though the adrenalin surges through him. Just five men strolling out into the hall, pausing for a moment to take in the scenery: glass and metal and walkways below high ceilings, the bright and open space lit by warning signs and directions and electronic boards, the queues for the security checkpoint three deep and lengthy, marshalled by a couple of crisply dressed police officers whose utility belts are laden with nowhere near enough for what is to come.

He studies the lines of men and women. Business people and tourists and nobodies waiting like sheep to be questioned and searched and scanned before they fly to another place where they will suffer it all over again. Control through fear. A cultural climate of terror and uncertainty. Everyone cowed and subjugated. All of them, pathetic.

He raises the assault rifle, the five of them take aim and some of the people become aware of the quintet fanned out in front of the elevator doors and turn to look, briefly confused, taking in the armed men for a moment as if their brains cannot grasp what they are seeing, as if it isn't happening, and that is all it needs because their inertia, their inability to recognise the unreal as real costs them vital seconds and turns it into a turkey shoot.

He opens fire. They all do.

His finger pressing down on the trigger, feeling the vibration in his hands, his forearm. Beyond the flame and smoke spurting from the muzzle of his roaring carbine he sees windows fracture and faces splinter and bodies dropping hard to the floor, his ears ringing with the terrible cacophony, the screams and agonised shrieks and the crashing of ruptured, twisted metal as one of his companions detonates a grenade.

And then they stop shooting because there is nobody left in the hall to kill. A momentary stillness. Alarms sound. People cry in the distance, on the other side of the security checkpoint. A sprinkler fans a circle of water droplets onto polished floor tiles, expelled bullet cases cooling with a hiss.

Quick breaths, taken while he reloads, the five of them striding over the queue, which is now three neat rows of bloodied corpses, the dull-eyed dead embracing one another with tangled limbs, past the fizzing, sparking X-ray system riddled with bullet holes, through the body scanners where they set off more alarms, to escalators which have stopped working, as frozen as the bodies he has just trampled on.

He takes the steps three at a time, following his companions, faster now, up to the stores and restaurants and bureau de change kiosks of the departure lounge, navigating the abandoned suitcases and rows of plastic seats, driving the crowd before them with more drilled arcs of gunfire. Scything people down. Finishing off the injured slumped against walls, those crawling on their bellies and calling for their mothers. Picking off crouching stragglers stupid enough to kneel in submission, to hold their hands up in surrender. As if it will do anything.

All around them, scorch marks and crimson streaks and items of clothing left by the panicked, the dying. Spider-webbed plate-glass windows, smashed liquor bottles and shrapnel-damaged novelties in the duty free, a small fire burning through the over-priced bookshop. The deafening superfast clank of his companions' weapons as they yomp and shoot and pick their next target, their next cluster of shivering tourists, their next cop who is already bleeding out on the floor and never stood a chance.

The sirens outside grow louder. The flight departures on the information display boards suddenly change, everything switching to 'delayed'. The airport locking down.

And he knows why.

One of his companions urges him: *check your weapons and ammo*. He reloads at the exit door, looks out onto the tarmac and sees the armoured vehicles screeching to a stop, the troops rappelling from a helicopter, kitted up with rifles and pistols and grenades, with belts of ammunition and ballistic shields, with everything. The response rapid and almost overwhelming.

He crouches, makes his way down metal steps, right into a basement service area, a concrete cavern of pipes and air con ducts and the electrical arcs of broken wiring then up the ramp to the airport apron – and here they come. Shielded special forces advancing, clad in black, a dark wave amongst the smoke and chaos, and he lets rip, lets rip with the carbine, joins his companions in mowing them down, hears himself shouting, *get some get some get some*, heart pounding as he quickly reloads again, huddles beneath the nose of an aircraft as he switches mags, bullets ricocheting off the concrete floor, the landing gear, the transportation dollies jammed with suitcases and he knows he is pinned down, can't see his companions, can't see shit in this chaos, and he is disorientated now, beyond tired, the long night catching up with him at last, has lost his bearings and can't even work out who is shooting and from where and he realises this might be over, this might be it, they've got him at last.

The bullets hit him.

Pummel him. He feels every one. Flashes of red in the corner of his vision. Blood clouding what he can see, the world tilting and fading as he collapses to the ground, his belly now roiling with a sickening feeling and he hears the nervous laughter and the voice, that voice asking him *you all right, you want to go again, is it over?* and he pulls off the headphones, throws the PlayStation controller to the settee and tilts his head back and roars at the ceiling, the sound coming from somewhere deep within, from the depths of his churning guts, an almost primeval growl of face-covering spittle and neck veins and bulbous eyes.

'*Fuuuuuuuuuuuuuuck.*'

His fists clench, so tight fingernails draw blood from the palms of his hands.

In his head he can still hear the question. *Is it over?*

They have him. The police, they have Timothy Coe in one of their cells right now. Working him. Questioning him. Pushing him. Their technical people, all over his laptop. His phone. His gaming rig.

One more of the team, gone.

Just like at the mosque. The police don't know about him yet, though. Don't know who they have and where he is: right under their noses. Right where he can be removed, too, when the time is right. Rescued. Brought back into the fold, when it is safe to do so. When he is needed so they can see this through to the end.

Because it nearly is the end.

It's salvageable. It's not finished. It's still doable.

He drops his head down to the television. Quits the game. The voice still echoing in his head. Bites down on his own tongue, swamping the anger with pain, drowning it, so it doesn't overwhelm him. Doesn't ruin everything. He kneels into the settee, head buried in the cushions. Shrieks. Shrieks long and loud and punches the upholstery, lefts and rights, swinging hooks, fists sinking into the padding, his voice raw and ragged. The frustration, spewing out of him.

The mosque. The shopping centre. Two of his people, out of the picture, despite their best efforts. Despite their misdirection. Despite taking care of the one person who was threatening to expose them before it even started.

He picks up his phone, brings up the messaging app. Pure end-to-end encryption, needed more so now than ever before. Sends the message.

No deviation. We will be ready for the grand opening. Make sure you are ready.

The immediate reply: *Yes sir. Will comply.*

Nothing more to be said. He clears the app, glances at the small screen, sees the time. Nearly seven a.m. He didn't realise it was so late. So early. He's gamed through the night. Lost time again, sliding into a fugue of gunplay and missions and controlling everyone he played with online, whenever he wanted, wishing that real life was the same, that he was the one everyone looked up to, everyone followed, everyone revered. He'd needed to do it. The pressure now, so immense. But it will be costly, this not going to bed. This locking himself away from them. He will be punished.

The walk from his loft room to the kitchen – ladder, stairs, hallway – takes fifty-four seconds. He has counted it so many times before. Made sure it is all he needs to morph back into the man he is in the real world. That everyone expects.

She is sitting at the wooden table in her ridiculously garish work uniform, a yellow and blue horror. Flanked by their children, who shovel cereal into mouths that drip milk. They have been up a while: the table top is a mess of paper, drawings, squiggles, bright faces, a house with a happy family and the sun shining down from one corner.

'*Daddy,*' the children beam. His son drops from the chair, skips over to hug his legs.

'Hey, guys!' he grins. Voice singsong, light. It hurts his face, his head, to do it.

'I suppose you'll be going to bed now,' she says.

He lowers his eyes. Cowers, almost. Hates himself for doing it. Loathes himself and the person he has become out here. In the real world.

Her look is one of disgust. She doesn't even try to hide it any more. It hurts so much. He feels it, more forcefully than the bullets that struck him in the game.

Then the phone buzzes in his hand. A number he does not recognise on the screen.

'Yes,' he says when he answers, his wife regarding him sullenly.

And he hears the voice on the other end of the line.

Knows it is time.

'I'm sorry but I have to go out,' he says to his wife, but doesn't hear her reply.

In his head, he is screaming.

Twenty-four

He hadn't meant to fall asleep, but it had happened, and his phone was vibrating in his pocket when he woke – neck at an odd angle, the muscles there cramping – and, for a full ten seconds, didn't know where he was.

Through the window: the Butetown skyline washed in dawn orange, the glistening water of the bay to the south. Beck, face puffy with sleep, stretching and yawning behind her desk in the CID suite, fresh coffee already made and in hand, a piece of toast on a paper plate next to her keyboard.

'You going to answer that, numbnuts?' she asked. 'It's been driving me up the bloody wall.'

MacReady pulled a face: *sorry*. Tilted the chair forwards, placed feet on the floor, surprised to find himself in socks; at some point during the night, exhausted and dozing at his desk, he'd removed his shoes. The time on the wall clock read 7.13 a.m. Sunday, yet the station was alive already, footsteps and the scrape of chairs audible above, the Major Incident Room in full swing, presumably already working through the information he and Beck had pulled from Paxton's equipment. His Airwave hand-held radio bleeped on the desk, a female controller putting out obs to traffic and response for a vehicle seen driving erratically.

A screensaver swooped and dived on the monitor in front of him as he fished out his mobile.

''Lo?' he managed to croak when he answered.

'All right, officer?'

A male. Full-on Cardiff gruffness. MacReady's head was stuffed with cotton wool; he knew the voice, couldn't place it. Far too early for calls. Far too early for anything, come to think of it.

'I'm, um, fine,' he replied, rubbing at his eyes. He checked around, looking for his mug. Needed coffee urgently. 'Who's this?'

'You gave me your card, remember? Man, you took fucking ages to answer.'

MacReady suppressed a yawn. He'd given plenty of cards out in the last five days. Then it came to him: the man on Ward A2 at the University Hospital. Peppered with shrapnel wounds, lying in his bed and thanking MacReady for what the police did to save him, to save his son. Then breaking down as he recounted how his wife had been mortally wounded in the Bessemer Market attack. Her name, now on the list of deceased on the boards in the Major Incident Room. He wasn't sure if he should offer his condolences.

'Mister Corlett?'

'Yeah, it's me. How's things, bra?'

MacReady smiled. 'All good here, thanks. What can I do you for?'

A soft chuckle from Corlett. 'Look, when you gave me your card, righ', you said to bell you up if I had anything, even if it probably wasn't important, yeah?'

'Of course,' MacReady said, sitting upright. He pulled a scrap of paper from the drawer, grabbed a pen. Thought it prudent to make a note of Peter Corlett's call, even if it was – as was likely – bollocks. 'What have you got?'

Corlett cleared his throat. 'It's well weird here at the minute. You know when you and your fat man came to see us the other day?'

'My fat man,' MacReady grinned, thinking of Harrison. 'Yeah, I know.'

'And you spoke to me and we was cool and all that and then you went over to the guy in the next bed?'

MacReady pictured the Asian male brought in from the Al Mahdi in Penarth. Remembered trying to speak to him. Feeling so awful for him, both hands amputated. Feeling terrible when he upset him, the man's head banging into the pillow, over and over as he whined from somewhere deep inside.

'Yes, I remember all this. What's weird, Peter? You said it was weird there.'

Corlett appeared to move his phone closer to his mouth. Speak quietly. 'Well, that guy, 'bout half an hour ago he got me to use the hospital phone gizmo for him. First time he's spoken, you know? But he asked me to dial a number so I did, feeling right sorry for him, and I tapped away and put the handset by his chin so he could talk, and then I got back into my bed. But I heard it all.'

MacReady was wide awake now. Coffee or not.

'And he was crying,' Corlett continued. 'Right crying but angry with it, you know? Saying he was ready and wanted to finish it and could do it, just *come and pick me up*, he was saying, *come and pick me up*, and then saying he'd already lost everything at the mosque, that he did it for them and now he had no hands left.'

MacReady closed his eyes.

The chill spreading from the base of his spine, out along his arms and thighs.

'And the nurses are going apeshit, man,' Corlett was still talking. 'They was on shift changeover and they didn't even know he'd gone. Someone came in here, another Asian-looking guy but with a stupid shaved eyebrow. I couldn't believe what I was seeing. He just unhooked the guy with no hands, cleared the telephone number from the screen, and then they were gone, man. Gone. You took too fucking long to answer your phone, bra. This was ten minutes ago.'

MacReady thought of Nazir Uddin and his shaved eyebrow.

Of the Asian male in the bed.

Of that patch of dark skin on the CCTV still.

The male's hands, missing.

Blown clean off.

And the female Ops Room controller, still transmitting on his Airwave set. Still repeating obs for a vehicle sighted driving erratically after leaving the University Hospital at speed.

'Oh, no,' he breathed.

Beck, glancing over. 'What?'

MacReady had forgotten about Corlett.

Said to Beck: 'The mosque bomber. We had him all along.'

*

MacReady, foot rammed to the floor, stamping on the revs. The diesel engine, screaming.

Beck had refused to stay behind. Had grabbed her cuffs and radio and CS incapacitant spray and led MacReady down to the basement car park, ruined hip nagging at her as she went, face set and determined as she pushed through doors, pushed people out of the way. Mobile clamped to her ear as she talked to Echols in the Major Incident Room, explaining what they had discovered, making sure he understood, that he'd be all over it, that Fletcher cancelled his meeting and came back, that the senior investigating officer would be updated immediately.

Her one hand on the dashboard now, the other clutching the Jesus handle above the front passenger window, steadying herself as the CID car rumbled through side streets, down lanes and alleyways, Beck's PR squawking transmissions and updates from Ops Room, from uniform, from traffic officers.

Echols had actually come good. Everyone was out within minutes, every station in the city emptied of officers, looking for the car containing Nazir Uddin and the handless man.

A black Ford Focus.

Such a mundane vehicle carrying such a dangerous pair of individuals. Driven away from the hospital at very high speed and reported on the niners by their security, who couldn't provide a registration number. Last sighted travelling south along the lake at Roath Park. The briefest of glimpses by a dog handler going the other way on the opposite side of the boating pond.

MacReady heading in that direction now, through the back roads and industrial estates of East Moors, along the streets and speed bumps of Adamsdown. Eighty-fiving it in thirty zones. Thumb jabbing the horn, beating out a rhythm of parps that would be almost comical if the situation wasn't so serious. Civvies yelling and cursing and throwing wanker hand signals as he cut them up, caused them to screech to a stop.

'You going to plot up somewhere and wait?' Beck asked.

'At the end of Albany Road. They were heading this way. We'll wait on the roundabout. Means we can go in any direction if they're spotted again.'

Sightings only, repeat, sightings only . . .

The warning from the control room inspector. Blaring every five minutes. No unarmed officers to stop or approach the car. They had no idea what Uddin had with him. What he was planning. How desperate he was to evade capture.

'Firearms are going to be twenty minutes away, I guarantee it,' MacReady shouted over the roar of the engine. 'Worst fucking time for this to happen, shift changeovers everywhere.'

Beck drew in a sharp breath, the CID car almost clipping a flatbed lorry as MacReady ran a red light. 'It's why Uddin chose this time to take him out of hospital. He's not stupid. We know that.'

'What if it wasn't Uddin's decision?'

Beck turned to him. 'You don't think he's the main man behind all this?'

'There's RakKap and RookSTAR still outstanding. The handless guy – he's one of them. Who's the other, though?'

Before they'd fallen asleep at their desks, they'd run the usernames through every system they had. Nothing. Not a hit anywhere. Emails to Special Branch, to the security services in London were yet to elicit a response.

MacReady joined Newport Road, running the CID car on to the wrong side of the carriageway, overtaking stationary traffic at the lights. Peeled left towards Albany Road. In the sky to the west a black dot, moving closer: Air Support, the police helicopter moving in.

'This'll do.' MacReady pulled over to the kerb, tucking the car alongside the wall of a church. Let the engine idle. A roar as the chopper passed overhead, going north-west, towards the lake.

'There were no black Fords at Bessemer,' Beck said, picking at a fingernail, working it, tense. 'We played every CCTV and video recording on loop, until I was seeing that car park in my sleep. Definitely no Focus. Definitely.'

'So they've got access to more than one vehicle.' MacReady was agitated, the sitting and waiting making his legs twitch. His PR, silent for a moment. Around them the world carried on its Sunday morning. A handful of cars queuing to enter the roundabout, two or three pedestrians walking towards the city centre, a couple of them shielding eyes with hands as they scanned the horizon for the helicopter.

Beck gave up attacking the nail with her fingers, chewed at it instead. 'Makes sense if there were four of them involv—'

Tango Echo Three One, vehicle sighted Ninian Road.

A traffic officer, voice an excited blast over the air, the words bleeding together.

'Shit,' said MacReady. Hand jamming the gearstick into first. 'Direction of travel?'

'Come on,' whispered Beck, eyes on her radio handset.

Vehicle making off, heading east along Ninian, towards Wellfield Road.

MacReady accelerated away from the kerb. 'They're coming this way.'

'Careful, Will,' Beck urged. Placed a hand over his on the steering wheel. 'OK?'

He nodded. Turned into Albany Road. 'OK.'

Speed seventy miles an hour. Still heading east. Road is clear of other traffic. Vehicle has . . . three occupants . . .

MacReady and Beck exchanged a look.

'Three?' Beck said.

Uddin.

Plus RakKap and RookSTAR. It had to be.

MacReady couldn't believe it. All of them, together.

He pushed the CID car up to sixty. Willed the Focus to come towards them. Heard the helicopter co-pilot, calmly advising they were en route. Heard the control room inspector again, calling for sightings only, for all unarmed officers to stand down, for the channel to remain clear of all transmissions other than those from the traffic officer following the car.

Vehicle straight on into Marlborough Road. Speed still seventy . . . Now left, left into Alma Road . . .

'He's going away from us now,' Beck said.

MacReady didn't reply. Wrenched the steering wheel to the right. Took a side street.

Temporary loss . . .

'No,' he cried. Shook the wheel. 'Don't lose them. Not now. *Please.*'

Silence on the air. Just a few seconds. To MacReady it felt like ten minutes.

From Tango Echo Three One, vehicle now on Westville Road, heading east.

A flash of livery to his right; a pair of firearms wagons overtook the CID car, screaming towards the traffic vehicle's location. MacReady eased in behind them, tried to match them for speed, the battered Peugeot failing miserably. He watched, frustrated, as they pulled away.

'Probably for the best,' Beck told him. 'Chopper will be recording. I don't really want the bosses to know we're here.'

'At least until firearms have our guys, anyway. Then we can, you know, just have a drive past . . .'

Beck shook her head. Was about to speak when the traffic officer transmitted.

Vehicle abandoned Westville Road. Driver out and running. Through the gate into Roath Mill Gardens, male, Asian, early twenties wearing a black hoodie . . .

'Shit,' MacReady said. 'I hope firearms are at scene.'

Silence on the radios again. He gritted his teeth, pushed the car hard, heading for the gardens, hoping they had all three men. That they were in custody. That this nightmare would be over at last.

MacReady turned into Westville Road. Heard Beck gasp at the jumble of police vehicles: firearms wagons, the traffic car, dog handler vans, unmarked motors. In the middle, the black Ford Focus. One door open.

Empty.

'Where are they?' he groaned.

Beck pointed into the park. At the cluster of uniforms and suits. At the black-clad firearms officers, weapons drawn, aiming at something on the ground. 'There.'

MacReady stopped the car, killed the engine.

'Wait!' Beck shouted. 'Don't go near the Focus, it might have an IED on board –'

He sprinted away from the Ford, into the park, warrant card aloft.

One of the firearms officers swung her Heckler towards him.

'CID!' he yelled. Raised both hands. 'DC MacReady, Cardiff Bay.'

Looked at the figure on the patch of grass, circled by firearms officers.

One male there. Handcuffed behind his back. Left eyebrow shaved. Looking up at his captors, a strange grin on his face.

Nazir Uddin. At last.

Beck at his side now. Breathing hard and fast.

'He's clear,' the female firearms officer said. 'No weapons. No explosives.'

MacReady shook his head. 'He might be clear, but what about the other two?'

She screwed up her face. 'What other two?'

'The Focus was three up. Where are the other two occupants?'

She gestured at Uddin. 'We closed at scene as it was abandoned. He was the only one in the car.'

MacReady let his eyes fall closed. Let out a groan.

Thought of the precious few seconds when the traffic officer lost sight of the Focus in the maze of tight side streets and weed-ridden lanes that surrounded Roath Park.

Pictured Nazir Uddin, smiling as he dropped off his companions.

Twenty-five

They deployed almost everyone they had.

Searched for three hours straight. Sheds and garages and back gardens. Porches, outside toilets, even a ridiculously over-sized treehouse. Woke anyone and everyone, not caring about the doughy faces and accusatory stares which greeted them on doorsteps, in bedroom windows.

Other than a guy in his late teens who'd decided to sleep off the previous night's drink behind a council bin – begging the cops who found him *not to tell me mam* – and a homeless old Para who'd fought with the uniforms who woke him, there'd been no sign of anyone in the alleyways and lanes.

And certainly no sign of the men who'd been in the Ford Focus with Nazir Uddin.

They hadn't gone to ground. The helicopter swept the area for the best part of an hour with its thermal imaging camera. Came up with nothing other than wildlife in the bushes and overgrown hedges.

MacReady knew it meant they'd had another vehicle nearby, and made off in it.

Or, as was most likely, one or both of them lived in the vicinity.

And they were now in a house.

Hunkered down.

Waiting for the uniformed patrols and parked-up ARVs to lose interest.

For the police to go away.

Uniform had checked the telephone system at the hand-less man's hospital bedside; it had, as Corlett mentioned, been wiped. Instead they'd traced the number dialled via the University Hospital's telephone system, called the mobile but got an automated voicemail message for an unregistered Tesco pay-as-you-go burner.

Whoever owned the phone had already killed it. The thing was probably in pieces and scattered around the area. There was no trace of the number on their systems either. Another dead end.

'Got the index?' MacReady asked, leaning forwards, fingers hovering over the keyboard. Fletcher, Echols and Harrison standing behind him, watching intently.

The index number of the Focus: negative on PNC. Previous Keeper Details only. Nothing listed on insurance details, too. A blank. They'd stood on Westville Road, watching while CSI inspected the car Uddin had been driving, wondering what to do next. Until Beck had suggested they return to the nick and check the plate details on the Automatic Number Plate Recognition database.

MacReady took a seat next to Beck at her desk. Waited as she launched the force intranet, clicked on the ANPR system, signed in.

'I can go back for ninety days,' she said.

'Then do it,' Fletcher grunted. 'If you need to do the full two years then so be it, I'll get the bloody authorisation from upstairs. Just find me something that I can give to the SIO.'

MacReady read out the car registration; Beck typed it in.

'There you go,' Harrison said from behind them.

Immediately there were numerous hits. A raft of them, listed on the right hand side of the screen. Registration number, locations, times and dates the Ford passed ANPR cameras. Still no keeper details, no names of the insured.

'Gets about, this motor, doesn't it?' said Beck.

MacReady looked at the most recent result: this morning. Just before seven. A fixed gantry camera on the A48 Eastern Avenue. Near the University Hospital.

'Let's see the photograph,' Echols said.

Beck clicked on it. A photo filled the screen, the black Focus travelling in the westbound carriageway, obviously heading to the UHW to collect the mosque bomber.

Nazir Uddin at the wheel.

In the front passenger seat, the lower half of what appeared to be a white-skinned male, his face obscured by the sun visor he'd pulled down.

'This our RookSTAR guy?' asked Beck. 'Or RakKap?'

MacReady stared at the image. The passenger in T-shirt and jeans, his forearms thin and pale, as if he spent considerable time indoors. 'Could be.'

'Check some of the others,' Fletcher urged. 'This guy has got to be on one of them.'

Beck clicked one from a week ago. Similar time in the morning, the camera located on the A4232 bridge over the bay, which linked Cardiff and Penarth. The Focus travelling west, towards the megastores and International Sports Village which lay on the headland.

In the accompanying photograph: a different figure at the wheel of the Ford.

'Wait,' Fletcher said, and leaned in. MacReady could smell last night's bourbon on his inspector's breath.

'That a woman?' Harrison asked.

A blonde. Early thirties. One hand draped over the steering wheel, the other up to her face, a finger rubbing at the corner of one eye.

'Nice clothes,' Echols remarked with a chuckle.

Several more clicks, Beck working through the list, choosing at random: morning, evening, lunchtime. Every one now showing the blonde female driving the car. Every photo with her wearing that gaudy outfit.

Beck went back to the first hit with the woman. Studied the ANPR photo. She was decked out in a bright-yellow short-sleeved blouse, thin blue vertical stripes cutting through the garishness. A name badge, blurred and unreadable, pinned to the left side of her chest.

'She's on her way to work.'

'Lots of different times, too,' MacReady said. 'Must be doing shifts.'

Fletcher tapped Beck on the shoulder. Pointed at the woman on the screen.

'Go there. Now. Print out that picture and take it with you. And take the tea boy. I'll update the detective chief super, you'll have firearms and crime scene coming over to meet you.'

MacReady glanced at the photo again.

At the store name stitched to the woman's right sleeve.

*

Ferry Road.

Thirty years ago it was a wasteland, the site of a colossal refuse tip, a mismanaged and neglected strip of oil storage depots, brickworks and scrap yards, along with a landfill which polluted the waters of the nearby River Ely. Until the canny folk at the council realised the potential of the area, and decided to turn the mountainous pile of human-generated shit into Cardiff's only hill by covering it with a bit of turf. Consumerville swiftly followed, changing the bluff into a paean to purchasing. Retail parks, superstores and global brands now jostled for space amongst the pockets of identikit housing estates.

The Ikea store rested on the northern fringe. Just a stone's throw from Bessemer Market, where all this began. MacReady pulled into a car park already crammed with civvy vehicles, turned to Beck.

'How do you want to play this?' he asked.

'Usual,' she replied. 'I'll do the honours. You just stand there looking average.'

Inside was busy. Families, couples, trolleys full of flat packs. A few bombings weren't going to stop people from getting hold of some Billy bookcases for their traditional Bank Holiday DIY fest, it seemed. MacReady and Beck made a beeline for the first member of staff they saw – a security guard, a painfully thin man with angry splashes of acne creeping across his neck, uniform swamping his scrawny torso.

Beck held up her warrant card, flashed a toothy smile. 'Manager about?'

The guard looked from the ID to Beck, back to the ID. Waited a moment, pretending to study it. Then: 'Wait one.'

MacReady gritted his teeth as the man muttered into his radio. Eyeing the police officers suspiciously as he did so.

'She's on her way here. Please do not leave the area.'

Beck hitched her eyebrows. Looked at MacReady, winked. Turned back to the guard. 'We wouldn't dare. But thanks anyway.'

'Pleasure,' the guard replied, giving a quick, humourless smile.

MacReady looked around. Wanted the manager here. Time was getting away from them. Today was the thirtieth. Paxton had the next attack listed for right now, yet they were standing in a home furnishings store being glared at by a typically overzealous security employee. MacReady wondered if, for once, they were going to hit the jackpot from the off. That the manager – *she*, the guard had referred to her as – was the female in the ANPR photo. That when he heard a polite cough and turned around it would be the blonde from the Ford Focus standing in front of them.

'Hi, can I help you guys?'

MacReady spun around. Sighed. The manager was early thirties, funky specs and nose piercing, her brunette hair yanked back in a loose pony.

Beck showed her warrant card, shook the hand that was extended to her. 'Can we talk,' she said, casting a sideways glance at an eavesdropping security guard, 'somewhere a little more private?'

In the manager's office MacReady stood to one side while Beck explained – without going into much detail at all – why they were there. *All routine*, she insisted. *No, your staff member is not in any trouble. We'd just like to speak to her if she's working today?*

'Do you have a name?' the manager asked.

'Unfortunately not,' Beck replied, then slid out the photograph MacReady had printed. Held it up for the manager. 'But this is her.'

The manager studied it for a second or two. Breathed in and out, an almost resigned sound escaping from her mouth. 'I don't think I'm supposed to be just handing out the personal details of staff without authority. It depends how serious this is, really. I'll have to ring head office, I think.'

Fuck this, thought MacReady.

'Look,' he said, and stepped towards her, 'you can waste time – ours and yours – making phone calls and waiting for some desk jockey boss who doesn't know how serious this is to make a decision. Or you can just tell us this person's name and where she lives so we can get on with our jobs.'

'Will,' Beck said quietly.

The manager blinked behind her glasses. 'I'm not trying to be obstructive or anyth—'

'I'll tell you how serious this is,' MacReady said, and pointed at the photo. 'This woman is linked to the people who have been blowing up the city this week. The attacks, you know? Where people have died? She may even be in a relationship with one of them. And we would really, really like you to just give us what we want, so we can go and speak to her, and find out just who is behind it. All right?'

The manager swallowed. Eyes shifting from MacReady to an apologetic-looking Beck. 'She's already called to say she'll be late for work today. I knew she was mixed up in some kind of bother. She's not been herself these last few months.'

Beck placed a hand on the manager's arm. 'Who is she, please?'

The manager looked at the photo.

'Her name is Sarah Rook.'

RookSTAR. MacReady felt he might punch the air.

'And do you know her partner?' Beck pushed, nodding slowly.

'Neil? I've met him a couple of times. They live over by Roath Lake. If you give me a couple of minutes I'll dig out their full address.'

Twenty-six

Neil Rook.

Another blank on their systems.

Another cleanskin.

Just the briefest of physical descriptions of Sarah Rook's husband from the Ikea manager. Male, white, slim, thirties. *Always, you know, a bit grumpy*, as if that would help. A landline telephone number for the address, and that was their lot. A request gone into the DVLA on the hurry-up for his driver's licence photo. In the meantime, the scant details they had called into the Major Incident Room by Beck and circulated force-wide. To neighbouring forces. Nationally, on PNC.

Nothing to the media. Not yet. They didn't want to drive Rook further underground. Didn't want him panicking and bringing any plans forward.

'Balaclava Road,' MacReady said, accelerating. The CID car's engine grumbling as the revs crept ever higher. 'I *knew* it.'

Beck looked up from Google Maps on her phone. Nodded. 'It's right next to the street where the traffic car lost sight of them. There's a tiny alleyway at the park end where the entrance looks like a garden gate, so you'd have to be local to know it was there. Uddin must have dropped them at Alma Street, then they ran to Rook's address.'

MacReady bit down on his lip. They'd been so close earlier this morning. Rook and whoever RakKap was; they'd gone in to a house overlooking Roath Mill Gardens. Had probably watched as Nazir Uddin was taken into custody.

Had been laughing at them.

Much to its manager's annoyance – she'd been angry with MacReady as it was, and he feared another complaint was forthcoming about him putting the arm on her – Ikea was now closed. Specialist Crime were taking no chances and had deployed firearms and bomb disposal to search and clear the building, including Sarah Rook's locker and any staff spaces she frequented. Via radio transmissions it appeared the firearms officers at scene had found nothing but a spare blouse, a pair of shoes and a half-finished packet of biscuits belonging to her. No improvised explosive devices. No tools, plans or traces of TATP.

So that left the house on Balaclava Road.

Neil Rook's home.

MacReady and Beck were minutes away from it.

In front, yet another convoy. Firearms 4x4s, more army bomb techs rattling along in a wagon, CSI, ambulance and fire. Everyone on silent approach. Blues only, no sirens. No announcing their imminent arrival. Fletcher, Harrison and Echols travelling behind MacReady, one of several other unmarked cars carrying CID, Specialist Crime, anti-terror police. The sense now that this was it. They had their man.

'I hope he's there,' MacReady said.

Beck chuckled. 'If it wasn't for your terrible driving making me cling on for dear life I'd be crossing every finger I had. And anyway, how do you know this RookSTAR is a he?'

'Got to be,' MacReady replied. 'Gamer? Rest of the attackers were male? Means he's got to be the same.'

'You thought the blogger was male. And you were wrong about that.'

MacReady was too tired to point out that it was in fact Klaudia Solak who'd been wrong about Heidi Paxton. But any mention of Solak now tended to turn Beck apoplectic, so he kept his mouth shut.

Beck glanced out of her window. 'We could go in there and find out it was Sarah Rook all along. A woman who got so sick of selling furniture that she turned domestic terrorist.'

'Yeah,' MacReady snorted, looking sideways at her. 'Happens all the time. Those self-assembly sofa beds can make anybody lose it.'

'They're stopping, by the way.'

MacReady checked ahead, saw the convoy slowing as it entered a library car park, jammed on the brakes, the CID car fishtailed a few feet before the engine stalled.

'Nice,' Beck remarked, and climbed out of the Peugeot.

Behind them the sound of a car horn: Harrison at the wheel of their motor, clearly unhappy at MacReady's emergency stop and the near-collision which had occurred. Echols and Fletcher, a pair of shaking heads beside and behind Harrison.

It was all so fast. By the time MacReady scooped up his radio from the footwell, the trucks in front were a blur of open doors and blacked-up Robocops checking kit, fastening ballistic helmets, looking down the sights of MP5s. Fletcher in amongst them, nodding as the detective chief superintendent and his coterie of rankers pointed and stroked chins, their faces drawn and anxious.

And then they were off. A long, crouched line of heavily armed cops cradling weaponry and tactical gear, of army EOD engineers with their robot and clearance equipment, scurrying across the main road. The library, just 200 metres from the entrance to Neil Rook's street.

MacReady checked for traffic, ran after his colleagues. Saw amazed faces in the stationary cars and vans of lunchtime traffic, in shop windows and on the football playing fields of the park, games paused and sweaty hands on hips, on smartphones as they recorded.

Fast. They had to be fast. This would go viral, and quickly.

Rook's house was midway along a narrow, quiet side street. Neat, redbrick, small front garden, resident parking only out front. As normal as could be, bar the clusters of coppers toting assault rifles and hiding behind bulletproof shields as they surrounded the place.

MacReady caught up with Fletcher, Echols and Harrison. His shirt now heavy with perspiration. Beck nearby, working her fingers into her hip, grimacing and hoping nobody would notice. Telling neighbours to go back inside and lock their doors.

'They're putting a call in on the number you were given,' said Fletcher. 'Get him out. Get them all out, if there are more of them.'

'You think if our bombers are in there they'll just throw the towel in?' asked Echols.

'Fucked if I know. But we've got to try the nicey-nice way at first or people will complain. You really want Professional Standards or the IPCC sniffing around you for the next four years?'

MacReady glanced across, saw the senior investigating officer on his mobile. Talking. Looking towards Rook's house, a good fifty metres away. Nobody at any of the windows.

Then: 'Armed police, let me see your hands!'

The shout came from one of the firearms officers.

MacReady watched, open-mouthed, heart thumping, as the front door of the house opened. A pair of hands, poking out. Raised. Empty.

Then the blonde from the ANPR photograph. Sarah Rook. Eyes wild and confused and terrified. The dazzling Ikea blouse at odds with the ashen skin of her face.

Clinging to her legs were two children. A boy and a girl. Both of them no more than six years old. Crying, loud wails which echoed along the housefronts and made MacReady think of Finlay. Of the kind of man who would subject his children to this insanity.

'Is there anybody else in the house?'

Sarah Rook shook her head at the firearms officer's question. Shook it hard. 'There's nobody. Nobody. It's just us.'

'Your husband. Where is he?'

'I . . . My husband?' she asked. Puzzled now. Hands dropping a little, until she remembered just what was being pointed at her and thrust them skywards again. 'He's not here. He went out. He went out earlier this morning.'

MacReady looked at Fletcher. Caught the flash of disappointment in his expression before his DI walked over to the detective chief superintendent.

'House is a dead end, I bet,' Harrison offered. 'I mean, look at her. Look at the kids. They know fuck all about this.'

MacReady said nothing. Silently agreed with Harrison, a sinking feeling in the pit of his stomach. Neil Rook was not going to be inside. His wife – clueless. The kids, beyond distraught. All three of them totally unprepared for what had just come crashing into their lives.

Sarah Rook followed the firearms officer's instructions. Came out into the road. Kneeled, hands still pointed towards blue midday sky. Placed her palms slowly to the hot tarmac. Dropped to her belly, the children still tugging at her clothes, still breaking their hearts.

As the firearms officers rushed over, submachine guns and Glocks and the red dots of Tasers trained on her, she lifted her head.

Through snot and tears begged, 'Will somebody please tell me what's going on?'

*

The Counter-Terrorism officers arrested her anyway.

Arranged for the kids to stay with relatives. Whisked them all away. Sarah Rook for questioning under caution, the children to the station for medical assessment then on to grandparents who were warned to say nothing to anyone who called at their home or rang their phones. To lock their doors. To ignore the plain-clothes firearms officers stationed outside their address in an unmarked car just in case their son-in-law decided to show up.

Then they ripped Neil Rook's house apart.

MacReady surveyed the aftermath. The search teams had gone as far as to remove suspended ceilings, wood panelling beneath the stairs, even tiles in the bathroom. It was, ironically, like a bomb had gone off in there.

And it was as they'd feared.

Rook's home was clean. No plans. No equipment. No pictures of the market, the mosque, or any clue as to what his next target might be. His gaming rig, another PlayStation found in some sort of man cave in the loft, had been bagged and taken away ready for a HQ technical wiz to interrogate. Plenty of pictures of the man himself, though. Recovered, copied, circulated across the force, to all officers and staff.

Neil Rook was Mister Average. Wiry, medium height, mousy hair, alabaster skin. In the photo MacReady now had on his mobile Rook appeared sullen, downtrodden. His eyes, looking at the camera but not really focused on it.

As if he was wishing he was somewhere else.

'So where are you?' MacReady asked, out loud.

Beck turned to him, paused sifting through the detritus of Rook's gaming hidey-hole to adjust a latex glove. 'First sign of madness, you know.'

He ignored her. Rubbed at his forehead with the back of his own gloved hand. It was like a furnace up here. He tried to picture Neil Rook, sweltering in his underwear as he practised running and gunning on a First Person Shooter, but all he could see was Duncan Jones, his almost permanently sozzled housemate. Rook's space was exactly the same as Jones's lounge: body-sweat-stained sofa, jumbo television, games console and little else. A handful of horror film posters on the walls, taped there haphazardly. Some graphic novels, a copy of the local free rag which was ninety-eight per cent adverts, a few leaflets and flyers for local events which, judging by the appearance of Rook in photographs, he'd never attended for fear of the sun alighting on his porcelain skin.

MacReady slipped everything into evidence bags, trying to avoid thinking about how his own life was just one small step from Rook's. All it would take is for the move to Jones's house to become permanent, which was increasingly likely given Megan's lack of contact and continuing anger with him for putting Fin in so much danger at St David's.

'But where is he?' he asked, looking at Beck this time. 'We're missing something. We need to find out who this RakKap character is. Where he lives. It must be nearby. They went there instead of here, there's no other explanation for it.'

A shrug from Beck. 'WECTU and Specialist are dealing, Will. They have a description of the guy with no hands, are doing house to house. From what I gather the wife doesn't even know Rook has an Asian friend, or that he spent so much time online talking to other people.'

'I find that hard to believe. I mean, come on.'

'Couples drift apart,' she said, pointedly. 'You above all people should know that.'

'Fair comment,' he replied, and sighed. 'But Rook is obviously with the handless guy. Looking after his injuries and waiting for us to drift away so he can come out and finish this.'

Beck straightened, a sweat moustache on her top lip. 'Look, all I know is the wife seems clueless. And all I caught is that her other half was up all night playing games until this morning, then had a phone call and decided he had to clear off. She said he was panicky, jittery. Not really there, like a zombie, and he took her car instead of his own, as well as *his* car keys which is why she couldn't get into work. And that's the last time she saw him. And that's the last thing I got to know about. So can we get out of this filthy sweatbox now? It's gone three and I haven't even had lunch yet.'

MacReady nodded. Sealed the plastic sack he was holding. 'Rook has a car?'

'I'm already on it,' Beck said, holding up a hand. 'Or rather my little bearded hipster elves are on it. I phoned them earlier. We're looking for a Blue VW Golf, fifteen-ish years old and a pile of junk, got the index number and everything. They're running some of the recordings, checking them again.'

MacReady titled his head. 'Some of them? Not all of them?'

Beck gave a cocky smile. 'I don't need to do all of them. Because I know I saw a similar vehicle leaving the market directly after the attacks. And I'll bet my next hip replacement money that it was Neil Rook who started all this at Bessemer.'

*

They waited.

The team, sitting in the CID offices, unable to bear the noise and heat and high-pitched, frantic nonsense of the Major Incident Room. Evening, sun dipping, tea and coffee running low, their biscuit supply exhausted thanks to Harrison, who'd bleated about having to skip lunch despite the appearance of sausage roll wrappers in the bin beneath his desk. Rook's vehicle had been circulated by Beck on PNC for sightings only, not to be stopped by unarmed officers under any circumstances. Rook's name and description also going out on everyone's personal radios every fifteen minutes.

And the clock, ticking. Ticking away on the day Heidi Paxton had marked for another attack. Ticking on the custody clock as Specialist Crime worked on Timothy Coe downstairs. Tried to break their new prisoner, Nazir Uddin, across town at Cardiff Central police station's cell complex. Uddin, already in the midst of a run of interviews. MacReady and the rest of Fletcher's department not a part of any interrogation tag-team after the run-in with Coe. He suspected Detective Inspector Lloyd Evans and his oppo from WECTU had a hand in that decision.

It was immensely frustrating.

Worrying, too, that Neil Rook and his handless co-conspirator were still out there somewhere. Doing their own waiting.

MacReady killed time by checking the Niche file on Uddin. For any updates from the interviewing officers. From the senior investigating officer, from forensics on the Ford Focus or a techie about Rook's game console. From *anyone*. Harrison was chummy with one of the civilian detention officers in the Central custody suite, and was picking up snippets from the CDO via brief phone calls as the afternoon bled into evening, but there was little for any of them to do except wait until the detective chief superintendent came out of the latest video conference with the chief constable and tasked them with things again.

Uddin was talking, though. And talking. His father was right: Nazir Uddin was king of the bullshitters. The antithesis of Timothy Coe, by all accounts. Wouldn't shut up, seemed to be revelling in the attention he was getting from officers, from solicitors, from designated Appropriate Adults who'd been asked to sit in on interview due to concerns for his mental wellbeing and because his own parents had declared themselves too ashamed of their son to do it themselves. But it was a lot of nonsense. He seemed to be making things up as he went along. Blagging it. Still boasting about his insurgent training in the Hindu Kush mountain ranges of Afghanistan. Telling his interviewers he was the mastermind behind the attacks, that there was nobody else involved. None of it making any sense. None of it tying in with what they already knew.

But he'd coughed to Heidi Paxton.

Had come right out with it. Suddenly lucid, serious. How he and Paxton were once in love. How she knew about all *his* plans and had written about them, lauded them online. How she'd suddenly dumped him, and he'd been paying her to keep quiet about his forthcoming campaign ever since. Until he'd run out of money. Until his father wouldn't give him any more, or let him take a bigger part of the business to earn more hush money.

Until he'd decided enough was enough.

Had lured her to the rear of Cardiff Central railway station.

Had jammed a knife into her.

Over and over before walking away.

Adamant that he was alone. No laughing along with Timothy Coe, despite the photographic evidence MacReady and Beck had recovered.

'She was a splinter,' was all he'd said about Paxton, before demanding a halt to the interview.

A splinter. A small part of a larger group. And Uddin wanted them to believe it was just him running the show.

MacReady spun slowly in his chair; Fletcher in his office, making calls, Beck writing out evidence labels for a mountain of DVDs and memory sticks. Echols tapping furiously at his keyboard, Harrison pretending to read his actions but probably checking bikini-clad celebs on the *Daily Mail* website.

He turned his attention to Paxton's laptop. Whispered, 'Let's see what else you have, Heidi.'

MacReady opened up her documents folder, marvelling anew at the amount of written work she'd produced. Pages and pages of text docs, journal entries, articles and opinion pieces, some of them 10,000 words in length. He leaned back in his chair, hand on the mouse. Clicked to Paxton's email account, found nothing new had been sent to it. Not even a spam message. Her Twitter and Facebook pages still dormant. Nothing to dig around in other than that vast collection of documents.

He exhaled, blowing air out from puffed cheeks, the scale of the task hitting him once again. Eyes scanning the window of items, scrolling down, down, then back again. Up to the top.

Down another two pages. So many documents. And an aimless way of searching them, with what he was doing. He began clicking on them at random, seeing titles – *Rage Against the Rapist Elites*, *A Slave's Life in a Patriarchal Society*, *Gender Fluidity in the 21st Century and Beyond* – that made his head spin.

Then MacReady saw it.

'Sarge,' he said over his shoulder. 'Can you come here a sec?'

Beck strolled across, lowered herself onto the corner of MacReady's desk. He clicked out of Paxton's documents, brought up her calendar. Shifted the laptop around so Beck could see properly.

'Remember this for August?' he asked.

On the screen: *Bess/AlMahdi. St. D's. N.Th8re.*

For today: *Venus.*

'The list of targets,' Beck nodded. 'And?'

He switched back to the documents. 'Here.'

One of Paxton's long rants flashed up. Unfinished, unpublished on the blog. Block capitals and exclamation marks everywhere. A diatribe about hedonism, about society's sense of entitlement, of people's disgusting self-absorption, how shallow and pitiful and obsessed with fleeting fame the world had become when there was so much pain out there. How she, along with her companions, was going to do something about it. Teach everyone a lesson. Show everybody that life is not all about enjoying yourself while others suffer.

Its title: *A Venus Flytrap.*

Fletcher was at his office door. 'Anything?'

MacReady explained. Showed the DI the piece Heidi Paxton had written.

'Set off any alarm bells?'

'Nope,' MacReady shook his head. Looked to Beck, saw her shrug.

'Send it upstairs,' the DI said, turning to stare at MacReady. 'All of it. And get it on the Niche system now. We don't have much time left.'

*

It took an hour to type everything up and then MacReady was back to chewing at a fingernail and wondering if he should call home. Speak to Megan. Apologise again. The clock on the wall showed nine p.m. She'd be asleep with Finlay now so he decided against it.

'Want something to do?' Beck asked.

He rubbed both palms across his face. Stretched his eyes and looked at her. 'Please.'

She walked across, carrying a towering pile of DVDs and Blu-rays wrapped in clear plastic evidence bags. 'You can file these for me. They've all been copied but the detective chief super wants them stored until we're sure we can hand them back to their owners.'

MacReady nodded. Back to the menial work. 'Charlie Alpha Nine Eight?'

'Security cupboard there, please,' she smiled.

The station's CCTV camera room – call sign CA98 – was a floor below. MacReady took the stairs, relishing the icy blast of air con that whipped around the central column of the building.

The camera operator's position was one for the old sweats, those uniform carriers who were nearing their thirty and didn't really fancy talking to troublesome members of the public anymore, as it usually meant lots of paperwork. Instead they spent their hours watching civvies go about their lives, using the city's huge network of cameras along with the council efforts the police could seize control of at the press of a button.

MacReady didn't bother knocking; most of the operators couldn't care less who came and went, as long as you didn't hassle them with anything other than very brief small talk and an offer of a cup of tea.

'Security cupboard?' he asked.

The grizzled plod just pointed to his left. MacReady looked in that direction, saw the tall metal cabinet designed to safely store precious recorded evidence, the door wide open, key in lock, completely insecure as always. He shoved Beck's items in there, filling a shelf with bagged discs, then turned and clapped the dust off his hands.

'Busy?' he asked, glancing at the array of screens. Cameras in every major part of the capital city, from the 'burbs and main roads in the north to the factories and industrial areas out west, and even further afield. He noticed new camera locations: Barry, Penarth, even some of the larger towns deep into the Vale of Glamorgan. The old sweat wasn't even watching the CCTV though; instead he had a small portable flat screen on his desk, tuned to the local news channel. MacReady chuckled when he saw Klaudia Solak broadcasting from someplace, gangs of teens and twentysomethings jumping around and waving behind her.

'Not much going on for a Bank Holiday weekend,' the opera-tor replied.

MacReady sensed the man wasn't overly keen on having a chat, no matter how brief. He studied a few of the CCTV screens embedded in the opposite wall. Saw the pedestrianised shop-ping thoroughfare of Queen Street. The castle, lit by floodlights. The Principality Stadium, or whatever it was called nowadays, its spires aimed at the heavens. Pockets of people drifting through the city centre's streets. A lone busker in the doors of a Sains-bury's, a small yet appreciative audience clapping along as he strummed an acoustic. All of them just rubbing along, living their lives, not bothering anybody.

And then he saw the queue of punters waiting to get into a nightclub.

'What's that?' MacReady asked.

A yawn from the old copper. 'Grand reopening tonight. Free entry. Refurbed the place. Licensing tried to get them to cancel 'cos of what's been going on but the owner wouldn't have it, said he's put too much cash into it to change dates. You lot have got the bomber now anyways, and the council are keen to get the city back to normal sharpish.'

MacReady looked from the old sweat to the portable flat screen, where Solak was still interviewing people. Over to the CCTV screen. At the long line of club-goers, queuing behind a rope, smiling and laughing and taking selfies while they waited, a slim figure in their midst, upper half of her body caught in the glare of her colleague's news camera.

'What's the club called?' he asked.

'Dunno, mate,' came the exasperated reply. 'I just fucking work here, y'know?'

MacReady was already out of the door.

Running for the stairs.

*

On his knees, in the office. Throwing evidence bags left and right. Bags they'd taken from Neil Rook's house that afternoon.

'What the hell?' Echols shouted.

'Will?' Beck asked, standing over him.

Fletcher and Harrison, swapping confused glances.

MacReady found the bag he was looking for. The small plastic sack containing all the paperwork and leaflets he'd found in Rook's gaming room.

Through the clear plastic: a brightly coloured flyer. Orange. Black lettering. Exclamatory.

Advertising the grand opening of the Vintage nightclub on Greyfriars Road.

The nightclub he'd just seen Solak standing outside, with hundreds of members of the public.

MacReady jumped into his seat, brought up the HOLMES2 system on his computer. Found the entries for the search conducted at Timothy Coe's flat. The list of evidence recovered.

Saw it listed there: *Miscellaneous papers/leaflets, including takeaways, massage parlours, Vintage nightclub reopening.*

Switched to Heidi Paxton's record on the system. The property recovered from her bedroom on the top floor of her parents' house.

Found the text entry. *Flyers/papers/magazines inc. concert in local public house, nightclub opening, local college leaflets offering various courses.*

'Shit,' he breathed. 'We should have noticed this.'

Fletcher, hand on his arm. 'Wait, Will. What have you got? Fast as you can, please.'

MacReady brought up Google. Searched for *Vintage Nightclub, Cardiff*. Scanned the hits. Clicked on one of them, his heart jackhammering.

'Paxton, Coe and Rook all had flyers for a nightclub opening,' MacReady said, looking at Fletcher and holding up the evidence bag, the orange flyer clear to all. 'The same club. The Vintage on Greyfriars. It opens this evening, a Bank Holiday Sunday special, I've just been to the camera room and saw it on screen. It's free entry so they're already queuing down the street, and the media are there. I think they were going to hit it. I think Rook and his oppo are *still* going to hit it. Tonight.'

Fletcher looked at the evidence bag with the flyer. Blinked. 'But Paxton's calendar mentioned Venus, yes? Not Vintage.'

MacReady swivelled his chair towards the computer. Jabbed a thumb at the Google result he'd clicked on. The local business report from two months ago.

'It was going to be called Venus,' MacReady said. 'But there was some wrangling with another so-called *superclub* down west that has the same name. So the owner here decided to change it. And it's the same owner as the cocktail lounge that was hit with the drone.'

Fletcher looked to the ceiling for a second, thinking. Then: 'Christ!' he yelled, and dug out his mobile. Pointed around the room as he dialled, placed it to his ear. 'Car keys, radios, cuffs and spray. All of you. Now. Yeah, hello? This is DI Danny Fletcher downstairs . . .'

'I need to make a phone call,' MacReady said to Beck.

He pushed himself up from the chair, fished out his mobile. Stalked out into the corridor. Dialled Solak's number.

'Bit busy here, Will . . .'

She was shouting. The background noise, so loud as to be almost deafening. Music. Laughter. A voice over the PA. She was inside the club. Had to be.

'Are you inside the Vintage?' he yelled.

'Will, I've got half a dozen Z-list celebs to interview about bloody strength and unity in the community. I was just about to go back on air –'

'Get out, Klaudia,' he yelled. 'Get out *right now*. Pull the fire alarm, any fire alarm, and get yourself out of there now. The bombers, they're going to hit the club. Can you hear me? *They're going to hit the club*.'

Dead air in his ear.

Solak was gone.

Twenty-seven

He mingles.

Talks, laughs.

Act natural.

Act natural. Ignore the pain. Swallow it. Smother it.

He becomes one with them. Stands alongside them and joins in with their singing, their jokes, their catcalls and whistles as yet another group totters past in their tight-fitting dresses, in their ludicrously high heels, faces thick with greasepaint, eyes already glassy.

He fits in. Blends in. Another face in this crowd. Out with his friends.

Just one of the guys.

Except he does not respond to their requests for high fives. Doesn't throw his arms around their shoulders. Cannot slap them on the back at their filthy jokes or vile comments about passing women.

The medication is just enough to fuzz his brain, keep him smiling. Keep him calm. Just enough to stifle the agony in his stumped wrists. Wrists which he keeps thrust into his jeans pockets at all times. If he removes them, if his new friends see his injuries, if anyone spots them, this will all be over. He stands away from them, too. Just a little. Not enough for them to notice. But just beyond arm's reach.

He has to.

The queue shuffles forwards, a heaving morass of shouts and shrieking laughter and aftershave and makeup, and he is at the entrance doors. The bouncers, the security, they give him the once-over and he deliberately avoids meeting their hard eyes, instead amps it up a little, grins harder, his face stinging from the effort, even – his breath captive in his chest for a few seconds, so dangerous is it to do – shoulder barges one of his new companions, just for shits and giggles. Just to show he is normal. One of the lads, larging it up.

Then a quick check across the road. Eyes only, a flash to his left.

At the figure, cast in shadow, tucked in the side doorway of a restaurant.

At Rook.

You can do this, Rakesh, Rook had said, not half an hour ago. *We've done our personal attacks, now this is for us all. The last thing we do together. We have nothing now, remember? But we don't want to be remembered as nothings, do we? We want to be remembered for* something, *right?*

And he'd been fine with that part of it. Fine with the shaving of his head, the piercing of his ear, the change in his appearance. Clear about what he had to do – but something had nagged at him at the time, something he couldn't quite put his finger on and he knew it was because of the drugs, the medication filling his brain with mud and before he knew it he was in the nightclub queue and it had gone from his head completely.

Now the rope is being unhooked by the giant security guy and he's being ushered through to a world of blue neon, then up a wide staircase and he can hear the *whump-whump-whump* of music, can feel it in the base of his spine, and he tunes out his new companions, lets them get ahead of him, the smile falling from his face – he is so relieved, the muscles there were *aching* – and he finally remembers what was bothering him back in his lounge, back when Rook was getting him ready after a day spent hiding from the police.

Despite all his talk of *we* and *us* and *togetherness* it was now him and him alone who was walking into a nightclub with bombs they'd constructed in his kitchen strapped to his ribs.

He climbs the steps, a small part of him annoyed with himself, confused now as to how he has managed to place himself in this position, but it is snuffed out in the instant he reaches the main floor, where it is heaving with people, with exposed flesh and glittery cheeks and elongated, fluttering eyelashes, and he is pushing through the crowd, towards the main part of the club with its huge dance floor, and he wonders what he should say just before he does it, wonders what the words should be before he sets them off, wonders if anybody will hear him over the pounding basslines.

Perhaps *I am Rakesh Kapoor and I am here to rescue you all from your sins.*

It's pretty poor. A cliché. He's been ignored most of his life, and this just won't do. Won't remedy anything. He ponders this for several seconds. The meds, knocking his brain off kilter. The music, knocking it further, such is its volume. He screws up his face, thinks as hard as he can, the effort it entails making one of his eyes thrum with pain.

Tries to conjure something memorable.

Something – when this is all done – people will remember him for. His family. Those few friends who drifted in, then out, of his life. All those people who he used to watch from the corner of the room at house parties, at pubs, at nightclubs, imagining just being with them, spending time in their company, laughing and loving and enjoying life and having someone to share it with, before realising his drink was warm and he'd been standing, alone, for three hours, and it was time to go home because not one of them had even looked in his direction once.

And the Al Mahdi. The only place he ever felt he belonged, until they turned on him. The imam and his circle of sycophants. The people who told him he would never amount to anything, ever. Who threatened him with expulsion, with turning him into a social pariah, all because he fell in love with another man.

If he gets this right, these people will remember him for ever.

And he is still thinking it over when he hears another sound, a sound as loud as the music being played by the DJ. A wailing, rolling whine that makes people turn and look at each other, then around at the walls and doors of the club.

Makes some of them head for the stairs. Head for the exits.

A fire alarm.

No. No, no, no, no. Not now. Not after all this.

Clubbers and staff hurry past him, running. Slamming open fire exits and disappearing into the night. Drinks spill, glasses smash in the rush. The music stops.

He runs himself. Runs into the main dance hall. Knows it is time. That he will do it here. Take them all out. Every single one of them, packed in here.

He struggles to rip open his shirtfront with his stumps, rushing not in the plan. A moment or two of fumbling and his vest is exposed to the world. Canisters of TATP, gaffer-taped underneath his arms.

'I am Rakesh Kapoor,' he shouts, 'and you will all –'

He stops.

The dance floor is empty. Fire exits and 'Staff Only' doors right the way around the circular room are wide open.

Everybody, gone.

'No,' he breathes, and sinks to his knees.

He can't believe it. Is sure it's the drugs Rook gave him. Is sure his brain has become unwired, somehow. That he is hallucinating. That the nightclub fog and flickering green lasers and vacant banquettes are an image from some other time and place that he cannot recall, his addled mind forcing it upon him in his weakened, altered state. It frightens him, this slipperiness in his thinking, this uncertainty that has suddenly overwhelmed him, and he wishes he was at home, running with Rook and Coe and Naz and poor Heidi while they destroy wave after wave of futuristic enemy soldiers, screaming into their mikes, controllers vibrating in their hands, racking up high scores and kill streaks and weapons upgrades to take out any Noob player who made the mistake of trying to join their ranks, so he just rests there, knowing this is just his imagination, his memory playing tricks, down on his knees with the club's strobes flashing on him, the fog shifting into myriad shapes, dancing and moving towards and around him, a peaceful grin on his face and his stumps dropping – fast – towards the canisters on his vest, just one hard thump and they'll go up and all this will be over.

Then it comes to him.

It comes to him and he knows just what to say.

Opens his mouth. Brings his eyelids down. Breathes in. Ready.

Because this will be so cool.

So brilliant.

Then he feels something hard and cold and cylindrical enter his mouth, something tasting of oil and metal, and says, 'That's really awful,' his words mangled and odd where his tongue cannot move around the object and then there is a bang between his ears, sparks and ephemeral zigzags of light in his vision, like somebody setting off a firework behind his eyes, and he feels hands on his arms, arms that have gone limp, hears *Lower him, gently, gently, he's rigged* and his eyes flicker open and he sees them, these dark angels wrapped in disco fog, sees their goggles and police helmets and glinting machine guns in their hands, their guns pointed at him and even jammed in his mouth and then there are more fireworks, four, five, six of them exploding inside his skull in quick succession, and the world folds in on itself, the strobes dimming.

Everything going black.

Twenty-eight

Amongst the crowds and the chaos and the cordons and emergency service vehicles – so many, Greyfriars Road clogged, brought to a standstill in seconds – MacReady stood on tiptoes and frantically panned his eyes left and right.

Looking for Neil Rook.

Searching for Klaudia Solak.

Barely able to breathe.

Clubbers screaming into the night air, running in every direction. Clambering over the bonnets of parked response cars, jumping into the backs of Public Order vans and slamming doors shut. Couples holding hands and sprinting away from Vintage. Dropping phones and bags and leaving footwear behind, such was the panic that had engulfed the horde who streamed out of the entrance, out of fire doors and staff exits and even windows on the ground floor of the building.

'We've lost control here,' he yelled to Beck. 'They could be running away with this lot. We're not stopping anybody.'

She was a few feet away from him, shifting at the waist, swivelling to allow frightened punters to run past her. Blue lights flashing on her tired face. 'How can we stop them all?' she shouted back. 'It's pandemonium. Everyone's legging it, so just keep scanning the crowd. That's all you can do.'

MacReady looked over at Harrison and Echols, waving hands, urging people towards them, towards the relative safety of the outer cordon at the junction with Park Place. A stupid thing to be doing, he thought. What if Rook or RakKap were among the very people they were trying to save? On the opposite side of the street, Fletcher was huddled together with the detective chief superintendent, with Counter-Terrorism officers, with – and MacReady was pleased to see him – Ken Cullen, the tactical adviser from Penarth.

As they'd rushed to the nightclub, Fletcher had called the officers interviewing Sarah Rook. The family were struggling financially, yet until recently her husband had been spending large amounts of money – paying Heidi Paxton for her silence, it had to be – despite being laid off last year by the building firm he'd worked for since his late teens.

The same building firm that had refurbished the Vintage club. That had given a complete makeover to the cocktail bar destroyed by the drone bomb.

The same building firm that was run by Dennis Afolabi, the man who also owned Bessemer Market and was wiped out in the blast.

Specialist firearm officers and army techs had already gone into the club. Two groups of four, parting the sea of fleeing clubbers as they went, one in through the front entrance, the second up an exterior metal stairwell and into the main dancefloor area. He could hear the faint wail from inside Vintage, knew it was the fire alarm. Knew Solak had set it off after he called.

But where was she?

'This is ridiculous,' he grunted. Turned and checked the wall behind him. No windowsill, no raised area. A council refuse bin wedged into a recess just a short distance away. He pushed through the fleeing bodies, checked the bin lid would take his weight, pulled himself up on top of it.

Stood there, eyes drifting over the bedlam.

Then over the pulse of the fire alarm he heard several bangs. Gunshots, he knew. Screams from the running clubbers. People crying openly as they ran. MacReady swallowed, fearful now. Turned to Beck, saw her looking up at him with wide eyes, knew she'd heard the shots too. Wondered if she was thinking about last year, and what happened to her in that basement garage.

MacReady gave her a reassuring nod.

Heard his radio squawk into life.

Tango Foxtrot Four-Five, one male in custody, urgent medical assistance required.

One male. Urgent medical assistance, the old euphemism used over the air, when things are recorded. So as not to give the game away that the target is probably already dead.

So one male was down and out.

But which one? And where was the other?

A sudden burst of light to his left, about 100 metres away, close to the outer cordon. Bright white amongst the sea of pulsing blue. He knew – relief washed over him – even before he looked that way.

Klaudia Solak.

Standing in front of the camera, broadcasting live from the scene. Ignoring Echols's demands that she move further away.

Calmly reporting what was going on while all hell broke loose around her.

Thank God, MacReady thought. And he stared at her for a moment. Let his eyes rest there. Pictured them together. The easiness. The lack of tension.

The feeling that he belonged.

Then his eyes shifted left a fraction. Drawn to a spot a few feet behind her, where a figure – bald, skinny – walked slowly towards the cordon. While everyone else shrieked and sprinted, this one was almost unfazed by it all.

Oddly calm.

He was reminded of Sarah Rook's description of her husband. How he wasn't really there. *Like a zombie.*

MacReady squinted. Tried to get a better look; the flashing blues and the cameraman's arc light making it difficult to see properly. To get a good view of the figure who strode away from Vintage.

Thought: *it can't be.*

'Sarge,' he called. Pointed. 'Take a look.'

Beck pushed herself up onto the balls of her feet, head bobbing this way and that. Too many people in the way. She looked up at him. 'What is it?'

'Shit.' MacReady jumped down from the bin. Ran towards the bright-white light. Lifted his PR to his mouth. Got hold of Harrison at the cordon.

'Male heading in your direction,' he shouted, breaths already heavy. Pushing his way through the clusters of panicked clubbers. 'White, thin build, shaved or bald head.'

'Any problems with him?' Harrison replied over the air.

'Only that he's calm as you like while every other person here is shitting themselves.'

'Roger. We'll pull him now.'

'I'm coming across, thirty seconds,' he transmitted.

Sensed somebody alongside him. Jerked his head left. Saw Beck, running with him.

'Sarge,' he said, shaking his head.

'My choice, tea boy.'

Another bang. More screams. Coming from the outer cordon. Shouts. It sounded like Echols, but his voice was reedy, terrified.

MacReady pushed himself. Faster, head low, fists punching air.

When they reached the tape they found Harrison sitting on his haunches, hands on a writhing Echols. An audience of silent, shocked clubbers clenching hands and bags and faces. Clenching each other. The DS was clutching his left thigh, fingers squeezing at the tattered fabric of his trousers, face contorted in agony. MacReady saw the blood. Saw the slickness of Echols's skin, the rolling eyes. Heard the groans through gritted teeth.

'Warren!' Beck shouted. Placed a hand on his shoulder.

Harrison tensed for a second. Took several breaths. Looked up at them. 'Rook . . .' he breathed, gulping for air. 'He pulled open his coat, he's got the sawn-off shotgun . . .' He dipped his head to Echols. 'He tried to grab it off him, the crazy bugger. Reached for the barrels and they started wrestling so Rook just pulled the trigger. Jesus, mun ... Where are the ambulance guys?'

'Which way?' MacReady asked.

Harrison pointed north, towards the Civic Centre. 'The gardens. The museum.'

'Will, wait for Armed Response,' Beck urged. 'He has a firearm and we don't know what else. We'll get Charlie Alpha Nine-Eight to pick him up on camera.'

'He goes to ground, he's gone,' MacReady said. 'Until he comes out again and finishes this. This is our chance, you know it. Wait here, Sarge. Please. I'll go after Rook, just keep him in sight until the Armed Response vehicles are on him.'

MacReady didn't wait for a reply, headed north along Park Place, along the side wall of the New Theatre. A stitch already in his ribs. Heard footfalls alongside him; Beck, keeping pace, despite her hip.

'You got something against detective sergeants?' she asked.

MacReady frowned, eyes searching ahead as he ran. 'Meaning?'

'They keep getting shot when you're around, numbnuts,' she grinned.

No traffic on the roads. No pedestrians. The city centre eerily quiet outside of the carnage at Greyfriars. Harrison, on the radio to the camera room. Updating them with Rook's description and last direction of travel.

'There,' MacReady said, pointing.

'He can't go anywhere now,' Beck said. Gave the location over the air.

A hundred metres away, a dark figure loping through the shadows in the manicured gardens next to City Hall Lawn. Long jacket, shaved head. Looking up at cameras which now swivelled towards him.

Checking over his shoulder at the pursuing police officers.

Twenty-nine

He runs.

Tired now. Beyond tired, everything catching up with him. The hundreds of hours spent planning and prepping and worrying and marshalling others, the exhausting, unending rage, all of it finally weighing down on him, making him feel hollowed out. Running on empty.

Adrenalin, a huge dump of it from firing the sawn-off at the plain-clothes copper – *Stop, police*, the man had actually shouted, and it had been almost comical, a pathetic wrestling match until he'd pulled the trigger – it's carrying him, pushing him on, but it won't last, he knows. It never does.

Nothing ever does.

And for a moment, arms swinging, pulling in deep, ragged breaths of sticky night air, he wonders what on earth he is doing. How he got here, to this point, where it all began and where it went so wrong. When he became this person, this thing he – now, fleetingly – tries to recognise but cannot. His mind is fractured and his lungs burn and his mouth is gum-numbingly dry and he cannot think straight, cannot focus, can only latch onto scraps and fragments and flickering images from these last few days.

From these last long, lonely months. The last couple of years.

It's like it all happened to somebody else. And he thinks about stopping, just lying down on warm grass and asking them for help, and they will envelop him in their arms and take him someplace safe and look after him and he won't have to worry about anything any more. Then it registers – a brief flicker, deep down someplace within – that such a thing will never happen because all that he once was has now unravelled. All that he had has disappeared. All that he could and should have been is lost.

There is his wife, and as he sprints and grips the stock of the shotgun to still it against his ribs he pictures her. Sees her expressions, how they have morphed over time, from open and smiling and warm and loving to worried and fearful. Disappointment. Revulsion. Disdain. Open contempt.

There is his career. Over. A silly argument with a work colleague, his temper getting the better of him, yet again, the red mist descending and his fists flying when words should have sufficed. When walking away and ignoring it would have been the best option. When he was already on his third and final warning and the boss had bent over backwards to keep him on the books. But no more. *Enough was enough*, he was told. Fifteen years working for them, gone in an instant.

His friends began drifting away. His wife became distant. Everyone, avoiding him. Talking quietly if he was around, avoiding eye contact. He couldn't understand why. The doctors and hospitals and social workers he eventually turned to, no help at all. Just tablets and leaflets and cancelled appointments and then a period where he was adrift, lost in a waking nightmare of sleeplessness and itching and stomach cramps and occasional bouts of lucidity where he'd find holes punched in walls and doors and crockery smashed, and after that it was just months of the room closing in on him and the thought of crawling out of bed striking terror into his heart.

The games, they saved him. He knows this. He found catharsis, and control, and meaning. Purpose. Found like-minded people, people he could corral and manage and direct and – for the first time in his life – *they all listened to him*.

But fuck it. *Fuck them*. Fuck his wife and his kids and his job and the boss and the people chasing him, fuck them all because who do they think they are? Treating him like this? Who are they to him, after all he has done, all that he has carried out in this city, making them cower and scream and bleed on the streets?

He feels drool fleck his cheeks, hears his deep breaths in his ears, realises he has been shouting at himself. Turns left, towards the fountains in front of City Hall, the buildings lit from below. He passes a floodlight, his elongated shadow – malformed, troubling, unrecognisable – thrown against the white Portland stone. Behind him, on the lawn, footsteps.

The police. Still coming for him. A voice: *Target heading west, still on foot*.

He wants to stop and turn and raise the shotgun and let them have it, but he can't.

One shell left.

A shell.

He is just a shell.

A voice he doesn't want to listen to, it nags at him that he is a coward. That after Bessemer he made everyone else do the work. Played them like it was a game. Sent them to carry out attacks. Pushed and cajoled them to carry out their fantasies, their revenge, to kill Heidi, and now they were either sitting in police cells or dead. Because there is no respawn point. There is no loading the last checkpoint. There is no starting all over again when you're out of ammo and health and the screen is showing *Game Over*. There are no saved games.

This is real life. And he is done with it.

And he thinks: *suicide by cop*.

No more cowardice. Take one of them, as many of them with you as you can.

He drops down into the underpass, out of sight. It's empty, dimly lit, the short tunnel from the Civic Centre to the bars and shopping centres of Kingsway and Queen Street.

He thinks of his family and how much he loves them and misses them. Begins to cry.

Here.

This is where the game ends.

Thirty

MacReady's lungs burned. His thighs, numb now. Beck was still keeping pace. Still keeping him going. He glanced at her, saw the effort etched on her face. The sweat, the grimace as she worked her hip, pushed herself. She caught him looking and he offered a weary smile.

Fletcher on the radio: 'I'm on foot with Ken Cullen, we're coming in from the western side, by the Crown Court. Firearms are coming out from the club and making their way. Do not approach Rook, do you hear me? *Do not approach*.'

'Target along the front of City Hall,' MacReady transmitted. He shot a look at Beck. 'I want to get there first.'

'No shit,' she breathed.

When MacReady turned back to Rook, the man had disappeared.

'No,' he moaned, and stopped running. Threw his head around, searching.

On his radio: 'From Charlie Alpha Nine-Eight, the target has run into the underpass beneath Boulevard de Nantes.'

The small subway. Rook was heading south.

'He's trying to head back into the city centre,' Beck said. 'He reaches the crowds on Greyfriars there's no telling what he'll do.'

MacReady scowled, hands kneading thighs. 'And we could lose him.'

They sprinted across the lawn, jumped onto the boulevard. Crossed it at full pelt. Streetlights flashing in MacReady's eyes as he willed himself onwards, willed himself to reach the southern end of the underpass before Neil Rook emerged. Beck, fading now, dropping back a little, dropping behind.

MacReady took a low wall at speed, weaved through a stand of trees. Down a grass bank, chest ready to burst. Feet on fire as he dropped to the paved slope and ran the last couple of metres to the underpass.

Where he came face to face with Neil Rook.

Neil Rook, his hair shaved to the bone.

Wet eyes wide and wild. Dried spittle on the blanched skin of his chin, his cheeks.

'*You*,' MacReady snarled.

Thought of Heidi Paxton. Her parents. Megan and Finlay. Shakima Corlett wailing as she reached for her terrified son. The faces of every single dead person on the photographs pinned to the Major Incident Room's boards. The last five days of sleeplessness and nerves and surviving on nothing but fear. MacReady tensed, ready to launch himself at the man in front of him.

Froze as Rook backed away. Tongue darting to lick at cracked lips. Hands pulling back the flaps of his jacket.

Raising the shotgun.

MacReady could barely catch his breath. Wanted to bend at the waist and gulp in air. Didn't want Rook to see any sign of weakness so stayed upright. Arms spread wide, palms out.

Calm, everyone. Calm.

'We all good, Will?'

Behind him, Beck dropped to the slope. Walking slowly down to join MacReady. Rook's eyes twitched left, over MacReady's shoulder to look at her for a fraction of a second.

'We're all good,' MacReady said. Nauseous now. Light-headed. He turned to Rook. Gave a shake of his head. 'There's nowhere to go, Neil. You're done, OK? This is done. Just keep your hands where we can see them –'

'One tap on the trigger and you're fucked,' Rook barked.

'We don't want that,' Beck said, keeping her voice soft. She stepped alongside MacReady, hands raised to the night sky. 'We want all this to stop now. Please. It has to stop.'

Rook stepped backwards again, further into the subway. His head, shaking. A quiet laugh coming from his mouth. 'You just don't get it, do you?'

'We get it, Neil,' MacReady told him. 'You want revenge. That's all this is about, isn't it? You and your friends, just getting revenge on the people you think have done you wrong.'

'Think?' Rook shrieked. 'Fucking *think*? We know. *I know*.'

'Well, we know too, now. We know you felt you were wronged, and needed to put it right. Needed to hurt the people who hurt you. Coe, he was humiliated by the girl in the restaurant, sacked by the security company. And Nazir, because he got dumped by Heidi and was treated like a dog by his father.' MacReady felt the surge of anger. 'And I don't know about your RakKap friend and why he did what he did at the mosque, because he's a bit fuck-ing dead.'

'Will,' Beck cautioned.

Rook looked to the floor. Closed his eyes for a moment.

'You really don't understand, do you? I have nothing. All of us, we had nothing. We're just the sad freaks who spend all day on games and the internet, right? On the fringes and ignored. Marginalised. Mocked on social media, by our partners. Just a bunch of . . . losers. But we took it back. Took the power back. Showed everyone. Became splinters in the sides of the establishment. And soon everyone will want to be us. They'll see what we've seen and do exactly the same.'

'I get that you think this is some sort of game that's spilled over,' MacReady said. 'Scoring points, winning, because you can't do it in real life. Because you have problems at home, at work. And I'll be honest with you, I have serious fucking problems at home, and plenty of them at work.'

'My heart bleeds,' Rook sneered.

'I'm not asking for your pity, because I deal with them, like an adult. Not with a pathetic childish tantrum that ends up with people dead. This *is* real life. This can't stand in real life. This sort of crap, killing people because they've hurt your ego, it doesn't get to happen, mate.'

'Doesn't happen?' Rook spat. Laughed, the hollow sound echoing along the walls of the subway. 'Doesn't happen? You're talking about a world where people get arrested by you lot for expressing a fucking opinion on Twitter. Or making a joke about blowing up an airport. Where a husband will stab his wife to death just because she's friended an ex on Facebook. Where politicians are murdered in the street by nationalists because of a stupid referendum. People are angry, angry all the time, and they're getting angrier. All bets are off. You want to talk Munich, or Orlando, or Paris, or Brussels? That's the world we live in, and now it's here. Right here. *Mate.*'

MacReady held out one hand. Wished the armed officers would appear *right now* and take this loon out. 'You're going to have to come with us, Neil. Please. Give me your hands. Keep them both away from the weapon.'

Rook looked at MacReady. At Beck. Breathed in deeply, turning his attention to the sky for a moment. The shotgun, still levelled at MacReady's guts. Then he looked down. His shoulders, slumping a little. His face, morphing from rage to wretchedness. A tiredness seeming to engulf him.

His eyes on MacReady's outstretched hand.

Rook snatched at it. Pulled, hard. Pulled MacReady towards him, causing him to lose balance, topple forwards, Rook's left arm scooping under MacReady's chin and turning him, hoisting him upwards, choking him from behind with the crook of his elbow. The man was thin but there was real strength in his arms. MacReady let out a strangled yelp as Rook tightened his grip.

'Don't,' shouted Beck. 'Please.'

Cold metal on MacReady's right temple: the shotgun barrels. Their ends jagged, gouging into his skin. Blood trickling down to his cheekbone already. Rook worked the wound on his temple with the barrels, the pain excruciating, until MacReady stopped pulling at his arm. Placed his hands up again.

'Good,' Rook breathed into his ear; the words wrapped in warm breath, stale and unpleasant. He could smell the man's body odour, a ripe mix of days-old fast-food sweats and unwashed flesh.

'Neil,' Beck pleaded. Hands out and up, shaking her head. 'Don't.'

'Stay where you are,' Rook shouted, and began backing away. Dragging MacReady, almost, his shoes scuffing on the paved floor as he tried to stay upright. Tried to shuffle backwards, anything to relieve the pressure on his throat. He was unable to speak, barely able to breathe.

Beck's face was contorted, fearful. Her head, shaking continually.

'There's nowhere to go,' she said. Taking small steps, matching Rook and MacReady for pace as they backed further into the subway.

'There's everywhere to go as long as I have your colleague.'

Sawn-off metal, needling beneath his skin now. Grinding against bone. It was agonising. MacReady closed his eyes and wished the pain away. His mind whirring, panicking, flickering images of Finlay rolling on his play mat, of Megan looking up at MacReady's eyes, of Klaudia Solak coiled amongst the bedsheets in her apartment. He truly did not know if he would ever see them again. And then his brother, always his brother, crowding in, ruining everything, just like their father had done over and over again. Then – for the first time in an age – he pictured his mother. Not battered and bleeding and weeping at the sink in their Edinburgh flat, doing dishes as she tried to hide the results of her husband's beating from her sons, but on the beach that time, over at Portobello, a rare trip away, the sun high in a cloudless sky and the sand soft between toes and his father nowhere to be seen because he was either in one of his mistresses' beds or on a weekend bender or sleeping it off in a police station cell. The one time MacReady could remember feeling at peace as a child. His mother, smiling. Content. Relaxed.

Relax.

Relax, copper.

MacReady could hear the voice and it was odd and slow in his ears but he felt himself nodding as best he could, agreeing with it, starting to go under. A suffocating tightness around his neck, blocking the air from his lungs, making him feel sleepy, making it difficult to move his legs. His vision blurred and speckled with pinpricks of white light. A dull and distant throb in the side of his head that wouldn't quit.

A woman's voice, afraid: *You're strangling him, you're going to kill him . . .*

So hard to open his eyes. The lids, so heavy.

That's the plan.

A man, answering her. Whatever it was around his neck, tightening further.

MacReady let the image of his mother fade. Gritted his teeth. *One last effort. One last go at this. Not game over yet.* His mother never gave up. Not until the very end, when she had no choice as his father took the knife to her.

MacReady pushed his eyelids open.

Saw her there. Charlie Beck. Pleading, reaching outwards, fingers grasping in front of her, towards MacReady.

Her eyes on the man squeezing the life out of him.

Neil Rook.

And he saw Beck swallow, and step forward, and MacReady felt the man hesitate for a second, and then Beck's eyes shifted a little, just the tiniest of movements to the right, a momentary flicker to something above MacReady, to something on Rook's shoulder.

'Wait –' Rook blurted.

And then another voice. Male. Familiar. Low and curt and northern.

'No you fucking don't, pal.'

MacReady felt a tremor shoot through Rook's arm. Felt it fall away from his throat. Felt the muzzles of the sawn-off pull away from his temple. Braced himself for the explosion in his ears as Rook pulled the trigger.

Except it didn't come.

He fell to the ground, squeezing at his neck.

Turned to see Ken Cullen standing over an unconscious Neil Rook, rubbing at the right fist he'd obviously just driven into Rook's face – the man was out cold, his cheek split and already swelling. Beside Cullen, Fletcher worked the shotgun free from Rook's limp hand, dropped the weapon to the ground and pushed it away from Rook with the toe of his shoe.

The DI winked at MacReady. 'Teamwork.'

MacReady rolled onto his back, breathing hard and fast. Felt hands on him, lifted his head to see Beck checking him over.

'I'm fine,' he croaked. 'Seriously.'

'Be quiet, or I'll throttle you myself.'

Screeches above them, the sound of radios blaring. Footsteps clomping at the northern entrance of the subway, down the southern slope at Kingsway. Over the air, firearms announcing they were at scene with bomb disposal. Finally. Now it was all over.

MacReady eased himself up on one elbow. Checked Rook, flat on his back and breathing quietly. Comatose.

'Glad there's no bloody cameras under here,' Fletcher said, shaking his head.

Beck looked at Cullen. 'Do we have to knock everybody out this week?'

Cullen dropped down to his haunches. Slapped a hand on MacReady's back. A smile appearing on his face. 'CID. Fucking useless morons, the lot of you.'

MacReady gulped on the warm night air. 'I really would like a holiday. Somewhere cold, please.'

One Week Later

Epilogue

With September came the rains, heavy and unforgiving, as if to make up for the glorious weather of the preceding month and to remind everyone that, yes, this was in fact Wales.

MacReady was relieved, much as he had been since Neil Rook was taken into custody. A week ago now, and this Monday morning saw the city finally returned to some sense of normality. Work, too. No more actions and briefings from WECTU. No more bombs going off or names to add to the casualty list – shockingly long, and still painful to read – they already had. Even the police and crime commissioner had reappeared, having presumably hidden in his office toilet for that horrible five days when Rook and his companions wreaked havoc across the capital.

They found Rook's battered car in the end. The Volkswagen Golf had been hidden in a garage at the home of RakKap – Rakesh Kapoor – who lived the next street over and whom Sarah Rook had no knowledge of. Neil Rook had shown himself to be the true coward he was and had been strangely amenable while in custody – as Beck had said when they were kitting up to go into Timothy Coe's flat, once under arrest the really guilty people become oddly calm, and Rook was as placid and pliable as you like. Happy to talk, to release the pressure at last, the antithesis of Timothy Coe, who'd refused point-blank to speak – on the orders of Rook – until he learned that Rook had given him up at the first opportunity.

And Rook gave it all up – everyone, every single thing – in interview. Was still giving it up, even after being charged with multiple murders and terrorist-related offences and remanded in custody courtesy of Her Majesty. Came good with everything. The reasons for the attacks. The components – frighteningly ordinary household items, the nail varnish, the hair dye – for the TATP bombs, those acetone peroxide specials so beloved of today's terrorists. The shotgun, his grandfather's, an antique he'd retooled and shorn of its barrels in order to conceal it under his jacket. The planning, his rage driving him: the job loss, the ostracism, the mental health issues, his retreat into an online world to escape the real. His online life allowing him to groom and cultivate a small yet worryingly obedient following of similarly damaged geeks and gamers that he bent and shaped to his will.

MacReady was glad it was over.

With the return to normality came the tidying up of other things. Outstanding crimes. The everyday serious assaults and creeper burglaries and convoluted frauds, the preparation of files for the coroner, for the Crown Prosecution Service.

The court cases.

MacReady sat motionless in Courtroom Number One at Cardiff Crown, Fletcher on one side, Beck on the other. Detective Sergeant Paul Echols absent, recuperating on a sofa at home and already counting the money he was planning to claim from the Criminal Injuries Compensation Authority – his wrestling with Rook's shotgun had been foolhardy yet fortuitous; Rook had missed, but a dozen or so 00 buckshot pellets had ricocheted off the pavement and, deformed and with their energy reduced, lodged themselves in the skin of Echols's left thigh. Echols had cried for an hour then immediately signed off sick. Then there was Warren Harrison, already pinched from the team and seconded to work down west on a double axe murder in Swansea, whose CID were thinly stretched and needed the extra pair of hands. As ever, Harrison was deliriously happy with the overtime. And as ever, the world continued to turn, and people went on doing terrible things to each other.

In the press section sat Klaudia Solak. He'd not been to her apartment for over a week. Since the night they had discovered who the blogger was. They'd exchanged texts and emails, nothing more. She kept glancing across at MacReady only to find Beck glaring at her so had to look away.

In the public gallery was Alex Castle's family. Unmoving. Eyes on the ceiling. Waiting.

In the dock, the five defendants. Still sniggering, still sneering.

'Here we go.' Beck, whispering. Her elbow nudging MacReady, not that he needed nudging of any kind.

The court went about its final business. The clerk handing the jurors' verdict to the judge. The judge studying the paper before handing it back to the clerk. The clerk asking the jury chair to deliver the result.

MacReady lowered his head, Alex Castle's parents the last people he saw.

Crossed his fingers.

Heard: 'Guilty'.

Felt Fletcher's hand on his arm, stopping him punching the air.

*

MacReady made his way to Courtroom Number Eight. Walked slowly, enjoying the sensation that they'd won. Won for Alex Castle. Won for his parents. For his family. Another group of shits off the streets for many years, and that was never a bad thing.

He was hoping the morning's run of good results would continue, that he would reach the court and hear another guilty verdict and see his brother sent away for a stretch, just a year or two, just so Kirsty and the children could create a new life for themselves without Stuart, that a spell over the wall might finally make his brother a better person, make him reflect on what he had done with his life, what he had done to the woman who loved him but wanted rid of him now.

He skipped down the stairs, turned the corner and froze.

Saw his brother, smiling and shaking his fists to the heavens, jubilant. A couple of suits standing next to him, files and brief-cases underneath arms, his defence barristers, a pair of well-fed fiftysomethings who looked ever so pleased with themselves.

Hanging around Stuart's neck was Kirsty. Kissing him. Hugging him. Closing her eyes and pulling him as tight as she could.

'Hey, baby bro!' Stuart shouted, seeing MacReady at the bottom of the stairs.

MacReady took a few steps towards them. The children, playing on the floor beneath their feet. A clear plastic bag in his brother's hands; MacReady saw items of clothing, a squashed tube of toothpaste, felt his heart sink. 'What happened?' he asked.

A shrug from Stuart. He raised the bag. 'No further action. Just picked up me things from downstairs. I'm out of here, mate.'

MacReady looked hard at Kirsty. 'I don't understand.'

'She had a change of heart.' Stuart turned to Kirsty, kissed the top of her head. 'Didn't you, girl? Decided to withdraw your complaint. You knows which side your bread is buttered, righ'?'

Kirsty snuggled into Stuart's chest. Eyed MacReady. Gave a small shrug of her own and pulled a face.

Sorry, it said. *But what can you do?*

Stuart whispered something to her then swivelled to face MacReady.

'A quick word?'

MacReady waited a beat. Nodded. Allowed Stuart to guide him away from Kirsty, into the corner of the waiting area. Just a potted plant for company.

'What now?' he asked his brother.

Stuart was smiling but his eyes had darkened. He leaned in, forehead almost touching MacReady's. 'I watched the news when I was over the wall. While my trial was on pause. What the fuck did you think you were doing?'

MacReady screwed up his face. 'Doing? My job, that's what I was doing –'

'With Finlay,' Stuart growled quietly. A quick check over at Kirsty. His finger, now jabbing at MacReady's chest. 'You fucking mad, bro? Taking my boy out then leaving him so you can roll around on the floor with some crazy bomber guy?'

MacReady recoiled. Swallowed.

My boy.

He looked over at Kirsty. Back to Stuart. Anger flaring in his brother's eyes.

Said quietly, 'He's not your boy, Stuart.'

'He ain't yours, though, is he?'

MacReady backed away. Away from this nightmare. Hands up, shaking his head. Turned on his heel and made his way up the stairs.

*

It was the usual crowd of nameless, solemn faces, of dark suits and black ties, of muted dresses and murmured conversation. One or two wept openly, hugging each other in the doorway of the crematorium's chapel as the pallbearers stepped by. Afternoon sunlight cut through the clouds, through the flowers atop the coffin: DAUGHTER. In the back of the hearse, more floral tributes. Muted organ music wafting out of the building.

MacReady watched from a short distance away. Hands clasped behind his back. Expression conveying condolence. Respect for the deceased and her family.

Remembering the last time he'd come here, and what they found in the funeral director's office. Where it led them.

A tug at his sleeve.

He turned, glanced down.

Simone Paxton, smiling up at him. Mark Paxton, crouched alongside her wheelchair, holding her hand. For his benefit more than hers, MacReady suspected. Heidi's father still looked broken.

'Thank you for coming,' Simone Paxton said.

'It's the least I could do.'

He'd done far more. Kept their daughter's other life from them as much as he could. Asked Solak to work her media friends and keep Heidi out of the reports whenever possible. Her level of involvement with Neil Rook and his plotters. Her secret, online life. How she'd cut her ties with Rook's group ten months before she was killed – hence that drop-off in contacts and appointments the previous September – then blackmailed them for money, money she planned to use, as MacReady had discovered from her laptop, to repay her parents and buy specialist equipment to enable her mother to get around the house more easily.

The Paxtons had suffered enough. MacReady knew it could all come out in the court case, but that was out of his hands. For now, he'd done what he could.

'We're putting her next to her brother,' Simone told him. 'With Jonathan.'

MacReady nodded. 'I think she'll like it there.'

'She's spent her life looking after everybody else, caring for other people. Caring for me. My sweet daughter. It'll be nice to have someone look out for her for a change.'

'Good.' He gave a gentle smile. 'We all need someone like that.'

Simone Paxton pulled him down, pulled him close.

Kissed MacReady's cheek.

Whispered into his ear, 'Thank you so much.'

*

It was late afternoon and raining, and he had no intention of going back to the office so was sitting in his car at the roundabout on Albany Road. Parked, engine idling. A text to Megan, typed but not sent, on his phone. Texts and calls and voicemails from Klaudia Solak, unanswered.

MacReady drummed his fingers on the gearstick. The windows, slowly fogging around him. Turn right, head for home. Turn left, head for Solak.

He dropped his head to the headrest. Closed his eyes.

Pictured Megan and Finlay, a curious mixture of pleasure and pain.

Thought of Klaudia Solak. Simplicity, but likely to dispense with his company within a couple of hours.

MacReady put the car into gear and just drove. Wipers flapping at fat raindrops, one hand on the wheel, the other draped over the handbrake. Letting the car take him where it wanted. Enjoying not having Rook or Paxton or Castle in his head for the first time in what seemed like for ever.

When he arrived the rain had stopped and the sun – weak now, the summer ebbing away at last – pushed through thick white clouds. He pulled out his key, unlocked the front door and walked in.

Knew he'd made the right decision.

'Hey, there.'

MacReady nodded. Grinned. Exhausted.

'All right, mate?' he said to Duncan Jones. 'Got any of those beers in the fridge?'

Acknowledgements

Huge, ongoing thanks to my agent Karolina Sutton, the redoubtable pocket rocket fighting my corner, and all at Curtis Brown, in particular Lucy Morris.

A very special thank you to my uber-editor at Bonnier Zaffre, the brilliant Katherine Armstrong: her nips, tucks and forensic attention to detail were incredibly important in shaping the finished book you now hold in your hands.

To every single person at Bonnier, but especially Mark Smith, Kate Parkin, Joel Richardson, Bec Farrell and the ace Emily Burns, who continues to field my ridiculous queries, emails and grovelling requests for freebies with astonishing good grace.

My beta reader extraordinaire and Hull crime lord, Nick Quantrill: you're one of the good guys. I'll remember to send you the correct draft next time.

David Watson, for the final, extremely thorough spit and polish to give the novel its shine – thank you.

Tony Platt, for listening to me drone on about this writing business despite far more important things going on in his life; and Liz McNally – I feel privileged to have known a human being who was so warm, inspiring and endlessly optimistic, even to the very end when it all, finally, became too much, even for as strong a person as you.

All on the creative writing faculty at the University of South Wales – thank you, as always.

I am beyond grateful to the book blogging and reviewing community – there are too many to name individually – who have been incredibly supportive since the first MacReady novel was published; what you do for authors is so important and self-less. Respect – and lots of free books, I hope – to you all.

My parents – I love you, miss you, wish you were here *para muita comida, bebida e risos*.

Deac, Tribester and Federico – sell some of those bike bits and move over.

And to my wife and children for packing life with All the Good Things – you are my reason.

Want to read
NEW BOOKS
before anyone else?

Like getting
FREE BOOKS?

Enjoy sharing your
OPINIONS?

Discover

READERS
FIRST

Read. Love. Share.

Get your first free book just by signing up at
readersfirst.co.uk